WHAT'S IN A KISS?

James grinned, then dragging his hand across his lips, he said, "I suppose I could give you a hint."

He reached for her hand. She felt a slight jolt from his contact, but then he lifted her fingers to his mouth. Annie snatched them away, jumping from her chair.

James's gaze jerked up to meet hers. "What's wrong?"

"Weren't ye going to bite me?" Annie rubbed the place where his teeth had nearly touched. "It might go septic."

James's lips spread wide with amusement. "No, I wasn't going to bite you, you scamp. It was a kiss. I was going to kiss your hand. Give it back."

"Are you sure?"

"Yes." His grin tinged his voice. "I promise you, I won't hurt you. In fact, you should like my kiss very much."

"If you say so, Captain." When he spoke in that voice, she couldn't resist him. She'd never heard that tone from any other man.

She offered him her hand. The captain bent over it and she braced herself, but she only felt the brush of his lips against her knuckles.

He raised his head, and looked at her expectantly. She paused. "That's it?"

CAPTURING ANNIE

PATRICIA WYNN

LOVE SPELL BOOKS   NEW YORK CITY

This book is dedicated to all those people who have the courage to set out to sea, especially my father, Charles W. Barnes. It is not dedicated to seasickness, which made a coward out of me.

LOVE SPELL®

March 2000
Published by

Dorchester Publishing Co., Inc.
276 Fifth Avenue
New York, NY 10001

ISBN 0-505-52367-1

The name "Love Spell" and its logo are trademarks of Dorchester Publishing Co., Inc.

Printed in the United States of America.

CAPTURING ANNIE

Chapter One

Off the coast of Jamaica, 1780

"Blow me, Cap'n! There's an English frigate—to larboard!"

"The devil ye says!"

Captain Sharkee's oath cut through the din of pistol shots, the clang of metal on metal, the roar of pirates' shouts and victims' moans.

With a cutlass grasped in both of her hands, Annie spun on bare feet to see what he'd seen. A blistering sun flashed in her eyes before she spotted the ship sailing toward the *Merrye Laurie* and closing in fast. It must have rounded the tip of Jamaica and made for their stern while their eyes had been fixed on the *East Indiaman* under attack.

Sharkee screamed to his pirates to man their cannons, but the order came too late. The frigate's sails loomed ghostly white behind them. A crash sent Annie tumbling to the deck. Bruised on one cheek, she struggled to her feet while the brig shuddered beneath her.

"Guard me left, lad! Me left!" the captain bellowed, but Annie had already scrambled to her post. She knew her place if they were boarded. Sharkee had drummed it into her.

His pirates had boarded the *East Indiaman* after ambushing it from their hidden cove. A bang-up victory it would have been, too, if not for this latest threat. Now the *Merrye Laurie* lay pinched between two larger ships, the merchant vessel at the fore and the frigate aft. It would take a miracle to save her, and Annie had never believed in miracles.

She tightened her grip on the heavy cutlass. The best she could do was to swing it, but that should be enough to protect Sharkee's left—his weaker side, he always said, and where she must stay in a fight.

Cries from the wounded filled her ears. Smoke choked her, bringing tears to her eyes. She tried to swipe at them with her shoulder, but her shoulder wouldn't reach.

"We're being boarded"—Sharkee's bellow ended in a furious rasp—"ye sots and swine!" As he whirled on his enemy, his tricorn flew, exposing his bald, shiny pate. A full, red beard covered his lips, but curses burst loudly from the tangled mass.

"Stay with me, Jem! Stay near me, lad!"

Annie obeyed. She had never heard such fear in Sharkee's voice. The thought that they might be taken—or worse—caused her gorge to rise.

Some of Sharkee's pirates had heeded his desperate cries. They leapt back aboard the *Merrye Laurie*, wood and steel in hand, to face the better-trained, better-armed British.

"Board her!" Two words, issued in a deep, sonorous tone, echoed above the rattling din.

Annie turned to search for the voice that had made her knees shake.

"Eyes *wider*, Jem!"

Sharkee's warning made her spin just as an English sailor lunged for her belly. She swung her cutlass with all her might, but it was Sharkee's quick swordplay that sent him reeling to the brink. A pirate threw the Englishman overboard while Annie struggled to catch her breath.

Pulse racing, she crouched to wait for the next assault. Snarls from the men caused the hair on the back of her neck to rise. She would have to stay on her toes if she wanted to keep her head—and if she didn't want Sharkee to make shark bait of her.

The *Merrye Laurie* gave a lurch, breaking Annie's hold upon her sword. As it clattered to the deck, the brig began to roll and heave like a harpooned whale. Its unmanned sails fluttered above like the wings of a dying bird. The helmsman had abandoned his post to join in the fight. The ship swung giddily to left and to right.

As Annie adjusted to its rhythm, the alien

voice boomed loudly again. "Mr. Shirley, attach the brig and secure her fo'c's'le."

The English sailors rushed to obey.

Annie had to marvel at their discipline. With pirates for mates, she had never seen much order, although the bite in Sharkee's voice had kept him captain and alive this many a year when a lesser man would surely have succumbed to mutiny.

This English captain had no need to rant and swear. His crew leapt to fulfill his commands.

From beneath a swerving yardarm, Annie spotted him, tall and strong like the oaks that mainmasts were made of. He gave another powerful blast, and the sound of his voice rang deep in her marrow like the clear, somber tones of a bell.

Distracted, she almost missed a sailor to her left, but Sharkee screamed another warning and plunged between them. With vicious jabs and swipes, he backed the sailor to the edge as Annie turned to find another bearing down.

Stranded from her mates, she pulled her knife and ducked in the nick of time. Backing up and bobbing beneath the sailor's cutlass swipes, she stumbled against the lurching wheel. One of its spokes hit her arm, spoiling her expert aim. The sailor's weapon rose above her head, poised to chop her in half. She was mouthing words to a prayer, when one of Sharkee's pirates jumped from the roundhouse roof and bludgeoned her assailant's noggin.

Billy Sams picked himself and his cudgel up.

With a snarl, he wiped the streaming sweat from his eyes before he darted around the corner of Sharkee's cabin, yelling over his shoulder, "Save yer bacon, Jem! This tub's lost. It's ev'ry man fer hisself!"

As Annie listened to his retreating footsteps, she gasped to recover her breath before a horrible thought entered her mind.

Mr. Bonny would be in the sick bay alone, with no one to defend him.

With a start, she saw that the decks of the *Merrye Laurie* were awash with the English sailors. Sharkee's pirates were all scurrying to hide.

Captain Sharkee was nowhere in sight. Peering fore and aft, Annie searched frantically for his rusty beard and strained to hear his raspy voice. She never should have taken her eyes off of Sharkee—never should have forgotten her duty.

A moan near her ear made her jump. If she wanted to save Mr. Bonny, she had better follow Billy Sams.

She struggled toward the quarterdeck, but the English crew had already secured it. She would have to find another way below. So she ran doubled up, stumbling over fallen corpses and dodging ropes until she arrived breathless at the ship's waist. The broad companionway yawned before her. Annie ran down the steps, hoping to work her way below.

But below was in chaos. She had retreated not a moment too soon. The *Merrye Laurie* was surely lost.

11

A pang for the only home she'd ever known narrowed her throat and weighted her chest, but she couldn't worry about the ship now. Not when Mr. Bonny needed her. Her heart was pounding like a loose jib in the wind.

What would the English captain do to them? Tales of Newgate and the gallows poured furiously through her brain. The horror of being dragged ashore and locked in chains made her shudder on her feet.

There was no way down to the sick bay. Mr. Bonny was trapped. Creeping back to the companionway, Annie climbed the stairs until she found a perch from which to peer out.

Firm on powerful sea legs, the English captain was gazing aloft at his sails, which flapped wildly above his head. He gave a sharp sequence of orders, and his crewmen rushed to secure the cloth. This signaled to Annie that their fighting was done.

They were done for—she and all her mates. Miserably, Annie watched as two English sailors struck the *Merrye Laurie*'s flag—a Jolly Roger with a dagger in one bony hand and a rummer in the other. With a burst of shame, she thought of Captain Sharkee. He had saved her many a time today, when it was she who should have been protecting him.

The English captain roared again. Rising on her toes, Annie was straining to see him when a sudden yank on her pigtail lifted her into the air. The sting brought water to her eyes.

Through a mist of tears, she saw a gap-toothed English sailor who pulled her to within inches of his face. His vicious leer curled her innards and his putrid breath made her flinch. "What've we 'ere?" he said as she swung her fists in fruitless circles through the air. "Just what kind o' pirate are you?"

Alone in his small cabin, the captain of the British frigate, Sir James Noble Avery, massaged his bruised and swollen shoulder. One of the pirates had hit him with a club, but that would be the last weapon that blackguard would ever wield.

In spite of the closeness of the call, James couldn't contain his grin at the day's results.

His *Flying Swan* had accidentally sailed into a pirate attack and had taken the *Merrye Laurie* without one wasted shot. Now, added to the reward for the French ship he'd recently captured would be one pirate brig, easy to convert into a merchant ship. And this particular vessel came free and clear. His letter of marque said nothing about pirate ships, only French and Spanish, which were forfeit to the Crown. He swore happily at his good luck.

A brisk knock sounded at the door, and Krebs, his steward, came in, followed by Mr. Shirley, James's first mate. With three large men crammed into the tiny space, the cabin was packed to the brim.

"Your tea, Captain?" Krebs asked.

"Put it here on my desk. Come to report on our victory, Mr. Shirley?"

13

"Aye, Cap'n." Shirley shifted his lanky body aside to permit Krebs's rounder one to retire. "We've got the whole lot in shackles aboard the *Merrye Laurie*, sir. A pretty scurvy bunch, an' I do say."

"Curse all pirates," James said grimly. "What sort of cargo did they carry?"

"Mostly loot. No treasure. Sixty barrels of flour, likely from a Frenchy ship. I can't rightly read the labels." Shirley's droopy eyes lit. "And twenty barrels of grog, Cap'n!"

James nodded. "A round for the men, then, Mr. Shirley. Two rounds for officers."

"Aye, aye, sir!" Shirley's mouth gaped in an eager grin.

Before he could be too elated by the prospect of more rum, James said, "Tell me about our losses first."

The order briefly sobered his first officer. "Three men lost, sir. Two topmen and the carpenter's mate. Not bad for a pirate attack, I'd say."

"We've the *East Indiaman* to thank for that. Send her captain ten barrels of the rum."

"If you say so, sir," Shirley said. His sagging face conveyed his opinion of such foolish generosity, but he would never dare question the captain's orders. "What about them men we lost? Want me to press some of them pirates?"

James hated to take on troublesome men, but it would be much worse to sail shorthanded. "What are their stories?"

"There's some has said they were pressed

14

when their ships were attacked." Shirley gave a skeptical hunch of one shoulder.

James sighed. "We'll have to accept them, I suppose. But keep a sharp eye on them, mind. I can't abide a cutthroat on my ship."

He thought about the danger a few villains could brew. Discord, even mutiny, were the threats he had to guard against. "What about Sharkee, then?"

"He's gone to Davy Jones's locker, sir. Took a dagger in the throat, Sharkee did."

James gave a grim twist to his lips. "Saves me the trouble of hanging him, I suppose."

The pirate Sharkee had been plaguing this part of the world for as long as James could remember. He'd been a ruthless captain and clever foe. James took no particular pleasure in sending a man to his death, but in his opinion, scoundrels like Sharkee deserved their rotten fates.

The other pirates would have to be tried, though they might as well be shot and have done. James appointed his second mate to carry them back to Jamaica and hand them over to the governor for summary justice. He told Shirley to form a skeleton crew to help the second mate limp back into Kingston aboard the *Merrye Laurie*, giving instructions for the brig to be overhauled.

"Anything else, sir?"

"Yes, tell them to have her ready to make sail as soon as I return from England. And send that flour with them. It will sell better in Jamaica, and the proceeds can go into the brig."

15

James reached for the tea Krebs had brought him and took a reviving gulp. His stomach was growling, but thanks to the battle, his dinner would be served late. "Is that all, Mr. Shirley?"

"Not all, Cap'n." The first mate bristled with an important recollection. "The brig had a doctor on board, sir. Name of Bonny."

James arched his brows. "A doctor? What does he have to say for himself?"

"Says he was pressed, too, sir. Taken and kept aboard this many a year."

"I've heard of such things happening before."

"But never once to escape? Not once in nineteen years?"

"That does seem peculiar." James pondered, then frowning, said, "Bring him aboard. He can see to our wounded for now. But keep an eye on him, too. I'll want to speak to him later today."

"Aye, aye, sir. And there's a boy, too, sir."

"A boy?" Looking up, James pushed back in his chair. "How old?"

"Hard to say. He's nothin' but a sprig."

James felt a wave of impatience. "Did *he* say how *he* came to be aboard a pirate ship?"

"No, sir. 'S'far as I know, he's not made any claims nor even asked for his freedom."

James sighed and rubbed the bump on his shoulder. No matter how the boy had landed on a pirate brig, he would have to be dealt with separately. "Probably too frightened to speak. Let's have a look at him, Mr. Shirley."

Shirley bowed himself out, and James finished his tea, reflecting on the worth of the captured ship. He could always sell her, but a glance at the letter he had received in Jamaica before sailing gave him a better idea.

The *Merrye Laurie* would make a wonderful gift for his affianced bride.

Taking up the well-fingered note, James repeated the lady's name. The *Lady* Olivia. Daughter of The Right Honorable Earl of Figg.

This engagement to the daughter of a peer, which had been negotiated by his agent in London, was the culmination of James's ambition and a fitting tribute to his father's memory. A merchant seaman, Seth Avery had thrived in the India trade, amassing enough in the way of sterling to have his son raised as a gentleman. His goal had been nothing less than to have his family raised to the peerage.

On his father's death, James had inherited a fortune large enough to tempt an earl. But it had been his own success in capturing French and Spanish ships for the Crown as a privateer that had led to his being knighted at the age of twenty-five. Since the revolution in the American colonies, French ships had been attacking British vessels and ports. James had found that His Majesty George III could be astonishingly grateful to those who protected his interests on the high seas.

Captain of his own ship at the age of nineteen, James had refused to be defeated at sea; losing a battle could have meant the loss of all he knew and loved. But the financial rewards of taking enemy ships had been enormous—enough to buy him the daughter of a peer if not his own peerage.

Olivia. Saying her name to himself, James leaned back in his chair and tried to conjure a vision of his future wife. But, as always since the letter had arrived, his imagination came up short.

His instructions to Pearson, his agent, had been clear when he had dictated them along with his other items of business: *a wife, daughter of a peer, one without heirs, in distressed circumstances. A willingness to enter into a marriage of convenience, favorable terms . . .*

According to this letter, Pearson had fulfilled James's requirements to a tee.

"His lordship's circumstances," Pearson wrote, "have been greatly reduced by his proclivities for gambling. Otherwise, his agent assured me, Lord Figg would never begin to entertain the notion of linking his name to a person whose birth he must naturally consider inferior to his own—"

The earl's superior attitude had irritated James, but he had foreseen it as one of the obvious drawbacks to such a union. It was only natural that a gentleman would resent the person to whom he must look for relief. He also understood that a man born to the ermine would consider any commoner inferior to himself.

But a man mired in debt from his own foolishness . . . He gave a grunt of disgust.

James had no patience with gamblers, at least not the cardplaying sort, although he himself had taken risks all his life. Every moment he was at sea, his life could be forfeit, not even counting the danger of battle. But he had no use for a man who spent his days playing at dice with his family's inheritance.

Still, he had expected some sort of vice from his future father-in-law. Who else but an impoverished wastrel would trade a daughter for money?

But gambler or not, Lord Figg was a peer with no heirs. This connection could help James and his sons to a peerage of their own.

He reread the remainder of the letter. Lord Figg, it seemed, had made some very stiff demands upon his purse, but his agent was still trying to negotiate a better settlement. Pearson went on to describe the Lady Olivia in general terms. According to Lord Figg's man of business, she could not be "a day over thirty." Pearson seemed to think that James would need to be reassured about his fiancée's attractiveness since she had been so long a spinster, but James's only concern was that she understand the nature of this marriage.

He did not intend to give up the sea. His principal reason for seeking an arranged marriage was that he didn't want the kind of ties strong affection demanded. He didn't want a wife who would be miserable when he was gone, as his mother had been every time his father had been absent for months or years at a stretch. James hoped Lady Olivia would relish the distance he would give her in exchange for his own.

As he reached the end of the letter, another knock on his cabin door announced Mr. Shirley again, this time with a prisoner in tow.

As the two entered, James caught sight of a boy with fair skin smeared with dirt and soot and blood, and he frowned with distaste. The lad's clothes were tattered, and so big they dwarfed his scrawny body. A long, tarred pigtail trailed down the center of his back. The expression on his dirt-stained face was mutinous, and it was plain from the odor that quickly overwhelmed the tiny cabin that he hadn't washed himself in weeks.

Something about that essence—an elusive sweetness or musk—caused the hairs on James's neck to rise, in spite of the years he'd spent in the company of unwashed men.

He shook the feeling off to examine the boy more closely. The last thing he wanted on his ship was a surly sailor who had lived under the influence of pirates. Still, he couldn't let a boy this young go so early to his grave.

The top of the boy's head barely came to James's shoulder. His eyes were bright and fair-lashed, and a glimpse of his wrists and neck showed that his bones were still small and delicate. James wondered how a child so fragile had survived among a crew of murderous brutes.

He started to speak. Then he noticed some chains about the boy's slim ankles.

Pointing to them, he said, "Was this necessary, Mr. Shirley?" He trusted his look would make his displeasure clear.

"The lad put up quite a fight, sir, till I told 'im we were comin' to see you."

Surprised, James searched the stripling's face. "You wanted to see me, boy?

"Aye, sir."

"What for?"

To his astonishment, the boy's gaze raked him up and down, pausing to stare at his expensive wig and his cleanshaven face, at the lines of his chest, and at the bulge between his parted thighs. Something about this bold, curious gaze caused James's muscles to contract. He snapped his legs together.

"Answer the cap'n!" Shirley snarled, giving the boy a vicious shove.

Jerked to his manners, the boy flushed rosily under his grime and a mischievous smile curled the corners of his lips. "No reason, sir," he mumbled, darting a glance James's way. "Just wanted to get a good look at ye, is all."

James raised a pair of startled brows. He looked to Mr. Shirley for enlightenment, but his first mate, as nonplussed as he, merely shrugged.

Somehow, the boy's sudden shyness had provoked James's own. He cleared his throat, which had begun to clog. "What is your name?"

"Jem."

"How old are you, Jem?"

"Nineteen, I thinks."

"You *think*," James corrected him automatically, but he had to snort at the boy's response. His voice was much too high to come from a lad of nineteen, not to mention his obvious lack of beard.

"I'm afraid your chin gives that story the lie," James said. "How old are you really?"

Jem wrinkled his brow. "Didn't I just tell ye, Capting?"

"None of your cheek with the cap'n!" Shirley was ready to deal the boy another blow, but James stopped him with an upheld hand.

"It's all right, Mr. Shirley. The lad may not know his numbers. How did you come to be on the *Merrye Laurie*, Jem?"

"Don't know, Capting." The confusion on Jem's face only deepened. "Been there all me life, I guess."

The boy seemed frank enough, yet he couldn't be telling the truth. "Think, lad." James acted stern. "Surely you remember the first time you came aboard the brig. Who were your parents?"

"Parents, sir?" Jem shifted uncomfortably under his gaze.

James was about to lose all patience with the boy. "Your parents, Jem. Your father and mother. The people who gave you life."

Jem looked relieved. "Oh, I han't got none o' them, Capting."

"The word's cap*tain*, not cap*ting*."

"If you say so, sir." He seemed surprised.

James tossed a frustrated glance at his first mate, but Mr. Shirley was at a loss to offer a clue.

James felt too tired, too hungry, and suddenly much too irritable to carry on a futile discussion with the boy, who was either a terrible liar or so starved he couldn't think. He couldn't possibly have joined a pirate crew before the age of eight or nine, even if he had been an infant when his ship had been captured. And that being so, unless Jem were merely a dimwit, he must surely remember when he'd gone aboard.

James gave him a disapproving look, but Jem's expression revealed he had forgotten the question entirely. He was staring at James's elegantly curled wig, while uncertainly fingering his own tar-soaked hair.

And for some strangely potent and unfathomable reason, James felt an unaccustomed heat invade his core.

He cleared his throat again, rising abruptly. "Is there something you wish to say to me, boy?"

Jem started as if he'd been caught peeping into a brothel. Then he grinned like a shameless imp. "You be just that clean an' all, Capting, I never saw such a like—Cap-*tain*," he hastily corrected himself when he saw the look of shock on James's face.

Mr. Shirley suppressed a snort of surprised laughter.

James felt a crimson heat rising from his neck into his throat.

"Enough of that, lad." Shirley had recovered enough to jerk on the captive's chain. "What'll we do with 'im, sir? Send 'im to Kingston with them other bastards?"

All trace of color drained from Jem's face. He threw a desperate look James's way.

James was still unsure about what he should do with the boy. "Let me think on it, Mr. Shirley. I'll give you my answer before the *Merrye Laurie* sails. Meanwhile, Jem can rest below with the second watch. That will be all," he said, turning back to his work.

"Aye, aye, sir."

"Er . . . Cap-tain, sir?"

James looked up from his desk to find the boy's stare firmly fixed on his face. Jem's skin still showed ghostly white beneath the dirt.

"What is it, Jem?"

"It's Mr. Bonny, sir, Sharkee's doctor." Jem's fingers played nervously with the rope at his waist. "What ye going to do with him, sir?"

"I haven't decided yet." He wasn't accustomed to being questioned by his prisoners. He was about to dismiss the boy briskly again when Jem drew himself up to his full, diminutive height.

"If Mr. Bonny goes wi' the others, then so does I."

"*I* will be the one to decide what to do with you both," James reminded him—but not without interest. This boy was a mystery. And so, in part, was the doctor. "Do you have a particular fondness for this Mr. Bonny?"

Jem's brows snapped together in confusion. "A fondness, sir?"

"Yes, a fondness. An affection." When Jem still seemed bemused, James said impatiently, "Is there some reason why you care what happens to this doctor?"

Jem's gaze darted about, as if he found the

question disturbing. "I just don't want nothin' bad to happen to 'im, is all."

"But he was part of your crew, was he not? Why should I spare any one of you pirates?" James hoped he might get an answer to this question, at least.

Jem squirmed. "Well . . . yessir . . . an' no, sir. Fact is, he's been aboard the *Merrye Laurie* long as I have, sir, but he weren't no pirate. Never did no fighting, Capting."

"*Any* fighting."

"No sir, none!"

Amused, but more than a little taken aback by his own reaction to the boy's grammar, James gave it up. Why should he let this boy disturb him? Why was he correcting Jem's English when he did not bother to correct his crew's? In the life most sailors led, equally divided between ocean voyages and Newgate, they had precious little use for grammar.

A fleeting image of Jem in prison unsettled James. He said hoarsely, "Never mind. I'll take your word for it that Mr. Bonny never took part in any attacks. Is that it?"

"Yessir. But, Cap'n, what will ye do with 'im?"

James sighed and rubbed his face.

"Enough, boy!" his first mate snarled. "Can't ye see the cap'n's not made up his mind? Don't talk back, or I'll have ye gagged!"

A glint of pure determination lit Jem's sea-green eyes. He folded his arms across his chest and stared stubbornly over at James.

Seeing that fearless look, in spite of the first

mate's powerful threats, James thought he understood how the boy had survived. *His size might be slight and his muscles puny, but inside he has a solid core of steel.*

As Shirley started to drag Jem from the cabin, James called, "Wait." On an impulse, he gestured for Mr. Shirley to remove the boy's chains. Then he said without a smile, "Jem and Mr. Bonny will sail with us to England. You can tell the *Merrye Laurie*'s crew to cast off." James pretended not to notice the boy's look of intense relief, though seeing it gave him an odd sense of pleasure.

The boy might be ignorant and dirty, but James had just caught a glimpse of a quality he prized above all others. The boy had loyalty.

"Aye, aye, Cap'n." Mr. Shirley sighed. "And what work can I give 'im? He's much too weak to work up top."

James considered for a moment, before saying, "He can train to be my cabin boy."

Jem's eyes grew round, but his look was wary as he asked, "Does at mean I sleeps in here wif you?"

"No, thank God. You will sleep—and it is *sleep*, not *sleeps*—in the fo'c's'le with the rest of the crew. But when you are on duty, you will stay close by and follow my commands with no questions asked. Is that understood?"

"Yessir!" Jem saluted, his back ramrod straight. "No questions asked, Cap'n! What sort of commands, Cap'n?"

James fought a grin. He had not been wrong

about the boy's spirit. But he would have to keep him in order from the start or lose control of his crew.

Therefore, he said, "None of your business, sailor. You may go. Mr. Shirley will find you a hammock. You will report to me tomorrow after you bathe."

"Bathe?" The word seemed to take Jem up short.

"Yes, you will bathe. And you will scrub."

"What for, Cap'n?"

"To remove your stench."

Jem blinked as if he'd been struck, and the excitement faded from eyes.

James had the ridiculous feeling he had been rude. "Sorry, boy. But I doubt you've bathed in your whole life. And I can't have you coming in and out of my cabin smelling like a pigsty. You'll need some clean clothes. See that the purser issues him a new set, Mr. Shirley."

"Then I'll be as clean and trim as you?" Jem asked.

Mr. Shirley reached out to cuff him for his impudence, but the boy nimbly ducked out of his reach. "Will I, sir?" Jem insisted.

"Close enough, Jem." James couldn't understand the boy's fascination with his cleanliness, and it made him uneasy. He couldn't let Jem start out on the wrong foot, however, so he gave the briefest of nods to show he'd been dismissed.

"Mr. Shirley"—James called his first mate back after the boy had left—"I want you to strip Jem naked and throw those foul-smelling

27

clothes overboard. Tell Cook to use rainwater, so the soap can make suds. And, if you need help, get the bosun's mates to scrub the rascal from head to toe."

"Aye, sir."

"And have them check him for lice," James said. "And check him all over."

Chapter Two

Annie couldn't believe her good fortune. As she crossed the maindeck in Mr. Shirley's wake, a tumult of relief made her take a running swipe at a rope dangling above her head.

She would not be sent to rot in jail with the other pirates. She would stay free and easy aboard the *Flying Swan* with its three tall masts and its sails that nearly reached the sky. The ocean breeze filled her nostrils with its rich, salty bouquet, and she inhaled deeply.

She would be a cabin boy, with Mr. Bonny safe as well.

Despite her pangs for the *Merrye Laurie* and her crew—especially for Captain Sharkee—Annie had always known that her future would lie aboard another ship. She had seen too many pirates come and go not to know that one day her own turn would come to be set adrift. She had feared that moment when Sharkee, enraged and in a fit of temper, would cast her off as he'd done to so many of his men.

The other pirates' lot, which she and Mr. Bonny had narrowly missed, was so terrible as to make her grateful for what she'd got. She had never believed she'd be so lucky as to take Mr. Bonny with her, even though living without him was a fate she had never wanted to face.

But now, when she'd least expected it, she'd found a safe berth for herself and for him. For a while again, she could breathe. She would always be at the mercy of a captain, unless she could become one herself. But if she could work her way to first mate, she would be able to protect Mr. Bonny forever. The thought that she might lose him had scared her more than any danger she'd ever faced.

Relieved of her greatest fears, she followed Mr. Shirley down the companionway onto the gundeck, where the ship's cannons framed the crew's well-arranged sleeping quarters. He found her a hammock and showed her where to hang it, before leading her to an open space outside the galley.

There, he and the cook, a strong-armed man with a wooden peg for a leg, seemed to forget her presence while they busied themselves over a steeping tub. Annie supposed they were going to soak some salt beef in it for tomorrow's mess, for they filled it with precious drinking water from the barrels. They didn't seem to need or want any help from her, so her attention soon strayed.

The captain—Captain Avery, that was—had looked even more formidable up close than he had in battle. A large, strapping man with a stern, unreadable face, he had dwarfed the wooden chair to his desk. With muscles that bulged under his tight-fitting jacket—and that powerful bulge between his legs—he had looked as magnificent as any ship of the line under full sail. The kerchief tied about his brawny neck had been trimmed in lace, a feature she had seen on no other man but Mr. Bonny. The captain wore an elegant wig, too, made of real human hair and gathered with a black, silk ribbon into a queue.

Dragged before him in all his finery, Annie had felt strangely ashamed as she'd fingered her scraggly pigtail. Then, the captain's disgust for her smell had almost made her flinch. No one she'd ever known had washed much, with the exception of Mr. Bonny and Captain Sharkee. And even Mr. Bonny had never worn a wig as fine as this captain's. She wondered what Captain Avery's hair was like underneath it. He hadn't worn it in battle, and from a distance, his hair had seemed short and brown.

She would like to get a peek at the captain's hair, as well as his body beneath those clothes. She had no doubt his chest and arms would be as strong as an anchor and his smooth, taut skin as cleanly white as the breeches that hugged those mighty thighs. And in those skintight pants, his codpiece had seemed bigger than any she'd ever seen.

Annie had seen more than a few male organs in her life. She had to wonder how Captain Avery's would measure up.

This bath he wanted her to have could be something of a problem, though. She would have to use her wits. Annie wasn't quite sure how she could manage to change her clothes aboard the *Flying Swan*.

She could bathe in the sea, fully clothed. She could swim and tread water as well as the next man—actually better—but once rinsed, she'd have to find a private place in which to bind her breasts and pull off her ragged breeches. Mr. Bonny would help her to find a place. Now that she knew he was aboard, she should have no fears.

"All right, lad"—Mr. Shirley called her back—"it's time to strip."

Annie gave a jump and found Mr. Shirley and Cook staring purposefully down at her, their arms tightly folded across their chests.

"Strip on down to yer birthday suit, and hop right quick into this tub. Cap'n's orders."

Annie looked from one grimly serious face to the other, then down at the rain-filled tub, and she felt her cheeks go pale. *Bathe naked*? "No, sir. The sea's good enough for me."

She backed toward the companionway, but Mr. Shirley and Cook split to go around her, arms wide to cut off her escape.

"Cap'n's orders, I said. Now, get yer hide into that tub!"

Annie recognized the warning in his tone. It said, *Obey, or you'll get a rare cobbing*. But she couldn't strip naked. Not ever. Not after what Sharkee had told her!

Mr. Shirley made a dive, and the cook grabbed.

Annie reached inside her pants.

"Captain, come quick!"

James heard his steward's voice at the door and bolted out of his chair. In the distance, he had heard the sounds of an altercation: voices raised in anger, shouts and curses, even a muffled crash. But he had faith in Mr. Shirley and his other officers' ability to bring the crew back in line. He had simply taken himself to task for allowing them to dispense the rum. It must have been too soon after battle for the men's excitement to be contained.

"Which fool was it?" he asked as he passed Krebs on the maindeck. "Harry Sikes or Turpin Brown?"

"It's one of the new ones, sir."

"Damn! I should have known." James started down the companionway toward the noise, which seemed to be coming from the gundeck. "I thought I told Mr. Shirley to have them watched."

Krebs hurried after him, his short legs running to keep up. "But they *are* being watched, Captain. They're down in the hold, locked up!"

James cast a look over his shoulder, never slowing his pace. "Make sense, Mr. Krebs. You've said it's one of the new men, but they're locked up?"

"Aye, Captain, but—"

Krebs didn't have time to finish. As they rounded the bulkhead to the galley, the ghastly scene before them spoke for itself.

Clutching a sodden red handkerchief to his shoulder, Mr. Shirley was leaning against a beam, shouting orders to the crew. Seated on the deck, Cook cradled his face in his hands. Blood oozed between his fingers. And if this weren't enough, half the second watch stood pushing and shoving at the galley door.

James forced a pathway through them. "What the—"

"Capting?" Jem's voice rang hopefully above the hubbub.

James elbowed a sailor out of the way to peer over the bosun's head.

There in the galley stood Jem, poised in a crouch in front of Cook's stove. A dripping dagger was gripped in one hand, a bloodied butcher knife in the other. A third, which he'd grasped between his teeth, had clattered to the floor when he'd called.

Water lay sloshed all over the galley and the seamen's mess. It was swirling pink with blood.

"Jem, for God's sake, *what is going on?*"

James's fiercest roar seemed to have no daunting effect on the boy. Jem beamed him a smile. "Well, Cap'n, thank the Lord ye've come."

"Jem—" James restrained his tongue, striving to keep his anger in check. He issued a sharp command to the bosun, who reluctantly stepped aside to let him pass. Determined to discover the reason for the quarrel before passing judgment, he stopped on the galley threshhold.

"What is the meaning of this?" he said, in a voice designed to promote instant calm.

Jem straightened from his crouch. In spite of his cheerful greeting, the boy looked pale and it was clear he was afraid. As he stood, some of the tension seemed to ease from his shoulders, but he kept both his weapons raised.

"I was just defending meself, Captain."

Shocked and displeased, James turned to look back at his crew. "Did anyone attack this boy?"

Shirley's voice came weakly. "Just followin' your orders, Cap'n. Tryin' to get the boy washed."

James faced Jem again. "Is this true?"

To his astonishment Jem nodded with a look that bespoke his outrage. "Aye, sir, but they tried to strip me, sir!"

A measure of relief came over James. A simple misunderstanding, that's all it had been. Not something vicious perpetrated by one of his crew. He hadn't liked the thought that one of them might have tried to hurt the boy.

"And what's wrong with being stripped? You have to strip to be washed. I gave that order."

Jem's eyes grew round. His grip on the knives tightened as he backed cautiously toward the stove.

"No, sir." He shook his head fast. "Nobody strips me."

James felt a sharp frown wrinkling his forehead. "Whyever not, boy? Surely you've disrobed before."

Jem shook his head vehemently.

This brat, James thought, guarding his patience, was proving to be much more trouble than he was worth. "Well, now we know what accounts for your stench. You've never seen so much as a drop of water."

"That ain't so! I does wash! In the sea, wif me clothes *on*!"

"Well, that's not good enough. You will strip and wash in clean water from now on. And count yourself lucky to be given the chance: we don't usually have that much extra water on board. Look at what you've wasted already."

As the frustration in James's voice mounted, the boy turned white, then red. "I will not. Ye can't make me!"

James clenched his fists. He would not stand to have his orders refused; he could already hear the men's grumbles behind him. Discipline was all that kept him alive with the sort of ruffians who often put to sea. But he could tell the boy was not going to give in without a struggle and, when that happened, he didn't want his crew to watch.

"All of you, back to your posts," he ordered. "Dims, Taylor"—he addressed the bosun's mates who had failed to capture the boy—"help these men to the sick bay."

Capturing Annie

Shirley stood. His voice trembled when he said, "Let me take care of 'im, Cap'n. With enough men, we can jump 'im and throw the dirty brat overboard."

James restrained the harsh words that flew to his lips. He could overlook a hint of insubordination in a man who'd had his arm carved up.

"I think not, Mr. Shirley. I will handle this myself."

"But, Cap'n—"

"Enough! Whatever you have to say about the lad, he's certainly proved he's good in a fight." The look he gave his men was enough to make them flush. "Retire. All of you."

The deck cleared while James kept a close eye on Jem. After seeing what he'd done to the other two, James had to assume he might throw a knife, though he'd be sorry if he tried. Jem had certainly been trained to use a weapon. James wanted to see if he could put that training to better use.

"Where'd you get that dagger?" he asked.

"It's mine, Cap'n. I keeps it in me breeches."

Oddly provoked, James snapped, "I *keep* it in *my* breeches."

"Ah, ye've got one in there, too?" His eyes falling to the bulge in James's breeches, Jem grimaced and nodded. "That would account fer it, then."

Resisting the same queasy feeling that had made him flush above deck, James drew in a deep breath.

"No, you little bantling," he said. "I meant

37

nothing of the kind. I was trying to teach you how to speak correctly—though God knows why! Jem, *put down those knives*!"

Jem eyed him warily. "No, sir. Can't do that yet, sir."

"For God's sake, Jem, you must obey me! And Mr. Shirley, too. You heard what he said. He wants to throw you over the brink."

Jem grinned. "That'd be all right, Cap'n. Then I could wash like I wants and still be yer cabin boy."

James was torn between a strong desire to strangle the lad and an equally powerful urge to laugh. He shook his head to rid it of such mingled emotions. "No, you will not. Not unless you bathe properly."

"Then I can't be yer cabin boy?" Jem's crestfallen look was ludicrous.

"No. If you want to be my servant, you must bathe. It won't happen any other way."

Jem sadly shook his head. "Then, that's that, I guess."

So. He would not give in. Weary of this futile argument, James knew he had no recourse. If he allowed this boy to get away with disobeying him, the result could be chaos and mutiny. James had a reasonably good group of sailors, but he was under no illusions as to the temper of a crew. Mr. Shirley's authority had to be backed by the bosun's lash, and James's own command must go unquestioned.

He would have to subdue the boy, though the

thought of injuring Jem gave him no pleasure. He turned to call for help.

"Cap'n? Where're ye going?"

James said curtly, "To call up reinforcements." Giving a glance backward and seeing the stunned look on Jem's face, he offered in a gentler tone, "You can't hold out against me forever, lad. You're a good fighter, Jem, but I've got some mean hands on deck, and I'm not too bad with a knife myself."

Jem seemed to wilt. He swayed briefly on his feet, before catching himself with one hand upon the stove.

With a start of realization, James saw how close to breaking the boy was. He cursed himself for not seeing it sooner. Of course, the boy was exhausted. He had fought a desperate battle this morning and lost, been confined with no meal in the hold of the brig, then brought aboard to face he-knew-not-what. Added to all that, he had just fought off two men three times his size and held out against two angry bosun's mates.

James took two steps closer to Jem and held out his hand for the weapons. "Come on, lad. Give it up—"

He stopped short. Jem had raised his dagger and was holding it to his own throat.

"No!" Appalled by the boy's reaction, James held up his hands. "Don't do it, Jem! Let's talk."

"I've already told ye, Cap'n"—the boy's voice was shaky but determined—"I'll not strip for no man. Not after what Cap'n Sharkee told me."

James's heart beat queerly. This was no mere truculence on the boy's part, he saw, but genuine terror. "What did Sharkee tell you, lad?"

"He said"—Jem swallowed before he continued—"he said that t'were better I slit me own throat than to take off me breeches."

"What?" James felt more befuddled than before. "For God's sake, why?"

" 'Cause every Jack Tar aboard would want to stick his poker in me."

James couldn't believe his ears. "His *what*?"

Jem gave him a wide look of surprise, then made a sudden swipe at the front of James's breeches. "Ye know, Cap'n—yer poker. Yer priggin' part."

James had been standing too close. The knife sliced near his manhood, making him jump back in alarm as he fought the urge to protect his member with both hands. "Of all—" A foul oath escaped him. "I know what you mean, boy! There's no need—"

Jem broke out into a grin.

At the sight of his ready amusement, James's temper sprang to the fore.

"I'll have you know, you little cur, that that sort of behavior would never be tolerated on my ship! Any sailor who even contemplated such a crime aboard my vessel would be flogged within an inch of his life, and my men know it!"

The boy's grin faded. Relief warred with skepticism as he asked, "Is'at really true, Capting?"

"Of course, it's true!" James had put up with too much. To waste time on this raggamuffin had been bad enough, but to have his discipline so impugned enraged him. "I don't know what sort of scoundrels Sharkee had on his ship, but let me assure you, a British gentleman's crew is quite another thing. I—"

"How do ye know?"

The question caught him off guard.

"I beg your pardon?" he asked in a frosty tone.

"I says how do ye know, Cap'n? How do ye knows what goes on down below?"

"I—well—" To his embarrassment, James heard himself begin to bluster. The truth was that half his crew, like every other, was made up of the scum of England. There would be very little difference between them and Sharkee's men. But to suggest that such things would go on aboard his ship and without his knowledge put him in a dangerous mood.

The infernal brat was still looking as if he didn't believe him. Jem gave him a knowing wink, still holding his dagger on guard.

"It's just like Cap'n Sharkee told me, Cap'n. Ye can't knows what goes on all over yer ship."

"I know my men."

"Do ye now? What about them few ye took from Sharkee's? They'd poke me, just as sure as yer standin' there."

A sick feeling came over James. "How do you know?"

Jem's eyes grew round with astonishment. "I told ye! Sharkee said so."

James rubbed a hand over his eyes. "So that's it, is it? The reason you won't bathe is because

41

you don't want to strip in front of my men. Because you're afraid?"

Jem nodded. James could see that nothing he could say would ever change the boy's mind. Perhaps, in time, if the lad began to feel safer on board, if he came to be better acquainted with the crew—perhaps then, he would learn to get over this unreasonable fear.

James mumbled a few curses directed at Sharkee and the sort of scurvy creatures he'd employed, but he knew he had lost. This boy was too exhausted to be reasonable, and it was hardly surprising after all he had been through. James himself had noticed Jem's fragility and wondered how he'd survived. By pure muleheadedness, it seemed.

"All right, boy," he said wearily. "You won't have to strip in front of my men." His heart gave a lurch when he saw the intensity of the boy's relief. "But you will bathe," he said. "And wear clean clothes."

"But how, Cap'n?" Jem's knife moved up quickly.

"You have my word," James said. His word must have meant nothing, for Jem didn't relax, not until he explained. "You can bathe here in the galley alone. Fill the tub with water and bolt the door. No one can come in while you're washing."

He pointed to a cake of soap which had fallen on the floor in the skirmish. "Take that and wet it, and rub it all over yourself until it makes a good lather. Then rinse it off in the tub. I want your head scrubbed, behind and inside your ears, under your fingernails, between your toes and your cheeks—and especially your poker, or whatever it is you call it."

"Aye, aye, sir!" Jem's face, in spite of his exhaustion, had brightened again. "I knew ye would fix it if ye came."

Such trust moved James, in spite of how painfully it had been won. To hide his feelings, he spoke sternly, "Just make certain you don't go cutting up my men again. Understood?"

"Yessir."

James turned to go, grateful that his men hadn't been there to see him when he'd jumped from that knife.

"And Jem."

"Yessir."

"I'll have one of the men bring you some clothes. After you strip, unlock the door and throw your old clothes out. They must go overboard."

"Yessir!"

"And you will have to clean up this mess."

"Aye, aye, sir."

James was relieved to see that the boy didn't argue about every order he gave. Merely two out of three.

When James reached the deck, the wind had risen. The *Flying Swan* was skimming over the water under full sail. He took a deep, healthful breath of the ocean air to clear his head. The tenseness in his neck made him realize just how worried he'd been.

He glanced astern in time to see the *Merrye Laurie* disappearing over the horizon on her way back to Jamaica. *Too late to send the boy*, James thought, and his stomach gave a curious twinge.

He couldn't define it, although in spite of his misgivings, he could admit he wouldn't be sorry to keep the boy. Jem was a bright, sharp-eyed lad. Brave as well as loyal. And turning him into a respectable sailor would certainly be a challenge. If he could only learn to obey, he would make a fine crewman.

James climbed the ladder to his quarterdeck and strode to the wheel, telling the helmsman, "I'll take her for now."

The sailor lounged across the deck to give the captain his sacred privacy. As James took the wheel lightly in both hands, he could feel each wave as it beat the hull, each pull or lapse of his sails as they tugged in the breeze. Nothing could soothe him better than guiding his own ship over a glittering ocean. Even after twenty years on and off at sea, he could still find peace when the wind ruffled his hair and he felt the craft responding to his every touch.

The scene in the galley had unsettled him badly. The boy might have killed himself. If Jem had, he would not have been the first to do so on one of James's ships. Men could grow despondent on a long sea voyage. But James would have blamed himself if Jem had taken his own life.

"Cap'n?" Shirley's head appeared over the ladder to the quarterdeck, soon followed by the rest of him. "What was that with the young 'un, sir?"

James waited until his first mate had drawn near. "He was scared."

"Scared of a bath? Huh!"

James shook his head, wondering how much he should say. But considering that Mr. Shirley had suffered a wound to his pride as well as to his body, James thought it best to inform him or harmony would never be restored.

"Not entirely," James said. "It seems he's been told that if he takes his breeches off, he runs the risk of being poked by the men."

"Buggered, ye mean?" Shirley's cheeks reddened in fury. "Aye, I'll bugger 'im if he—"

"Mr. Shirley, you forget yourself!" James was surprised by the visceral nature of his reaction. He couldn't bring himself to laugh at the boy's fright. "You will remember that Jem has led a rough life. Rougher even than most sailors'. It will take time for him to understand that we do things differently aboard the *Flying Swan*."

Even as he finished speaking, a sickening thought caused a rise in his stomach. What if the boy were speaking from experience? His lack of memory, his unreasonable fear, seemed strange at best. What if the lad had been used by one of Sharkee's men?

James signaled to his helmsman to take the

wheel. "Mr. Shirley," he said, "I want to see this Dr. Bonny in my cabin at once."

"Aye, aye, sir. It's him who fixed me up. Did an uncommon good job, too."

James searched his first mate's face. "Did you tell the doctor who had wounded you?"

"Yessir."

"What did he say?"

Shirley scratched his grizzled head. "Didn't say nothing, sir. Just asked if the boy'd been hurt. When I told him no, he looked a bit relieved, that's all."

James nodded, but his mind was awhirl. This relationship between the man and the boy—it might have been an unnatural one. Men grew restless out of port; and, some, if there were no women around, could be tempted to settle for a boy.

Was that it? he asked himself. Had his nose sensed something unhealthy about Jem? Had it picked up a scent of illicit sex and tried to warn him?

James would be damned if he would allow someone to use a boy thusly on his ship. Besides his own revulsion, such a situation on the ship could only lead to unrest among the men.

"Send Bonny to me," he said grimly. "I'll be waiting in my cabin."

Chapter Three

Annie obeyed her new captain, filling the tub again with water from the barrels. One of the sailors had brought her a new homespun shirt and a clean pair of breeches.

With the door firmly closed, she stripped off her filth-soaked garments, cracked the door to throw them out, then slammed it shut and threw the latch. A long strip of cloth was wrapped tightly about her chest, but she would have to keep it, for she would have no other until Mr. Bonny could find a replacement. This one had been torn from a dress she'd found in one of the seaman's chests they'd plundered. A lady's dress, she'd been told by a mate. Of course, he'd never known what she'd meant to use it for. Only Mr. Bonny and Sharkee had known, and Captain

47

Sharkee had never referred to it again, not since the time he'd told her to keep her breeches on.

Naked now, Annie stepped into the tub of water, so clear it was fit to drink. As she sank down, she gave a blissful sigh. If this was the way they lived aboard the *Flying Swan*, she thought she could get used to it. Even her breasts felt good, and Annie had always hated her breasts. She had never understood why they had to be such a pain when the other pirates were never bothered with theirs.

But now they felt wonderful, floating in the coolish water with the tub's waves tickling their crests.

She lay back against the tub's wooden edge, loving the touch of this sweet, clean water as it whirled gently between her legs. As much as Annie loved the sea, its sting had never made her feel nearly this good. She closed her eyes and gave herself up to these welcome sensations, until an ugly image snaked through to her thoughts.

Captain Sharkee.

Dead . . . because of her?

Annie swallowed, but her throat seemed to have closed. A momentary weakness made her eyes fill with tears. It was almost impossible to imagine life without Captain Sharkee. He'd been so big and fierce, and he'd raged the way a pirate ought to rage. Sure he'd boxed her ears and cuffed her across the deck. And there had been times he'd been so rough, she'd wanted to take her knife to his throat. But he'd never flogged her.

And there had been other times, when none of the other pirates had been watching, when he'd given her a pat on the shoulder or a friendly tap upon the cheek.

Well, she reminded herself, fighting the lump in her throat, Sharkee would not expect her to mourn him. They'd seen too many pirates come and go, he and she, ever to waste time mourning for a companion lost. If she had been the one to go, Sharkee would have thrown her body overboard without a backward glance. So, why did she feel so rotten about him?

Things would be different on Captain Avery's ship. Its decks were clean. The captain's cabin was neat. And this captain seemed different, indeed. Annie didn't know why, but when his voice boomed, she wanted to move closer to hear it. When his face grew hard in anger and his body loomed, something inside her wanted to melt.

A pair of drops slipped past her eyelids. Annie was both astonished and ashamed. *I haven't cried since I was a baby*. If a little knife fight was going to turn her into a water spout, then the captain would surely send her back to port. The fear of being marooned in a city made her sit up and reach for the soap.

She rubbed herself vigorously. In a short while, she had lathered her whole body, and the grime of years had floated away. Excited, she went over certain parts again: her breasts and under her arms and in that place she should have had a poker. Of course she didn't have one, but the captain would never know that. She imagined she smelled as good about now as one of those bright purple flowers from the tropical isles.

Annie saw that the marks from her tight bindings had nearly been erased. She lay back against the wall of the tub and closed her eyes. An image of the captain floated into her mind, and a flush started in the spot between her legs before rolling to the tips of her breasts. The feeling surprised her, but, then, this whole bath felt strange. She knew she should get up and get to work, but the water felt so good . . . and she was so tired. Her neck lolled against the metal tub's edge. The rocking of the ship sent the water in the tub back and forth across her breasts like waves against the rocks. . . .

As James paced in his cabin, he prepared himself for a confrontation with the doctor. This was a situation he had never faced. He had long ago decided that the vices of his crew were their own business so long as they did not endanger his ship. But, in this instance, there was a boy to protect.

"You wished to see me, Captain Avery?" A hesitant voice broke in on his thoughts.

James looked up, and was astonished to find that the ogre he'd half-expected was nothing but a thin, stoop-shouldered, old man with a pair of crooked spectacles hanging on his nose. The doctor's ancient wig had retained no more than a handful of hair, tied into a thin, wispy tail. Though worn through at the knees and elbows, his sober black suit had once had a Puritan cut.

Pointing to a chair, James swallowed the remarks he had planned to make, convinced that his suspicions about the doctor and the boy had been unfounded. "Won't you come in, Mr. Bonny, and sit down?

Once the old man was settled across from his desk, James asked, "How long have you sailed on the *Merrye Laurie*?"

"About nineteen years, I believe."

"And, you say, you were kidnapped?"

Mr. Bonny bobbed his head. "That is correct."

"Then, how is it you never managed to escape?"

The doctor gave a deprecating cough. "Some things are not so easily managed, Captain. You flatter me if you think me capable of overcoming my captors."

"But surely there were opportunities—"

"I was of some value to the crew." Mr. Bonny shrugged. "Captain Sharkee had me heavily watched. And later . . . well, other matters tend to interfere."

"Such as . . ."

The doctor sighed. "Such as one's age, Captain Avery. I am not a young man. You young, virile men cannot possibly understand the feebleness of age."

James took a short turn about his cabin, his

51

hands clasped behind his back and his gaze fixed on Mr. Bonny.

"This boy . . . Jem."

"I hear you intend to make him your servant. I do not think you will regret it."

"That decision is not final, sir. What I first need to know is something of the boy's history."

"Oh, as to that . . ." Mr. Bonny waved an age-freckled hand. "The boy has no history, as you call it. He's been aboard for most of his life, as I imagine he told you."

"Yes, he did. He also told me he had no memory of ever living on shore." James had paused to stand in front of the doctor, to watch his face.

"There, you see," Mr. Bonny said. "The boy can answer for himself."

"For God's sake, man!" James lost his temper. "The boy is no half-wit, yet he remembers nothing about his life before the age of eight?"

"Did he say that?" Mr. Bonny looked surprised.

"Not precisely. But if he could not have come aboard before that age, and he has no memory of doing so, surely—"

But the good doctor was shrugging again in a gesture James was coming to resent. "I really could not say, Captain. I do not understand all the fuss. He will make you an excellent cabin boy, as soon as he learns better manners. If you like, I can instruct him as to the way he must behave. There wasn't much point before, but now . . ."

James's frustration was building. What was

there about this boy that got under his skin? Why was he certain that something was wrong?

Bang. Bang. "Open up!"

Annie jerked awake, sloshing water on the floor. It took her a moment to realize where she was, before she heard the angry men on the other side of the door, yelling to come in.

She jumped up, spilling more water, and reached for the clothes the sailor had brought her. She had no time to bind her breasts. Hurriedly, she yanked the shirt over her head. Her wet breasts stained the front, but it was big—she hoped big enough to conceal their shape.

She grabbed the breeches and lunged out of the tub. Her legs and hips were dripping. Hopping on one foot, Annie shoved her other inside the pants leg. Soaking wet, her skin clung to the material with every inch. Her old breeches had never been this tight. With men cursing and pounding on the door, she struggled quickly with her next foot and nearly toppled over. She could barely pull them over her legs they were so damp.

Then, when she tried to jerk them over her hips, they wouldn't budge.

Annie cursed the roundness of her bum. Her panic mounted. She pulled and tugged and jerked, but the blasted breeches wouldn't move. Her hips were too wide.

Desperate, she glanced around for something, anything with which to cover herself. . . .

53

Patricia Wynn

But there was nothing between herself and those men but that door.

"Captain!" The shout came loudly, interrupting James's talk with the doctor. "You've got to come again, sir!"

"What is it this time?" James cursed as he threw open the door.

"It's the boy again, sir!"

"For God's sake! Who's he cut up now?" James hastened for the companionway.

"No, sir. That's not it." Kreb's voice came more faintly as he fell behind. "He's not answerin' us, Captain. We've knocked and pounded and near broke the door down, but he don't say a word."

James froze for a moment, before doubling his pace.

Good God! A memory swam before him of Jem holding a knife to his throat. *Oh, dear God, no.*

"Jem!" James pounded on the galley door. "Are you in there, boy? Open up!"

Silence greeted him, except for the ominous breathing of his crew behind him.

"Mr. Lucas." James spoke quickly to his carpenter. "Bring me an axe. The rest of you"—he jerked his head toward the companionway—"clear out. Go back to your duties."

The men shuffled reluctantly back to their posts, leaving only the first mate and Cook behind with James.

James waited tensely for the axe. A jumble of feelings churned inside him, threatening to

smother him: fear of what Jem might have done
to himself, frustration at his failure to get at the
truth, and a growing anger—at himself for
bungling his job—and at Jem for making him
do it.

The axe should have been nearby. Mr. Lucas
seemed to take an unconscionable time in fetch-
ing it.

James waited a moment longer. Then—"Out
of the way." He waved the other two aside. He
braced himself against the beam behind his
shoulders and gave a massive kick.

With a splintering sound, the door cratered at
the latch. He kicked it again, and the door
swung freely, hitting the wall with a crash.

The sight of Jem, standing in one piece in
front of the tub, shattered James's fear, leaving
him with nothing but fury. He loomed, blocking
the doorway, and glared menacingly at the boy,
who shone pale from the neck down to his
shoulders. From there down, he clutched a shirt
that covered the rest of his body except for two
white legs and two sunburnt arms. His eyes,
showing white, rolled with terror back at James.

Two angry strides brought him within reach.
A silent warning—something about the slim-
ness of those legs, the angle of that chest—rang
an alarm in James's ears, but he was too furious
to heed it.

"What the devil do you mean—" Before he finished swearing, he snatched the shirt away—

—and froze, dumbfounded by what he saw.
Two of the sweetest, roundest breasts he'd ever

glimpsed. Two tender pink nipples, tinged purple with cold. A short, narrow waist perched above smooth, spreading hips and a triangular strawberry thatch.

"Captain Avery, sir?"

Mr. Shirley's voice came from behind him. Swallowing, James thrust the shirt back at the boy—*no*—*girl*.

"What's wrong with the lad, sir?"

What's wrong? James's mind screamed loudly. *He's a she!*

Then, as James's startled gaze met the girl's frightened one, he realized his body had blocked the view of his men. This girl—Jem or whoever she was—was gazing mistily up at him like a lamb sent to slaughter. Her green eyes—now, he could see they were green—both begged and dared him with one stare. Beneath the shirt, her woman's breasts gave a quivering heave.

A response from below his belt startled him out of his inaction. Quickly, he turned his back. "Jem"—he paused to clear his throat—"remain here. Mr. Shirley and Cook—outside."

He followed them across the threshhold and closed the splintered door.

"What is it, Cap'n?" Shirley's round eyes demanded an answer. Cook, too, was agog.

"The boy has . . ."

"What, Cap'n?"

James struggled to find a lie. ". . . A slight deformity."

"What?"

"Two . . ." James started to raise both hands to

his chest, but caught himself just in time. He lowered them and closed his eyes.

The truth was he was shaken. It had been so long since he'd been with a woman. His circumstances—fear of the pox, long sea voyages—conspired to make him celibate for long months out of necessity rather than choice, and the sight of this girl's body had nearly sent him overboard.

He had bunched his hands into fists beside his arousal. He dropped them suddenly, afraid his crewmen would notice his state, but Shirley's face was already clouding over with sympathy.

"Kind of a goiter, eh?" he said. "An' two? There? Poor little bugger."

"No wonder he wouldn't strip fer us then," Cook said, wincing.

"Aye, no wonder." Shirley rubbed his jaw.

James felt a burst of relief. He wouldn't have to invent a lie; they'd done it for him. "You men, keep this to yourselves. No need for the rest of the crew to know." He glanced over his shoulder at the door. "Wait here. I'll see what the—what the boy needs."

Still unsettled, he paused before entering the galley again, then rapped twice and stepped inside.

Jem stood just as he'd left her, the shirt clutched across her breasts, her slim legs shivering beneath it. James closed the door as best he could, but the latch was broken, so he leaned his back against it and faced her in silence.

"Why didn't you tell me?" he finally asked in a whisper.

"Tell you what?" She stared back, confused.

Impatient, he gestured toward her body.

"Oh . . . that."

"Yes, that! Why didn't you say you were a girl?"

" 'Cause Sharkee told me not to."

Jem was staring at him sullenly. Now that she was washed, James could see how fair her skin was. Her face and hands and feet had been scorched by the tropical sun, but where the sun had not touched her, she glowed a marbled white, with blue, narrow veins beneath a milky skin. Her hair was still tarred, but he could see a glimmer of color at its roots, a soft strawberry fuzz surrounding her sunburned face. A whiff of memory teased him. But other than the fact that the color of her hair matched her thatch below, the connection eluded him.

What could be done?

Staring at her shapely legs below the shirt, he recalled that she had no clothes on. He swallowed, tamping down the surge between his legs.

"Why didn't you dress?" He glanced away.

She answered in the same loud whisper. "The breeches don't fit me."

"What?" He looked back to see her pointing at one bare hip, and his pulse began to throb.

"Me bum's that big, I can't get 'em over it."

"No . . . well . . ." Her honesty took him aback. "I suppose your hips would be wider than a man's of the same height. They're supposed to be."

"They are?"

"Yes. Didn't you know?"

Jem shook her head. But, then . . . she wasn't Jem.

"What's your name?" he asked.

"Jem—" She seemed surprised at the question.

"It can't be. You must have a girl's name."

"Oh, yeah." She looked ashamedly at the floor. "That would be Annie, I guess."

"You only guess?"

"I never uses it. But Mr. Bonny—he said I should know what it was."

"Ahhhhh. Mr. Bonny." Straightening, James folded his arms and braced his feet against the rocking of the ship. "Do you mean to tell me that he and Captain Sharkee both knew you were a girl and still they let you aboard?"

Annie pulled a frown. "I told ye, Cap'n, I've always shipped aboard the *Merrye Laurie*. But Cap'n Sharkee and Mr. Bonny, they did know. They're the ones who told *me*."

James gave a jerk, and the hair on the back of his neck began to tickle, as if he'd come upon a trap. But then, Annie's hand, the one that was holding her shirt, slipped an inch. He could see the smooth, white mounds of her bosom, the cleft between those breasts. And the pulse in his groin grew more insistent.

"Can I still be your cabin boy?"

An image of her naked in his cabin—in his berth—rocked him with temptation. He started. "No! Of course not. I can't have a woman in my cabin!"

"But why?"

Her innocent confusion brought him to his senses. "We shouldn't be discussing this here. I'll return to my quarters, and you'll report to me there—after you dress. Does the shirt fit?"

She nodded glumly.

"Just a minute." James stepped outside and asked Mr. Shirley for another pair of trousers—a larger one.

His first mate *tsk*ed. "Aye, poor lad, that'll be just the thing."

James waited until Shirley had brought them, then told him to go up on deck. "And when the boy comes out, make sure he reports to me. Mr. Bonny should still be waiting in my cabin. But if he's not, get him in there at once."

James was determined to get answers this time. And now that he knew what to ask, he thought grimly, he would.

He squeezed back inside the galley. Annie, her tarred head bowed, held the shirt with both hands crossed over her breasts, her thumbs hooked underneath her armpits.

"Here," James said, handing her the trousers. "And don't look so dejected. As soon as I can get to the bottom of this, I'll know what to do with you. For the moment, at least, it would be best if the men still thought of you as a boy."

She glanced up at that. "Is it true, then, what Sharkee told me?"

He paused. Now he saw why her fear had been so great, and why Sharkee had cautioned her. "Part of it's true." He stumbled over his answer. "At least . . . you will be certain to be safer if the men don't know the truth."

"And what about you?" She eyed him warily.

"What?"

"Don't *you* want to poke me?"

James's stomach lurched. His heart hammered in his throat. "Of course not!"

"But Cap'n Sharkee said every man would. And yer a man, ain't ye?"

He had been willing himself not to think of her body, but now, she was forcing him to recall those firm, young breasts and creamy thighs. The soft, bushy mound pressed so tightly between her legs.

Just the thought of running his hands over those legs made his throat thicken with desire.

But he chokingly said, "A gentleman wouldn't think of abusing a woman on board his ship, nor would any man with a speck of decency. But Sharkee was right. It would be impossible to trust every man to behave if they knew you were on board."

Annie hunched her shoulders miserably. Her gaze was more desolate than ever, and it was at this precise moment that the extent of her naiveté struck him.

She was a virgin undoubtedly, thanks to Sharkee and Mr. Bonny. But much more than that. Annie seemed to have no understanding at all of what it meant to be a girl. Or a woman—he corrected himself—for she surely was a woman now.

"We can discuss this later, Jem—er, Annie. Do

as I said. Put on those clothes and come to my cabin. I need to have a word with Mr. Bonny first."

"Aye, aye, sir." Her dejected tone followed him outside.

Leaning against the splintered door, James took a deep breath, relieved to be out of her presence. The longer he'd stayed with her, the more his eyes had been drawn to the place where her slim legs emerged from beneath her shirt. The way she held it had concealed her imperfectly, just enough to make him long for another glimpse of the cleft between her legs.

If she could do this to him, what would she do to his crew?

What in God's name am I going to do with her? he thought as he made his way back up to his cabin.

Mr. Bonny was still sitting where James had left him. At the sound of the door, he looked up long enough to read the truth on James's face, and his thin shoulders seemed to bow.

James took a seat before he spoke. Fixing the doctor with an unwavering stare, he said, "Perhaps now you will be good enough to tell me what you know about Jem."

Mr. Bonny removed a tattered handkerchief from his pocket and wiped his forehead. "I knew it would come to this one day, but believe me, Captain, my greatest interest in all these years has been to protect her."

"Annie."

"Yes. Annie." With the speaking of her name, a

look of relief swept over Mr. Bonny's features. "How much did she tell you about herself?"

"Nothing. To be honest, I got the impression that she knows very little. Scarcely, in fact, that she's a female."

Mr. Bonny stared at him in deadly earnest. "For all intents and purposes, Captain, that was how it had to be. If either Captain Sharkee or I had given her any cause to think herself different from the men—if we had given them any cause to suspect the truth—she could have been in terrible danger."

"She was in constant danger already!"

Bonny shook his head. "No more than any boy who goes to sea. Captain Sharkee, for all his failings—and they were many—taught her enough to keep her safe."

"To keep her breeches on!"

"Yes. That, as well as other things. It certainly kept the men from guessing."

"But my God, man! Surely any one of them could have guessed it from other things! Look how quickly I found out."

Bonny smiled. "Your standards of cleanliness are much greater than the average pirate's, Captain. No one ever told her to bathe naked before."

"But surely—Did no one ever notice how she was growing? Surely her—" He felt himself growing heated at the memory of her rounded breasts and hips, and he strove to cover his reaction. "The changes in her figure must have caught someone's eye."

"No, they didn't. The crew changed constantly, as pirate crews do. And you see, it fell to me to watch for the signs. A sudden spurt of growth—I made certain she was given a larger set of clothing. The emergence of her breasts—I taught her how to bind them. Then, of course, the onset of her womanhood—"

James's head jerked up in anger. "How did you handle that one, Doctor?"

Mr. Bonny stared back at him unhappily. "Yes, that was very difficult, Captain. When Annie's time came, she thought she had been wounded. She thought that she was dying. I've never forgiven myself for not preparing her. As it was, most fortunately, she had the good sense to come to me. I explained her condition to her as best I could and how she must go about hiding it. She never has understood, really, why this torment comes upon her and not the men."

"But certainly she knows she is different from a man?"

Mr. Bonny nodded a bit doubtfully. "Certainly she knows of the anatomical differences. I told her of them myself, but—" He sighed and wiped his forehead. "Annie has no real comprehension of what a girl truly is."

James let this knowledge sink in slowly. What Mr. Bonny had said tallied with every impression he'd had from Annie herself and explained much of her apparent confusion.

But it did not explain all.

"Tell me one thing, Doctor. Why in heaven's

name would a pirate as ruthless as Sharkee allow a girl to board his ship?"

He expected the doctor to show some embarrassment. Something, at least, to show that his conscience pricked him for endangering a girl in this fashion.

But the doctor betrayed only a hint of disappointment. "I had supposed you might have guessed the reason, Captain, but since you have not, I will tell you a story.

"Some nineteen years ago," he began, "I was passenger aboard a ship sailing to the Colonies. Certain ventures of mine of a business nature—we need not go into them—had failed to prosper, and I was persuaded to try my luck in the Americas. With nothing to stay me, and no one to leave behind, I nevertheless left with a sense of trepidation, aware that success or failure would depend upon my own enterprise, when I had never considered myself a very enterprising man."

Mr. Bonny stared into the distance before shaking his head with an embarrassed little laugh. "But that is neither here nor there. What will interest *you* is that I never reached my destination. Our ship was attacked by the *Merrye Laurie*. We were boarded, robbed, and of all the passengers, I was the only one taken aboard."

Mr. Bonny had James's full attention now. James knew that attacked sailors often signed on as pirates: some when pressed; others who feared they would not be paid at the end of their voyage. Doctors were particularly vulnerable to being kidnapped. But it was strange that Bonny should have been the only one. "Go on."

"When I boarded the ship, I was taken at once to the captain's cabin. I had expected to be put in chains, but instead I was ordered to assist at a birth."

"Good Lord!" James knew he should have seen it coming, but it was so hard to believe. "Who was the woman?"

"I've never known." Mr. Bonny took his handkerchief and wiped his eyes. "The poor woman died that night. No one ever told me her name."

"And Annie was born."

"Yes. Fortunately for her, if not for her mother, she was on the large size. A sturdy, healthy baby who survived everything, even the inexpert handling of a scurvy crew." The doctor's voice softened, and he stared at his hands as if he recalled the moment she'd first slipped into them.

But James's mind had skipped to something else. "Had the woman been kidnapped?"

"I could not say. It is possible, but I did not think so at the time."

"Why was that?"

Mr. Bonny looked back at him. "I could only surmise by the affection she was shown by Captain Sharkee . . . and then, of course, by his overwhelming sorrow when she died."

Of course. James could have kicked himself for not guessing the truth. No other girl would be allowed on board but the captain's own daughter.

He had noticed the girl's fringe of reddish hair—and he was trying very hard to forget the strawberry curls between her legs. He had encountered Sharkee only this once but, of course, he knew him by reputation. Sharkee had been called, among other things, "the Barbarossa of the Caribbean."

"And you countenanced this?" James asked "Her being raised aboard ship?"

"Oh, no, Captain! Not at first. I begged and pleaded with Sharkee to let me take her with me. I promised to find a couple who would raise her as their own, but Captain Sharkee wouldn't hear of it. The child was his, he said, and must stay with him."

"But you stayed as well."

"Yes." Mr. Bonny crossed his arms over his chest. "Yes, I stayed to take care of her. At first, I don't mind telling you, because I was kept as a prisoner for that purpose. Not that I ever would have left her," he added. "My departure, assuming no other doctor came aboard, would have meant the death of the child. But I could not manage to escape and take her with me.

"And after a time"—his voice lowered—"I had no wish to give her up. And if we had escaped together, how could I have supported her? I am much too old and, as I said, not a very enterprising man. But it was I who fed and cleaned her. And I who tended to her needs. And I who insisted eventually that she be raised as a boy."

"You? Why?"

"Don't forget, Captain. I had seen what pirates

were capable of. I had witnessed episodes I would prefer not to relate. As Annie left her babyhood, I determined she would be safer as a boy. Captain Sharkee had no objections. Indeed, I believe he preferred to think of her that way. He certainly never gave any indication that he remembered her otherwise."

"Except to tell her to keep her breeches on."

"Ahem . . . yes." Mr. Bonny's lips curved upwards. "In the beginning she needed some encouragement to keep *any* clothes on, but she eventually got the hang of them. Then the crew was let go, another was taken on, and to them—Annie was Jem."

James remembered the scene in the galley and felt a little smile. Annie had not mastered the problem of dressing yet.

Mr. Bonny was clearing his throat.

"Yes, what is it?" James hastily pushed his vision away.

"There is one more thing you should know, Captain." Bonny's look had a pleading quality. "Annie does not know who her parents were."

"What?" *But she had told him as much.* "Why?"

"Captain Sharkee's orders. And, for once, I agreed with him. He told me that such men as he would have sailing under him would be sure to take their anger out on Jem if they knew him to be his son. They might even hold Jem hostage in a mutiny. Sharkee could not leave himself so vulnerable."

"Hummph!" James exploded. Sharkee had been right. And yet the bastard seemed to have had no further consideration for his daughter. James remembered his own father and the love they had shared. For that reason, he would have liked to think that the old sea dog had cared for his child.

But what did this imply? Had she never been hugged or caressed? James remembered that Annie didn't seem to know what affection meant. If she felt any at all, regardless of her lack of understanding, it seemed to be not for her father, but for this doctor.

James raised his eyes. "So," he said. "Now what, Mr. Bonny? Shall I leave you two ashore in England?"

When Mr. Bonny paled, he added, "I can give you the funds you need to get by—call them the proceeds from the *Merrye Laurie's* cargo."

"No, Captain." Mr. Bonny shook his head. His color matched the gray of his hair, but there was a firmness in his tone. "At one time that would have been fine, but not now."

As James waited for an explanation, a sinking feeling invaded him. He saw the trace of pain in the doctor's eyes.

"I have said that I am old, Captain Avery." The sadness in the doctor's tone belied his gentle smile. "But it is much more serious than that. I am ill, and I doubt I have long to live. Certainly not long enough to teach Annie all she needs to know to live as a girl."

His dim eyes lit in earnest. "You might say it was providence that made you discover her when you did. The burden is yours now."

James stared. What was his burden? A girl? A woman, who didn't even know what she was? Whose behavior was so far removed from a female's that the thought of changing it was too daunting even to contemplate?

He wanted to say no. This girl was not his responsibility. His only duty was to his ship. But he knew that, of course, she was. He had taken her from the only life she'd ever known, and, even if she remained ignorant of the details, the fact was, one of his crew had killed her father.

What kind of life would Annie lead if he left her on shore? As a woman, what would become of her? James had seen enough seaports to know what became of poor, unattached women, and if he hadn't, his own reaction to Annie's body would have told him. He couldn't condemn her to that.

"Does she have any other relatives?" he asked, with a hint of desperation.

"None, except perhaps her mother's people, but no one knows who they were."

"Have you no clues?"

"No, Captain. Except that Annie's mother seemed to be of gentler birth than Sharkee."

"Why do you say that?" In spite of himself, James's interest was piqued.

"I am judging by the little I heard of her speech and her dress, but of course, that was long ago, and there are no other witnesses. I have no proof."

A bristle of irritation raked along the back of James's neck. "Could she learn a trade?"

A trace of some emotion, perhaps a slight darkening of the doctor's features, made James wince.

"It is possible, certainly, but she would be safer as a sailor. You see, Annie's never been ashore."

"What!"

"Oh . . ." Mr. Bonny gave his gentle wave. "She's been on beaches where there were no towns. But she's never been in port—another of Sharkee's orders."

"Why—" But James could imagine why. For the very same reasons he had thought of.

He pondered, putting his elbows on the desk and sinking his face into his hands. No matter what solution he came up with, the facts remained the same.

He had taken an innocent—at least, an innocent of sorts—from her family, and he was responsible for her.

"Well, then . . ."

He straightened to find Mr. Bonny's eyes upon him. James could see the doctor was trying hard not to tense.

"It appears we have a rather large task in front of us, Mr. Bonny." James could hardly restrain his sigh. "We will instruct the boy, Jem, in how to become the girl, Annie, without the crew's

71

catching on. For the time being, I suppose she should become my cabin boy as the men expect. That will give me a chance to work on her manners and tutor her in deportment. You will do what you can to correct her speech, as will I. If we want her to have a decent life, we must make her sound like something better than a pirate hand."

"Aye, aye, Captain." Grateful teardrops glistened in the doctor's eyes.

Moved, James pretended not to see them. "By the time we get to England," he said reassuringly, "I shall have thought of a plan for her future. You may trust me to see that the best is done for her."

"I will."

Mr. Bonny stood. James could see how frail the doctor was now, as if the removal of his burden had given him permission to own his illness to himself.

"And I thank you, Captain, for saving my girl."

James heaved a louder sigh. "Don't thank me yet, Mr. Bonny." An image of Jem in his grime and tatters seemed to taunt him. "Somehow, I don't think our row will be an easy one to hoe."

Mr. Bonny chuckled gently. "Well, at any rate, Captain, I hope you have a better notion of what a female is than I. I have scarcely seen one for the past nineteen years."

James grimaced, but he could not laugh. He didn't know that much about women, either. Only that their bodies drove men wild. Throughout his long terms at sea, he tried his best to forget they existed. When on shore, he avoided deep entanglements. No sense in getting attached to someone he wouldn't see for months on end.

And besides, for mere companionship he preferred men, who knew that the sea was the sea, and not some loathsome monster or a flat, lifeless image in a painting, but a creature of moods, sometimes alluring, sometimes fearsome.

Women wanted to be coaxed, courted, and catered to. He didn't have time for any of that nonsense. His ships took all his life and all his love. He would marry Lady Olivia, of course, to fulfill his ambition and have a son to pass his ships to, but he would not expect to know her.

He knew one thing, though.

His ship was no proper place for a girl.

Chapter Four

Drooping like seaweed on the beach, Annie emerged from the galley only to be waylaid by Mr. Shirley and Cook. She reached for her knife and ducked past them, but their anticipated attack never came. Instead of taking their due revenge, the two wounded sailors proposed a pax. Then Mr. Shirley pressed her to sit at a table, while Cook dished her up some hardtack and pork.

The smell of salted meat reminded her that she hadn't eaten a mouthful all day. In spite of her hunger, though, she had to protest, "But the cap'n wants to see me."

"The captain'll bide, but ye'll need yer strength. He won't mind if ye have a little bite."

As she plopped her bottom on the bench, Mr. Shirley winced.

Cook turned pale. "Eat up, ye poor li'l bugger," he said.

Thrown off by the pity she saw in their eyes, Annie complied. If they didn't know she was a girl—and the captain had promised he wouldn't tell—then, what was there to pity her for?

A sudden thought robbed her of all appetite.

She was going to be marooned. The captain had said she couldn't be his cabin boy. She had her stupid breasts to thank for that. For the millionth time, Annie wished she'd been born a boy like everyone else.

Mr. Shirley began to hover as if he were about to take her spoon and feed her himself. "Captain'll be waiting now. Best hurry it along."

Annie stuffed the last of her biscuit into her mouth, which was so dry she could barely swallow. For the second time that day she felt an unaccountable urge to cry. Why had this had to happen? She'd been going along just fine until Captain Avery had captured the *Merrye Laurie*. Now her life was ruined.

When she'd finished, Mr. Shirley led her to the quarterdeck. Annie lagged behind. The familiar rocking of the ship beneath her feet and the lap of waves against its sides helped to soothe her a bit. The sea had always been her refuge. If she hadn't just bathed, she would have flung herself overboard to feel its healing warmth and be cradled in its calming swell. But deep inside, Annie knew that even the sea would be powerless to comfort her this time.

"Come along, boy. The captain won't hurt ye," Mr. Shirley said.

He already has. He shouldn't have gotten her hopes up like that only to dash them like so much jetsom on the rocks.

When Annie entered the cabin alone, James stood quickly. His sudden motion seemed to take her aback, for she checked at the door.

"Please be seated," he said, gesturing toward a chair.

In spite of her wary posture, she betrayed no consciousness of the embarrassing scene in the galley. Unnerved himself, James could only wonder at her lack of bashfulness as she sat, legs splayed wide and hands clasped between them. He resisted the temptation to examine those legs for signs of feminine curves and focused on her face instead.

Faded tar still framed her sunburnt cheeks, which glowed with a newfound cleanliness. Pale emerald eyes stared back at him defiantly. If he hadn't been so aware of the luscious body beneath her clothes, he might've been able to convince himself she was the courageous boy whose fierce loyalty and spirit had so intrigued him.

He resumed his own seat behind the desk, and she crumpled her brow, as if wondering why he'd stood in the first place.

"Annie," he said. "What do you know about women?"

She slumped, unhappily crossing her arms over her chest. "I know that men pokes 'em," she said with a grimace. "And that they've got diddies that are much too big for anything and hips that don't fit in breeches like they should."

James suppressed a smile. "Is that all?"

She hunched one shoulder, and the cast of her face was pure misery.

"What's wrong?" he asked.

"What's wrong!" She screwed up her mouth. "Ye says I can be your cabin boy and then ye says I can't. That's what!"

"*You say* I can be your cabin boy."

"Huh?"

James sighed, leaning forward to rest his elbows on the desk. "Annie, I'm trying to improve your English. If you're going to pass for a respectable woman, you have to sound more ladylike."

"But I don't wants to be a woman!"

"Annie . . . you *are* a woman. And the sea is no place for a girl. You're not safe living this way."

"I was safe enough until you came along."

A spurt of unjustified anger made him frown. Annie tossed him a glance from beneath her lowered brows, and her expression seemed at once contrite.

"You have reason to say so," James admitted. He couldn't doubt his part in her sorrow. "But

77

I'm responsible for you now, and I've decided you must live as a woman."

"But, why—" She halted, as a question took shape. "Just how do they live?"

James took his time, leaning back to make a steeple of his fingers on his chest. "Have you never seen *any* women, Annie?"

"Some, I guess." She shifted on her chair, mortification in every gesture. "But never up close. Captain Sharkee never brought none aboard."

"*Any* aboard."

"What?" She flashed him a confused look, before remembering. "Oh. All right. But I have seen 'em on other ships."

"What did you notice?"

She seemed taken aback by the question, before her expression lightened. "I saw their clothes."

"Their dresses, you mean?"

"Yeah."

"What else?"

"Well . . . they hadn't got no weapons."

"*Any* weapons."

"Oh. Yessir."

"Anything else?"

She frowned, as if trying hard to remember. "They wore their dresses so their diddies showed."

James felt a rush of blood to his thighs. "And that surprised you?" he said, trying to keep a straight face.

"They should've been ashamed of 'em, shouldn't they?"

"No." James grinned. "Not at all. They should be proud to show them. Don't you know what they're for?"

Annie shook her head, her eyes opening wide.

"For feeding babies."

The breath seemed to vanish from her lungs. She went white as a sail. "Lor' blind me," she gasped. "They don't eats 'em, do they?"

James burst out with a laugh, before he remembered his duty. He rubbed a hand across his mouth to hide a smile. "Good Lord, no. When babies suckle a woman's breasts, they get milk."

Wondrously, Annie raised her hands and gathered her breasts. "If ye sucked on one now, would ye get any?"

James felt the pit of his stomach falling as his gaze flew to the mounds beneath her shirt. In his mind's eye, he could see those pink-tipped crests. "No." Heat rose steadily to his face. "You'd have to have a baby first. But"—he cleared his throat—"Annie, we shouldn't be discussing your breasts."

"Ye're the one who brought 'em up."

"I did—" *Not*. As heat tingled up into his buttocks, and his throat began to close in embarrassment, James saw how futile it would be to reason with the girl like this. He dropped his face into one hand, before he said, "All right, Annie. Forgive me. And may God do it, too.

79

What I was trying to do was determine how much tutoring you need, and I can see it's quite a lot."

"Tutoring?"

"Yes. Mr. Bonny explained to me how you were raised, but you're a woman now. You should be living like one. I propose to teach you about it myself."

"Do I be your cabin girl, then?"

"Not exactly, no. Captains don't have cabin girls. But for the moment, you will appear to be my cabin boy. You'll perform most of the duties, but when you're closeted with me, I'll give you lessons on how to conduct yourself. Then, when we reach England, I'll put you ashore."

Her face had brightened during his speech, but now she surged in her seat. "Put me ashore? But what'll I do?"

James turned away from the fear in her voice. "Don't worry. By the time we get there, I'll know what to do with you. But I promise you'll be cared for."

"I don't want to be cared for!"

"You must. It's the only proper role for a woman."

Annie drew herself up and spat in disgust.

James stiffened. He stood to lean on his fists and gritted his teeth. "First lesson, Annie," he said. "Ladies don't spit."

"Well, I does."

"You *did*. But from now on you *will* not or I'll set you ashore with no lessons!"

80

The threat of being marooned seemed to daunt her. It reminded her that he was the captain and must be obeyed.

She hung her head. "Yessir."

After a moment, James stepped around his desk and raised a comforting hand to her face.

Annie bounded out of her chair and flung up one arm as if to ward off a blow.

James froze. A wealth of emotions coursed through him. "I wasn't going to hit you, girl."

"Ye weren't?" She lowered her arm.

"No." Tension strangled his speech. "Second lesson, Annie. Gentlemen do not strike ladies."

"They don't?"

"No. Have you been hit before?"

"Sure, lots o' times. By Cap'n Sharkee. The pirates. Anybody who felt like it, I guess—except Mr. Bonny."

James sensed a pain in his lower jaw, and he found that he had clenched it. "That will never happen aboard my ship."

Her brows rose up in surprise. "Are your crew all gentlemen, then?"

"No. Far from it, I'm afraid."

He raised a hand again, more cautiously this time. At first, she leaned away and her eyes grew round. She couldn't seem to resist the urge to flinch, as he touched her chin. "They are none of them gentlemen, but they will obey me."

"Are you a gentleman?" Her voice had turned into a hoarse, dry whisper.

James carefully restrained his movements. He

81

felt as if he were taming a wild, frightened fawn. With one gentle hand, he turned her sun-beaten face to examine its profile.

Annie's nose was small and straight. Beneath the burn, her cheeks glowed with health.

James smiled as her eyes returned to his. "I say I'm a gentleman. Others would say I'm nothing but a wealthy social mushroom. I plan to prove them wrong."

"Are ye rich then?" Of all he'd just said, she seemed to understand only this much.

"Rich enough to buy a noblewoman."

"Are they for sale?"

James chuckled. "Some are. But that is my business. Yours is to start acting like a girl." He took back his hand, but not before lightly skimming her cheek once. "I think you'll make a pretty one, too."

"Me?" Annie reached up to touch her face. Their hands brushed in midair, and a spark seemed to fly from her fingers to his.

James felt an instant awareness. He cleared his throat. "Yes. Your face is pretty enough. And when you let your hair grow, you'll look even better."

"My hair?" She mimicked his words like a dazed parrot.

"You mustn't tar it again."

"If ye says so, Cap'n."

Her incorrect speech provoked him like a mosquito under his skin. He tossed his wig on the desk and raked his scalp.

"Annie." He faced her again and tried to curb

an irrational exasperation. "Try, if you will, to speak more like me. Or Mr. Bonny. One doesn't say, 'I says' or 'you says.' It's, 'I say' and 'you say.'"

"Is that right?" She seemed pleased to know. "I always wondered, but Mr. Bonny didn't sound like the others, so I thought he must be wrong. But I can sound more like him if you want."

"I do." He experienced a flicker of hope. "I'm surprised you noticed the difference."

"I'm not deaf, Cap'n." Her scowl told him she wasn't stupid either.

"Cap-*tain*."

"Aye, aye, sir. Cap-*tain*."

"Very good."

"But—" A new question wrinkled her brow. "Captain, how do you know the way you talk is right?"

At the challenge in her voice, he bristled. "Mr. Bonny and I both speak like gentlemen."

"Is Mr. Bonny a gentleman, too?"

"No." His patience was growing thin. "Mr. Bonny is a doctor."

"Well, what's a gentleman, then, if it's not somebody who talks like you?"

"A gentleman is someone born to lead a certain life, a life of luxury. A doctor is not. But Annie, social distinctions are too much for you to comprehend as yet. We should begin with simpler things."

"Like what?"

"Well . . . for instance, if you were on shore, or even a lady traveling aboard my ship, you would not address me as your captain."

"No? How would I, then?"

"As Captain Avery or Sir James."

"Sir? James? What's that?"

"That's my title and my given name. The way your given name is Annie."

"James." She seemed to try it on for size. "I like that. Do I call you James?"

"No. As my female acquaintance, you must call me Sir James or Captain Avery. Only an intimate of mine would call me James."

"What's an intimate?"

Her question took him unawares. "An intimate would be a family member or a close friend or a sweetheart, but—"

"What's a sweetheart?"

James became flustered. "Annie—this conversation is getting out of hand. You mustn't ask so many questions."

"Why?"

"Annie . . ." He looked at her sternly. "*Why* is a question, too."

She sighed and scratched her head. "I'm sorry, Captain. But you do say the strangest things."

He approached her again to take her by the shoulders. The warmth from her body spread through his palms and up his sleeves. She smelled of soap and tar and something harder to place. James struggled against an urge to rub her shoulders with his thumbs.

He wanted to be kind.

"This is all very confusing," he said gently.

"But you'll understand it all in time. Just not all at once." He gave her a smile.

Annie stared at his hair as if she'd never seen hair before, then at his mouth as if she'd never seen teeth. His eyes were drawn to her lips.

Her lips separated. A quickening in her breath caused a tightening in his loin.

She gave her head a sudden shake, and James released her, chagrinned.

"You look tired, Annie," he said, wondering why the sight of her sun-baked lips had aroused him. "Is that enough lesson for today?"

His voice seemed to startle her from a dream. She met his gaze of concern. "I—I guess so, Captain. I don't know what's wrong with me."

"Too many changes, I suppose. But you'll soon be all right."

"Yessir, James."

"Yes . . . *Sir James*."

"Yessir, James."

Exhausted, James decided not to press the issue. She had clearly had enough for one day. He had felt her quiver beneath his touch.

And that trembling had been contagious. Even now, his hands would not be still. The stress, no doubt, of having such a secret on board, one that would be hard to hide from the men. He worried that he might treat Annie differently. At the moment, he didn't see how he could prevent himself.

"Annie, whatever I teach you in here, is for *in here*," he added hastily. "You must act like Jem for the crew, you understand? It won't be easy to keep the two roles apart."

"I'll try." She looked more composed now. Her pale green eyes lured his to her sunburnt face.

"You need to wear a hat. Do you have one?"

Numbly, she shook her head.

"Then find one. Keep it on when you're out in the sun, so your skin will clear."

"If that's what you want, sir—James."

She had got the inflection wrong again. But he told himself it would just be a matter of time. The more she heard him speak, the better she would imitate his voice.

She yawned with her mouth wide open. "Shall I go now, Captain?"

"In a minute." With a stab of worry, he realized she would be sleeping in the forecastle with the men. Surely someone would notice her feminine shape. Scanning her body for signs, he felt almost certain her breasts were unbound.

"Annie"—he paused to swallow— "when you dressed, did you have time to . . ." Pointing at his own chest, he gestured from side to side with one finger.

She stared at his motion before getting his drift. "Oh, me breasts!"

"It's *my* breasts."

An impish grin lit her features. "No, I didn't wrap yours. Would you like me to?"

"Annie . . ." he warned, but he knew he'd asked for that one. It was simply that the shape of those mounds beneath her shirt seemed so obvious to him now. Her waist turned in unnaturally for a boy's, and her new soft breeches seemed to drape the curve of her buttocks and thighs. The men would have to be fools not to—

James pried his eyes away from her hips. "Whatever you do, Annie, for God's sake, keep your breeches on!"

"Aye, aye, James. You, too. But you don't have to worry about me." She reached inside her waist and pulled out a knife. "I've still got me dagger," she said, swiping at the air. "And if any one of those dogs comes near me, I'll cut 'em to shreds."

"Annie!"

But with a laugh she had already left.

James dropped into his chair and sank his face in his palms. After a moment, he straightened and said with a sigh, "Well, at least I know what to cover in lesson three."

Instead of heading for the sleeping deck, Annie searched below it for the sick bay. She had asked, and had been told that Mr. Bonny would be setting up his cabin in the cockpit below the gun deck. On the way down, she tried to make sense of what the captain had said.

She wasn't sure what he'd meant about learning to live like a woman. She didn't want to be a woman, but it *had* been fine to hear that part about her breasts. Maybe Captain Avery could teach her something about the rest of her body, too. Somehow, when he mentioned it, she felt more curious than when Mr. Bonny did.

As for his other plans, there was nothing

much she could do at the moment. A captain would always have his way. But she would do her damnedest to change his mind about putting her ashore. She would show him she could make a good sailor, and maybe he'd decide to keep her on.

One thing had disturbed her, though. The captain's touch had made her mind start to dim. It had robbed her of breath, and her lungs had gone desperate trying to feed her some air. His fingers had stroked her as lightly as a breeze, but instead of coolness, they had brought heat. Her nipples had ached as if they'd been scorched.

Bothered by this unnatural reaction, she found Mr. Bonny in a low, dark compartment, lit only by one smoking lamp. He was unloading a small crate that seemed to contain the medicines he had accumulated aboard the *Merrye Laurie*. At the sound of her knock, he glanced up.

"Come in, Jem, lad." His face easing gently, he pushed a bundle of lint out of the way to make a place for her to sit before lowering himself onto a chest.

Annie noticed that his stiff back seemed to pain him.

"I had hoped you would come to visit me," he said. "Are you faring well?"

Annie shrugged. She felt uncomfortable under his searching gaze. "I guess so. I likes our new ship. What about you?"

"You *like* our new ship."

"Oh, not you, too!"

As Annie rolled her eyes, Mr. Bonny leaned

forward to whisper, "You must do as the captain says, Annie. He's your only hope."

His anxious tone made her stop. "Only? But he said—you and me—"

Mr. Bonny was shaking his head. "No, child. I have told the captain, and now I must tell you. I am a very sick man."

"Can't you doctor yourself?"

"Yes, but some things cannot be cured. The symptoms are not unique, and I cannot deceive myself."

A chill stole through her.

At the sight of her stricken face, a tender smile touched his lips. "But you must know, child, I would never leave you unprotected. Captain Avery has given me his word—"

Annie spat to show her opinion of the captain's plans, but she felt instantly guilty when she saw Mr. Bonny's frown of disapproval. He never had liked her to spit. She remembered James's warning, *Ladies don't spit.*

"Annie, has the captain explained his intentions to you?"

"I guess so. Yeah."

"Then, let me add a word. I want—That is, if you have any affection for me, my dear, I want you to do what the captain asks in every particular."

A strangling pain began in her throat. She didn't promise right away, but strained to ask over the lump, "What is affection? The captain asked me if that's what I have for you. Is it?"

"I hope so, child." He colored faintly. Then,

choosing his words with great care, he explained, "There are many different kinds of affection. A father's for his child may take the form of pride, whereas a mother's will manifest itself in the feeding and dressing and other care she lavishes on her—"

"Like you did for me?"

Mr. Bonny was taken aback. Moisture glistened in his eyes as he chuckled. "Yes. I suppose so. Undoubtedly."

Annie wished the pain in her throat would go away, but ever since he had said he was ill, it had been building.

"What other kinds?" She wanted to change the subject.

"Well . . . the others are a bit more difficult to describe, but I hope you will experience them all one day." Mr. Bonny seemed as gun-shy as the captain when he'd talked about her breasts.

Annie fixed him with her gaze.

"There is another sort"—Mr. Bonny looked away—"it is the kind a person feels for a close friend."

"Like Billy Sams and Curly Pete?" Those two would have died for each other.

Mr. Bonny gave a dismissive nod. "Precisely. You see what I mean." He reached for one of his instruments, brought from the *Merrye Laurie*, and polished it with a cloth.

"But—" Annie knew there was more. "What about sweethearts?"

His hand paused. "What about them?"

"Who are they, and what do they do?"

"Where did you hear the word 'sweetheart'?"

"From the pirates." *And from the captain.* Annie didn't know why she kept this last bit of information to herself.

"Ah, yes. Well, even a pirate may love a woman and miss her when he is at sea."

"Is love the same as affection?" Annie tried to understand. She knew how some of the pirates felt about women. She had heard the insults that had made her cringe. Nothing was worse than to act like a woman. She had also heard the sneers and threats, the foul plans some men made before going ashore, which had made her shudder with distaste.

But at other times, she had heard them confess how much they missed their wives or sweethearts. She had heard the yearning in their voices and seen the ache in their eyes. Then, once in port, there had been the joy of being back home, the anticipation of something even the meanest pirate had understood and laughed about. Only she had not understood.

Even now, Mr. Bonny would not meet her eyes. She remembered how Captain Avery had cut her off when she had asked about intimates. What were they being so secretive about?

Something to do with women.

Mr. Bonny reached out to pat her hand. His rare gesture confused her.

"My dear, it would be difficult for an old stick like me to answer all your questions. Perhaps, another woman could do it. Even another medical man, but—"

"Maybe the captain?"

"Yes . . ." His voice had turned dry. "Although I trust he will not explain too much himself. Better for another to make all clear. And someday, someone will."

Annie didn't like the way she was being treated. The captain had completely changed his manner since he'd discovered her secret. And now, even Mr. Bonny was acting differently, and he had known she was a girl all along.

They both were hiding something from her.

Something to do with being a woman.

Something they knew she wouldn't like.

Chapter Five

"Morning, Cap'n!" At three bells precisely, Annie carried James's tray through his narrow cabin door.

Krebs was inside, helping James with his shaving. The captain stood shirtless in front of his mirror, his broad, muscular back turned toward the door. At the sound of her voice, his hand gave a jerk, and he swore. A red stream of blood trickled down his lathered chin.

"Did I startle ye, Captain?" Annie set the tray on his desk and turned to watch him shave. She admired the wide expanse of his shoulders and his smooth, tapered back.

James grabbed the towel Krebs was holding to dab at the nick on his face.

"No, of course not. Krebs, my shirt," he said, clasping the towel over his chest.

"But, Captain, ye haven't finished shaving," Krebs protested.

"Never mind that now. *Just hand me that shirt.*"

Annie rested her fists on her hips and eyed James with interest. His big chest was covered with full, hard muscles above a narrow waist. Before he'd covered himself with the towel, she'd caught a glimpse of the coarse, dark hair that disappeared where his breeches hugged his hips.

As Krebs shook his head, James struggled into his shirt, still holding fast to the towel. He seemed to be having a rough time managing both.

"Can I help ye on with that shirt, Captain?" Annie asked, wanting to be helpful.

"No! That is . . . no thank you, sailor. That will be all."

"But Mr. Shirley said I should stay and get me orders."

"And *I* say, come back when I've finished dressing. And from now on, you may bring my breakfast at four bells instead of three. And knock before you enter."

"But Cook said—"

"Jem. *Goodbye.*"

Annie knew better than to argue with a captain when he took that tone of voice, so she left and closed the door. But she wondered what she'd done wrong. She'd made sure to wake at the start of the watch so she could get the captain's breakfast on time. She wanted to do her best at this job.

Disgruntled, she wandered out on deck and found the men struggling aloft with a torn royal. A rope had broken during the night. The canvas it attached had flapped in the high winds until it had been caught on the topgallant mast. It couldn't be lowered without tearing further. Sails being costly, Mr. Shirley was doing what he could to salvage it.

A man had climbed the mast and was trying to push the sail over it, but he had stopped far too short of the tip. He tried tossing the canvas repeatedly. Then, when his right arm tired, he threw with his left, which worked even less.

"Why don't he shinny on up that topgallant and push the royal over?" Annie asked Mr. Shirley.

"That mast be tapered so"—Shirley kept his eyes on the man, shading them with both hands—"a big man like Zeke wouldn't have nothing to hold on to."

"I could do it." Sharkee had always let her help when there'd been problems aloft. He said she climbed like the veriest monkey.

"Could ye, lad?"

"Sure." *And if I do this, maybe the captain'll see what a good sailor I am.*

"That's good, then. Zeke," he called up to the sailor. "Come on down!"

Annie spat on her hands to make them sticky, then strolled to the ratlines and started to climb.

Halfway up, she crossed Zeke coming down.

They hung side by side in the ropes, catching their breaths.

"Good luck with it, boy," Zeke said. "There's a fierce wind ablowin' up top. It don't look like much, but when it puffs all sudden-like, it near takes ye with it."

Annie thanked him and climbed again, resting briefly on the trestletree. Holding on to the top-mast with one arm, she let her body sway in the breeze. The *Flying Swan* was in the Atlantic now. Not a speck of land was in sight. Row upon row of gray-green swells topped with white foam surged relentlessly beneath a colorless sky. Far down on deck, the men looked like moving specks.

Annie breathed deeply of the thick salty air and licked it off her sunburnt lips. She was used to their cracks. She remembered the captain had wanted her to wear a hat for some reason—something about her skin—but she was glad she wouldn't have to contend with one up on the topgallant mast.

Collecting herself—for a fall from this height meant certain death—she spat on both cal-loused hands again and wiped them on her new trousers. When she judged them to be just right, she started to shinny up.

She needed to work quickly. No time to waste before she tired, as Zeke had done. The wind was gusty, as he'd said, but nothing to fear. She just had to hold a little tighter, which meant tir-ing faster, too. But in a minute, she had reached the skewered sail and could start to push it up.

"Good God!" The captain's voice boomed up at her, making her jump.

She nearly lost her grip. She started to slip, then caught the mast and hung on. *Bloody hell!* Her heart was beating like the wings of a frightened duck. *He shouldn't ought to startle me like that.*

"Come down this instant!"

Peering down at James over her elbow, Annie saw him standing on the main deck, his brown hair gleaming like a fine mahogany rail. But she couldn't obey. She had got this far, and there was nothing for it but to finish the job.

What's got into him, anyway? Does he have a crab in his breeches?

The anger in his voice troubled her. She'd thought he would be pleased when he saw how useful she could be.

Ignoring his command, she slowly inched the royal up, then herself, then the royal, until she was close enough to the tip to push it over.

As she stretched as far as she could, the sail broke free. With it flapping wildly around her, Annie tightly grasped the mast. Her arms were straining, and her legs shook from holding on, but she could hear the men's cheers floating up from the deck. The captain had stopped his yelling. Everything would be fine now. He had seen what a good crewman she could be and he would want to keep her on. Good crewmen were hard to find.

She started down, so much faster and easier than going up. Her legs slid quickly over the wood, polished by countless pairs of sailors' trousers. As she reached the ratlines, she got her second wind and swung down, deliberately skipping every other rope step.

When she'd almost reached the deck, she looked down and found James glaring up at her. He clutched the bottom of the ratlines in an iron-hard fist, his face set in a relentless mask, his lips pinched to a terrifying white.

"You will come down this second, you brat, and you will never climb the riggings again."

"But, Captain—"

"Obey or I'll have you thrown overboard!"

Annie had slowed. Now, as she slipped lower, he reached up to grab her; she stopped, uncertain of his temper.

Her bottom came to rest in his palm.

A shock went through her. It started where his palm warmed the V between her legs, then spread like lightning to her breasts. As the tingling spread, Annie knew she had never felt any pleasure so great. She wanted his hand to stay there forever.

He grasped her leg instead and pulled her down onto the deck. His lips compressed in an angry line, he grabbed her roughly by one arm and drew her along behind him.

"Captain—" The first mate stumbled in their wake.

"Mr. Shirley, this is none of your affair. The boy must not disobey me."

James dragged her toward his cabin. Mr.

Shirley fell back in confusion, as James reached the cabin door.

"A word with you, sailor." He practically tossed her inside.

Annie found she could hardly stand. Her knees had been weakened by the exertion aloft; and then, his touch, so near that funny place between her thighs, had made her legs go all wobbly.

James slammed the door. "What was the meaning of that?" He paced about the tiny space.

Annie tried to answer, but her throat had dried.

"Did you want to kill yourself?"

"No, sir, James!" His question made no sense at all.

He stopped and faced her.

Annie cringed, ready for the worst. Her legs still trembled, but it seemed he was holding back his temper.

"I told you to report to me after I dressed."

"I forgot. Mr. Shirley needed help, and I thought you would like it if I got your sail down."

"I—" He paused, and a shudder seemed to ripple right through him. "Annie, I never want to see you doing anything so dangerous again."

"But Cap'n Sharkee—"

"Damn Sharkee! Good God! Do you tell me that cur had you working up in the riggings?"

Annie felt the cut to Sharkee as sharply as if

James had slapped her instead. "He said it made him feel proud." She squeezed back tears. What was wrong with her? Why would she cry?

"Good Lord." James's anger seemed to weaken on a breath. "He might have . . . He might have lost you."

When Annie saw that his fury had sprung from concern, she relaxed. Immeasurably cheered, she said, "Oh, no, sir, James. I'd've been fine if ye hadn't made me jump. Ye shouldn't ought to do that."

"I *shouldn't* do that."

"No, sir, James, ye sure shouldn't," Annie agreed. "Remember how I surprised you this morning and ye cut yourself? Well, ye did the same to me. Only it's much more dangerous up where I was."

James closed his eyes. She saw him struggling with an emotion before he opened them and said, "Annie, you only startled *me* because a lady shouldn't see a man before he's dressed."

Annie felt floored. "Whyever not?"

Her question seemed to distress him. Color seeped over the captain's neck. He stumbled with his words. "It just isn't done."

"Well—" Annie marveled. She'd wondered why he seemed so upset. "It's a good thing I didn't know that before, or I'd've had to go about the fo'c's'le all me life wif me eyes closed. I've seen more Jacks in the buff than rats in a hold."

With a moan, James collapsed into his chair. "For God's sake, Annie, you've got to stop saying such things. And you must *keep* your eyes closed from now on."

"What's the matter, Captain?" she asked sympathetically. "Think ye got somethin' to hide? Ye shouldn't worry none. There ain't nothing I haven't seen. Why, we had a fellow aboard who had the smallest poker ye ever did see. The other pirates gave 'im a rough time about it, but never me. Not when I haven't got one meself."

James made a strangled sound. "Annie, this has to—"

"It's nothin' like that, is it? Ye look just fine to me. Why, that codpiece of yours looks as jam-packed as a pistol."

"Annie!" James sprang to his feet before, quickly skirting the desk, he clamped a hand over her mouth. She stood, gazing over his fingers with surprise.

"Annie, that's enough." His angry eyes were mere fingertips from hers. She found it hard to breathe. "You will stop this talk right now. When I lift my hand, you will not speak until I give you permission. Is that understood?"

Annie nodded as best she could with his hands clasped one in front and one in back of her head. He pressed his fingers to her lips a moment longer, as if he dared not believe her, then slowly removed them, one by one.

"There"—he took a cautious step backwards—"that's better." In a moment, he shook his head and a look of pure bewilderment filled his eyes. "Annie, you are something else."

She hoped he meant that kindly, but she didn't think he did. She would have asked, but his stance still warned her.

"Now. Sit," he said, pointing to a chair. "Sit and listen while I give you your orders.

"Number one"—as he continued, he took his own seat—"you were told to wear a hat." He reached behind his desk and brought up one made of straw with a wide, stiff brim. "Wear this always."

"But—"

"Not another word! You will do nothing from now on that will make wearing a hat a burden to you. You will not be climbing up into the riggings. As my cabin boy, you will not stray from my side. Understood?"

"Yessir, James."

"Number two"—he seemed to falter—"I cannot erase the things you've seen below deck, but from now on, you must try to forget them."

When she started to ask why, he flung up one hand. "You don't have to know the reason—not yet—but ladies and gentlemen do not share quarters unless they are married. No great harm has been done, but as a woman you will never mention to *anyone* the parts of men's bodies you have seen. Say, 'Yessir.' "

"Yessir, James."

"Good." He closed his eyes briefly, as if relieved. "I promise to explain this more fully at a future date. When you need to know.

"Now, for number three: No more daggers."

Alarm made her start. "But what if somebody picks a fight with me? What'll I do?"

"No one aboard my ship will hurt you. If anyone tries, you will report the incident to me. Part of my job is to ward off such events. Give me your dagger. Please." He reached out one hand.

Reluctantly, feeling as if she'd been stripped of her honor, Annie stood and shoved a hand inside her baggy breeches. The captain's eyes followed her motion.

All at once, they seemed to darken. His face was hard and unreadable, but his gaze narrowed until it fixed on the place between her legs. His lips must've suddenly gone dry because he licked them. Something inside Annie jerked in response.

A bubbling heat began to simmer in the spot where he'd touched her before. Savoring the pleasant feeling, Annie did all she could to prolong it. She clutched the hilt near her waist and squeezed her empty V. The captain's rapt stare never left it for an instant. His will seemed to orchestrate her every move, as if it were his hand inside her breeches, his fingers placed between her legs. James showed no sign of impatience, but as his face grew tense, her flesh grew warm. Annie shivered from the heat. Moisture seemed to dampen her thighs. Moving slowly as if her hand were stuck in a bowl of syrup, she withdrew her knife: the hilt . . . the blade . . . the tip.

James let out a shuddering breath. "Hand it over," he said. His voice had gone raspy.

Annie took the step to his desk, clasped his hand and closed it around the dagger. Her knees were trembling again.

"Take your seat," James said, averting his gaze.

Annie sat.

She didn't feel like crying, so she didn't understand why she was shaking. She wasn't scared, and she couldn't be that tired from her climb, not when she'd made them so often.

"I don't know why it is, Captain," she said, noting the quiver in her voice, "but you make me go all squooshy between me legs."

"Dear Lord!" His oath came out weakly. "Annie . . . you mustn't say that, either. To any man! You see . . ." He struggled with his words. "That's precisely why no woman should be on board a ship."

"What?" He must have misunderstood her. "What do my legs have to do with anything?"

"Everything. Just knowing you are here makes . . . *might* make some men feel squooshy, too."

Annie pondered his words, but they made no sense. She hadn't said *all* men made her feel squooshy. Just James.

She started to say this, but he interrupted her with, "Please, no more speech. Put on your hat and go outside. Stay near my cabin door. I have work to do."

"Aye, aye, sir, James."

James waited until she'd gone before looking down at his lap. He'd gone as stiff as a cannon.

He balled his hands into fists. This torture had to stop. But how was he to stop Annie's mouth? The girl had no idea what she was saying. Appalled as he had been by her revelations, he knew she was an innocent. How was he to cope with such a blatant, inviting innocence aboard his ship—and in such tight quarters?

British society had ways of protecting men from gross temptation by females. Guarded speech for one, but no one had ever taught Annie how to mind her tongue. Her brazen honesty had left him aching.

He grimly faced the facts. Her tempting presence on board had already caused him more grief than even he'd expected.

From the moment she'd stepped inside his cabin that morning, his whole day had been overturned. For the first time in his well-ordered life, he had not finished shaving. How could he, when it would have meant explaining his strange behavior to Krebs? What could he have said? *It unnerved me to see this girl walk in while I stood half-naked?*

Perhaps because he'd seen her naked body, and all night long she had haunted his thoughts.

He could almost strangle Mr. Bonny. Why hadn't the doctor at least taught her something that would help her now? Such as not to look a man up and down as if he were a piece of raw beef. And not to talk about men's members as if she were a judge in a county fair.

And that knife. Good God. James could almost

feel it coming out of her breeches. It might have been the part of him that throbbed.

The thought made him sweat.

He had to get a grip on himself. He had things to do. He had his course to plot. Ships to capture. A wedding to plan. He couldn't let Annie distract him from important business. She was nothing but a girl. A female like any other. He would have nothing to do with her.

He would teach her the bare minimum she needed to know. Then, he'd turn her loose on London and let London fend for itself.

He had never let anything rattle him, neither Spanish marauders nor Barbary pirates, raging storms or the mightiest winds.

And, if he could handle all those things, he could certainly handle one slip of a girl for the time it would take him to get her to London. And once they arrived, he would get married and would be safe. She would not get under his skin again.

This last episode, however, had revealed how much Annie had to learn. She couldn't be placed safely on shore if she didn't understand the worst about men. He'd have to explain to her the baseness of their desires or she'd be in instant peril. James shrank from the task.

Then, a welcome idea made him smile.

He would make Mr. Bonny tell her.

A knock at the door made him call, "Come in."

"Cap'n, sir?" With his hat in his hands, Mr. Shirley slinked in. "Sorry about the boy, sir."

James sighed. "That's all right. But I meant what I said. Jem must stay out of the riggings. You said yourself he wasn't fit for such work."

"Aye, I did, sir. But did ye see the little scamp? Why, he shinnied up that mast like a sail under hoist."

"Yes, he did." James had already cursed himself for his outburst. He might have made Annie fall; but when he had seen her up there, his heart had leapt into his throat.

Now that she was safely down, if he were to be honest with himself, he would have to acknowledge that he had been impressed with the courage and devotion to duty that had made her persevere with her task in spite of his anger. But he couldn't let her risk her life again, no matter how valuable her service had been.

"All the same," he said to Mr. Shirley. "the boy's supposed to serve me here. I can't have him wandering off on other jobs when I might have need of him. Remember, he's not used to discipline."

"Aye, sir." Shirley rubbed the back of his neck. "I could have him flogged, if ye want."

"No." James's stomach gave a lurch. "I don't want him whipped. If he needs to be punished, I'll do it."

"Yessir." Shirley looked relieved but puzzled all the same. It was the bosun's mate's job to dole out punishment.

James decided he had better give his first mate

Patricia Wynn

a reason or he'd stay uneasy. "What with that swelling he's got . . . between his legs . . ."

"Oh, aye, sir! No telling what the cat would do to it!" Shirley winced in revulsion.

His reaction gave James an idea. "Mr. Shirley, I want you to send the doctor up to me."

"Yessir?"

"I want to ask Mr. Bonny if the boy's condition could be contagious."

Shirley's eyes bugged. "You mean, catchin', sir?"

"Don't say anything to the men." James lowered his voice. "I don't think it is, but I'd keep my distance if I were you. And I don't think he should sleep with the others."

Shirley gulped and drew a cross on his chest. "Aye, aye, sir."

"Now, fetch me the doctor. And remember. Not a word to the men."

"No, sir."

As Shirley hurried from his cabin, muttering a prayer under his breath, James suppressed a chuckle. He didn't like to fool his first mate. Still, his idea had been a stroke of genius. Shirley would never betray an order. He would never repeat what he'd heard, but he wouldn't have to. As soon as the other men caught on that there was something wrong with the boy—which they *would* when they saw the first mate avoiding him—they would all follow suit.

And Annie would be safe from that quarter.

James sighed with relief. He credited his men with eyes, and sooner or later, if they stayed too

108

close to her, someone would notice the delectable curves beneath those baggy breeches.

Mr. Bonny reported to the cabin right away, but in his step there was a shuffle James had not noticed the day before.

Change could be hard on the old, James knew, but still his stomach gave a flip when he saw how Mr. Bonny held on to the chair before sitting down.

"You wanted to see me, Captain?"

James hesitated. It would not be easy to discuss this with the old man. "It has come to my attention," he began after a moment's pause, "that Annie understands nothing about the relations between a man and a woman."

"Yes, that describes her condition exactly. It was necessary, you understand."

"Yes, I can see that. What troubles me, however, is that she has no knowledge with which to protect herself. For instance, her . . . vocabulary is such that she might be misunderstood if she were—"

"What you mean to say, Captain, is that Annie swears like a sailor. I know. I trust you will help her to change that habit."

"But I—"

"She has no one else."

"But what about you!" James had not meant to sound so frustrated, but Mr. Bonny was being no help at all.

"I?"

"Yes, you! You're her parent as much as anyone." The doctor chuckled, then colored. "Yes. Last night, she came close to suggesting that I was her mother."

"Her mother! That's how much she knows!"

"And when, Captain, have you ever known a mother to teach her daughter anything about men? At least, the things I presume you refer to. In my years in England as a doctor, I cannot tell you the number of poor girls I consulted who did not know the first thing about their bodies."

"But this is different! This is desperate!"

"Is it?" Bonny's curious gaze brought a warmth to James's cheeks.

"Well, not desperate, of course." He forced a little laugh. "Nevertheless, she has no one else."

"She has you. You are her governor now."

"Somehow I . . . don't think a captain's role is to discuss such things with his crew."

"No, but perhaps you could find a woman to take the job."

James sat bolt upright. *A woman. Yes.* He could hire a woman in London. Better yet, his fiancée could help him find Annie a governess. "That's a brilliant idea," he told the doctor.

"Not brilliant, no. Just cowardly."

James's eyes found his, and he laughed. "Yes, we are both cowards. I admit it. Well." He stood and held out one hand. "I shall engage a woman to do our dirty work."

"Never dirty, Captain!"

James looked away, feeling guilty again. "No, of course, not. Just awkward. You may rely upon me."

The doctor stood. His back no longer straightened entirely, and he seemed tired. "I do trust you, Captain. And not a moment too soon."

As Mr. Bonny shuffled from the cabin, James didn't reply. His throat had begun to close. The old man trusted him. He must not betray that trust. If he were tempted to forget himself, by anything Annie might say, he had only to keep this image of Mr. Bonny in his mind.

He would need that image to avoid disappointing himself. He couldn't deny the threat Annie presented. As long as she continued to arouse him with her provocative talk and her winsome smile, he would run the risk of betraying his honor.

But now he could relieve himself of the necessity of teaching Annie all she needed to know. Lady Olivia ought to be able to find some sort of tutor for her. Perhaps not a tutor in the classic sense, but a woman who could teach her to be a female.

James wasn't sure that kind of teacher existed. If they had not left Jamaica so far behind, he would have consulted Therese, his friend Pierre's widow. She would have been the perfect person to take Annie in hand. But surely Olivia could take care of the matter just as well.

Meanwhile, let Annie say what she liked. James vowed to keep his head cool and his ramrod limp if it was the last thing he did.

Chapter Six

I wish I had been marooned, Annie thought three weeks later, as she languished on the deck. She'd been sitting outside James's cabin for what seemed like a year already, waiting for the lessons he'd promised.

A breeze ruffled the short, red roots of her hair, which had grown about an inch beyond her scalp. But even the cool northern air, threading through her hair for the first time in ages, could do nothing to ease her surly mood.

Nothing had been going right. She took the captain his breakfast at four bells each day, and his dinner when the first watch gathered for mess. He always greeted her with his wig on, thanked her with a frown, and dismissed her, looking away. The captain had promised her lessons, but so far they hadn't consisted of much.

"Ladies don't curse" and "ladies don't squat." "Ladies don't hoot" and they "don't dance the hornpipe." If she heard that word "don't" one more time, Annie thought she'd scream. Ladies didn't do anything, as far as she could see.

Bereft, she glanced up at the sails and watched them billow in the wind as the masts creaked forward. A sailor was swinging gently in the ratlines. She felt a strong pang of envy for his freedom. "Ladies" didn't climb up in the riggings. Neither did they jump overboard with their clothes on—or *off*. They didn't roughen their hands, didn't expose their skin to the sun . . . they just didn't, didn't, *didn't*.

"Jem!"

Annie dragged herself slowly to her feet. She didn't rush the way she used to, because ladies didn't rush. The captain could just wait.

As she closed the narrow cabin door behind her—softly, since ladies don't slam—she found the captain in his usual stance behind his desk. He pointed politely to her chair, then seated himself after she did.

"Good afternoon, Annie."

"Good afternoon, Captain Avery."

"Very good."

Maybe he *thought* the way she said it was good, but he sure didn't act that way. A stern look was always on his face. He studied his desk-

113

top intently, as if there were papers on it, which there weren't.

"I want you to repeat after me," he said. "How do you do?"

"How do you do."

"Very well, thank you, and you?"

"Very well, thank you, and you."

"It is not a statement, Annie. You are inquiring after someone's health. You must give it some inflection."

"Very well, thank you, and you?"

"Excellent." James frowned. "Have you worked on your English with Mr. Bonny today?"

"He wasn't feeling good."

"He wasn't feeling well or he felt unwell."

"Sorry, captain."

"*I beg your pardon*, Sir James."

"I'm sorry, James, but he wasn't," Annie couldn't keep from wailing. "He looked bad."

James finally raised his eyes, and his gaze softened. "I know, Annie, and I'm sorry. He is very ill."

"Yessir. That don't make it easy."

"That *doesn't* make it easy."

"That's right. I guess I've just heard that word 'don't' so many times, I forgot."

James studied her. His eyes were guarded but not unsympathetic. "Perhaps this is not a good day for a lesson."

"Perhaps not."

"Do you wish to be excused?"

"I guess so." When he grimaced, she added, "Yes, please."

114

"That's quite all right. We'll resume tomorrow."

Lord ha' mercy, Annie thought.

As she rose to go, James stood and bowed. He seemed disturbed, as if he really did care about Mr. Bonny. Annie was sorry she had displeased him, so she bowed back.

James started. "Annie, ladies don't—"

"Don't what this time?" she breathed wearily.

James gave a glimmer of a smile and waved her away. "It doesn't matter. We can discuss it another time. Perhaps you'd like to visit Mr. Bonny or go for a stroll on the deck. You don't have to sit outside my door all day."

"Mr. Shirley said I did."

James nodded. "If you were really my cabin boy, I would expect it of you. If Mr. Shirley speaks to you, tell him I dismissed you for this watch."

"Aye, aye, Captain."

Annie didn't wait to be corrected before leaving his cabin. She knew she had erred, but today she felt rebellious. All her freedom had been taken away.

She could almost regret that she had not stayed on the *Merrye Laurie*. The brig would have taken her to Jamaica. She could have gone into Kingston for the first time, roamed the docks and—

But no, she would have been taken to jail with the others. Annie shivered at the thought of a ball and chain. She sickened when she tried to imagine no sight of the sea. At least, here, she was still on board a ship. She could still smell

115

the ocean salt, still feel spray upon her face and sense a swell beneath her feet. If she was a prisoner here, it was of her own stupid body.

She sauntered to the edge of the quarterdeck, ran to the companionway, and picked her way down the narrow railing. At least, as Jem, she could do such things without being scolded. Even the captain had to let her act the boy for the men.

The door of the sick bay was closed. Annie waited until it opened and was surprised to see Cook emerging again. She always ran into him here.

When he saw her, he gasped and flattened himself against the opposite wall of the passageway. "Jem." He nodded as he sidled past.

"Boo!" Annie yelled after him. For some strange reason, he seemed to be afraid of her now. It must have been that knifing, though she had thought he'd got over that. For the past week, all the men had seemed to avoid her, as if they thought she had the plague.

And it made her mad.

On top of all her other troubles, she had no friends to talk to. Even Mr. Bonny would be leaving her soon.

Annie took a deep breath and willed herself not to show the distress the sight of him always roused. With every day, Mr. Bonny grew more infirm. His skin had dried and cracked like old parchment. His color was as gray as a morning cloud. It was all she could do to go see him and not cry, but weeping over him wouldn't do him any good.

Annie greeted him brightly. His old eyes lit for a second when he saw her, and her heart twisted in pain. *If this is affection,* she thought, *it is no fun at all.*

"Is Cook sick?" she asked, to divert her thoughts from Mr. Bonny's illness.

He wrinkled his brow. For the moment, professional interest put some color back into his cheeks. "No. It is most peculiar. I have witnessed a similar condition in men before. It is usually accompanied by melancholia. But I have never seen the same, precise condition in any two men simultaneously."

At her puzzled look, he peered over his spectacles. "Both Mr. Shirley and Cook seem to be under the illusion that they might have contracted a disease of their nether persons."

"And they haven't?"

"Not that I can see. It is most peculiar." He shook his head and tsked.

Annie crossed herself. "I hope it isn't catching."

Mr. Bonny's eyes twinkled. "This particular affliction, even if they had it, would pose no threat to you, my dear. You may rest assured.

"Now, tell me," he said, easing himself onto a stool. "What progress are you making?"

"None."

His eyebrows rose above his spectacles. "None at all? Dear me! I hate to contradict you, but I see progress in you already."

117

"You do?"

"Yes, in your speech."

"Oh, in my speech!" Annie sneered.

"Do not disparage the worth of gentle speech, my dear. It has an enormous value in the world you will enter. You may consider yourself fortunate that the captain has taken pains to instruct you himself, when he might have left you to discover this alone—the hard way."

Annie didn't mean to argue with Mr. Bonny. Though she doubted what he said, she kept it to herself.

"This *world* you talk about . . . would that be London?" she asked.

She had heard the other sailors talk about London. Some couldn't wait to get back there; others seemed to fear it as if a shark were waiting to catch them there.

"It is possible." Mr. Bonny turned his back to study one of his books. "That will be up to the captain, not me."

His distant reaction was becoming all too familiar. Mr. Bonny did not want to discuss her future. If she asked him anything about it, he always referred her to the captain.

Mr. Bonny cannot help me, she thought. *He cannot help me any longer*. His illness had made him so weak, he had given her up.

"I'll probably like London, won't I?" She tried to sound cheerful.

"I daresay you will." He turned to face her. "That's the spirit, child." His look softened. "I am proud of you."

118

Annie struggled to smile. Mr. Bonny wouldn't be there to see her in her new life. And even if he were, she thought he would be sad.

That's why he won't discuss it, she realized with a quick stab of fear. *He doesn't want to lie to me*. Mr. Bonny couldn't be glad to see her turned into a lady. Not when ladies didn't do anything.

Hiding her inner turmoil, she bid him good day. She climbed up on deck and wandered to the gunwale, feeling the truth with full force.

Being a lady was being a prisoner. She leaned over to stare at the water. Being a lady was four stone walls and a chain.

I just won't be one. The captain can try, but he can't make me be a girl. I'll jump ship before we get to London. Then, I can sign on with another crew, and no one will ever know.

She didn't want to hurt Mr. Bonny, but she thought he might be glad for her if he knew she had escaped.

Music from a pipe broke from the deck behind her. Sailors from the second watch had formed a circle to entertain themselves. As the musician blew on his pipe, the Greek they called Nikos, one of Sharkee's former men, began his dance.

The sound of the reed had always raised Annie's spirits. Now, it heightened her despair. The other sailors pointedly ignored her, causing a deeper pain than she had known. And worse, James would keep her from dancing with them forever if he had his way. An anger that had been building in Annie over his cold, distant

119

treatment boiled up until she could contain it no longer.

She danced a fine hornpipe. Throughout her childhood, she had amused the pirates by dancing for them. Maybe her skill could break the barrier the crew had made to shut her out.

"Hey, look at this," Annie said, as she hopped into the circle, shoving Nikos to one side.

When she would have started her dance, the piper stopped. The other sailors backed away.

"Eh! You, lad! What you doing?" Nikos asked, a mixture of fear and pity on his face.

Annie glanced at him, then at the others. Every pair of eyes stared back at her uneasily. "I was only going to dance," she said. "Same as you."

"You not wanted here."

"Yeah. That's right." The others nodded and grumbled.

Hurt and bewildered, Annie stood fast. Even Nikos, her former mate, had turned against her. And for no good reason that she could see. She had to get to the bottom of this.

"Why? Why can't I dance with ye like I used to?"

The men fidgeted. They eyed Nikos and began to edge away from him, as if she had infected him, too. He couldn't fail to notice. Fear of ostracism widened his eyes.

He growled, "I don't know why, but you just not wanted. Begone with you! Now!"

Annie felt as if she'd been kicked in the ribs. First, she'd lost the *Merrye Laurie* and Captain Sharkee. Then, Mr. Bonny had taken ill. The captain's lessons had turned into torture sessions. And now—this.

With a flash of outrage, she rounded on Nikos and screamed an insult.

A gasp of horror rose from the crew. Nikos reddened, and his eyes began to bulge.

"Take that back!" he demanded, one hand reaching for his cutlass.

"No!"

"Take that back, or I eat your liver!"

"Go ahead and try!"

As he grabbed for her, Annie ducked. She reached inside her trousers, itching for a fight. But her knife was gone.

"Yikes!" She'd forgotten that James had taken it away.

She ducked again and made a run for it. Nikos had already drawn his cutlass and taken a long, fierce swipe. Her maneuver sent him spinning, but he recovered, coming after her at a fast gallop.

There was only one hope. Annie scampered down the long deck, reaching for the ratlines. Nikos's stride was longer than hers, his reach enormous. He nearly winged her before she swung a barrel in his path.

With a grunt, he bowled the barrel aside. It went crashing down the swaying deck. Men were shouting. The piper blew a shrill call upon his pipe.

James strode out of his cabin in time to see a pair of running sailors reach the mast. He saw a

121

Patricia Wynn

commotion down on his main deck, and he cursed.

"Mr. Shirley!" he bellowed.

His first mate came running. "It's the boy again, Cap'n."

"Jem?" Fear gripped James's stomach. He had not glimpsed Annie, but he had seen one of Sharkee's men running after someone with a cutlass. James turned back in time to see Annie leaping for the ratlines.

She had outstripped her pursuer. Heavier and weighted down by his weapon, Nikos was no match for her nimble climbing. Frustrated, Nikos could only stare up after her, with curse after bloodcurdling curse spewing from his lips.

Even as he spied her, James's fear ebbed, but his relief gave vent to his fury.

"Mr. Shirley, take as many men as you need to subdue the Greek and throw him in the hold."

"Aye, aye, sir. But, Cap'n, it was the boy what picked the fight."

James gritted his teeth. "Now, why doesn't that surprise me? Tell him to report to my cabin, and if he gives you any trouble, then—" *What . . . put her in chains?*

He couldn't bring himself to issue the order. With a snort of disgust, he strode back into his cabin to wait.

She arrived only a few minutes later, hands free and her chin jutted in the air. James was glad the men had not needed to use force, but her defiant air did not bode well for ship's discipline.

"Well, Jem . . ." James waved his first mate away.

Mr. Shirley paused. "Shall I tell the bosun's mate to ready the cat, Cap'n?"

"When I ask for it."

His curt response made Mr. Shirley's eyes narrow. He stared resentfully at Annie before he left.

Annie paled, and James felt a wicked spark of pleasure. *Little scamp deserves to be scared.*

He sat without offering her a chair and faced her across the small desk, knowing that at any moment he could reach out and grab her.

Which is what he wanted to do. He wanted to grab her and shake some sense into her silly, thick skull, to make her understand why she mustn't act so foolishly. But, clenching his fists into balls, he realized he must not touch her for the same reason he found it hard to look into her eyes during her lessons. His awareness of her was a constant problem. A constant temptation to forget himself and his duty.

Fortunately, at the moment, her eyes avoided his. No matter how proud her manner, she wasn't looking forward to this little chat.

"Annie, do you mean to tell me the meaning of what I saw on my deck?"

"They wouldn't let me dance."

"They?"

"Them." A jerk of her head encompassed the whole crew. "They don't let me near 'em anymore."

James felt a stab of guilt. He was the one who

123

had caused Annie's isolation. It was just what he'd wanted, but he'd never considered how losing the men's companionship would hurt her.

"And you were angry?"

She nodded.

"Angry enough to pick a fight with a man *twice your size*?" As much as he'd tried, James couldn't keep his voice from rising.

Annie only scoffed, "Oh, that ain't nothing. I could've beaten him if I'd've had my knife." The look she gave James told him whose fault that was.

As reluctant as he was to admit it, James did see that he'd left her vulnerable. Sailors would fight. The men thought of Annie as a sailor, like them. Only now, because of the rumor he had started, they feared her, too.

James knew too well how fear could lead to violence on a ship.

"Well"—he cleared the guilt from his throat— "we can discuss that later. But for now I want to know what you did to provoke Nikos. I told you ladies don't fight."

She bowed her head, and her voice dropped to a mumble. "I *saidizmothradarrytits*."

"Pardon?"

Annie looked up and shouted, "*I said his mother had hairy tits!*"

James recoiled. A hoot of laughter threatened to escape him, before he schooled his lips into a firmer line. "My God, Annie. Don't you know the worst thing you can do to a sailor is to insult his mother?"

124

"Yessir."

"Then why did you do it?"

She shuffled and refused to meet his gaze. "I felt like making trouble, that's all."

James chewed the inside of his mouth. He could press her, but somehow, he knew he would not get the real answer. Still, he could not let her get away with fighting on his ship.

What could he do? If she were a man, it would be so easy. He could throw her in leg irons or have her dragged on a line. He might even resort to flogging.

But the thought of doing any of those things to Annie made him sick, even more than flogging one of his men, which he seldom did. He saw the need for such a punishment as a failure of his leadership.

Annie was still staring down at his cabin floor, maintaining her graceful, boyish posture in spite of the frigate's rocking. Clearly, she expected some punishment, but what?

Torn between punishing her and letting her go, two impossible choices, James stood up and ran his fingers through his hair. "For mercy's sake, Annie! I can't have you fighting with the men. One of them's likely to kill you!"

"Not if I have my knife."

"Forget the knife! I told you not to fight. I want you to forget all that pirate nonsense."

She raised her chin then. "It's not so much nonsense," she said with unconscious dignity. "What's nonsense is being a woman. It is no kind of life at all."

James felt as if he'd been kneed in the chest. He had meant to protect her, but she was telling him that instead, he had taken a bright, resourceful creature and smothered its life. He had taken away her freedom and replaced it . . . with what?

Still, he grumbled, "I ought to spank you, that's what."

She went pale. "Spank? What's that?"

For a split second, he thought she was trying to fool him. How could she not know what a spanking was? Then, he remembered she had been with men all her life, not children. And men did not "spank" other men.

Seeing her fear, unable to imagine what she must be thinking after the horrors she had witnessed, he relaxed his expression for the first time that morning. "It's only a child's punishment," he said gently. "It means that I should put my hand to your backside."

Almost immediately, her color deepened into a rosy glow. Annie stared back at him, considering slowly. Finally a shy smile transformed her mouth into the coyest of smiles.

"I wouldn't mind that so much."

A river of heat gushed suddenly from his core. He remembered pulling her down from the mast, the feel of her womanhood in his palm. The mistaken touch that had nearly scorched him. It had taken rigid discipline to forget.

She couldn't possibly be thinking of the same

126

thing, could she? She couldn't have enjoyed his touch as much he had. Could she?

He felt himself go hard and aching. In a last-ditch effort to keep his distance, he purposely recalled his oath to Mr. Bonny and turned away from her, muttering the first thing that came to mind, "Hairy tits. For God's sake, Annie, what does that mean?"

He played with the ledgers on his desk, giving himself time to recover, expecting no response to a rhetorical question.

But before long, Annie piped up. "I think I know what it means, Captain. Men have hairy ones, but women don't. See?"

James dropped his head into his hands. "Annie, it's just a crude expression. It doesn't have to have a meaning."

"But it does, James, and I can prove it. Remember when you saw mine? They weren't hairy, were they? And then I saw you with your shirt off, and your chest was hairy all over yours. And other men, they've got—"

James leapt to his feet with a groan, his manhood throbbing.

He reached across the desk and clapped his hand over her mouth. "You've got to stop!"

Her eyes grew round, and a muffled voice teased his palm, "Stp wht?"

"Stop talking about your breasts. Ladies *do not talk about their breasts*!"

Her lips moved warmly against his fingertips. The moisture sent a thrill through his palm and down his spine. He jerked away as if she'd bitten him.

"Why not?" she demanded. "Men talk about them all the time."

Heat infused his face. It pulsed at his temples. His thoughts were muddled.

"I know they do, but such talk is not polite. And ladies don't do anything that is impolite."

Annie clutched her fists at her sides. "You've told me a great deal about what they don't do. What *do* they do, for Pete's sake?"

"What?"

James searched through his mental fog and found he had little memory of what women did. He had seldom seen his mother since he had been old enough to go to sea. When he had visited her, he had sat in her parlor and made polite conversation about the events that had transpired between visits, always careful to leave out anything his father said would be unsuitable for her ears.

It wasn't that he hadn't been happy to see her. In his own way, he had loved his mother very much. It was only that he had always ached to be back at sea.

"Well . . ." he told Annie, groping for something to tell her. "They sit."

Disgust crossed her face. "I've been doing a heap o' sittin' already."

"No, it's different." His head was clearing now. "They sit in their parlors, and they . . . they sew!"

Annie gazed at him speculatively. "I don't

know what a parlor is. But this sewing—you mean like sails?"

"No." James knew where he was now, and what was wrong. He ought to have taught Annie more, but there was so much for her to learn and he knew so little about it. He had danced with ladies, of course. He had bedded many women, but they had not been what one would call ladies. And he had wasted little time wondering what his mother did when he was at sea.

"A parlor is a room in a house where company is received. And ladies mend things like clothes."

"I can do that. Any sailor can. That's not so different from sails."

"No, it's not." A picture of his mother's embroidery came into his mind. "And I daresay that other stuff is much the same."

"What other stuff?"

"Embroidery. Fine needlework." When Annie looked confused, he elaborated, "Things with flowers worked into them with stitches."

She raised a skeptical brow.

James waved the subject aside. "But that's for some other woman to teach you. Not me."

"But you've got to teach me something!" Annie gazed at him pleadingly. "You promised."

James could finally see the burden under which she'd been laboring. She'd been told she must not be a boy, but as yet, she knew nothing about being a woman. Even *he* knew more about women than she did.

He had planned to teach her, but her remarks

had been so provoking, he'd had to distance himself. Now, his neglect had led to her fighting with the men.

With a sigh, he conceded that he had to face up to his responsibility. "Very well," he said. "I will teach you what I know. But, Annie, it will not suffice. Sooner or later, some woman must take charge of you. Only another woman can teach you what she does of a day."

"That's fair enough." Annie's frown was clearing. "But you need to answer my questions."

"Fair enough." James agreed before he considered the words, and immediately he regretted them; but he could not take them back. He only hoped that Annie would not ask anything too uncomfortable for—

"Then why don't women talk about their breasts?"

He winced. "They—It is considered impolite."

"Why?"

"Why? Because—because it is."

Annie's expression forced him to continue, while he fought the sudden rise in his temperature. The heat of embarrassment filled his throat. "Because such talk can be provocative to a man."

She cocked her head in question. "Provocative? You mean provoke? Like a fight?"

"Sort of."

"You mean, it's an insult?"

"No, not that." James nervously shook his head. He felt like squirming. His cabin seemed to have grown tinier . . . his neckcloth much too tight. "You remember what Sharkee told you about keeping your breeches on . . . Well, it's like that."

"Ye mean, men wants to poke 'em?"

Annie's vocabulary had lapsed. She blanched again.

He did not want to frighten her too much. Something deep inside him did not want Annie to fear sex.

"It's not as simple as that, Annie. When a man thinks of a woman, he likes to see her breasts, because they're so . . . beautiful. Then . . . some men can't help themselves from—from doing certain things, and if a woman speaks about her breasts, a man might think she's issuing an invitation for him to touch her."

Annie scoffed. "Are they that stupid then?"

James's hackles rose. "It's not so stupid," he said.

Annie studied him closely for a few moments, remaining quiet. He waited for her to speak, but she never did.

He cleared his throat, feeling a rush of blood inside his temples. "I hope that answers your question. We should proceed to something else. I'll teach you how to sit."

She laughed out loud. "Any baby knows how to sit."

"Not like a lady." He smiled, liking the sound of her unrestrained laughter. "A lady sits much differently."

"How?"

"Sit down and I'll show you."

Annie sat, with her knees wide apart, her heels resting on the legs of the chair.

"Not like that. Your knees must come together."

Annie moved them in, but her heels were still out.

"Bring your heels in, too."

She did, but her knees bounced outward.

"No, here." He circled the desk and placed his hands on her knees. "Bring them together, so. Then—" Kneeling, he ran his hands down the back of her legs. Trapping her ankles, he pulled them together.

"Ouch!"

"Did that hurt?" He let her go.

"No. But it did feel strange. Sort of twisted." She shook her head. "Show me again."

James tried to be gentler this time. Perhaps, after so many years of striding like a boy, her legs had bowed and they wouldn't meet.

But they certainly felt all right. Beneath his fingertips, he felt the press of fine muscle over delicate bones. Her ankles were slim and straight. He remembered that they had been his first clue of her sex. These slim, small ankles.

His hands passed over them. His chin came near her shoulder. He raised his head.

Annie was staring, not at her legs, but directly into his eyes. And despite her sunburnt skin and the tar upon her hair, he felt as if her eyes were the green eyes of a siren, calling him.

"Show me again."

James tried to stop himself, but her voice was the soft musical notes of a siren. The feel of her legs in his palms was too right. He began at her knees again, or a little higher—he did not see. His gaze was still trapped by Annie's gaze.

As he felt her hips and her thighs, then her knees, moving downward, her breath came quicker. It echoed the racing beat of his heart.

With a sudden move he jerked his hands away, reminding himself how unwise it was to think of her as a woman. She was an obligation of his and nothing more.

"Do you see now?" He cleared his throat of its huskiness and stood.

"Yes, I see." Annie's voice came in a soft whisper. It sent a thrill shooting through him, which he tried to ignore.

"Well . . . that is that. That is how ladies sit."

He backed away, putting his desk between them like a shield. "That'll give you something to practice."

"But that's easy. Show me something else."

"Not today." He made a great show of consulting his timepiece. "I have to get on with my work."

Her face fell.

"But, Annie"—he stopped her, reaching across his desk to trap her elbow—"I promise to teach you more each day."

She smiled shyly and looked up. "What about my knife?"

James had forgotten the knife, had forgotten

133

her fight during the moments before. Now the reason for her being in his cabin came back to him with force.

After a moment, he said, "I will give it back to you, but on one condition only. You will not provoke fights with my men. You may use a weapon to defend yourself, but only when needed. Agreed?"

"Aye, aye, Captain!" Her face brightened, and it pleased him to see her joyful again.

He reached inside the chest by his berth and handed her the dagger.

Annie licked her finger and tested the blade. He could not correct her for such a rough gesture. Not now.

"Thankee, Cap'n." She smiled, and he knew she was only teasing him with her careless speech. She tucked the dagger neatly into her waistband. "Same time tomorrow?"

"Same time tomorrow . . . if I live that long."

"Pardon me, James?"

He shook his head. "It's nothing. Get away with you now." *Before I run my hands over those shapely legs once too often.*

"Aye, aye, sir, James."

Chapter Seven

When James next stepped onto his quarterdeck and sniffed the wind, he knew immediately that trouble was brewing.

He could see it in his men's eyes when they glanced at him through lowered lids. He saw mutiny in the sloppy state of their work. He heard it in their low murmured growls. Their slouching posture and crude gestures confirmed the threat of what he most feared.

It wouldn't be long before the worst of his sailors began rolling shot.

Discipline aboard a fighting ship was both delicate and crucial. A crew looked to their captain for control. If for any reason the men lost respect for him, they soon found ways to bring him down. And rolling cannonballs to trip his unwary officers was often the first sign.

James knew what had angered his crew. Something would have to be done. He called Mr. Shirley. "Assemble the men," he said. "I have something to say."

Mr. Shirley saluted him before calling down to his mates. The cry went up, "All hands to the main deck. Step lively now!" The slap of hundreds of bare feet on the companionway, the creaking of ropes as the top men slid down, and the sound of voices calling down every hatch covered James's few moments of indecision.

Unbidden, Mr. Shirley had ordered the bosun's mate to fetch Nikos from the hold. Dragged up the ladder from his dank, black prison, the Greek blinked confusedly at the bright sunlight. He had to be anxious to see a rope in the bosun's mate's hand, for in the case of a flogging it was the offender's job to make his own cat-o'-nine-tails.

Amidst the scurry of assembly, Annie appeared to stand side by side in the first row of men. With a curt gesture, James ordered the bosun's mate to "take charge of the boy."

He saw flickers of contentment in his crew's eyes and tried to ignore the fear in Annie's.

Expecting to see the punishment that had been unfairly delayed, the men quickly settled into their rows. The quartermaster blew a signal upon his pipe. James stood and faced his men squarely on, his expression grim.

"I had intended to assemble you today for a

celebration; however, a breach in ship's discipline has caused me to reconsider. An armed fight was nearly averted on the maindeck, involving these two men." James let a jerk of his head in the offenders' direction speak his contempt for their actions.

He had not missed the ripple of eagerness at his mention of a celebration. To sailors that could mean only one thing: more grog. Rum was what every sailor lived for day to day, but it was measured out in strict units. Victories at sea were some of the only reasons for dispensing more grog, but fortunately, James had just remembered another.

Staring sternly at his men to allow them time to absorb what the fight was to cost them, James inwardly rejoiced at their discontented expressions. His men blanched at the treat they thought had been denied and cast sideways glances at the two that promised retribution.

Meanwhile, Annie had stoically raised her chin along with Nikos. The promise of punishment would unite the two. When James thought he had allowed everyone's disappointment to reach a pitch, he changed his tone.

"After careful consultation, I have come to the conclusion that only these two were at fault. Consequently, I see no need to deprive the rest of their pleasure. What I have to announce will come as no surprise to some of you; however, I hope you all will toast me on my upcoming marriage to the Lady Olivia, daughter of The Right Honorable Earl of Figg."

Patricia Wynn

The prospect of an increased ration of grog instantly revived the men's spirits. With Mr. Shirley leading the cheers, they huzzahed at the top of their lungs.

James let their enthusiasm mount. A careless glance, however, at Annie's face revealed that she'd been startled. His announcement had surprised her, even to the point of erasing her fear.

The men finally quieted, aware that no barrel of rum would be cracked until this assembly was over. James took the opportunity to give them a strict lecture on the consequences of starting a fight. He made them bow their heads to pray for forgiveness and the strength to govern their tempers.

Then, staring at the two offenders, he went on. "In this instance, no blood was shed; but I cannot countenance any fight aboard this ship. In light of the ship's celebration, I have decided to reduce these two men's punishments. They will receive no extra allotment of grog, and they will each be given additional duties.

"Mr. Shirley"—James turned to go—"have the bosun's mate release these men. I want them to swab and caulk the quarterdeck. After that Nikos may return to his normal duties, but for starting the fight, Jem will have to report to me for more schooling. You may dismiss the men to quarters."

"Aye, aye, Cap'n!" With a sharp salute, Mr. Shirley betrayed his satisfaction at his captain's resolution of a nasty problem. He had undoubtedly sensed James's reluctance to whip the boy.

138

But if Jem received the same punishment as the Greek—or worse with that extra schooling—Mr. Shirley's sense of justice would be restored.

James strode briskly off the windy deck to seek his quarters. Behind him, he heard the rapid sounds of scattering men. He hadn't missed Nikos's and Annie's expressions of relief, although Nikos's had quickly dissolved in disappointment at the loss of grog. He would miss it, but he had to be grateful to have been spared a flogging for such a serious breach.

A little backbreaking work wouldn't hurt Annie, either, and it just might save her life. Witnessing her punishment would make the men feel sympathy for her.

And maybe, just maybe, the little scamp would learn to guard her tongue.

The next day, when she had finished her swabbing, Annie reported to James. Other than a bit of stiffness in her shoulders, she barely felt the effects of her hard work. For weeks, she'd been next to idle, a much worse condition. She was grateful to James for the way he had handled her transgression since it had restored her to the men's good graces. In every respect, he had shown himself worthy of the title of captain.

And while her hands had been busy with her swabbing, she had pondered all the things James had told her.

The captain had said her breasts were beautiful. He'd said her breasts were so beautiful, men would want to touch them.

Patricia Wynn

At first, she hadn't believed him. She had no basis to believe anything so strange, but then James had reacted testily to her scorn. And she had known.

He wanted to touch them, too. And, for some mysterious reason, that desire embarrassed him.

His every touch had given her pleasure. And, if his touches could give her a thrill, could it be that he found them a thrill to give?

Even though the captain had promised to answer her questions, this was one she meant to guard to herself. The process of discovery had become too delicious to make her want to rush toward its conclusion. Annie decided she would give this being-a-woman another chance.

Her lessons proceeded apace. At one, James said that she must work on her walk. He made her cross his cabin several times as he tried to explain what was wrong, but she couldn't get it right. No matter how hard she tried, his frustration only grew.

"Nevermind," he finally said, throwing his wig on a chair. "Let me show you what I want."

Annie tried to make room for him, but the only way was to retreat behind his desk. James took her place.

"Just watch." He paused and pondered. Then, with a look of concentration, his head barely clearing the ceiling, he took three tense little steps from one wall of the cabin to the other, one hand held out in front of him.

Annie choked. She laughed so hard she nearly fell into his chair.

His voice rumbled like thunder. "I was only trying to show you. For God's sake, Annie, be serious!"

"Sorry, Captain." She covered her mouth. No man liked to be laughed at, she knew, not that it had ever stopped her from poking fun at the pirates. But she didn't want to make fun of the captain or get into a fight. "Why do ladies walk like that?"

"It doesn't matter why. But"—scratching his head, he gave her question some consideration—"it must come naturally to them."

"Well, it sure doesn't come naturally to me."

"Annie . . ."

"Sorry, James. Do you want me to try it?"

He nodded. Then, as he moved aside so she could join him, his hand brushed the base of her spine, and a bolt of lightning shot through her. She stiffened.

"Uh-hmmm." He cleared his throat. "Carry on, sailor—er—Annie."

Annie moved away from him reluctantly. Focusing on her task, she did her best to imitate his walk.

"No, you are bobbing too much. Try to walk evenly."

Annie bent her knees and scurried levelly across the floor.

"Straighten up. Move more slowly."

She locked her knees and walked stiff-legged. James swore and rubbed his face.

"I'm trying, Captain! Don't I look like you?"

"Perhaps you do, but it's still not right."

James rested his head in his palm. He stayed there for a long moment, then glanced up. "Books," he said, reaching for his captain's chest.

"Are we going to read?" Annie watched him rifle through his belongings.

James paused with a stack of books in his hand. "Can you read?"

"I can read a little," Annie admitted, not sure how he would take it. "Mr. Bonny taught me a long time ago."

"Good Lord." It was said very quietly, but James was staring at her as if she'd been born with fins. "And he never thought of mentioning this to me?"

Annie eyed him warily. "Likely he forgot. He only had three books, and only one we read. It's been a long time since we did it."

"That was his Bible, no doubt."

"Yes. Is that what you have?"

"That book and others. But, Annie"—excitement filled his voice—"do you know how few sailors can read?"

"I know." Her guilt lightened when she saw his admiration. "Most of the pirates couldn't. Even Captain Sharkee. When Mr. Bonny taught me, he told me not to tell anyone."

"Well, I'm glad you told me."

Annie suddenly felt as if she couldn't meet his gaze. The wonder in it warmed her far too much. And all just because she could read. "Are we going to read, then?" she asked after a moment.

"No, but someday we will." He turned back to his chest.

Annie admired the way his coat stretched across his broad shoulders. Two ripples of muscle ran the length of his back beneath the dark blue material. Annie wondered what it would feel like to touch him there.

The captain extracted two heavy ledgers. "You are going to walk with these on your head."

"Why? How will that help?"

"You'll see. You must try to balance them."

Understanding, Annie took the ledgers and stacked them on her head. It took some practice, but they would balance.

"Now, walk."

She started across the cabin. With every step, the books threatened to fall. She could see what the captain had meant about not bouncing.

When she had made the short trip across the space several times, she asked, "Is this better?"

"Much better. But there is something . . ."

Annie glanced up, and the books toppled. She caught them, but the captain was concentrating on something else. He was staring at her hips and frowning.

"What is it?"

His eyes met hers, and confusion came over him.

"What?" she insisted.

"I . . . It was nothing. I was trying to imagine how you would look in a skirt. For the walk, you know. To see if it was right. But that was impolite."

143

"Oh." Annie couldn't see why anything so simple should be impolite, but she didn't ask. Sometimes, when the captain looked uncomfortable, she felt uncomfortable, too.

"Well, do you think I was doing it right?"

"I think you nearly had it right. But . . . Annie, when women walk, they do different things, all at the same time. They seem to glide, as if they're taking no steps. But then they sway, too. I can't describe it, and I refuse to show you myself."

"Why?"

James grinned, a knowing look cocked her way. "Because you would laugh."

"No, I wouldn't. I promise." She would promise anything to see him repeat his ladies' walk.

"Liar." James's grin faded as he studied her. Then, he stood and rounded the desk, and Annie felt a curious fluttering in her breast.

"Put those books up again," he said. And she did.

"Now, turn your back toward me."

Annie complied. She could feel him behind her, as if her back was warming in front of an oven.

"Now take one step."

She took one, a short one. She could feel James coming along behind her. And, in the next moment, his hands took hold of her waist and she gasped.

"I'm only going to show you how I think it's done," he explained from behind her. "Are you paying attention?"

"Oh, yessir." *Lots of attention.*

"Good. Now, sway this way with this step, and that way with that."

Annie felt his palms gently pushing her hips to the side. They guided her warmly, the way a wave might catch her and pull her with its tow. She caught the motion from him, and swung her buttocks with his rhythm.

Keeping the books on her head, she glided forward, swaying left and right with his motion. She concentrated hard, and when they reached the wall, she halted, expecting to repeat her steps the other way. But James kept moving. "Take another step, Annie."

His eyes must have been focused elsewhere, for she was into the wall and couldn't budge.

"But, Captain—"

"Take another step." When she'd stopped, his hands had slipped around to the front of her breeches, and his voice had suddenly turned hoarse.

"But, James, the wall!"

"Wall?" In a flash, his hands flew from her thighs. "My God! The wall."

Then, after a second's pause, he did a strange thing. He reached gently around her waist again and pulled her back until her body nestled against his like two stacked spoons. Annie's buttocks pressed warmly against his thighs. She felt the heat of his whole body coursing through her.

She wanted to stay, stay right here where she felt safer than ever before; yet, despite the safe feeling, her heart was beginning to pound like a hammer and her breaths came in gasps.

It seemed as if the captain wanted to stay here, too. He gave no sign of letting her go. Then, Annie felt a quiver inside, something leaping into her throat, and the captain sighed.

"Annie— These lessons—"

"What's the matter, Captain, didn't I do it right?" Annie spun to face him and found her nose just inches from his. Her breasts brushed his chest.

"You did fine, Annie." His expression was glued to the wall behind her head as if he dared not move. "It's not you."

Something had gripped him, she could tell by the way his jaw had tightened; but she didn't know what it was.

"Aren't you feeling good? Can I help you, Captain?"

He stepped back abruptly and gave a groan. "No. No, Annie. You've done quite enough for one day. That had better be all. We'll do better tomorrow."

As he returned, almost stumbling, to his seat, she couldn't help feeling that she'd failed him. She didn't want to let the captain down, or he might stop these lessons, and Annie couldn't bear for them to stop.

"But ye did just fine, James. See?" She turned her back toward him. "Now, I think I can walk just like a lady. I'll practice some and I'll show you tomorrow." She moved for the door in a swaying glide, her hips rolling left and right for him.

She hoped her walk had encouraged him, but as she closed the door behind her, she thought she heard him groan.

The next lesson, James resolved, would have none of the pitfalls inherent in the walking lesson. The mistake, he knew, had been in touching her.

He had *tried* to teach her without resorting to physical manipulation, but it hadn't served. He told himself he had done the right thing. At least she knew how to walk like a woman now—if all too well. The way she had rolled her hips when she had left . . . well, he just might never sleep again.

The fact that Annie could read began to trouble him. With a skill like that she could lead a better life than he had hoped. He began to wonder if he shouldn't teach her to move in a better milieu than he had planned. He decided it would be safe to teach her some table manners. With the table between them, he should be safe from temptation, too.

He instructed Krebs to deliver two trays to his cabin, telling Krebs one would be for Mr. Bonny. Then he called Annie in and explained to her that he would teach her how to dine with the proper manners.

"You're going to teach me how to eat?" she asked.

"I thought you knew how to eat." His teasing remark drew a grin from her.

"But not like a lady, I don't," she teased back.

"That's right, so take this chair, please."

Annie plopped herself down.

"No, not like that. Stand again, and then sit down slowly with your . . . with your limbs pressed together."

The captain kept holding the chair as if it might fall over. Annie did as he said, and he said, "Good. Now, as I advance the chair under the table, you should raise yourself just a bit to make it easy for me to slide it in."

Annie cocked her buttocks out. A choking sound came from behind her. "Like that, James?"

"Close enough. I suppose a skirt will hide it."

James came around the table and seated himself across from her. He sighed, as if he'd just managed to escape a danger.

"Now, your napkin." He showed her how to place it in her lap, and Annie copied him.

"There, that's fine."

When she would have made a grab for her knife, he stopped her. "Depending on the circumstances, someone may pass you the food or else cut some and put it on your plate. If it is a guest of yours, you may do the same for him. Why don't you let me serve you?"

"Very well." Annie put on her best behavior. If James could hold her chair so it wouldn't fall over, the least she could do was try to speak well.

Polite speech was coming more easily to her. She had heard Mr. Bonny speak it all her life. The captain's voice was slightly different, yet she could see the similarities enough to sense what was simply polite and what was peculiar to each man. Their inflections were the same, as were the way they put words together and the forms they used. Annie found she hardly needed to think anymore about what to say.

James had given her a generous portion of boiled meat and vegetables. She was starving.

"Do we get to eat now?"

"No, not just yet. The purpose of eating in a polite setting is to enjoy the company of one's guests."

"Are you enjoying mine?"

James chuckled. "I'm sure that I will."

"And I'll enjoy yours." Annie looked him over. He seemed to have taken even greater pain than usual with his clothes. He had been freshly shaved that morning, of course, but his coat looked newly brushed and pressed, his lace cravat was neatly knotted, and his shirt, breeches, and stockings were gleaming white. Even though the wonder of his fine clothes, the washings and ironings, had lost their mystery for her now, she still thrilled to see him so handsomely turned out.

But now, with James looking so swell, and herself still dressed like Jem, she began to feel less than beautiful again.

She continued her scrutiny in silence.

James's gaze began to waver. "Well, then, we can begin now." He cut a piece of meat, stabbing it with a fork, and raising it to his mouth. "You should use your fork in the left—"

"James"—Annie's words cut across his—"I think I need another bath."

149

He choked on a gasp.

James coughed so violently that Annie leapt up, rounded the table and clapped him on the back. He held her away, and still coughing, pointed her back into her chair.

"It's quite all right," he said, raising his hands as if to ward her off. His coughing had subsided, but his heightened color lingered on. "Another bath, you said?"

Annie nodded. "I think I need it."

"I hadn't noticed. But, Annie . . . I just don't know."

"But I need it. You want me to smell good, don't you?"

"Annie, a lady does not discuss her odor."

"But you're the one who said I stank."

"But I didn't know! Annie . . . no."

"I could take it in the galley again."

"*No.*"

"Why not?"

"Because of the men. Someone might see you."

"No one did last time."

He glowered. "*I* did."

"But that was different. You wouldn't burst in on me again. Would you?"

He glanced away. "Of course not." He stared at his plate. "We are supposed to be eating here, Annie. Aren't you hungry?"

"Oh, yes. I'm starving." She took her knife and cut a bite the way he had shown her.

"And be sure to eat with your lips closed."

"Yessir, James."

He seemed to be having trouble swallowing. He watched her eating until Annie grew self-conscious under his gaze and chewed more slowly. His eyes seemed fixed upon her lips as they moved round and round.

"What about my bath?"

He started and glanced away. "Let me think about it."

Annie stayed silent while he thought.

Finally, James cleared his throat and said, "We could do the same thing with the bath that we have done with dinner. I could order a bath for myself, and you could use it first before me."

"Use your bath water? But what about you?"

He wiped his mouth. "I could bathe after you. We could share the water."

"You wouldn't mind?"

"I'd try not to think about it."

"I beg your pardon, James?"

"That is, I would not regard it. Neither should you."

"If you say so, James. Thank you."

He pointed to her food with his knife. "May we eat now?"

"Oh, yes." With the matter of the bath cleared, Annie turned to her plate with gusto.

She had observed the way James held his knife and used his fork to scoop his food instead of his hands. She tried to hold hers in a similar way and found the movements to be quite easy. Before long, with the captain's approval, she could use the tools without thinking.

James, she saw, ate with a measured pace that

she tried to imitate. Every few bites, he would ask her a question and she would reply. He started with the weather, but that was not surprising for a seaman. Annie told him about the rising swell outside and, thinking of it, excitement tinged her voice.

"The *Flying Swan* will be a fair sight in a storm, I'll wager."

The captain's lips curved up in one corner. "You want to see my ship in a storm, Annie? Why is that?"

She flushed, confused by his amusement. "I like a storm, that's all. And she's a lusty ship."

He muttered, "And getting lustier all the time."

"Beg your pardon, Captain?"

"It's nothing," he said wryly. "So you like my ship, do you? She meets with your approval?"

"Aye, she's comely." Annie could see that he welcomed the praise, as any captain would for his ship.

"And you are not afraid of storms?" His eyes teased her.

Annie started to spit in disgust, then remembered to use her newly learned words instead. "Poppycock!" she said, imitating the captain at his haughtiest.

He laughed. "Well said. What is it that you like about a storm?"

Annie thought. "I like the way the ship heaves beneath my feet as if the whole world is turning over. I like the crashing sounds, so you can hardly hear the men's shouting. It's like the sky and the sea are coming together at last."

The captain's eyes gleamed in the cabin's dim light. He studied her intently until she felt heat curling through her veins.

"That's the way I've always felt about it," he said. "Though I've never expressed it so well before."

He cleared his throat. "But what about sea monsters, Annie? Any good sailor believes in a few of those."

She leaned toward him and lowered her voice. "I shall tell you a secret, Captain. Most sailors are quite superstitious."

"Is that so." James's lips gave a twitch. "And how do you know?"

"Mr. Bonny told me."

James stared at her from across the table. "Mr. Bonny taught you a wealth of things you must always be grateful for, Annie."

"Aye, sir, I know." His serious turn had brought a lump into her throat. "I won't forget."

"Good girl." James reached for his tankard of ale and, eyes still intently on her, tossed it back.

Unsettled, Annie groped for something to say, something to take her mind off Mr. Bonny.

"Captain, if ye order the bath for yourself, then won't ye have to stay in here while I take it?"

His ale spewed over her. In a fit of coughing, he jumped to his feet.

Startled, Annie jumped, too. She wiped at her face and clothes with her napkin.

The captain made some effort to dry her. Reaching across the table, he swiped with his handkerchief at her face and her lap. Then he moved his hands about her throat.

Tightening his grip, he gave her head a gentle shake. "Annie, you're going to be the death of me yet."

"What did I say, Captain?"

"Nevermind."

Chapter Eight

"That will be all, Krebs."

The next night, after thanking the steward for bringing his bath water, James dismissed him as usual, grateful, at least, that he would not have to invent an excuse for making him go. James had long ago established the policy that he would bathe and dress without help. Though such behavior might lower him in the eyes of some people, he could not stand to have another man hovering about him.

Moments after Krebs had left, Annie slipped inside with an air of excitement. She gazed down at the tub between them.

James watched her uneasily, suppressing the need to shift from one foot to the other. He felt as if he were covered with ants. Just the sight of that water between them was enough to make him want to rip his clothes right off.

"Annie . . ."

She looked up and smiled. Her eyes were bright and green. The skin on her face had peeled, leaving it fresh with a sprinkling of freckles beneath the hat he'd given her. With her head turned toward him, he could not see the queue of tar, only the ring of curly red about her face.

He sucked in his breath. The girl was proving to be as pretty as he had expected, but James had never thought she would take his breath away.

He focused on her baggy clothes and the dirt beneath her fingernails to remind himself that she had been raised as a pirate.

"Shall I hop in, Captain?" She startled him.

"You *do* mean to undress." It was more a statement than a question. He knew she had been used to bathing with her clothes on, but he thought she had learned otherwise.

"Of course." She tugged at the buttons at the top of her shirt.

"Not yet!" James silently cursed his own jumpiness. "Let me make a screen for you," he said, and he reached for his blanket.

He had needed to wait for Krebs to leave, but James had never had any intention of watching her bathe—for all the pleasure it would give him to do so.

And it would still not be easy, it seemed, to

156

teach Annie to preserve her guard. He would have to talk to her about it again. Later.

James lifted the blanket and spread it out. He had already called the ship's carpenter and ordered him to affix two hooks to opposing walls of the cabin. The carpenter had complained that James was certain to snag his sleeves or his wig on them. James had replied that he needed the hooks to accommodate an instrument.

It was no less than the truth.

He had checked, and his blanket would just span the distance between them, making it impossible to see her.

"There." James examined his work and was satisfied to find that Annie was now invisible to him on the other side of the screen. He would be free to sit at his desk while she, no more than three feet away, would have complete privacy in her bath.

"Should I take my clothes off now?"

James found that Annie, disembodied, lost none of her allure. Just the thought of what would go on beyond his vision set him to quivering.

"Yes. You may go ahead, but please hurry. I shall be working here."

"Aye, aye, Captain."

James sat down at his desk, and with complete determination, started checking the clerk's entries to his inventory log.

Then, Annie began to whistle. It was some sailors' tune with a merry lilt.

In his imagination, James could see her lips puckering while she quickly disrobed. The small sound of cloth falling on the floor told him that she had stepped out of her trousers. Then, for a brief second, her whistle was muffled, and he knew that she had pulled her shirt over her head.

The whistle changed into a hum, as if her chin were lowered, and he wondered if she was unwinding the band from about her breasts.

A whistle again. Then, the unmistakable noise of a foot plopping into water, followed by another.

James felt his throat begin to thicken.

He cleared it with a deep cough, and forced his mind to his work.

"Hah!" The one syllable made him jump.

"What is it, Annie?"

"You should see my goosebumps, James. They're very amusing. They've sprung out all over my body."

He started to reprove her, but before he could speak, she gave another laugh. "You should see my breasts! They're sticking up like cannons!"

"Annie!"

"Oops! Forgot. I'm not supposed to talk about them. But if you could see them, James, you would understand why I drew them to your attention."

James put his head in his hands. He didn't know whether to laugh or cry.

But he did not respond. There was no way he could speak without letting his appetite show.

After a few moments of silence, except for Annie's whistling, she called out, "Are you still there, James?"

"I could hardly fit through the porthole, if that's what you mean."

Annie laughed, as if she had never heard anything so witty. James could almost see the gooseflesh that would break out as a result. A surge of pleasure shot through him that he could tickle Annie with his humor.

"Are you working?"

"I am *trying* to work." But he wasn't. Only a eunuch could work, knowing that Annie lay naked on the other side of that curtain. Any normal man would be biting his knuckles by now. James didn't need much help to remember the sight of Annie, fresh from the bath.

He could see her now: her fair, gleaming skin, the contrast of white and dark in places where the sun had darkened the mundane and heightened her more secretive parts. The nipples he longed to bring to peaks with his thumbs. That thatch of red that would haunt him until he'd buried himself inside someone else.

"James, what are you thinking about?

James moaned. "Annie, I told you. I am trying to work. Can't you take a bath without talking?"

"You sound so strange."

"I'm just—frustrated." He could tell that much of the truth. She would be unlikely to know what he really meant.

"You know, James. It feels very strange knowing you are on the other side of that blanket."

159

God, does it. And more than strange. It feels like bloody torture.

"What do you mean?" he couldn't keep from asking her.

For once, she paused before speaking. "I'm not sure. I don't really know how to tell you."

"Try." No matter what she said, James knew he must restrain himself. But he had to know what she was feeling.

"I know you're there," Annie began. "It's like you're here in the bath with me, almost." In her voice, he could hear a certain wistfulness.

He clutched his fists. "And . . . ?" He shouldn't encourage her, but an enchanting possibility had just arisen in his mind.

Those hooks. Just perhaps, they wouldn't hold the blanket. The whole arrangement looked distinctly insecure. He should have thought of something safer, but perhaps he had not wanted to. Perhaps, just one corner of the blanket would slip. Lower and lower. And then, with a sudden flourish, the other would fall, and all at once, they would be sitting there, he and Annie, facing each other, and Annie would stare at him in wonder . . .

James's eyes glazed over. If he exerted any more restraint, he feared his member would burst.

But maybe he wouldn't need for the curtain to fall. Maybe she was feeling a portion of the desire that was making it near impossible for him to stay where he was.

What if she said she wanted him, too? In the bath. Now. With her.

"And what?" Annie said in response to his question.

"And . . ." He held his breath. ". . . Is that all you're feeling?"

"I guess so."

With a whoosh, James expelled his breath. "Annie, you've got to get out of that tub."

"Why? Do you want to come in?"

"Yes— No! That is, it *is* my turn. But you must get dressed."

"As you will, Captain."

No, God help me, it is not at all as I will. It must never be that.

He heard the sound of water sucking as she rose from the bath, and then the drips as the water trickled to the ends of her breasts and fell.

Aphrodite, rising from the sea.

At that foolish thought, James had to laugh. And with his laughter came relief. Annie was no Aphrodite. Her hair was still tarred, she strode like a boy, and her language was more suited to a sailor than a goddess.

That didn't mean, of course, that he had any less desire to bed her.

Shame rolled over him. If she had spoken on, would he have been able to restrain himself? One more word, one more tantalizing word, and he might have deserted his code of honor. He might have done something that he would have regretted for the rest of his days, deflowered a virgin under his protection.

Annie was humming again as she dressed.

"James, these clothes need a washing."

"I can't help that, Annie. If you washed them, the men would surely suspect. But we'll be in England soon, and I will buy you more clothes."

"I can't use this binding again for my breasts."

"Why not?"

"I just can't make myself do it. It's dirty."

In England soon. Much too soon. He had still not told Annie enough about being a woman to protect her. She had no earthly notion of what marriage was, yet marriage was her one hope. She must have a man to take care of her.

"I'm dressed now, James."

"Thank God."

"Pardon me, Captain?"

"I said, thank God. Now, Annie, you are dismissed, but I shall speak with you later today."

"Aye, aye, Captain. Enjoy your bath."

James gave a grunt. As he heard the door close behind Annie, he wished with all his heart that the water would be cold. Ice cold. With an arctic—no, a polar frigidity. It would have to be, or his desire would be too prominent for him to face his crew for the remainder of the day.

Another week rattled by. From his quarterdeck, late one evening, James gazed out over a starry horizon. The moon was so slim and delicate, it left the waves in shadow and cast the sea as a surging bed of mystery. It was as if the powers that be refused to shed light upon the widening world, to assist him with his task.

The sun had set many hours ago, and still James had not found his courage.

He had shot the sun at noon with his sextant and experimented with his new chronometer. If his readings with the latter were even remotely correct, they should land in Liverpool within the week, give or take one day, then sail on to Portsmouth.

James knew that Annie had been sitting outside his cabin even though her watch was long over. He had told her to wait there for him until the ship's crew was mostly settled for the night. It was far past time they had a serious talk.

Heaving a sigh, James did his best to get a grip on himself. His present duty was clear. Annie must never discover the arousing effect she had had upon him, how she'd fired his desire. At the same time, he must finally do whatever it would take to make her understand the effect she would have on most men. *On any man* who had a shaft between his legs and wanted to use it.

James knew she needed a woman to teach her how to sew and how to laugh in moderation; how to curtsy and how to guard her tongue; how to fend off men's advances and how to keep her eyes affixed to the ground to keep from tempting them.

But what if this woman were curt, what if she refused to understand the world Annie had left, what if she purged every shred of honesty and joy from Annie's soul?

When James thought of the life she had led, and the life that was to come because he had discovered her, he knew he could not live with himself if he said nothing to prepare her. If Annie must leave Eden, then he must be the one to soften the way.

"All's well, Captain." His second mate's voice floated up to him on the hour.

"Very good, Mr. Petty. Make her ready for the night."

"Aye, aye, sir."

"And Mr. Petty . . ."

"Yessir?"

"I am not to be disturbed until first watch."

"Aye, aye, Captain."

James had no need to explain himself. His mates always knew that such an order was to be considered annulled in the event of an emergency; but the request for privacy would be respected until he was truly needed.

James strode with purpose to his cabin and ordered Annie inside. She leapt up to follow him.

"You wanted to see me, Captain? Are we going to have another lesson?"

Annie eyed him eagerly. His lessons had become her life's blood. No matter how much the captain puzzled her, she enjoyed every moment spent with him. But there was a mystery about him tonight that had started her pulse to racing and her limbs to trembling.

"Annie . . ." The captain's voice was kind. "I want you to be seated."

"Yessir, James."

He started to take his customary place across from her; but after a moment's hesitation, he came near her and settled one hip across his desk instead.

As he leaned there in the lantern light, one hand resting on his extended leg, Annie felt a curious sense of longing. The muscles of his thigh were splayed over the desk just inches from her face, so near, that she could almost feel the power in his leg. She wanted to stroke it.

"Annie." James cleared his throat. "Annie, I'm afraid these lessons will have to stop."

"Stop?" Her head jerked up. "But why?"

"We are almost to England. I have done my best to teach you some of the things you need to know, but I cannot do more. Annie—"

She felt her heart was breaking. The captain would be leaving her there.

He continued, "There is more you need to learn. It would not be fair or proper for me to be the one to teach you. When we get to England, I shall have to find a woman to do the job."

"But, Captain, haven't I done well? I've tried to speak the way you want me to. And I can sit right and walk right enough, can't I?"

"Yes, of course, you have done very well. But, Annie, there is so much more."

He frowned, and at first she thought she had displeased him, but then he took one of her hands in his and held it gently. Annie stared down at his hands.

They were big and callused. For all that they

were clean and his fingernails evenly cut, they still had the strength of a working man's. Their roughness pleased her. As his hand moved, almost imperceptibly against hers, she felt a thrill in her palms, a thrill that mounted along her nerves, from her wrists to her heart and set it pounding. Shimmering heat seemed to swirl about them. She felt encased in a haze created by his touch.

"Annie, are you aware of marriage?"

"Marriage?" She shook her head to clear it. The captain would be wanting clear answers, not some parrot's mimicking. "I think I know what it is."

"Tell me about it."

"Some of the pirates used that word. I think it meant they visited a woman when they were on land. One particular woman. At least"—she pondered—"no more than one in each port."

James grimaced and gave a sigh. "It is something like that, but so much more. Annie, some day you will marry a man. That means that you will live with him. You will share his bed and have his children."

"But why?"

"That is the fate of nearly all women."

"Why?"

His lips twisted. "Somehow I knew you would ask. All I can tell you is that it's the way of the world. The same as why the sun sets at night, and why the ocean is deep."

Annie thought about it. If she had to live in a house, she would rather some man lived with her. She was used to men, a whole shipful of men, and to being their companion.

As far as sharing someone's bed . . .

She looked at the captain. She liked it when he touched her, and she thought he liked it, too. Why else would he have started stroking her hand with such tenderness? If marrying him would mean lying down beside him and feeling his body next to hers like a pair of stacked spoons, she knew she would like that.

But children? Annie knew what they were. She had seen them from the deck of the *Merrye Laurie*. They were shorter than grown, the way she had once been. Mr. Bonny had explained that to her. If the captain had children, and he wanted her to share them with him, she supposed she had no objection.

"Very well, Captain. I'll marry you."

A look of shock came across his face and he dropped her hand. "No, Annie, you misunderstand me. I was speaking of some other man."

"Why?"

"Why?" He looked astonished and dismayed. "Annie, we are not of the same world."

She cocked her head and studied him. "You're a sailor, aren't you? Well, so am I."

"Yes, but you're a crewman and I'm the captain." James shook his head and grimaced as if at a loss. "At least, you're not a crewman," he corrected himself. "You are a woman. But, Annie, I am afraid it is something like that."

"Like what?" If he had left it as it was, she would have understood.

"I am a gentleman."

"Oh." A pang of disappointment shot through her. She supposed that meant that he must marry another gentleman.

"Then who will I marry?" She was not so sure she wanted to share a bed with another man.

"Someone you choose. If possible, someone you love."

Love. Such a mysterious word. "So I get to pick him?"

"Yes. At least, at first someone may pick you, but you may always refuse if you wish."

That didn't sound so bad. "And then what?"

"Then?"

Sometimes the captain could be worse than she was for sounding like a parrot. He tried to peer through the porthole above her head, but of course, it was dark. He stared at his lap instead. "Why then, Annie, you will have his children."

"Is that all?"

"All?" His head came up, and he studied her closely. "I am afraid there is more to it than you know."

She let her eyes question him.

He chuckled nervously. "Annie, this is where some woman must take over."

"Why?"

"Because it would be improper for me to speak to you about the secrets of marriage."

The secrets. There. She had the truth at last. For once, someone had spoken of these secrets out loud.

"Are they bad?"

"Bad? No." He shook his head strongly. "Some might say they are the best part. If you live with someone—even you know this, Annie—you might get tired of him, or he might even make you angry at times. But in marriage, there are certain benefits that compensate."

"Like what?"

"Like . . . kisses, for example."

"Kisses?"

James smiled at her. "Don't tell me you don't know what kisses are?" Then, he sighed. "No, of course you don't."

"Well?"

"Annie, someone will teach you. You needn't worry."

"I'm not worried. I just want a hint."

"A hint?" He considered her. "Just a hint?"

"Yes."

James grinned, then dragging his hand across his lips, he said, "I suppose I could give you a hint."

He reached for her hand. She felt a slight jolt from his contact, but then he lifted her fingers to his mouth.

Annie snatched them away, jumping from her chair.

James's gaze jerked up to meet hers. "What's wrong?"

"Weren't ye going to bite me?" Annie rubbed the place where his teeth had nearly touched. "It might go septic."

James's lips spread wide with amusement. "No, I wasn't going to bite you, you scamp. It was a kiss. I was going to kiss your hand. Give it back."

"Are you sure?"

"Yes." His grin tinged his voice. "I promise you, I won't hurt you. In fact, you should like my kiss very much."

"If you say so, Captain." When he spoke in that voice, she couldn't resist him. She'd never heard that tone from any other man.

She offered him her hand. The captain bent over it and she braced herself, but she only felt the brush of his lips against her knuckles.

He raised his head, and looked at her expectantly.

She paused. "That's it?"

He brows snapped together. "What do you mean, *that's it*?"

"That was a kiss?" Annie shook her head. "What's so secret about that?"

"I never said it was a secret." James looked disgruntled, as if he had expected a different reaction from her. "And that was only a hint. Remember?"

"A hint of what?" Annie sat down again, disappointed. "More kisses?"

"No. A hint of different kisses. If a gentleman is meeting a lady, he might kiss her hand. But once he knows her better, he might try to steal a kiss from her lips."

"How can he steal something like that?" The whole deal sounded stupid.

"It's an expression, Annie. What it means is

that the lady might give something of herself when he kisses her."

"That doesn't make sense."

"Oh, yes, it does." He sounded angry.

"Then show me."

James's jaw clenched, as if with a challenge. "You want me to show you. Are you certain?"

"Of course."

"You don't know what you're saying, Annie. This kiss will be quite different from the other."

Annie really didn't see what all the fuss was about. "If you say so, Captain. Go ahead." But she was still disappointed.

He studied her. In the lantern light, his hair was dark and gleaming. He seemed poised on the brink of a dive, his lips fixed in a determined line. "Very well," he said tightly. "But I think you'll notice a great difference this time."

What he meant, Annie could see, was that she *would* notice a difference, or he'd be damned.

She prepared for a light, quick touching, the way his lips had brushed her knuckles. But the captain was not in the mood for that.

He stood and yanked her to her feet. Annie felt herself pressed the length of his body. Her breasts, which she'd left unbound since her bath, touched his chest and her nipples sprang to life. His fingers spread like a warm fan across her lower back. He pulled her closer, and the warmth of his legs made her ache to move nearer still.

But that would be impossible, she thought.

James grasped her pigtail and pulled her head slowly back until her neck lay open to him. "Now, hold still, Annie," he whispered. "Hold very still."

The sound of his voice, with a fresh hint of huskiness, sent chills down her spine. She might have struggled, but his chest felt so delicious. It warmed her nipples where they had peaked.

The whisper of his words was like the hiss of a magician's snake drawing her closer.

James bent his head toward hers. Annie's lips parted on a gasp, just as he met them with his own . . .

They were so soft. So smooth and moist and soft, like a warm Caribbean tide. At first, merely touching like the lap of a small wave on the beach, and then stronger as he rubbed himself against her. His lower lip moved against hers. She took a rasping breath and plunged back, just as his teeth flashed out to bite her.

A nibble against her mouth. James groaned, and his groan spread through her like a ripple through a sail. Annie played with his lips and tasted of their salt with her tongue. She ran her fingers through his hair, and his tongue found hers.

The sudden roughness made her jump—but jump toward him. Annie grasped at his chest. She felt his muscles quiver beneath the cloth and she began to rub.

"Annie . . ." He tore his mouth away, and his hand moved to cup her jaw. "Annie, don't touch . . . Don't touch. . . ."

He brought his forehead to hers and rested. They both were breathing as if they'd climbed the ratlines to the stars.

After a moment, he took her hand and pressed it to his heart. "Do you feel the beating, Annie? The danger?" His voice was rough. "That's the secret, Annie. That danger is the secret."

Danger? Annie sensed no danger. She felt gloriously alive.

James pushed her from him. "That was the hint you asked for. Are you satisfied?"

No. How could she be satisfied, when all she wanted was more? She wanted to sail on the wind they'd raised until she reached that place he had promised to take her.

Except that James had not really promised. Only his lips had hinted at a secret island that no one knew of.

"Annie, are you all right?" The captain spoke to her in a rigid voice. "Annie, this is why these lessons must stop. Someone else must teach you the rest."

"If you say so, Captain." Annie found her voice. Now that he'd released her, she felt foolish. Her limbs were wobbling like the veriest landlubber's.

"Now do you see what a kiss is?" James glanced at her out of the corner of his eye.

"I suppose so." She shrugged. She mustn't let him see how silly she'd become.

"What in the blazes do you mean by 'suppose so'?" His color had risen.

Annie studied him. Her indifferent response

had clearly offended him. "Oh, that was fine, that was, Captain."

Her hasty words hardly placated him, which gave her the inspiration to play a little game. A game to get what she wanted.

"I expect that was a prime kiss, James, but since it's my first, I really don't know. If you'd just do it again, then I could tell you what I think."

James started toward her, then abruptly stopped. He gripped the desk behind him tightly with both hands.

"No, Annie. That would not be wise. I think you have had enough lessons."

"Tomorrow then?"

"*No*! Annie, you don't know what you're doing."

"But if you showed me, Captain, I would be sure to get better."

"*That is not what I'm worried about!*"

"Then, what is?"

"Annie. . . ."

It was no use trying to trick him when he got that threatening tone. "All right, then, Captain. But I sure did like that kiss, and I was only trying to please you."

James squeezed his eyes shut. "Dismissed!"

"Aye, aye, James."

With a sinking heart, and her limbs still shaking from his kiss, Annie let herself out. One week, just six or seven days, and she would never see him again. And no more lessons before then?

She *must* be alone with him again. She must make him kiss her at least one more time. If she had to go ashore, she must first get as close to him as their bodies would allow. Just once more. So that possibly this furious curiosity that was making her shake with dissatisfaction would finally leave her alone.

She thought of the threatening note in his voice and felt a shiver. What would he have done if she had not stopped teasing him?

His threats were so different from Captain Sharkee's, more intense and more restrained, as if he could barely keep his fingers off her. She remembered the white of his knuckles against the desk. What would those wonderful hands do if they captured her?

She must make him touch her. Whatever trick it took, she would goad him until he broke.

Chapter Nine

The next day, when Annie went looking for Mr. Bonny, he was not in the cockpit.

"He's laid up," Mr. Shirley informed her when she inquired. He went so far as to lay a hand upon her shoulder. "He's feeling mighty sickly, lad."

"I see." Even knowing he was ill, Annie was shocked to hear the news. Mr. Bonny had never failed to rise from his berth before.

"I'll go and see him," she said, while her heart set up a quicker beat.

"Aye, you do that. That'll cheer the old bugger up."

Annie hurried to the cabin that had been assigned to the old physician. It was smaller than the captain's and had to accommodate two men, since Mr. Shirley had made room for an extra berth when Mr. Bonny had come aboard.

Annie rapped softly upon the door. When no one answered, she quietly pushed it ajar.

Mr. Bonny was alone and, to all appearances, asleep. He was lying crammed into his makeshift bed, his face as colorless as a wintry day. His mouth hung slightly open, and Annie could hear his raspy breathing even from where she stood.

After a moment, she started to leave, but a creaking of the ship from a sudden gust caused him to open his eyes and see her.

"Jem!" His feeble voice accosted her eagerly. "Stay, lad, stay."

Annie entered, feeling strange to see him in such dishevelment. A curious odor filled the tiny space, a whiff of decay. Though the pirates had mocked him, Mr. Bonny had always maintained himself fastidiously. Now Annie understood that it was this preference, along with his perfect speech and gentle courtesy, that had elevated him above the other men.

With one limp hand, he waved her to the cabin's only seating atop a seaman's chest. Annie sat and drew up her knees, wrapping her arms about them. Surreptitiously, she wiped her damp palms upon her trousers. For the first time in her life, words eluded her.

With a tightness in her throat, she began, "Mr. Shirley said you were feeling poorly."

"Feeling ill. Yes. Or rather"—he smiled weakly—"feeling that to get up this morning would be something of a trial."

"Is there anything I can do?"

He gave the impression of shaking his head, though Annie realized the movement was little more than the ghost of a shake. For how long had Mr. Bonny's phantom gestures fooled her into thinking him more alive than he was?

"Nothing, child, except"—his expression held a plea—"I pray that you will keep getting along with the captain."

"Oh . . . the captain." Annie felt a rush of blood stealing up her neck. "I guess you could say we're getting along all right."

She wondered if she should tell Mr. Bonny about the captain's kiss, which had made her knees shake every time she had thought of it. But something held her back, some budding sense of discretion, as if the captain and she must cherish their shared secrets.

"Annie . . ." Mr. Bonny groped for her hand. His touch brought sudden tears to her eyes. He had seldom touched her, knowing that to do so would reveal her gender to the pirates.

Instinctively, Annie warmed his weathered flesh between her palms.

"My dear . . ." He paused for a long moment. "I have not done all I should to prepare you to leave the ship. I am afraid I have wronged you."

"No, it's all right, Mr. Bonny," Annie said quickly. He mustn't be allowed to fret or he would waste his strength. "The captain's been doing all that."

"What?"

"All those lessons. He's already taught me to

sit and walk and speak like a lady." *And to kiss like one*.

"Like a lady? Well, that is most curious." An anxious frown marked his features. "Has he told you of any plans he has made on your behalf?"

For Mr. Bonny's sake, Annie suppressed a grimace. "He said I would need to learn the rest from some female."

"The rest of what?"

"Oh . . . things like marriage, I guess."

"He has spoken to you about marriage, then?"

"Yes, but he said that I couldn't marry him."

"Oh?" His brows rose. "How did that arise?"

Annie screwed up her mouth. "I said I wouldn't mind it."

"You did?" A flicker of anxiety touched his eyes. "But he refused?"

Annie nodded. "Yes, he says because he is a gentleman."

"Ahhhhh." The captain's reason seemed to make perfect sense to Mr. Bonny, but even so, his voice held a certain sadness when he added, "Of course, he is right."

"Don't gentlemen have to marry?" The question had bothered her all night.

"No, my dear," Mr. Bonny said wryly. "Gentlemen may do exactly as they please."

His words seemed to hit her like a slap across her cheek. "Then, it wouldn't please him to marry me. Is that it?"

The pain in her voice must have struck him, for he answered quickly. "No, child, no. You misunderstand me. What I meant to say was that a gentleman may choose not to marry at all, but if he does, he must marry a lady. A woman of gentle birth."

The distinction confused her. Annie had always thought that a captain was all-powerful, but it appeared that, at least in some matters, he had no choice. "That's all right, then," she said. She remembered the captain's announcement the day of her punishment. He had said he was engaged to a lady. That must have been what he meant.

The more Annie had thought about his words to her last night, the more troubled she'd become. She was not at all certain that she would find another man she wanted to share a bed with. She had known many men. She had seen different pirates come and go from the *Merrye Laurie*, and not a one of them had drawn her the way James did.

Mr. Bonny was studying her intently. He seemed troubled.

"Annie." His dry lips worked to form a message for her. "When we reach land, do you perfectly understand that Jem will be no more?"

Annie stared. Of course, she knew. The captain and Mr. Bonny both had told her, but even so, hearing Mr. Bonny's words, she was rocked. The person she had been all her life—all nineteen years—in less than seven days would exist no more. And who would live in his place?

Who was Annie? She didn't feel like a new person except when she was with James.

The only answer she could give Mr. Bonny

was so vague that she merely nodded. Then, to change the subject, she said, "The captain says we'll be in England in another week."

"In England?" His eyes hazed over. He looked past her as if he saw something she could not see. "I never expected to see England again." His fingers plucked at his sheets.

For the first time, Annie wondered how Mr. Bonny felt about going home. She knew how much she missed the *Merrye Laurie* at times, especially when the captain was too busy to see her.

"Are you glad, then, to be going back?"

His gaze slowly focused, but even now he seemed to be somewhere else. A fretful note entered his voice. "I had thought I would be buried at sea."

Buried. It was the first time he had spoken of death out loud. Annie felt a growing lump in her throat.

"I should like to be buried at sea," she spoke softly and clasped the hand still held in hers. "When the sea opens its waves for you, it can take you anywhere you want to go."

"Yes." Mr. Bonny's eyes misted over. "That is a lovely thought . . . my dear . . ."

And you will float forever and ever, Annie wanted to say.

But Mr. Bonny had closed his eyes. Slowly, his hand went limp within her grasp. His lips parted, and once again she heard his raspy breathing.

Annie stayed with him for a while, for once

181

letting tears roll unguarded down her cheeks. There was no one here to see her cry. And Mr. Bonny deserved her tears.

Mr. Bonny stayed abed the next day and the next, and each time that Annie tried to see him, he was asleep.

The captain went to check on him once, and then assigned Krebs to wait on the doctor. He told Annie that she might sit with Mr. Bonny as much and as often as she liked.

She was determined, nonetheless, to perform her simple tasks as cabin boy. She took the captain all his meals, and though he thanked her kindly, he kept his distance. As James had threatened, there were no more lessons.

Annie tried to fight the feeling that some kind of fuse had been lit, one whose spark was racing briskly to a disastrous end. Mr. Bonny would die, she knew; in some ways he was already lost to her. And with Mr. Bonny's passing, so would pass the boy, Jem.

No one else would remember the boy she had been. And no one else but James knew that she was a girl. Annie felt trapped between two worlds and shunned by both. Mr. Bonny's death would close the door forever on one; she had no choice but to go forward.

England. The word hovered above her like a threat. As the ship sailed nearer and nearer to her destination, the crew grew eager and restless. The deck was awash with seamen, day and night. Arguing and grumbling, responding to more whistles and orders, each sailor ached to be the first man to sight Land's End.

Even the captain, himself, was infected.

Unlike his men, however, James maintained his calm. Annie first noticed a change in him when he stepped up his orders. All the decks were to be washed and scrubbed, all the riggings mended. He examined the yardarms for soundness and tested each sail against the wind. With more sail aloft, they flew ever faster toward her dreaded future and its loneliness.

No more James and no more Mr. Bonny. The two men who had come to mean everything in the world would be gone. Annie knew she would not survive their loss. All her worst fears roiled to the surface like seaweed in a storm: land, but not beach; people, but not sailors; the sea at some great, unfathomable distance away. Women for mates. Different clothes, different manners, different ways.

She wanted to talk to the captain about her fears, try to make him see that she must stay aboard. But James kept busy now with his charts and his logs and his ship. He excluded her from his days in every way.

Yet, she knew that he sensed her presence. Whenever she drew near, something in his posture changed. He straightened his shoulders and propped his legs as if to brace himself against a surge of tide. He clasped his hands behind his back as if to keep from touching her.

Just the thought of his touch set her pulse to racing until it even throbbed in the nub between

183

her legs. In her sleep, she dreamed strange things: about seahorses so great that she could ride them; about mermaids who slithered through the waves, and she was one of them, the water gliding over her body as if she'd been greased. And in these dreams, her nub kept beating, beating, until she had to press her legs together to still it.

Such delicious dreams. Almost like being with James.

But she never *would* be with James, not the way they had been together when he had taught her how to kiss. The imprint of his lips upon hers had begun to fade, leaving them desperate for more. A restlessness had seized her that she couldn't comprehend. She hungered for his taste and his touch, but James wouldn't touch her. Not again.

Not . . . she thought a minute . . . not unless she could find some way to trick him. Annie felt like a ship whose sails had been fully hoisted, but the wind had died, leaving her becalmed and quivering. She would almost prefer James's anger to his calm indifference. Something had to change. If her sails needed a boost to get them going, then, by God, she would think of some way to heave them herself.

Another day passed. James sat at his desk in his cabin and wondered what he could do next. He had already had the decks swabbed and buffed to a dazzling shine, and the twelve-pounders polished till they reflected the sun like glass. The men had been checked for lice and scurvy. The stores had been counted, the rum strictly rationed, the crew's prize money figured. It always made sense to pass out their prizes just before they pulled into port, with a promise of more if they signed on again. A lure of sorts.

The trouble was that they might pull in tomorrow or in several more days. No way to tell to the hour or the knot how much more sea lay ahead. His scouts were all aloft, and any moment one might cry out, "England ho!"

England. James had always felt the excitement of coming home, even though hoisting sail again moved him more. But this time, he could feel only dread about leaving Annie.

He must leave her, of course, and he would, but not before speaking to her again. He must make her understand he was doing the right thing.

He had sensed her misery. He didn't have to know Mr. Bonny's state to guess her fears. He saw them in her eyes.

He could almost suffer with her. He could imagine how he would feel if he had to leave the sea forever. But Annie was a woman. Things were different for women. No woman could love the sea like a man.

Yes, Annie would form new attachments. Women were good at that. She would make new friends, some silly girls, no doubt. She would learn to love her new governess or whatever the woman would be. She would make a life for herself the way women were supposed to. She would even marry.

The specter of Annie's eventual marriage hovered ominously below his belt. Some other man possessing Annie. Some clumsy brute of a tradesman taking his due with her beautiful body.

Even perhaps . . . Annie enjoying it.

James could almost swear she had enjoyed his kiss. Before God, *he* had. Her kiss had been anything but timid. Without pretense or artifice, like the unschooled little savage she was, driven by instinct and nothing else, she had torn into his mouth. He had nearly lost control.

James cursed himself and drove such thoughts from his mind. Annie was a burden to herself and to him. The sooner she found a life on land, the safer they both would be.

Standing suddenly, James decided this would be the right time to talk to her. If he waited until they were in port for their final chat, he might be too busy to be fair.

Abruptly, James crossed the cabin, threw open the door, and shouted, "Jem!"

Annie was lounging on the quarterdeck. Though her head snapped around at his call, she stood very slowly and dragged her feet the whole way to his cabin.

James knew he mustn't let his feelings for her weaken his resolve. His decision was made, and there was clearly no other. He stiffened himself against an onslaught of senses. He took his place behind his desk and waited for her to sit.

She sat, all right, but not the way he had taught her. She slouched against the seat with her legs splayed in front. She glanced at him strangely from beneath her strawberry lashes.

He tried not to mind.

"Annie," he started, curbing the unease she always stirred, "we shall sight land soon. I think it is time that we review all I've taught you."

"Aye, aye, Cap'n."

He bristled. "Have you forgotten? When we are alone, you are to behave like a lady, not like a pirate. My name is Captain Avery."

"That's right, sir, James."

He let that one slide, but her continued slouch was making him angry. She had glued her eyes to the deck like some wretched servant.

"Do you remember your greetings? How do you do, and so forth?"

"Very well, thank ye."

"Thank *you*."

"Aye, aye, Cap'n."

"Cap-*tain!*" He restrained himself.

She darted him another glance he couldn't read.

"What is the matter with you today?"

Annie looked up and hunched one shoulder in a vulgar shrug. "I don't know, sir, James. Seems like I've forgot is all."

"I have *forgotten*," he said between his teeth, before shaking his head in frustration. "You could not possibly have forgotten already. Perhaps if you sat correctly, you would remember."

"Like this?" Annie brought her legs together. She pressed them so tightly that the apex of her trousers bunched into a tight V.

James's eyes were inevitably drawn to it. "Yes . . . that is correct, but . . . perhaps not so tightly."

She spread her knees slowly, her eyes unwittingly daring him.

For one moment, he allowed her to continue; his dreams had carried him away. Between those legs.

Angry with himself, he muttered, "That will do. That will do."

"Aye, aye—"

"Yes, Captain."

"Yes, Captain."

Before going on, James tried to clear his head. He had planned for this meeting to go differently. Annie was to behave, and he was to retain control. They would review what she'd learned, and then he would talk to her of his plans. Then, if she wept or looked even remotely sad, he would lend her his handkerchief and comfort her calmly with words—

She had slouched in her chair again, and her eyes were cast down.

What the devil was wrong with the girl?

"Then, let's see. What else do we have?" he asked aloud, grasping for a thread of thought.

"Ye taught me how to sit and to walk and to kiss," Annie answered.

"You taught me."

"No, Capting, it's you what taught me."

"You were the one who taught me. And the word is 'captain,' not 'capting'!"

"Aye, aye, sir."

Blood pounded in James's head. "For God's sake, Annie, why are you doing this?"

"I don't knows, Captain—"

"I don't *know*—"

"Mebbe it's the wind—"

"Maybe, it's the wind—"

"—or else that me breasts are *that* big—"

"Or that my breasts are so *big—"*

James winced as her chin flew up. A grin broke over her lips and she started to laugh, clutching at her sides.

"Why, you little . . ." James's heart skipped a beat. She had set him up. Like the brat she was, she'd— Something inside him snapped. A vicious smile burst from his mouth. "You little villain! I'm going to get you for that!"

Her eyes lit with fright. No, those were Jem's eyes. Jem's green eyes taunting him.

James lunged across the desk, and she shrieked with delight. Her pleasure jolted him with energy as she dodged his lunge. He gripped the desk with both hands and spotted her the way a tiger eyes its prey as she tried to avoid him darting left and right.

Her emerald gaze was lit with a dare, sparkling with the green of the sea. Like a mermaid's gaze, taunting him from the deep.

James's blood beat faster.

She feinted to the left and he pounced—

"Got you!" He pulled her into his arms.

She swung, and they both reeled, falling on his chair, Annie on his lap.

James had meant to shake her . . . to shake her

until her teeth fell out. But the feel of her buttocks on his lap disturbed his plan.

Her shrieks of fear had changed to hiccups of laughter. Well, if she wanted to laugh, he would make her pay.

He tickled her. His fingers climbed along her ribs, under her arms, along her thighs and back to her sides. He pressed his chin into her back.

And Annie squirmed. She wriggled and jerked, bouncing in and out of his lap, her bursts of laughter growing silent as she sobbed for breath.

"You're going to pay for what you did, you little wretch," James whispered in her ear.

His whisper sent laughter blazing along Annie's neck. Goosebumps sprang along her flesh, from her ears to her breasts to her toes. She struggled against his body. His breath warmed her spine and made her shiver with thrills. The strength in his thighs tickled her buttocks.

Then a ridge began to develop between her legs, and it tickled there, too.

"Annie . . . don't move." His hands came to a rigid halt. He grasped her arms and pulled her down against the quivering ridge.

But it kept growing and pushing against her. Harder and harder, it brushed her nub, and a pounding itch took hold of her.

Annie wriggled her bottom to scratch it.

"*Annie*— Don't move." James's voice filled with strain.

"But—I have to—James." The tickle was filling, and throbbing. Her attempt to stifle it had only made it worse as the ridge felt as if it would burst through her breeches.

It was a delicious itch. It promised to carry her to her dreams, if only she could reach it.

"Annie—"

She rocked against him, and he groaned and wrapped his hands about her shoulders. She felt his hot breath against her neck.

She arched her back and his hands slipped to her breasts. They both gasped.

"Annie . . ." The captain pleaded. His hands moved down to her thighs.

She would have stopped, then. But his hands moved again to come up beneath her shirt. They found her bare breasts and covered them with a wonderful roughness. Annie felt a jolt pass from his thumbs, through her nipples, and back again. She squirmed again to scratch the tickle.

She rocked while his fingers played over her nipples, flicking them to hardness. A surge whirled between her legs like the sea. It formed a pool around her nub and and heated and teased it.

Annie rubbed deeper and deeper against him, circling, and now he was helping her . . . back and forth . . . back and forth—he rubbed her across his lap.

She felt a sudden rush inside her nub as if a breaker had crashed against the shore, but still it crested and crested, sending wave after wave over ripples of light. She heard herself shout, and then her shout withered. The wave had

raged and raged as long as she had moved . . .
but then . . . it had left her. She tried to bring it
back, but no matter how much she wriggled, it
was gone.

Then she heard James cry out behind her. She
felt a thump beneath her as he bucked just one
more time; then he collapsed with her against
the back of the chair. His hands still rested over
her breasts, and his thumbs made circles over
their tips.

"Annie"—his voice was ragged—"oh, my
God."

"What was that?" She felt a softer thump as if
the sea might waken again, but his ridge had
begun to fade.

"Dear God, what was it?" James's throaty
chuckle tickled her ear. He kissed her neck, so
softly. Then his palms passed over her nipples,
teasing them, and he shivered with her as if they
were one. His voice grew deadly serious. "It
must have been an earthquake or a tidal wave at
the very least."

An earthquake? But she had sailed on a tidal
wave before and it had never felt this good.

She wanted to question him, but his fingers
moved gently against her breasts, as if he
wanted to fill his hands with her. She began to
shake again.

"Dear God," James groaned. "What have I
done?"

His misery slapped her. She had felt so . . .
alive.

"Captain!" A loud hammering struck at the door.

James jumped to his feet in one motion, knocking his chair down and dropping her onto the floor.

As Annie hit it, the door flew open.

"Captain, sir?"

"What is it, Mr. Shirley?" James ran a hand through his hair and straightened his cravat. As Annie struggled to her shaky legs, their eyes met. His spoke a command.

Mr. Shirley surveyed them and the disordered room. His gaze darted to the floor where Annie had been, to James's face, to the capsized chair.

"Is everything all right, sir? The lads thought they heard a scream."

"No harm done." James looked down at a spot of dampness on his breeches, a spot that had caught Mr. Shirley's eye. "The lad—the lad tripped and spilled some water on me. It . . . startled me. That's all."

Annie held her tongue. She had never known the captain to lie, but she could sense his nervousness, even as she was still trembling.

"Sorry for that, Captain," she said, feigning regret.

Mr. Shirley accepted their story, even though there was no tankard of water about. Something more important seemed to have claimed his attention.

"Sorry to tell you, Cap'n—" He ventured a glance Annie's way. "It's Mr. Bonny, sir."

193

"Mr. Bonny?" Fear and shame washed through Annie. For the past few minutes, she had forgotten all about him.

The first mate's face told the tale. "Yeah, lad, he's gone."

Chapter Ten

Mr. Bonny was buried at sea just minutes before England rose into sight. Annie stood on the deck, surrounded by her mates, their hats removed and their chins lowered. In the brief time that they had known him, the sailors had all come to respect the good doctor, and whatever they had held against Jem, they gave no sign of it now.

Mr. Bonny had been shrouded in canvas. Annie had helped to prepare him for this last ocean voyage. James read from a book, the one he used on Sundays to read to the crew—words not unlike the ones Captain Sharkee might have said—but this time his words had a special meaning for her.

He read about the roaring of the sea and the

compassing of the waters, the spreading of the heavens and the storming of winds, about the depths of misery and the jaws of death.

His voice, which had been the first thing she'd ever noticed about him, wrung at her heart as she faced the fact that she would soon hear it no more. But she mustn't think about that now, when it was all she could do to keep from crying.

". . . Lord God, at whose command the winds blow and lift up the waves of the sea, and who stillest the rage thereof . . ."

Annie squeezed her eyes shut and offered up her own prayer. *Dear God, please don't take the sea away from me.*

"Man that is born of a woman hath a short time to live and is full of misery. . . ."

Woman and misery . . . Man that is born of a woman and misery . . . The words seemed synonymous.

James paused in his reading to take a step near her. His presence warmed her even as the sun was lost behind a sea of clouds. He laid a hand upon her shoulder. If they had been alone, perhaps he would have taken her in his arms and let her cry, but with his men watching, this was all the comfort she would be allowed. Mr. Shirley had let drop that James was going ashore to meet his fiancée. He soon would be married, and she would be lodged with a stranger to live forever away from everything she had ever held dear.

A cry of "Land ho!" sent the sailors scurrying to their posts. No sooner had Mr. Bonny's body been consigned to the deep than James had to turn his attention to the important task of bringing his ship safely into port. He wished he could have offered comfort to Annie, but the tides waited for no man or woman.

In Liverpool, a message from his agent urgently requested his presence in London. James hurried his men through the unloading of their cargo, then directed them toward Portsmouth. From there, he hired a carriage to take him up to London, and for the first time since Land's End had been sighted just a few days ago, he had a moment alone to reflect.

He had left orders with Mr. Shirley that no women were to be allowed aboard ship. He was grateful to have made this his habit, so the men would be sure to obey. The sailors could take turns going into port for whatever vices they cared to indulge, but he would not have Annie exposed to them. If her father, a reprobate pirate, had managed to shield her from such sights thus far, James would be damned if she would witness them on his watch.

Knowing she was safe, however, was a far cry from feeling comfortable about her.

The announcement of Mr. Bonny's death, coming so soon after his sensual encounter with Annie, had plunged James into a jumble of feelings, not the least of which was guilt. He did not know how he could have let things get so out of hand, particularly when his intentions had been so good.

He was going to be married, for Christ's sake! If all went well, within the next few days. And he was going to have to ask his fiancée to take under her wing a girl with whom he had nearly had sex on a straight-backed chair in his cabin. A girl whom every man aboard took to be a boy. Only their clothes had stood in the way. And, *evidently*, their passion had been too intense to be bothered by a little thing like clothing.

He had been bound by his word to Mr. Bonny, a gentleman if there ever was one—regardless of the accepted definition. James had been bound by his word to take care of Mr. Bonny's adopted daughter, an innocent virgin in his care. Yet, knowing that, he had still not been able to keep her off his lap or to keep his hands from caressing her breasts.

The fact that he had let things get so out of hand had both puzzled and infuriated him. He supposed he would have to attribute the whole sequence of events to the danger of having a woman on board. He had seen the danger, and he had sworn not to give in to it. But . . . he had.

What had surprised him more, though, was how quickly Annie had responded to the dictates of her body. He had tried to stop her before she discovered the extent of his arousal. But, little savage that she was, she'd given in to ravishment without one iota of restraint. She'd proven to be as amorous as she was brave—and James had helped to make her so.

Even now, as he struggled with his conscience, he couldn't help feeling pleasure at the thought.

Throughout the few busy days in Liverpool and the sail to Portsmouth, he had tried to come to terms with his responsibility. He couldn't deny his attraction to Annie. He could only be relieved that they had arrived in England before something irreversible had occurred. The sooner he handed Annie off to Lady Olivia or a governess, the safer she would be from him. And the safer he would be from himself.

Still . . . he couldn't be happy about the solution. It genuinely pained him to think of leaving her with a complete stranger. She had lost the only person who had been a parent to her, not to mention her friends and her home. She had borne her grief with an incredible maturity for one so young, with a grace so patent that the crew had forgotten the lingering resentment they had harbored for her. She had spared them all her tears and had taken her place as Mr. Bonny's kin in the preparation of his shroud. No person could have shown more fortitude.

James had been amazed by her grace, especially after he had peered into her eyes and seen the depths of misery inside them. It was then that he had realized just how much Annie had lost. And yet, still she had not reproached him.

Never once had she railed at him for taking away her ship and her crew. Not once had she treated him to tears for Sharkee's loss. She had borne her defeat with the honor of an admiral.

He did not know any woman who could have suffered so much, yet carry no grudge.

And, still, she reported for duty each day.

If he had to admit it, he would wish he had a shipload of sailors exactly like her—minus, of course, her troublesome sex.

He would never forget her generous spirit, her loyalty, her courage, or her grace.

And never, no matter how many seas were put between them, would he ever forget the sight of so much misery in Annie's eyes.

James arrived in London, expecting to be informed of the arrangements that had been made for his wedding. By this time Pearson should have negotiated the rest of his contract with Lord Figg and the papers should be ready for James to sign. But, when he was ushered up into Pearson's busy office near the Strand, he saw no papers waiting for him amidst the stacks of counting books.

Pearson greeted him with all the friendliness of a man who had been his father's agent when James had been no more than the child of a merchant seaman like himself. Josiah Pearson was a squarely built man, who always dressed in a sober, brown suit and a modest, unpowdered wig, befitting a man of his class. He never made any pretension of being anything else; he despised the wasteful habits of the aristocracy and had no wish to emulate them, even though James suspected that his personal income amounted to a level that many an aristocrat would envy.

Never one to waste time any more than money, he adjusted the pair of tight spectacles over his nose and quickly apprised James of the reason for his urgent note. "Lady Figg, Lord Figg's countess, has died quite suddenly this fortnight past, so the marriage cannot take place immediately as planned. Even had she not, no agreement has ever been reached. The earl's demands have been as outrageous as you might expect from a man who's lost his family's fortune. He hasn't got a penn'orth of sense as far as I can see."

James heard the news with relief and frustration—a surprising mixture, which he could only blame on his confusion over Annie. Relief—that he would not have to face a *wife* immediately with his sins so fresh on his mind—and the more conventional feeling that circumstances had conspired to thwart him of a goal.

This last, which prompted his impatience, was much more comfortable than the first, so he seized it. He was accustomed to getting what he wanted, and he wouldn't settle for less. If the earl wanted the deal to be sweetened, James could soften his position, particularly since he would be asking the Lady Olivia to take on a girl whom he had nearly taken to bed.

"How much is he asking for? I wouldn't wish to put him off for the sake of a few guineas a year."

"It would amount to a great deal more than that, I'm certain." Pearson peered wryly at James over his pince-nez. "His lordship seems to think that I can persuade you to back his wagering habit for the rest of his life. Now that you're here, though, he'll see that you are as firmly resolved against it as I've represented you to be. Never fear. Your contract will be ready to sign before you take to sea again or I'll eat my hat. And you'll be married to her ladyship one of these dockings or another, if that is still what you want?"

The question in his tone caused a flutter of doubt in James's stomach—about taking another woman to wife when so lately all he had thought about was Annie's beautiful body and the less tangible qualities he had just discovered. But he couldn't let a temporary obsession with a girl who was quite unsuitable upset his lifelong plans.

Realizing that Pearson was staring at him, he started guiltily. "Of course, I still wish it!"

Pearson continued to eye him with a hint of concern over the rim of his spectacles. He'd clearly been surprised by James's defensive tone. "No need to fret about it, lad. I'm sure that between us we can bring his lordship around."

Pearson gave him the address of Lord Figg's lodging in London with the message that his lordship would like to be waited upon as soon as James came up to town. Then he filled him in on the terms of the latest discussions.

Later, when they turned to James's other business, the results of his recent voyage and the status of his many ships, James was at pains to keep his mind from wandering. He couldn't seem to care whether his crews had fulfilled their obligations or if he might have made more money someway else. For the first time, his thoughts were less taken with his fortune than with the safety of the *Flying Swan* where Annie would be anxiously awaiting the news of her fate.

A long day later saw him perched uneasily on a frail, reedy chair in an ornate drawing room, balancing a cup of tea on his knee.

He had followed Pearson's directions to Lord Figg's lodgings. A note had preceded him, so he had found Lord Figg and his daughter at home. The house, with its door heavily draped in black crepe, had been far more modest than he had expected for the residence of a peer, but Pearson had explained that Lord Figg had been obliged to rent out his London townhouse and his country estates under pressure from his creditors.

The businessman in James had taken this for a sign that Lord Figg would soon be made to sign the marriage agreement on Pearson's terms.

He had been shown to a tiny drawing room by an inexperienced footman, who had badly bungled his announcement. James would have raked his men over the coals for such incompetence, but again, he'd interpreted this as a sign of weakness in Lord Figg. Clearly this family stood in need of a stronger man to manage its affairs.

But, as James had been confronted with the combined receptions of Lord Figg and Lady Olivia, his earlier confidence had ebbed. Lord Figg was an arrogant man in his early sixties of meager height and weight, with watery eyes and a face permanently splotched by hard drink. When James had bowed, his lordship had inclined his head in a manner clearly designed to let James know he had no intention of ever treating him as an equal. At every opportunity he had tried to put this upstart seaman in his place.

Lady Olivia, fair, pale, and plump, had been blessed with greater dignity; but, when James had bowed over her hand, she had snatched it back with a visible shudder of distaste. Her powdered wig concealed her hair, but her eyes were a pale, limpid blue and her skin an alabaster white. He had been surprised to find a still-unmarried aristocrat even remotely so pretty, although her wan, high-strung air would not have attracted many beaux.

Then with dismay, James had surveyed the drawing room, which had been crowded with a surfeit of furniture likely brought from their larger estate. Sevres and Meissen porcelain figurines dotted every surface, while thin-legged tables and chairs endangered his every step. Lord Figg had taken a chair by the fireplace. Lady Olivia had taken the other, relegating James to an inferior position by the window with its accompanying draft.

He was almost grateful for the chill air that

seeped past his legs, for a combination of factors was making it hard for him to breathe. His starched clothes—a white lace cravat tightly knotted about his neck and a newly curled wig made him sweat. The delicate figurines at his elbow—he did not dare move for fear of knocking them all over. Lord Figg's intolerant distain constantly pricked at James's temper. And a chilliness on the part of his fiancée, which James had tried his best to thaw, refused to give way. He had been used to feeling at his ease, but there was no earthly way that a man of his size and character could feel at home in a setting like this.

He shifted cautiously in his chair, rattling the porcelain at his elbow. The chair he was seated in had been carved out of reeds, its delicate feet showing traces of chipped ormolu. He prayed it wouldn't collapse under his weight and leave him lying in a heap at Lord Figg's feet.

The teacup was much too small for his calloused hands, and for the thirteenth time, he wished he'd refused a drink.

Lady Olivia had hardly addressed him a word as he had struggled to converse. She quailed as if his large frame were a personal affront. James was doing his best to seem gentle and kind. He had no wish to intimidate her, nor could he help it that his skin had been toughened and bronzed by the sun. Unfortunately, it seemed he would have no opportunity to show Olivia the kind of just man he was as long as her father was around.

"These accursed laws!" Lord Figg continued the rant he had started almost the moment James had arrived. "They are all designed to ruin the aristocracy. It's rebellion, I tell you! Rebellion and democracy!"

James had acquiesced once for politeness's sake and had tried to restrain his impatience, but he would be damned if he'd stay quiet any longer just to please Lord Figg. The man's remarks had all been aimed at convincing James that it was not only his duty but his privilege to be bailing a man of his lineage out of debt.

The Lady Olivia was clearly cowed by her father. She threw an occasional wary glance James's way, but she seemed not in the least curious to know anything about him.

Which was perfect, he told himself. Exactly what he needed. Someone for whom he would find it hard to develop strong feelings, who was highly unlikely to miss him when he was gone.

James could sympathize with her, but the facts were that Lady Olivia must marry for money. Her father would insist that she did. Better it be to a man like him, who would seldom be at home, and when he was, would do his best to be kind, than to another man who might change her life in more unpleasant ways.

"A gentleman can scarcely breathe these days without losing the comfort that is rightfully his!" Lord Figg snarled.

James finally lost his patience. "In that case, sir, you should be glad that our agreement will restore at least a measure of comfort to you." Although he was sorry for Lady Olivia's wince, he could not regret his wry tone.

Still, he tried once again to draw her out. "Did your father say you would be willing for the marriage to take place in one year?"

Lord Figg grumbled, "My fool of a daughter insists on a full year of mourning for her mother. This unnecessary delay does not suit my convenience, I assure you."

"Under the circumstances, a year's engagement does not seem at all uncustomary."

Lord Figg scoffed. "There is nothing at all customary about this affair, sir, I assure you. Nothing at all!"

"Then, my lord, we must endeavor to give it the appearance of normality. For your daughter's sake."

"I have told Olivia that she has nothing to say on the matter. She knows her place, sir, even if you do not!"

James felt his gall start to rise, but he held it in check. "In this situation, Lord Figg, I know it all too well." He turned to his fiancée, who blanched again under his gaze. "And I assure the Lady Olivia that her sentiments on any matter regarding her well-being shall always be of importance to me."

To his surprise, this act of kindness only appeared to make her more unhappy. Another shudder ran through her, as though he had proposed to rape her on the spot. But, though after a moment, she thanked him politely enough, he still felt like a man whose offer of a bone to a starving dog had been rebuffed.

"Forget my daughter, sir." Lord Figg demanded his attention. "Your business is with me, sir. Have you considered my changes to our agreement?"

James said firmly, "I am not prepared to discuss the details in front of your daughter, my lord."

Lord Figg made a sound like a harrumph, but James was relieved to see that the commanding timbre of his voice had had a slight effect. Apparently, the great man could be put in *his* place, on occasion.

Lord Figg had asked for an annual allowance, a sum that would break James if his ventures failed to prosper. He had assumed that his lordship would ask for a reasonable amount to sustain his daughter, not that he would demand to be backed at the gaming table for the rest of his life.

But James was a cool businessman, and so was Pearson. Neither would give in to senseless pressure from a desperate man. Lord Figg's debts were so pressing that he would soon come around or find the bailiffs ensconced in his house.

Turning to the occupant of the other chair, James tried again to make headway. "I shall be most eager to get better acquainted with you, my lady, but I have made plans for this year's voyages, and they must be kept."

James ignored his lordship's grumblings about *trade* and *damned merchants* and went on. "You do understand, do you not, that I shall always be gone for the better part of the year?"

Her shoulders seemed to lift a little at this assurance. "Yes, I do."

"But I shall leave everything in place to assure your daily comfort." *Even if your father does not*.

Lady Olivia's eyes filled with tears, the first sign of warmth she had shown him. "That is very kind of you, Sir James."

James smiled down at her, though he wished she would stop darting looks at him as if he might devour her like a lion in the Tower. He had thought himself reasonably attractive to women, but he could not appear to the best advantage when everything around him seemed as if he might break it with his teeth. "Not at all. I am sure we shall make each other very happy."

The words were no more than a platitude, but even so, she turned such a sickly pale that he was afraid she might faint. She swallowed nervously, as her gaze fell to a handkerchief knotted in her lap. As if contemplation of the marriage act with him made her want to retch.

It occurred to James that she might have an attachment to another man, one without the fortune to satisfy her father. He could not ask her in front of Lord Figg, but thought he might find another means of discovering the reason for her extreme revulsion.

He turned to his lordship, before Lord Figg could gain the upper hand again, and said, "Perhaps you would not object if Lady Olivia and I were to enter into a correspondence over the year. Then, when the time is up, we will each know more of the other's tastes."

James suspected that these porcelain figures—which were fine in their way, no doubt—unfortunately represented his fiancée's taste. He doubted that Lord Figg, with his fidgeting impatience, brown tobacco stains on his fingers, and a venous face, had collected these falderals. His lordship had the air of a man who was seldom at home.

And, James realized, he ought not to have said, "when the time is up" as if he meant when his reprieve was up. It had sounded as if he were facing a sentence. Which he was, in a way. He would not be eager for the year to pass.

Nor would Olivia, it seemed. For the first time that day, she ventured a more elaborate response. "I seldom write letters, although I will make an exception in this case if the need arises. I shall want to know how to reach you if anything should occur that might nullify your agreement with my father."

James wanted to ask what might occur to alter their agreement, but Lord Figg interrupted her with a snarl. "That will be enough of your nonsense, girl. You would not want Sir James to take you in disgust."

At James's frown, he snorted, "My daughter's got expectations, she says. An old aunt of her mother's—a harridan, seventy-three if she's a day, but still going strong." He turned to Olivia. "Better give up on that possibility, girl. I told you long ago there'll be no pickings off that dry old bone."

So Lady Olivia was still hoping for some way out of her engagement. James felt mortified.

For a moment, he wondered if he ought to break off negotiations with Lord Figg. He felt he had to know the reason for Lady Olivia's reluctance, for he would not be a party to ruining a woman's life.

"If it is a question of your comfort, my lady, I can assure you, I shall provide amply for you."

Lady Olivia straightened in her chair. Her father's words seemed to have touched on an old argument, but she seemed to recognize that James deserved an explanation. "It is not comfort that concerns me, sir, although I should be grateful for the independence of my own establishment and I am grateful for your assurances. It is merely"—she hesitated—"that I had determined not to marry at all."

Not marry? James was surprised to find any woman so inclined, but he was relieved that she appeared to have no other suitor. It seemed the state of marriage itself was repugnant to her. He could read it in her face.

Well, he shrugged to himself, it was as he had thought. Better he than another. And much the better for his purposes if she had no intention of forming an attachment to him.

After a few more unsuccessful attempts on his

part to inspire a civil conversation, Lord Figg began to rant again, so James stood to take his leave.

As he did, his chair tipped behind him. He was used to heavier furniture, and most of it bolted down. In his hurry, he had forgotten how fragile his chair was.

He caught it, but not before Olivia sprang to her feet with a cry of dismay. A Meissen shepherdess was falling on the table next to James; a Sevres courtier trembled near the edge. James lunged for them both and managed to trap them without upsetting any of the others. Avoiding his fiancée's horrified gaze, with a flooding of red to his cheeks, he righted them both with clumsy hands.

He saved his apologies for a future date when he would undoubtedly need them and backed gingerly from the room.

James was eager to make his goodbyes and to escape his lordship's dainty house. So eager, in fact, that he almost forgot to ask Lady Olivia about Annie.

He remembered as he bowed over his fiancée's reluctant hand, a hand so cold and white that it made him shiver. The memory of Annie's warm clasp rushed back to him then, her small brown hands, nearly as rough and as strong as his own. And other comparisons came to him: Annie's strong, lithe body to Olivia's plump, stiff one; Annie's beaming smile to Olivia's fearful wince; her passionate response to his fondling to this woman's impenetrable dread.

212

James fought the trembling in his loins as he looked up into the white face bidding him good-bye with such revulsion, and he remembered his obligation to Sharkee's daughter. With a sinking heart, he swallowed and forced himself to say, "I forgot to mention a matter that I hoped you might assist me with, my lady. I need to find a governess."

Lord Figg's cheeks took on a purplish hue. "What is this? Your man made no mention of brats."

James frowned to let him know that he did not appreciate the unwarranted interruption. "Pearson knows nothing about her. She is neither my heir nor my child. She is a young—a young . . . wo-man. Recently orphaned."

"I fail to see her connection to you."

"She is—of Jamaican family. The daughter of a—daughter of a colleague." *You might say*.

"Jamaican!" Lord Figg snorted, his cheeks both veined and mottled. "The West Indians are all commoners, sir. Do not think you can foist this common girl on me."

A hot, bursting rage surged its way through James's veins. He raised himself to his full, imposing height until he towered above Lord Figg. His lordship's color receded and he looked up at James with a startled air.

In a cold, controlled voice, James bit out his words as he would to his lowliest crewman, "I can assure you, *sir*, that there is absolutely nothing about Annie that is at all in the common way."

213

"Annie?" Lord Figg's eyebrows rose. He tried to recover even as he took a step out of James's reach. "That is not a name for a lady."

James silently cursed himself for letting his temper get the better of him. He should not have introduced her so clumsily if he wanted to secure these people's graces in her behalf.

"Her name is Anne, my lord. Miss Anne—" James searched his mind desperately. He had forgotten she would need a name. He couldn't very well call her Sharkee. Not when that surname would ruin her chances before she had ever begun, and he had promised Mr. Bonny he would never divulge—

A sudden, welcome thought rushed in to fill the troublesome void.

"Her name is Anne Bonny," he said to Lord Figg, repeating the name because he liked the sound. "Miss Anne Bonny. And I have no intention, Lord Figg, of foisting her on you at all."

"Hummph!" His lordship's nostrils flared. "Still sounds like a common name to me."

"You are quite wrong." Though James lied, he had never been more sure of anything. "Mr. Bonny was a noble man in the very truest sense."

"There is only one sense." His lordship's shrewd eyes narrowed. "But I take you to mean that the girl is an heiress. I must be assured that my daughter will not be made to skimp as a result of her."

Now he'd done it. James could only wonder why he'd dug such a deep trap for himself, even

214

as he realized Lord Figg's concern was for his own pocket and not for his daughter's. Then, as before, a revelation came to him. An inspiration that might have come directly from heaven—though more probably it came from hell.

"She is an heiress," he said, and for once he spoke the truth. "Her father"—*bless his murderous, black heart*—"left her considerably endowed. He left her with a sailing ship, Lord Figg, the prettiest, neatest little brig that ever hoisted sail." Or she would be, by the time he tidied her up. "She's called the *Merrye Laurie*, my lord."

"Sailor's language, sir! Such terms mean nothing to a real gentleman." He made a dismissive gesture with a show of offense, although James could see that he was impressed.

More and more *gentlemen* were investing in ships and cargoes, and making their fortunes in trade. His debt-ridden lordship could not be so ignorant as not to know what an entire ship could be worth.

As he did himself, James thought with a sigh, and again he wondered that he had given away his prize on the spur of the moment like that. But then, the *Merrye Laurie had* belonged to Annie's father. It was only fair that the brig be hers. And fortunately he had never informed Pearson of his intention to give her to Lady Olivia on the signing of their marriage contract.

Lady Olivia had been listening to this exchange without the slightest show of interest.

215

The issue of a governess for Annie had still not been resolved.

Before James could pose the question again, Lord Figg said, "You should send the girl to school. That will take her off your hands."

"She is too old for school I'm afraid. What she needs"—James turned hopefully to Olivia—"is more in the nature of . . . town polish. About . . . how to go on in London . . . how to get on in society . . . and so forth." He finished lamely, certain he had made a mistake in bringing Annie's name up at all.

"She doesn't need a governess, then, just a chaperone. Hire the girl a companion," Lord Figg said, dismissing the subject out of hand.

"That has been my intention all along, sir, if only Lady Olivia might be persuaded to recommend one. Someone . . ." James did not know how to go on. How could he tell them what he needed without giving Annie's history away?

"Hah!" Something had occurred to Lord Figg that seemed to afford him considerable amusement. "Give him that harpy's name, Olivia. The one you like so much, eh?"

James started to say that he wanted no harpy to get her claws into Annie, but a hurtful cry came suddenly from the woman at his left.

He turned his head in time to see Lady Olivia flush before a ghostly pallor invaded her cheeks. With tears in her eyes, she drew herself up, and her lips parted to utter one contemptuous word. *"Papa."* She confronted him with a withering look. "I have tolerated many things from you,

216

sir, but I shall not stand by for one moment to hear Miss Thurston so maligned."

James was impressed by the way she came to the other woman's defense. Someone, at least, could engage her devotion. As always, the evidence of loyalty inspired his good will. It made him feel better about his choice of wife.

"I am sure," he said, "that if Lady Olivia considers Miss Thurston to be a worthy person, I shall find her ideal for the task."

But his thoughtful words merely provoked more of her scorn.

"Sir James"—she spoke with the same contempt she had shown her father, as if they both crawled the earth at the level of a worm—"Miss Thurston has no need for employment. She is comfortably situated at present, and I do not think she would find a position such as you describe a challenge to her quite superior talents."

Oh, it would be a challenge all right. But James kept this thought to himself. He had had enough of these two for one day. In truth, for a lifetime.

He made his apologies and left as quickly as he could, as an ugly question reared its head. How would he stand their greater intimacy when he could hardly wait to get away from them now?

But that was not the point, he reminded himself. He didn't have to enjoy his wife or her family. He should see to his marriage as he saw to his ships and to his other business. And Lady Olivia had not been as intolerable as her father.

James believed he could arrive at an understanding with her once they were free of Lord Figg's company.

So—one earl's daughter wanted.

One job accomplished.

Pearson would have to find someone to teach Annie, it appeared. The more James thought about it, the angrier he became that he had even mentioned Annie to them. Lord Figg would never understand the kind of life she had led at no fault of her own. And after one look at Annie's dagger, Lady Olivia would be so frightened she would hide beneath the bed.

As he strode down the street, he wished he had not thought of a bed, for it conjured up all sorts of images he must not think about. Lady Olivia, not Annie, would be the woman to occupy his bed. She would undoubtedly come wrapped in lace and doused with expensive perfume, but her coldness—

He had to remind himself that this was what he had wanted when he had instructed Pearson to find him a wife, someone who would not care when he left her alone. He could always find women to satisfy his baser needs if Olivia couldn't, the way his father had always found.

He hailed a passing hackney, trying hard not to think about Annie's extraordinary passion. She was his ward now by reputation if not in truth. That made her his legal responsibility, even though the whole story had been a sham. He should begin to think of her as his ward, the girl he must protect. Inviolate.

And, as his ward and an heiress, she would need many things. Dresses. Jewels. At least, in some modest number.

James found that the prospect of endowing Annie, of clothing her the way an heiress should be clothed, gave a needed boost to his spirits. He had begun to feel despondent as soon as he had met his future father-in-law. Buying Annie something would be a welcome change of subject. Suddenly he had an uncontrollable urge to see Annie in silk and satin with the tar cut out of her hair.

And it was not at all remarkable, he told himself, that he should suddenly want to see Annie gowned. He had always taken his responsibilities seriously, and seen to them without delay.

If Annie was to be made presentable, then he should take care of the matter right now.

Chapter Eleven

It was with that same sense of duty, after a two-day shopping spree, that James rejected the last applicant Pearson had found for the post of governess. She was much too strict, he decided, as he showed a woman with a ramrod spine out of the inn. He had reserved a private parlor so that he might talk to each applicant personally, but after a day of interviews he had come up with no one. This last pedagogue would have come to blows with Annie before her first day was up, and would quite likely have been stabbed.

And if Annie did stab her, he mused as he shuddered over the interview, he might not blame her properly as he ought.

In desperation he went over the list of applicants again. The first woman had been far too easily shocked. She had raised a hand to her lips and gasped at the thought that Annie had arrived on his ship with no maid. What would she do if she knew the truth, that Annie had been acting as his personal servant for the past six weeks, had shared his bathwater, and had slept all her life with a shipful of men?

The next had been far too flirtatious. She had cooed and hung on his every word. James had crossed her name off the list immediately. He didn't want Annie to learn to flirt like a dancer at the opera. *For God's sake*, that was the last thing a girl with her talent for passion needed.

Then, there had been the motherly sort. James had been fooled at first, until she had divulged her regime.

"Tighter stays, Sir James. Tighter stays and a purging diet of vinegar are the best way to cultivate beauty in a young lady. They lend an attractive pallor that will captivate the most hardhearted male."

Annie did not need torturous tricks to catch a man, especially tricks that would make her sickly. Her charm was in being so radiant that in comparison she made everyone else look pale.

James tossed the remaining names aside. There had been something wrong with each and every one of them. What he needed was a woman who knew all the ways of her sex without being a slave to its restrictions. A woman who was affectionate and understanding, who nevertheless could hold her own. A person who had seen enough of life not to be shocked by

Annie's salty tongue or the truth of her past, but who would know how to correct it. What he needed was Therese Dubois.

Her husband, Pierre, had been James's friend and competitor on the high seas. Such a friend that they had exchanged an oath to leave each other's ships alone, which had been in direct defiance of their letters of marque. But who would not have been friend to a man like Pierre Dubois?

Even now, James missed the man who had taught him how to enjoy society, but Pierre had died in a sea fight against another Englishman. Such were the rules of war. But his loss had made James feel the loneliness of a captain's life.

He sighed, wishing that Therese were here to advise him. The past few days had taught him that Annie did not belong in London. No one here could understand her. And she did not belong in a country with so little sun.

Therese would take Annie for him if they were only in Jamaica. Take her and teach her what she needed to survive on shore. Turn her into a lady who could pass as his ward and ready her for marriage.

As Annie's guardian, *he* would have to be the man to approve her husband. She would need his permission to marry. The thought made him strangely sick.

If he had realized this fact sooner, he doubted he would have made her his ward. But he had committed himself legally now. He had declared her his ward before a peer of the realm, and his agent was even now drawing up papers to convey the *Merrye Laurie* to Annie, naming James as her trustee.

There would be no going back. Pearson, with a flourish of efficiency, had completed his negotiations with Lord Figg's solicitor. James's wedding had been scheduled for a year from now, the announcement put in the mail. And Lady Olivia, too, considered Annie to be his ward.

Well, there was nothing for it but to take Annie back to Jamaica, to Therese, who loved the warmth of the island and preferred the freedom of Jamaica to her native Paris. Living in a villa on the beach, she had the benefits of Kingston society without the rigidity of a court. Viceroys came and went. Jamaica changed from French to Spanish to English, but Therese remained queen of her own little kingdom.

The only question was how to get Annie back unharmed. As the familiar sense of lust washed through James, he remembered, as he had every waking moment since their last encounter, how she had cried out in shattered innocence. He had not seduced her. He had not taken her. But he had not left her untouched.

Annie didn't understand what had happened. It might be years before she truly understood, and by that time she would be safely married to someone else. To a respectable fellow, perhaps to another man raised from the merchant class like himself, not too refined but neither too rough, who would know how to manage her inheritance. A man who could be a companion to her.

One of James's ships would be sailing for Jamaica in another two days, a ship with a different crew. It wouldn't seem strange if he were to decide to sail with her, taking his new red-haired ward along. He could join up with the *Flying Swan* when she docked in Jamaica a few days later.

The decision made, James felt a load lifted off him, a leaden weight that had burdened his steps since he'd come ashore. It was because he had found the right solution, he told himself.

Now that Annie was his ward, he would be certain to resist the temptation to take her to his bed. His sense of honor would be reinforced, and his promise to Mr. Bonny would keep her safe. He could conclude his normal business and get back to sea where he belonged.

That would be why he felt so eager to join his ship and make the arrangements, although he could hardly wait to see Annie's face when he told her the *Merrye Laurie* was hers.

It was late, dark, and cold by the time the captain fetched Annie off the ship in Portsmouth. As he led her onto the dock, she shivered with dread. James had only said that he had a surprise for her, but considering the plans he had described before, she wouldn't be too eager to hear it.

For the first time in her life, she felt hard pavement thrusting up to meet her feet. It was impossible not to stumble when her legs wouldn't move for the lack of swell. The world all around her seemed hard and stiff, except for the horses and carriages that whizzed past. They were faster than a mail packet under full sail. The clatter of the horses' hooves, the rumble of carriage wheels, were almost deafening compared to the long, cool silence of the sea.

They took a hack, as James called it, from the docks to a place he called an inn. Annie thought she might be sick from the ride, which was nothing like the smooth rocking of a large ship or even the roiling heave of a tiny barque in a storm. Her backside was bruised by the constant jolts of the carriage seat, and the sudden jerks when the horses shied made her feel as if she'd left her stomach back on the dock.

This land was certainly queer. And its people were, too.

There were so many of them, with their heads bowed or their eyes set straight ahead. It was a wonder they managed not to bump into each other. She could see why they stared straight in front. They must be worried that their legs would fail beneath them just when someone else was coming about. A helmsman would have to be very alert with this many vessels packed into one harbor.

Annie didn't know the words for half the things she saw, but James told her not to worry about it now. He told her to keep her head down and her questions to herself as he led her into a place with more decks than she'd ever seen. Fires were burning in shallow caves in the walls, and the air smelled of tobacco smoke, burning meat, and ale.

There was a grand cabin on the main deck— James called it a public room—where men stood about or sat and drank ale. She figured they were idlers, men who had burst their stomachs hoisting sail over many a year and were good for nothing now but deck duty.

Then, there were stairs. At first Annie balked about climbing a ladder with no rails that went up into the air instead of below deck where it should. The space above looked far more threatening than a hold. It seemed the whole structure had been built upside down, and she had to fear that the top part might come crashing down on their heads. But James showed her how to climb with no hands, and it was surprisingly easy. Or it would have been easy, if her legs had behaved.

James caught her as she fell and held on to her arm the rest of the way up. A stranger led them to the top of the hatch, then awaited them in the doorway to a cabin.

He eyed Annie strangely as she ventured cautiously inside. She had pulled her hat brim down in front to hide her hair, as James had ordered.

"Seems the lad 'as 'ad a bit too much to drink," the man said.

"Who? Jem?" Laughing, James shook his head. "He's just not used to being on shore. He'll get his land legs before too long."

He patted Annie on the shoulder before motioning to the man to leave them. Then he said, "My ward will be arriving before morning, but I will wait up and let her in myself."

"Very good, sir."

James closed the door. At a signal from him, Annie removed her hat and looked about the enormous cabin. It was so large she could move around as if she were outside on deck. It had square windows partially covered by cloth which looked down onto the street. There was a huge bunk plopped in the middle of the room, taking up the space of nine hammocks. She wondered how many people could sleep in it, and what they would do with the rest of the space.

Several captain's trunks like the one James used were piled against one of the walls.

"Where are the Jacks that go with these?" Annie asked, pointing to them.

James stared at her for a moment, before his smile reappeared. "Those are all yours, Annie. Those are the dresses I bought for you." His eyes held an odd, expectant look. "I promised to get you some decent clothes, didn't I?"

"All mine?" What could she possibly do with so many things?

"Yes." He seemed uneasy. "Don't you want to see them?"

"Of course." She hurried to the first trunk and pried open the lid. "Oh . . ." A gasp escaped her. She had never seen anything so fine. Annie stroked the gown on top, which had been made of cloth as blue as the Caribbean Sea. It shone as if the sun had touched it.

"Do you like them? They're mostly silk. I had to choose them myself since I couldn't tell anyone why you weren't doing your own shopping. They may not fit exactly right, but I told them how tall you were and—Well, your maid will surely be able to adjust them for you."

Annie turned to face him. "My maid?"

"Yes. Annie, when we leave this inn, you will leave as my ward. I'm taking you back to Jamaica. A friend of mine there can teach you how to go on better than anyone I've found here. But as my ward, you must have a maid to escort you."

This last part meant nothing to Annie. All she heard was the first, and her heart leapt for joy. "It's true? I'm going back aboard the *Flying Swan* with you?"

"No, we'll take another ship. I don't want the crew to know that Jem was a girl."

Without thinking, Annie launched herself toward him. He caught her in his arms. Instinct drove her to press her lips to his face in loud smacks. She sought his lips.

"Wait! Hold on!" James laughed. After one strong hug, he pushed her away and kept her at arm's length with a firm grip on her shoulders. "You mustn't think I've changed my mind. You're a woman now. I'm taking you to Jamaica to learn."

Gazing up at his smiling features and his sun-bronzed face, Annie felt an overwhelming desire to kiss him. She stared at his mouth and felt a hunger that made her ache.

James's smile faded and his expression dimmed. He pulled away from her, releasing his hold. He was silent for so long, Annie felt a strain between them. "Annie, I have to make you understand. You mustn't kiss me again. We mustn't touch each other any more."

"Why? Don't you like it?"

At the sound of her dismay, he gently smiled. "I'm afraid I like it far too much. But I am about to be a married man. And you are my ward."

"What's that?"

"It means that I take full responsibility for you. I shall manage your affairs until you marry."

"Marry who?"

"Whomever you choose."

"Well, I like kissing you, so I choose you."

She heard him catch his breath, but just as suddenly his eyes took on a pained look. "We cannot marry, Annie. I've already told you, I'm engaged to someone else. Besides"—he looked down—"it wouldn't be a good idea."

"Why?"

"You should marry someone who will keep you company. Someone who will stay at home."

"Where's home?"

"Annie—" He got that exasperated look. "I can't tell you where your home will be. But after you learn to be a woman, it will become clear."

She would have pressed him for more answers, but he cut her off. "And there is one thing more you should know. I have deeded the *Merrye Laurie* to you. The brig is yours."

Annie felt her knees buckle with the shock. "The *Merrye Laurie*? Mine?" She stared into his eyes. "Why, James? Why would you give your prize to me?"

"She's not really mine to give. I took her from you, so I'm giving her back."

"But—you won her fair and square!"

"I did, but this is something I need to do." His smile teased her. "Don't you want her?"

"Of course I want her." Annie felt dazed. "Do I get to be the captain?"

The pleasure faded from his eyes. "No. She is yours only in name, and all the money she makes will be yours, but someone else will have to sail her for you."

"Why—" But Annie could read the answer on his face. "It's because I'm a woman, isn't it?"

"I'm afraid so."

They stared at each other for a long, long while. Annie could see that he was as unhappy as she was that she could not sail the *Merrye Laurie*. She wondered why being a woman was so prohibitive.

"Well, thank you, James," she finally said. He deserved her thanks for the gift of the brig. "And thank you for all these fine clothes."

Her words seemed to cheer him a bit. He looked about him, then strode to one of the trunks. "I bought a pair of shears." He dug beneath the dresses. "Before we hire you a maid, we must make you look more like a girl."

He held them up before his face, and his next words were uttered in a momentous tone. "Annie, it is time to cut off that pigtail."

She gasped and grabbed for her hair, but James was too fast. She closed her eyes and felt a sharp tug on her head. After a while, the pulling ceased. James stepped around in front of her and ruffled the hair on either side of her face.

"That's much better," he said, as his fingers lingered there.

Then his gaze crossed hers, and his expression filled with heat. Annie heard him gasp again before he stepped away.

"Come here." He moved toward a table set against the wall. "Look into the glass."

Annie followed him. He grasped her by the shoulders and turned her around to face the mirror.

A stranger stared back.

Blunt, uneven curls of a light red color circled her face. Her cheeks were clean from a recent wash. Wearing a hat had turned her skin soft and white. Her eyes seemed two enormous slits of green between the billow of hair. Except for the clothes she wore, there was no sign of the boy she had been.

She didn't know what to think or what to say. She looked in the mirror at the captain. But what she saw in his eyes turned her knees to rubber.

He still stood behind her, his fingers gripping her shoulders. His chin nearly brushed her ear, and his eyes were burning with a warm, liquid light. She had seen him stare like this before, once when he watched his crew hoisting his sails at dawn.

He saw that she watched him, and his gaze caught hers in the glass. He parted his lips as if he would speak. Annie tried to turn slowly so that she could feel his breath caressing her face, but he abruptly pulled away.

"There." He backed hastily toward the door. "You look much prettier now. Don't you agree?"

"Do I, James?"

"Yes. By far."

"Does that please you?" Mr. Bonny had said a gentleman could have what he pleased.

But the captain kept moving toward the door.

"I should leave you to get some sleep," he said, not bothering to answer her question. "Before I come in the morning, put on one of those gowns. For tonight—" He halted suddenly, as if he'd remembered something, and he groaned.

"What's the matter?"

"I forgot to buy you shoes. Or a nightgown. Or a shift. I tried to think of all you would need, but there was so much—paniers, gloves! I remembered stockings, but forgot a corset or shoes."

"I can get along without all those things."

"No, you can't. A lady has to wear them, and I can't pass you off as my ward if you don't."

"Does that mean I don't get to be a lady or have the *Merrye Laurie*?"

"No," He sighed. "It only means that we put it off a little longer. I can't delay the ship. We have to sail with tomorrow's tide." Clearly annoyed, James removed his wig and ran his fingers through his hair.

"Then, I'll still be Jem?" Surprisingly, Annie was a little disappointed. She had wanted to try on her dresses.

"I suppose so," he said. "If it will still work. Let me have a good look at you."

He made a signal for her to turn around.

His eyes roamed over her body, lingering at her breasts and at the place between her hips. He frowned and muttered, "If I can bloody see it so clearly, what's wrong with the crew?"

"What, Captain?" Annie placed both fists upon her hips and faced him.

Something about her pose brought his gaze back up to her face and made him laugh. "That's the answer, I suppose. Perhaps we can fool them again, after all, with a little dirt. You haven't forgotten how to be a boy, have you?"

"No, sir, Captain."

"That's my girl." For an instant, he seemed taken with those words. Then he heaved a wistful sigh. "I had better leave."

"Can't you sleep with me?"

"Wh—No! We mustn't ever do that!"

"Why?"

"It wouldn't be proper."

"Oh."

Her answering sigh brought a grin to his lips. "Would you like me to?"

She nodded. "I don't like to sleep alone."

James took a ragged breath. "Neither do I. But

233

what we want and what we can have are often two different things." His voice changed. "Annie, I swear I will try to do right by you, in spite of us both."

Annie felt as if some force was holding him back, something over which neither he nor she had any power, a force that made her heart ache. "That's all right, Captain. We can sleep together after I get my dresses on."

He choked. "No, Annie. Not then, not now." He touched one hand to his forehead. "I have really mucked this up."

"Have you? How?"

"Nevermind. Therese will explain everything to you, but suffice it to say for now that only married men and women can share a bed."

"Can I take off my breeches now?"

"No!"

"Not even to try my dresses?"

The disappointment on her face made him hesitate at the door. "Very well," he said, "but later. Not here. Just before we get to Jamaica. Understood?"

"Yessir, James."

"Remember, you're still Jem."

"Aye, aye, Captain."

"Very good." He smiled, and his voice came so softly, she felt it like a breeze blowing over her body. "Good night, Annie."

And so, Annie went aboard a different ship, with a different crew. James assigned her to help the cook. It should have been a safe occupation, but from the start they were in for stormy weather.

A strong stern wind tossed them along. Annie kept busy, lashing down their provisions, tending to new sailors who got seasick, and helping the cook prepare each mess even though the sea threatened to capsize them at any moment.

Throughout the voyage, she was conscious of James's eyes upon her. If the ocean got too rough, he was certain to send for something from the galley in order to make sure she was all right. Otherwise, he kept a distance between them, hardly addressing her a phrase. But, even so, she could feel him watching her. And when he did, something inside her seemed to roil.

At times she wanted to speak to him so badly, she could hardly contain herself. Her pulse beat wildly just at the sight of him, tall and sober on his quarterdeck. But she had to be careful, too. The tendency to smile was much too strong whenever he appeared. And in the back of her mind, she couldn't forget that at the end of this voyage she would suffer the end of their friendship. With every puff of the wind in their sails, she was rushing to a different life.

James hadn't told her much about this woman, Therese. Nor had he said just how they would part. Annie was terrified that her last glimpse of him would take place in front of the crew, when she couldn't be herself. For she was becoming a girl, just as Mr. Bonny had said she would. She could no more go back to her previous life than she could forget the taste of James's mouth.

The ocean tossed them about, and the wind fiercely howled. Before Annie could quite credit it, James had assembled his crew to announce that the storms had blown them faster toward Jamaica. His instruments told him they should sight land at any time.

Annie felt a surge of panic. The voyage was too short when at the end of it, she must say goodbye to James. She couldn't bear to think that her life at sea was nearly over, nor could she face a life with strangers.

She thought that James would call for her, but he didn't. For the past few weeks, he had worn a perpetual frown and snapped orders at his men. If his eyes strayed often to her, they had not lit when they had. If anything, he had seemed angry and curt. The men had been puzzled by his attitude, and Annie had, too.

But angry or not, she wouldn't allow him to break his promise. He had said she could try on one of her dresses, and something inside her wanted him to see her in one. She would make him, and when they were alone, they could say goodbye.

Chapter Twelve

On a moonlit evening, when the tip of an island had been spotted off the bow, and the second watch had all been fed, Annie knocked on the captain's door.

She found him poring over a set of sea charts, a half-drunk bottle of wine at his elbow. He peered up, frowning, to see who had disturbed him, and surprise widened his eyes. Something about his look set her pulse to thumping.

"I want to try on one of my dresses," Annie said, with her back pressed to his door.

He seemed to swallow, and she could see a refusal forming in his eyes. "Annie . . ." He seemed uneasy. "I don't know . . ."

"But you promised!"

James sighed. "That's right. I did." He stood and rolled up his papers. "Very well. I shall have one of your trunks brought up. You may change in here. I'll stand guard."

"Thank you, Captain."

He smiled reluctantly. "I did promise you, didn't I? No harm could possibly come of it?"

Not that she could see.

But uneasiness remained on his face. "Can you manage alone?"

Annie scoffed. "James, I've been pulling on my own trousers for years."

He glanced at her hips, then back up to her face. "That's right. How hard could it be?"

Annie grinned, and James gave a nervous grin back at her. "It will give me great pleasure to see you in one of those dresses." The confession seemed wrung from him.

"Why?"

He chuckled. "Nevermind why. To see if they fit, I suppose, since I bought them." His gaze met hers and his appreciative glow warmed her. "Annie, do you know you are a unique creature?"

"Is that good?"

"Yes, it is. Please promise me that whatever you learn you won't change too much."

"Could I?"

"There are . . . things that might make you change." A shadow clouded his face. "But avast with all this. I'll have your trunk sent up. You can't stay in your skirts, mind, only long enough for me to see you. Then it's right back into your trousers. I'll give you plenty of time before I knock."

"Very well, Captain."

James left, feeling a flutter in his lower abdomen, as if a creature inside him were fighting to get free. At last, he would see Annie in a gown.

Her attractiveness had burgeoned over the weeks. Her hair was now a few inches long and curled in a luscious mop about her piquant little face. To all the crewmen, she must appear as a fragile, unkempt boy, but to him she was a fairy, a sprite, a nymph. He could only envy the man who would win her.

He gave the order for a trunk to be delivered to his cabin. It didn't matter which one. Each was filled with the stuff of his fantasies. Silks and satins, bows and laces, materials that would set off her pearl-colored skin, curves to emphasize the perfection of her figure, colors to bring out the green of her eyes.

He paced the deck outside his cabin, ignoring the curious stares of his men. They would never know the reason for his restlessness.

Annie chose a dress of shining green. It took her fancy, being the color of the ocean at rest. She took it out and laid it on the captain's bunk. With shaking fingers, she removed her sailor's clothes, until she stood in nothing but her skin. Though her hands and feet were still dark, her limbs were evenly pale. She held the dress up to

239

figure it out. One side had a delicate piece of open-work, sewn loosely at the neck, and some sort of shiny twine tied in fancy knots. The other had a long row of buttons.

No question which went in the front. Annie threw the voluminous skirt over her head. The sleeves seemed tight, as if sewn out of place, but James had said her maid would be able to fix any problem.

Annie started to work on all those buttons. . . .

At the sound of one bell, James stopped pacing. Eight o'clock and the start of the night watch. He had given Annie a good half-hour. Surely enough.

He paused outside his door and tried to listen through the wood. He supposed, if she had run into any trouble with the fastenings, she would have called to him.

James looked about, then tapped softly, holding his breath.

"Come in."

Reassured by her jaunty voice, he found that his knees were shaking. Feeling foolish, he kept his gaze to the deck until he moved inside and the door was shut.

Annie stood in the middle of the space, looking shy but proud. The large skirt, without hoops or pads, fell in heavy drapes to the floor, where it bunched. The bodice was—

James peered closer in his dim cabin light. Something was definitely wrong with the bodice. It shouldn't grip her breasts like that, with the front of it straining and the back in lumps.

Then he saw what was wrong and hooted with laughter. He clamped one hand over his mouth, but his tension had found its release in loud guffaws.

"What is it?" she demanded. She blanched, then color surged into her cheeks. "Why are you laughing?"

James tried to speak. Her anger waved a warning flag, but he choked on a chuckle.

"What the bloody hell's wrong with you?"

"Annie—sorry," he gasped. "You've got the dress on backwards."

"No, I don't!"

"Yes, you do, you goose. Look at the buttons."

"I am looking at the buttons, and I say I did them right!"

"No. The buttons on a dress go in back."

She squeezed her eyes closed, balled her hands into fists and launched herself at his chest. "You're bloody wrong!" She pounded at his face and his neck. "Stop that stupid laughing, James!"

With a grunt, James fell back, one hand flung up to protect his face. His temper flared, and he blocked her fists, trapping her wrists and twisting them behind her.

"That's enough! Annie, stop!"

He felt her teeth coming through his clothes, a sharp, hard bite on his nipple.

"Ouch! You're going to regret this, sailor!" But

his anger vanished when he felt her tears, soaking through his clothes. In astonishment, he heard her sobs.

"Oh, Annie, I'm sorry," he said. "So sorry. Go easy now, please."

His remorseful tone brought her struggles to a halt. She fell against him, weeping, her cheek pressed flatly to his chest. James dropped hold of her wrists and quickly gathered her to him, sitting in his chair to hug her on his lap.

He rocked her in his arms, crooning words of comfort. "You didn't know."

"It isn't fair!" With one last gasping breath, her sobs came to a halt. "You should have told me," she whispered into his cravat.

"Yes, I should, but I didn't think. I never have put on a dress, you know."

At this, she gave a watery chuckle. But she wouldn't look up. "I did it wrong." Her voice was so full of misery. "I'll never be a lady if I can't even put on a dress."

"Yes, you will. You'll be the prettiest lady there ever was."

She peered up him, her eyes still rimmed from crying and the dampness from her tears clumping her golden eyelashes. "But I wanted to be one *tonight*."

James hid a smile. It would be far too soon to laugh at this notion now. "You can be a lady whenever you wish."

"Even with my dress on backward?"

"You can always turn it around."

Annie sat up and looked hopelessly down at the multitude of buttons. "I don't think I could do them by myself in back."

"Then I'll help you."

As soon as he said it, James winced. He had begun to feel her buttocks on his lap. He should never have made such a reckless remark, but he hadn't wanted to leave her so despondent.

Annie started eagerly to her feet, and he helped her to move away. Better to put some distance between them.

Then she started on the buttons.

James gasped when he saw the skin covering the delicate bones at the base of her throat, a luminescent glow of ivory by the light of his lantern. He opened his mouth to stop her, but her fingers had moved again, and a widening V was delving between her breasts. The cloth of the gown still concealed her nipples, but its shadow failed to hide the soft, white globes he had cradled in his palms. She wore no underclothes.

"Annie—"

Annie raised her head at the strangled sound. James was watching her strangely, his eyes appearing drawn against his will to the opening in her dress.

"What is it?" Fingers moving rapidly, she unfastened two more buttons at her waist before he said, in a wavering voice, "You . . . have to stop."

"Why?" She started to comply, but his eyes belied his words. They begged her to go on. His gaze locked on her hands, poised at the button on her navel.

Slowly, Annie undid it and the captain let out a ragged breath.

If a woman talks about her breasts, then a man might think she's issued him an invitation to touch her . . . Breasts are beautiful. . . .

The sum of his words came back to her now, and she thought she understood at last. If she wanted him to touch her, she must invite him to. No need to talk about her breasts when they were right here for him to see. Annie unfastened more buttons.

James seemed paralyzed, as if the sight of her skin from her neck to her stomach had robbed him of speech. He didn't repeat his order for her to stop. His eyes seemed to glow with a fire, and his glow fired her from within. His breaths came in shallow gasps.

Annie felt her own pulse responding as if their hearts beat in harmony. As his gaze followed her fingers below her waist, heat pooled between her legs. She was not so far from the place between them, that little place that had nearly burst the last time they had touched.

Scarcely knowing what she did, only that she followed an imperative of his, Annie kept on with her buttons, until she passed the red thatch between her legs. When he saw it, James moaned as if in pain.

But it couldn't be pain; craving and hunger stared out from his eyes, making her weak in the knees.

"Annie," he whispered, looking up at her face. "You are so very beautiful."

Her heart gave a leap. She had pleased him. Her undressing had pleased him. Who needed a dress?

The garment still covered her nipples, which had grown painful for his gaze. Annie spread the dress slowly, revealing more of her body inch by inch, the pulse between her legs growing stronger as his lips parted. James looked as if he would like to drink from her nipples. Annie felt a tingling in them as if they'd filled for him.

She let the dress slide over her shoulders, along her arms and past her waist, over her hips and buttocks, and onto the floor.

James let out a enormous breath. "Annie . . ." His tone was like a prayer. He stared at her body as if she'd opened a box filled with pearls.

"Why, James?" Annie asked, her own voice trembling. "Why is it that when I think of you at night I ache so here"—she moved her fingertips over her nipples and felt them go hard—"and here." She touched one finger to the place between her legs.

"Dear Lord—" As if a force had wrenched him from his place, James came toward her. "Annie, you mustn't tell me that." He took the hand she had placed over her thatch. Her finger was damp and sticky from the moisture it had found there. James took her finger into his mouth and closed his eyes.

He was close now, oh, so close. Annie felt his clothes brush the tips of her breasts and tickle

245

the hair between her legs. "James, sometimes I want to climb straight up you the way a sailor climbs a mast."

He opened his eyes again and reverently grazed her nipples with his thumbs. "Annie, I've tried not to touch you, but you're all I can think about. I lie awake at night wanting to stroke you like this."

"But I *want* you to touch me." His hands, so softly running over her, were all she had ever wanted. And his look, when he'd tasted her, as if of the finest wine. . . .

"Annie, I don't want to hurt you."

"Ye mean . . . poke me?" Annie felt the blood draining from her face. But James was so gentle, she couldn't believe he would do anything to hurt her.

"No, Annie. Poke is the wrong word." He shook his head in a kind of agony. "I would want to make it special for you. Dearest, most beautiful Annie."

Dearest. James had called her dearest. If what he wanted to do felt even a tenth as good as what he was doing to her now, she knew she would love it.

"Do it," she begged.

"Ah, Annie." James swept her up. He held her as if she might break. "I promise you won't regret it. No matter what."

Annie moved against him, rubbing her breasts across his chest.

She felt him groan inside, the way the ship moaned when it turned too rapidly. James clasped her buttocks in both hands, and going wild, Annie started to climb.

She felt his trousers brushing against her tiny nub before her legs had reached his waist. James pressed her to him there, and she felt the ridge that had teased her before. She rubbed against it, a frenzy growing in her, but James held her away.

"Not this time, you little beast. I want to take my clothes off, too."

"You do?" Annie liked that idea. She had a sudden desire to feel his skin against her nipples. His legs against her thighs.

"Help me, Annie," his whisper encouraged her, even as his fingers guided hers to the knot in his neckcloth.

Annie fumbled with it. Her knees were trembling, even as the air became filled with a sweet smell, coming from the sticky spot between her legs.

As she loosened his cravat, James kissed her on the lips. His fingers parted the hair over her nub, and he touched it.

Wave upon wave of thunder rippled through her. *This is what I wanted.* She was dazzled by sensations. The feelings from her dreams fluttered through her as James teased her, coaxing her. Annie pressed her thighs close together to keep from crying out.

"Annie, take off my shirt," James urged against her ear.

The sound of his voice, as dazed as her mind, sent a rush of happiness through her. James wanted her to touch him the way he was touching her.

She fought the weakness his hands had brought upon her to make short shrift of his buttons.

"Annie—" He ran his hands down her buttocks as if he couldn't stop himself, and her blood felt on fire.

When his shirt lay open, Annie touched his chest tentatively, flattening it with her palms.

"Don't stop," he said quickly, when a sudden fit of shyness seized her. "Please, don't stop."

She brushed his nipples and felt him shake, as if a quake had passed through him.

"I've dreamed of this." His head fell back. "Of your little brown hands, rubbing my chest."

How did he know? she wondered, as she felt his muscles contract beneath the hair. She moved her palms over his nipples and felt them stiffen like hers. *How did he know how this would feel?*

James brought her hands to the flap at his waist. He didn't need to tell her what he wanted. As his fingers sought the place between her legs again, she wanted to see for herself the ridge that had made her gasp.

His manhood was straining against the cloth of his breeches by the time she finally freed it. She had never seen one so engorged.

"James . . ." Annie breathed admiringly, as she took it in both her hands. "You've sure got a big—"

His low chuckle surprised her. "Don't say it."

"Yessir."

"Don't call me 'sir,' Annie." He kissed her ruthlessly, holding her against him, pressing her against his body until his member squeezed between her thighs. "Call me 'sweetheart'."

His voice trailed off as she began rubbing herself along his member.

As her frenzy mounted, Annie thought she knew at last what all those secrets had meant. Not a poke, but this lovely, aching burn that made her want to yell. James's fingers tickled her at the base of her buttocks, and she thought she might scream.

"Go ahead," he said raggedly. "Do whatever feels good to you."

"James"—her urge was getting stronger—"I still want to climb you."

"Go ahead. I'll help you do it."

He did more than that. He lifted her until the tingling place between her legs just pressed the tip of his manhood. The feeling of it poised there made her head spin. Annie curled her knees up under his arms. The insides of her thighs rode his chest, and she started to play with his tip, rubbing it up and down, feeling it press closer each time, as if burning an entrance.

"Annie." His voice was rough with strain. "I think you're going to drive me mad."

"Do you want me to get down?"

"No, not ever."

She knew relief because she didn't think she could. That delicious feeling was mounting inside her, the one she had had before when the earthquake had struck. The room was spinning down into a whirlpool that began and ended between her legs. "James. Oh, James."

"That's the way. Give in to it." His husky voice sent chills down her spine, prolonging her ecstasy. Annie rode the waves and prayed they would never stop swirling, those waves that bit like teeth and raged like pounding storms. But then they faded as before, and she collapsed.

"It happened again," she said, gasping for breath.

"Don't stop," James pleaded in her ear. "It's too late to stop this now."

"What comes next?" There couldn't possibly be more.

"It's my turn now," he said, holding her back so he could see her.

"It is? What do you want?"

"I want to move inside you." With those words, James pressed her harder against his manhood. At first, his pressure stung a bit, but then as she stretched, Annie felt the swirling rising again. She craved his pressure. When he pulled away, she whimpered.

"Did I hurt you?" The fright in his voice startled her.

"No. Don't pull away."

"Oh, Annie." A deep, contented rumble issued from his throat. "If you even guessed how good you're making me feel. You're everything I've ever dreamed of and more. I don't want to hurt you. Take me in slowly."

She wasn't certain what he meant, but she felt

herself stretching for him. The place he had teased with his fingers was slippery with her essence. The feel of his smooth tip, sliding against it, made it open wider as she pressed herself against him.

The ship lurched and James staggered beneath her. "Annie, we can't do it like this. I might fall on you if I don't set you down."

"Do we have to stop?" She couldn't stop. Not now, not with the swirling coming on again.

"Not on your life." James held her firmly against his chest and walked with her. The movement of his manhood against her nearly made her scream.

He laid her on his berth. Trembling, Annie looked up into his dark eyes.

"I'm going to look at you." He knelt beside the berth, and his gaze moved slowly over her, his fingers following along.

"Ever since I saw you the first time, I've been dreaming of this. Of these perfect pink nipples—" He brushed his fingers over them one by one. A shiver rippled through her as James bent over her body. He brought his lips to her nipples and kissed them, then licked them into hard pebbles.

"Ooooh, I like that," Annie crooned, arching her back to meet him and thrusting her breast into his mouth. Chuckling, he took her in his teeth, and she writhed against the cushions, and his breath became ragged again. When he started to move his head, she yanked it back. "Don't stop," she nearly begged.

"Annie, trust me," he said hoarsely. "It's my turn to steer."

She let him go with a sigh, but then she found that he had not gone away, he had only moved lower across her stomach. He kissed the sensitive skin of her ribs.

"I love to watch you squirm," he said, running his eyes over her again. "It makes the light dance over your skin like moonlight on the water. And something else I dreamed of . . . this." James gently parted the hair covering her nub and kissed her on it, long and hard, and dragging with his tongue.

Annie couldn't stand it any longer. All her nerves were on end. She didn't know whether she loved or hated it, but she was urging him to do something, gripping his head between her legs.

"James!" she cried out, needing something he had not given her.

"Shhhhhh, love. You'll have the whole first watch beating down my door."

Annie had forgotten about the ship, forgotten about the other men. All she knew was James and her craving.

He poised on top of her, the tip of his manhood nestled against her again, making her open for him.

"Annie, this may hurt."

"No, it won't," she said, yanking him toward her.

But it did. A little. A sudden sting made her

252

wince. Then, the pain receded and she realized James was inside her.

Inside her. James was inside, all hers, a part of her in a way she had never imagined.

He started to pull back, and she clutched at him.

"Did it hurt?" he whispered, his voice a tight band of restraint.

"It doesn't hurt now. Please don't leave."

"Then move with me, come with me, Annie." He started a motion, one so familiar that she had known it from her cradle. It was the rocking of the ocean and the rolling of the waves.

Annie helped him, meeting his thrusts, feeling her opening stretch to draw him deeper. James was inside her, filling her, bringing her to the crest of a wave and then down the other side.

Her nub grew warm again, warm and ripe with the beating. Annie felt it surging, surging, as if it would burst with delight. She cried out, just as James began to shudder. His back arched and he drove himself deeply into her once . . . twice . . . three times before gasping her name.

Then, as if they had both run out of strength at the same moment, they lay together panting.

"Dearest, sweetest Annie." When James could speak again, he shifted so that he leaned on one elbow beside her. He kissed her gently and brushed the hair from her temple. "I never knew it could be so perfect. You are so . . ."

He didn't finish, but kissed her on the nose, the cheek, then the nipple.

As his lips moved over her again, Annie felt a burst of gladness. Happiness shimmered along her skin and brought a smile to her lips.

"I didn't know it could be like that, either, James, especially that part with you inside me, but I really liked it. Can we do it again? And are we married now?"

Chapter Thirteen

James fell back against the wall of his berth, staring at Annie in stunned dismay.

"Annie, I never lied to you. I never said we would marry."

"But aren't we sharing your bed?" Confusion and a suggestion of pain budded on her face.

James fell back on his pillow and threw an arm across his eyes.

What had he done?

She was Eve incarnate. Sensual. Savage. Yet so innocent that she had no notion of what they had done with the apple. Annie had only obeyed the youthful stirrings of her body, never once having the least idea of what would result. While he, knowing it all full well, had let himself be tempted beyond the bounds of mortal man.

He looked at her. "Annie, I've told you before," he said, inwardly pleading for her to understand. "I cannot marry you. I am sorry."

"But—why?"

Surely he had explained this before. But what had he told her? James searched his memory and came up with very little. Something about the differences in their stations.

He *had* told her he was engaged.

He seized on that now. "I know I told you I had a fiancée."

"But aren't we sharing your bed? You said only married men and women shared a bed."

He could see he hadn't been clear enough. "Come here," he said, urging her to lie against his chest. Once she had settled, he tried to explain in a repentant voice. "I should never have made love to you like this, Annie. It was wrong of me."

"Why?"

"Because . . . in society, the rule is that a man should only make love to his wife, although in practice . . ."

Caressing her hair, he remembered all too well what the practice was. His father had often taken other women over the course of his long sea voyages. As he had matured, James had understood his father's need, but still, it had added to his guilt whenever he had visited his mother, that he should know a secret that could hurt someone he loved.

Annie sat up beside him. Her red curls clustered about her face like an angel's halo. Her green eyes, shaded in this half-light, took on the color of the sea in storm.

"James, you said that I could be a lady now. You told me you had to marry a lady. You shared your bed with me. So why aren't we married?"

Sitting there erect and naked, she took his breath away. Her smooth, white skin shone like marble. Her high, perfect breasts with their large, rosy nipples, still ripe from his avid love-making, lured his fingers, but he knew he must not touch her again now. Not until he could make her understand.

And understand what? That he had never even thought of her as an appropriate mate? That he had preferred to marry someone else, even though he couldn't bear to think of Olivia when Annie was here? How could he explain all that?

Dismayed, he studied her. She had sat back on her heels, completely unaware of the erotic picture she made with her flushed white skin and her enticing curves. No Fragonard could be more tempting. Just the sight of her in his bed, so bold and unashamed, felt so gloriously right, he had to fight a shifting in his heart.

How could he have tempted himself with a girl no man could resist?

It was time to answer her in a way that she would finally comprehend. James realized that he had skirted the issue before, avoiding an honest talk because he had been afraid of his own weakness. He had wanted Mr. Bonny, Therese—anyone but himself to talk to her about love because he had feared that, if he broached the subject, he would not be able to stop himself from touching her.

Now, he had crossed the line he had drawn. He had erased it with the part of him she had swiped at with her knife. Better for her if she hadn't missed it that day.

There was no cause for secrets between them now.

"Annie, marriage is a contract. Nothing more. It's a business transaction. In order to be married, a man and a woman must sign a paper before a parson, a man of religion, and have their union consecrated before God."

She waited for him to finish, her chin held high, as if she knew his next words would hurt her. James had no intention of making this any more painful than it had to be. He would never tell her—could never explain to her really—all the reasons for his social ambitions. She would never understand the falseness of society—or its importance.

"Annie, we cannot be married. I made the decision years ago that I should marry someone who wouldn't mind my long absences from home. I have already engaged myself to marry a woman who meets that qualification."

"Who?"

"A woman in London. Her name is of no importance. She is a lady, however, and in need of this marriage."

Annie pondered what he had told her. She looked away as if she could no longer stand to look at him, which hurt, he discovered, more than he ever would have thought. Then she noticed his manhood, lying limp.

"Why does it do that?" she said, taking it carefully in her hand.

"It's tired." Despite the seriousness of their talk, James had trouble restraining a smile. Annie's frank curiosity had always been a large part of her charm, and he couldn't help being pleased as a lion that she could be fascinated by his body. "Give it time, and it will wake up." And indeed, under her handling, he felt it recovering all too fast.

He knew he should stop her, but the temptation to let her continue was too strong. In a moment he would be ready to satisfy her again. At the thought of doing it, his pulse began pounding, and his member grew hard. Annie's red hair bounced about her beautiful face, which she leaned over his throbbing part. Her lips were still swollen from his ravenous kisses, and he longed to bite at them with his teeth.

Then, suddenly, Annie released her hold on him and looked up at him with a glare. "Do you mean, if you marry this other lady, you'll be putting *that* inside her, too?"

She poked him hard where it hurt, and the pain in his pulsing arousal made him cry, "Ow!"

Her accusation shocked him into shame. The withdrawal of her hand from his aching part made him sick and desperate.

With his heart still beating loudly in his ears,

James saw her anger, then denial, then a sentiment greater than fury come over her face, and he knew he had no need to respond.

She started to get up from his berth.

"Annie, wait, don't go. Please don't leave just yet." He pulled her back to lie beside him. "Let me figure this out."

So much had occurred, so much had changed. He had never felt this confused in his life, and the feel of Annie's womanly body against him did nothing to clear his brain.

He had told her he would figure it out, but how could he? He was engaged to be married. He had signed the contract in London, and in London society a marriage contract was almost as binding as a warrant. He had achieved the apex of his ambition, and the merchant inside him had triumphed, even if the man had not. At that moment, when he had gained Lord Figg's agreement to lesser demands, nothing had mattered to James but the assurance that his father's spirit had watched approvingly at his side. For, in spite of a few issues between them, Seth Avery had been a good, affectionate father, supportive of his only son. Together they had forged a future for their descendants.

No, nothing must unsettle his father's plans.

Annie's question about Olivia, though, had sent inevitable misgivings flittering through his head. Olivia instead of this divine creature in his bed? How could he bear her after what he'd just tasted?

He knew that no other woman could ever satisfy him the way Annie just had. Good God, but he had never felt so indescribably good!

His loins still ached from her tender stroking. He wanted to bury himself inside her again. He had never felt so sated, yet so hungry for more. Her body, nestled beside him, made a perfect fit near his heart.

If he had only known how good it could be. If he had only known.

His mind turned rapidly. He knew of captains who sailed with women in their cabins. He had always despised the habit, regarding it as low and beneath the dignity of a gentleman.

But, Annie . . .

There would be no greater heaven than having her here, right in his berth.

For no more than a second, he let himself dream of keeping her here, but soon he realized he was letting his hunger think for him. He couldn't countenance keeping a woman on board—look at the trouble she had already caused. She would have to live ashore, but he must see her.

He would set her up with a life ashore. And when he wearied of her . . . but he suddenly realized that he would never tire of Annie. He could never grow weary of her endearing frankness or her fascinating passion. He could hardly wait to discover what she would do next. Something told him that they had just scratched the surface of her potential. The thought of her ready appetite, her lack of restraint, made him squirm in a fever of delight. He would surely go crippled from excess before he would stop making love to her, and when he was old, he would have her cheerful companionship, her boundless courage, and her loyalty to keep him happy.

And until then, they could make hot, rabid love until the stars fell from the skies.

Olivia need never know.

Lust clouded his eyes. It thickened his throat as he said. "Annie . . . love . . . I cannot marry you because I have given my word to another, but we can be together whenever I come into port. I can visit you where you live."

"Where I live!" She pushed herself up and turned angrily to face him. "And where would that be, pray?"

James blanched. He could see that his idea was not exactly what she had had in mind, but for the life of him, he couldn't think of a better plan right now. The sight of her tousled and naked in his bed lured him so much that he could only think of how much he wanted her.

"You would have to live in Jamaica. I could find you a house right on the beach. And I would come as often as I could."

"Why would you want to come?"

If she could only see herself now, James thought, she wouldn't ask such a silly question. He could almost wish she didn't look so good. Then, maybe, his mind would work.

"Well . . ." Trying to coax her into a better mood, he gently brushed the back of his index finger over her nipple. He saw her eyes turn liquid for him, and he smiled. "I should think that would be pretty obvious after what we did tonight. But we could do whatever came to you . . . I suppose."

Slowly, like a sensuous feline, Annie crawled on her knees until she loomed over him. Her breasts were almost within reach. He reached with his tongue to taste one, but before he could lick it, her angry whisper stopped him cold.

"These *things* we would do . . . would you be thinking of doing them with your wife?"

James froze, and guilt from the anger in her tone gave him a kick in the gut.

He faced her squarely, though, still unable to make himself give her up. "I would have to lie with my wife. But only for a few times. The law requires it! I would stop as soon as she had borne me a few sons."

"What do *sons* have to do with *this*?" She gave his manhood a furious flip.

He winced, moving his hands quickly to protect himself. When he opened his eyes and saw a relentless question in hers, he swallowed. "They have everything to do with it, I'm afraid. What we just did is how men and women make babies, and I will have to have heirs."

"Did *we* make a baby?"

Her question started him out of his sensual daze.

"Oh, God. We might have—or we might not. We won't know until you miss your monthlies."

For just a brief second, the angry look left Annie's eyes. She even looked hopeful. "Making babies takes away your monthlies?"

"Yes, but just for nine months each time."

"Oh." Her face fell again.

"Annie, the point is that we might have made a baby tonight, and if we did I promise to do the right thing by you."

"How do you know what the right thing is?"

James decided it would be better if he didn't discuss this right now. "Don't you worry about it. Just know that I will. But chances are, you won't be pregnant."

"Why wouldn't *I* be pregnant if you think your wife would bear you a few sons after just a few times?"

Why wouldn't Annie have his children? If she had them, they would all be bastards.

With that one horrible thought, his conscience dealt his dreams a mortal blow. He would never put Annie's sons in that position, not when their mother was the mate of his heart.

In his fever of desire, he had forgotten all about Annie's interest and the promise he had made to Mr. Bonny.

James looked up at her still face with its cluster of soft, copper curls, and he knew that he could never make Annie his mistress.

A hard, dull ache started in his loins and spread rapidly to his chest.

"You are right, Annie. I cannot sleep with two women and not expect them both to have my children. It wouldn't be right. I am so sorry."

She pushed on his chest, making him "oof," as she scrambled up from his berth. She snatched her boy's clothes off the floor and started to dress.

"Annie—" He wouldn't plead for her to come back into his arms, for he mustn't touch her again. He sat on the edge of his berth and miserably ran his fingers through his hair.

"You deserve better than me," he told her and meant it. "You deserve a man who will be a companion to you."

It nearly killed him to watch her cover her body, knowing that he would never see it again, never feel her against his heart. One episode of perfect lovemaking would have to last him for a lifetime.

"What if I don't want another husband? Maybe I don't want another man coming inside me."

Her statement ripped him in the gut. He had been so sure he could figure out a way to have his cake and eat it, too, that he had forgotten.

Annie's husband would have those rights.

But he mustn't let his selfishness make him overlook her interests again. "You will feel differently when you meet other men."

"I know a shipload of men already."

"Yes, but you've only known one gentleman before. When you meet others, you may find that you prefer them to me."

Annie glanced at him speculatively. "You mean I'll want to climb those other gentlemen, too."

Again, that hard boot in the gut.

"No! That is, maybe one—but you mustn't— until you marry—"

"Why not, James? Didn't you just put yourself inside me? And *we're* not going to be married."

This last was no question, but a blow of revenge. And a very effective blow, he had to concede as a painful lump in his chest became unbearable.

He wouldn't let her see that she had hurt him, though. Not when he was doing the right thing for her for once. But neither could he speak, as Annie let herself proudly out of his cabin.

In Kingston, James hired a carriage to take them out to Therese's plantation. Sitting wrapped in a cloak beside him, Annie gawked at the scenery, leaning dangerously out to crane her neck at the novel sights. At a rapid trot, they whirled past the cane fields with their armies of slaves, groves of cacao trees swaying in the warm, humid breeze, wagons filled with bunches of indigo, and baskets heaped with vanilla beans. A scruffy boy gaped back at them, a string of crabs slung over his shoulder.

James sat silent with remorse, ignoring the pungent odor of donkey dung and rotting fruit that littered the Kingston streets. The tropical aloe, the yucca and cacti were all too familiar to him. Nothing could distract him from his shame.

He had debauched a virgin in his care. He had broken the faith placed in him by a dying man.

He couldn't excuse himself, either, on the grounds that he'd been seduced, not when Annie hadn't known what she was doing. All he could plead was that his conscience had fled him when desire had grown to such a pitch. And Annie had wanted him, too.

Now that his head was cooler, he would have to resolve what could be done with her. He had corrupted her, but he could not make her his mistress. Even if Annie would agree—and she had made her conditions fairly clear—his conscience wouldn't let him.

He was bound by law and a contract from which a gentleman was not allowed to escape. His oath to Olivia would consign Annie to an inferior position. If she had children, they would all be bastards. His children with Olivia would be his legal heirs, who could lord it over their half-siblings the way Lord Figg had sneered at James.

Annie and her children would have to live in a port without the honor of his name and with little property to call their own. He had no doubt they would all come to hate the man who had left them there.

James didn't want to condemn Annie or her children to such a dismal fate—not when she could have a better life with someone else. She had slept with him because he was the first man to treat her with gallantry. She'd been thrown into his hands without ever knowing the courtship of other gentlemen. She had lost her home and the one man who had ever shown her any affection. In such close quarters, with temptation driving him mad, where his own judgment had abandoned him, how could she fail to turn to him for passion, when she might rather have found it with someone else?

There was only one way to know. Annie must be given the chance to choose. She must live with Therese and learn about society and meet eligible men. Then, if she chose a husband from among the eligible bachelors of Jamaica, James would know. And the harm he had done her might be forgiven.

They drove a few more miles, until a sweet smell of flowers brought him to his senses. He turned into a seashell drive. Ahead, the stucco plantation house, with its vermillion bougainvillea draped in garlands over sun-bleached walls, gleamed like a porcelain teacup beside the blue water.

At his side, Annie took one look at the place, so alien and beautiful at once, and she gazed at James with a silent plea. He looked down and covered her hand. "It will be all right. You'll see." A flicker in his eyes belied the confidence in his words.

Annie tried to be brave, but she was taken aback by the servant who answered the door. He was an imposing black man, dressed in such clean finery that he made her feel grubby and dirty and scared. The man led them down a bright, clean passageway with a floor checkered in light and dark woods, then into an airy room full of delicate chairs, where he asked them to wait. The space had glass-paned doors that looked down over the Caribbean. The emerald-blue sea shimmered below them in the sun.

The sight of the water made Annie's throat ache. She didn't know how she could stand to leave the sea; but ever since James had been inside her, she had hardly known herself anymore. She had begged him to let her stay on board. She had even promised not to touch him again, but though he had almost wavered, he had ended by saying that they must separate for a while. He said they must carry on with the plan he had made.

A noise made her turn to look at the door. A tiny creature was moving through it with loose black curls gathered on her head. When she saw James, she gave a high-pitched shriek and ran on high, red heels to throw herself like a siren upon his chest.

Annie started forward, sudden fury burning a hole in her heart. She grabbed for her knife, but James's kindling eyes fired a warning shot across her bow.

"James, *chéri*, at last you 'ave come to see me. What do you mean by it, eh?" Therese cocked her head sideways, and her eyelashes fluttered. "Two years, and not one visit! You think I have not pined for you, eh?"

James's traitorous laugh made Annie want to cry. "No. I know very well you have not pined. You have swains aplenty and no need for an old seadog like me."

"But such an 'andsome seadog, *n'est-ce pas?*" She turned to Annie. "And who is this charming little boy?"

"Therese . . ." With a nervous sigh, James

stepped to Annie's side and drew back her hood. "She's no boy. Please receive my ward, Miss Anne Bonny."

Therese gasped and exclaimed. Her fingers flew to cover her lips.

The link of Mr. Bonny's name with hers, which Annie had not expected, brought sudden tears to her eyes, so that for a moment she hardly heard the woman's speech.

"*Ô là!* So this is why you 'ave come. I begin to see."

She swayed up to Annie, who noticed that Therese was several inches shorter than she. She would be easy to beat in a fight.

"And where did you find this little *gamine*, eh?"

"I'll tell you all about it." James's manner was stiff and uncomfortable. "Annie's been raised a little . . . unconventionally, but she's a quick learner and she needs your help. Annie, will you greet our hostess the way I showed you?"

Annie threw him a mulish look, but his answering nod was firm.

"How do you do?" Stiffly, she thrust her hand forward for a shake.

"*Ô là!*" Therese said wryly. Then she laughed, and taking Annie by the face, planted soft, feathery kisses on both of her cheeks. "Welcome, *chérie*. Now perhaps you would go to a room to wash yourself, while I chat with *ce cher* James. But first, I must ask my servant to prepare one for you. I shall only be a moment."

As Therese tripped lightly from the room, Annie whispered in desperation, "I can't stay here, James! That woman's an idiot! All she knows how to say is '*ô là*.' "

"That's just what French people say when they exclaim."

"No, it's not. I've known lots of French pirates, and they say '*ô merde*,' which means 'bloody hell.' "

The corners of James's mouth tugged upward for the first time in days. "Loosely translated it may," he agreed. "But '*ô là*' accomplishes the same thing and it is far more respectable."

"But—she kissed me! I don't want to kiss her. Let's go!"

"Annie"—he grasped her by the elbow, and the smile fell from his lips—"you must stay with Therese. It's the only way."

She was shaking her head when Therese came wriggling back into the room—her walking surely looked like wriggling to Annie, who could only watch it with her eyes agape.

"Mademoiselle's room is ready. Marie-Paul will conduct you to it, *ma fille*."

Over by the door, a large servant woman in a white apron and cap was waiting. She dropped a curtsy to James and smiled at Annie with a mouthful of big, white teeth.

James gave Annie a nod. When she didn't budge, he shoved her gently, then more firmly toward the hall.

"You're not going to leave?" she said, clinging to his arm.

"Not yet."

He was stronger than she was. He could pick

271

her up and throw her over his shoulder if he wanted and force her to obey. On top of that, he was still her captain. There didn't seem much point in fighting. With a tentative glance behind her, Annie followed the servant woman, hoping that James would never lie.

James watched her leave, and his whole chest began to ache.

"Well, *chéri*." Therese's voice came dryly from behind him. "I am ready to hear you explain yourself."

With a heavy sigh, he turned to see her pointing toward a chair. He found it hard to meet her knowing gaze.

"You 'ad better sit down, *mon cher*. This is going to be a complicated story, *n'est-ce pas*?"

Chapter Fourteen

Marie-Paul left Annie alone in a room overlooking the sea. It had a bed as big as the one at the inn in Portsmouth, but when she stood on top of it and bounced, she found that it was even springier. She peered about and saw a chest full of drawers made of fine inlaid mahogany. The mirror had a sharper image than the one in Portsmouth, too, and the porcelain washbowl and pitcher had been painted with flowers.

She waited for something to happen; but, when nothing did, she began to fidget. There was nothing to do inside these vast shore quarters. No one ever seemed to work.

She hopped from the bed and went to stare out the window. From here she could see along the beach. A square-rigged brig like the *Merrye*

Laurie lay at anchor offshore. Looking down into a gated garden filled with green leaves and purplish flowers, Annie saw how easy it would be to escape when she wanted.

After a few moments more, Therese knocked and entered, followed by a smiling Marie-Paul. "Here you are, *chérie*. I hope you 'ave rested well?"

Annie glared at her with suspicion. "Where's James?" She started for the door.

At a signal from Therese, Marie-Paul moved her bulk in front of it. "He is resting, *chérie*. You mustn't worry."

Alarmed by the trap, Annie crouched and prepared to fight. "You're lying." James didn't need a rest. Why should he, when he'd done no work?

A tiny sound between a gasp and a sigh was all the protest Therese made.

Despising it for the pitiful complaint it was, Annie whipped out her dagger and jabbed it toward the women to frighten them away. Everyone knew that women were easily scared.

Neither one ran. Marie-Paul's smile faded, to be replaced by an angry, stubborn look. She threw back her shoulders and crossed her arms, seeming to double in size.

The smile on Therese's face had frozen. A steely glint hardened her eyes.

"Ah, no, *chérie*. You cannot play with knives in my house. I will not permit it."

"I'm not playing." These women were obviously too stupid to tell the difference. But it was a little disconcerting that they had not fled. "If you don't want to get hurt, you'd better move out of my way. I want to see James."

"And this is how you would see 'im?" Therese, also, folded her arms. "This poor James. He said you were a smart little girl, and I believed 'im. Poor besotted fool."

Annie remained in her crouch, but one word arrested her. "What's that? Besotted?" She waited, her gaze darting from one woman's face to the other.

"Besotted? That is to say that James is so foolish in love that he cannot see that he is wrong about you."

"Love?" Annie straightened suddenly, and her knife almost slipped from her hand. "In love with who?"

"Why, with you, of course! He has quite tormented 'imself. And for what? For a foolish girl who does not even know how to help 'erself."

"Yes, I do!" Annie's eyes filled with tears, and she angrily raised her hand to brush them away. "I can take care of myself. I don't need you or any other woman to teach me. You're nothing but fools."

"And who told you that, *chérie*?"

"My mates."

"Ah, these pirates of yours, I suppose. And do they know everything, these pirates?"

Annie began to nod, but she couldn't in truth. The more she had seen, the more she had realized that her pirates could sometimes be wrong.

Therese pressed her silence. "Your precious

James does not think me a fool. If he did, would he bring you to me?"

A lump the size of a cannonball had clogged Annie's throat. Unable to speak for it, she merely shook her head.

Therese's eyes softened. "You are not so foolish, then, are you, *chérie*?"

"Don't call me *chérie*! I don't like it." Sulkily, then, she added, "And you shouldn't call James that, either."

"In my own house, I shall call you what I like, and I call you that out of pity, my little one." Therese's voice now held a note that Annie had only heard from Mr. Bonny.

This unlikely thought could do nothing but produce more tears. She pushed them away. "Has James already left?"

"No. He will stay for a few more days to make certain that you are all right, but you will want to look *très élégante* for 'im, *non*?" Turning her back on Annie's dagger, as if it had ceased to exist, Therese clapped her hands and said to Marie-Paul, "Ask Jean-Luc to bring in mademoiselle's trunks. And *vite, vite*! We must turn Mademoiselle Annie into a vision."

Turning back, Therese reached a tiny hand out for the knife.

Annie jerked it behind her back. "James said I could keep it."

After a moment, Therese gave a sharp nod. "My 'usband always said that a hidden dagger can be very useful. But, in my house, you will never use it or show it to my guests."

She reached a hand to Annie's cheek, a soft, cool hand. "You are a good, brave girl, as James has said, and I shall help you, *chérie*."

"How can you, when no one can?"

"*Non*? Well, we shall see. Do you love this idiot James?"

"James is not an idiot! And I don't know about love, but I want to marry him."

"Why?"

"I want to be with him, and I want to share his bed."

"But that is love, *certainement*!"

"Did"—the sparkling gleam Annie saw in Therese's eyes made her ask—"did James tell you he's already engaged to another woman?"

"Yes. The foolish boy. We shall have to see what we can do to change all that."

"We will?" Annie felt a sudden glimmer of hope.

Therese placed her hands on her hips. "But of course! You do not plan to let him marry this other woman, do you?"

"He says he must."

"Bah! Men are crazy about their honor. But James will soon learn that he cares more for something else. What 'e really wants is for *you* to decide his future for 'im."

Hope leapt like a porpoise in Annie's mind. She had never known she could make a captain change his course. She grasped Therese by the upper arm. "Can you tell me what I need to know?" The ache in her throat made her voice come out raw.

Patricia Wynn

"I shall tell you everything and more," Therese
promised. She pried Annie's fingers loose, but
instead of releasing her, she gently pulled her
closer until Annie's head rested on her bosom. In
this curious position she began to stroke Annie's
hair, while she crooned in a soft, sympathetic
voice. "I shall do what I can for you, *petite*, but
the rest will be up to you. You understand?"

Annie wanted to push her away, but the pil-
lowing under her cheek, and the sympathy, did
something very unexpected to her. She broke
down in sobs.

"That's right, my little *chérie*. Cry as you 'ave
never cried before. It will only make you
stronger."

Annie's throat felt thick. Her eyelids burned,
and she soaked Therese's gown. "I never cry,"
she blubbered.

"Neither do I, *chérie*. Even when my Pierre
was gone and I thought I would die, I found it
'ard to cry. But it feels so very good."

What a strange way of seeing things this
woman had! But Annie was glad for the strange-
ness now. To her surprise, Therese's puzzling
advice *had* made her feel better. And, as her sobs
began to cease, she found that she did feel
stronger.

"Now"—as soon as she'd finished crying,
Therese pushed her away and clapped her
hands, all business—"your trunks are coming
up. Let us see what this James has bought."

Marie-Paul soon appeared at the door, followed by three men who hauled in Annie's

trunks. Therese threw open the first one and exclaimed in rapture, "*Mon Dieu!* You see what love can do! They are *formidable, non*?"

"Do you think they're pretty?" Annie heard her own anxiety.

"Pretty? They are *ravissantes*! And so many! How many are there?"

"James said twenty-five. Is that enough?"

Therese's musical laugh was like a flock of birds singing. "Enough! Marie-Paul, do you hear? Is that enough? It's enough to get you six 'usbands, at least."

"But I only want James!"

"Of course, *chère* Annie. I was only teasing. But where are your underclothes?"

"He didn't buy me any."

Therese turned to look at her with raised brows. "He would rather see you without, I think."

"I think so, too," Annie agreed.

Marie-Paul giggled, and Therese plopped on the bed in laughter. "We shall have fun with this one, eh, Marie-Paul?"

Annie wasn't sure why they were laughing, but she found she didn't mind. She might be enjoying herself, too, if she weren't already missing James.

"Shouldn't we check on the captain?" she asked. "He might be needing me."

"*Non, non*, Annie." Therese's words came laden with caution. "You must never be eager to see James, not until he is yours. You must make 'im suffer first for what he has done to you. Now is the time to twist the knife."

"That's right." Marie-Paul suddenly spoke, nodding vigorously.

"But I don't want to hurt him!"

"*Chérie*"—Therese's voice was patient—"James 'as behaved very badly, *non*? Then he 'as decided to marry this other woman. He must be made to suffer."

"But he never stabbed me!"

Therese stared, then clapped one hand across her mouth. "*Ô là*! We shall have to be careful with this one, *n'est-ce pas*, Marie-Paul?" She shook her head. "Nevermind, *ma fille*. All will be clear very shortly. But from now on, you must obey me if you want to win *ce cher* James. Understood?"

Bemused and feeling helpless, Annie could only agree.

Three days later, after tradesman after tradesman had been called to the house, Annie possessed a full complement of clothes. Slippers and fans. Stockings with clocks woven onto them. Gloves to hide the sun on her hands.

Her hair was to be held back with ribbons. She had wanted to wear a fine, heavy wig like Therese's, but Therese had declared her Titian hair too *formidable* to hide. It would make her unique, Therese had said, and provide an excuse for whenever her speech was not exactly *comme il faut*, for everyone would expect a redhead to speak her mind.

They had rehearsed her walk and her curtsy. She had been made to sit and rise over and over from a chair until she had it right.

Now, she was ready to be introduced to society before James left to pursue the taking of enemy ships.

"What will James think?" Annie asked anxiously, as she stared at the woman in the mirror. "Will he think I'm pretty?"

"*Chérie*, you were already pretty. We 'ave made you *magnifique*." Therese fluffed out Annie's short curls. "You 'ave not much hair to work with. But I 'ave done my best, and my best is very good."

"Will it grow?"

"Of course. And by the time your James comes back, it will be much longer. But, *petite*" —Therese looked up and smiled—"he is already in love with you, even with short hair. A few more inches will not make a difference, *n'est-ce pas*?"

"Are you sure?"

Therese nodded secretively. "I think 'is mind will be less on your hair than on the other parts of you. And we 'ave done miracles with those."

A half-hour later, Annie descended the stairs, feeling more rigged out than a Royal British Navy ship-of-the-line.

She had been swabbed with sweet-smelling soap; her fingernails and toenails had been filed; her hair had been scrubbed and ruthlessly combed. Her underclothes now consisted of a lacy chemise, a French pair of drawers, and a basket-like rigging to make her bum look wide. A villainous instrument called "stays" kept her waist nipped in so tightly that Annie could hardly breathe, but Therese had assured her that it would do fabulous things to her breasts that would drive James wild with desire. So Annie had suffered the pain and allowed her breasts to be bolstered until they nearly popped over the top of her dress, though she was certain no one in her right mind should wear a rig this strangling.

Downstairs, Therese's guests had been gathering. As Annie neared the last step, she saw James waiting in a corner to escort her in. He seemed to have frozen at the sight of her. The hunger in his eyes as he swept his gaze from her nipped-in waist to her pushed-up breasts and up to her face both burned her with its heat and rewarded her for the pain. She felt a rush that slowly tinged the nipples of her breasts. She could feel them glowing beneath her lace, and her blood hummed. She remembered what it had felt like to climb James's body, and her knees went weak.

Just in time, she remembered the advice Therese had repeated over and over the past few days. Instead of running to meet him, Annie swayed, touching the end of her fan to her lips.

"Sir James . . ." She made him a much deeper curtsy than the one he had taught her and allowed him help her up with one hand.

"Annie . . . My God!" The oath seemed to have escaped from him. "You look absolutely . . . beautiful."

"Thank you." Therese had prepared her to

accept his compliments cavalierly. "Shall we go in?"

Her poise obviously took him aback. "Yes—of course. Annie, you won't be afraid to meet these people?"

She had to laugh. "No, James. How could I be afraid of a set of people who can hardly move in their clothes?"

He laughed. "You have a good point."

James looked down at her. He had been nervously waiting for this moment. Therese had kept Annie hidden away for days. She had refused to let him see her, saying that if a break must be made, the sooner it were made would only be better.

She had informed him of the clothes she had ordered to augment Annie's wardrobe. She had talked about petticoats and camisoles, long silk stockings, and things too unmentionable even for Therese to mention. James had found these discussions had the power to make him squirm. He knew that women wore such garments. Of course, he knew that Annie would need them, but did Therese have to remind him with every word?

It was unlikely that he himself would be the man who would see Annie in those garments. But he could picture her in them all too well. He had no trouble remembering the joys that satin and lace would hide. And being reminded of the pleasure that might fall to another man when he urged them off of her made him want to growl.

Patricia Wynn

Looking at her tonight, he was more impressed by the beauty in her face. By the radiance in her smile as she'd seen him. By the softness of her emerald eyes. His Annie had always had that little edge of coarseness to remind him that no matter how much he might desire her, she would never be for him. Now, that protective reminder was gone, and with that last barrier broken, he had never felt so vulnerable to her charms.

She walked beside him with all the grace of a duchess. Her back was so strong, it gave her a regal air. Her neck was so fine, it might have belonged to a princess. And her eyes were so brilliant, he was reminded that behind this image of female complacency lurked a brain that was every bit as sharp as a man's. It must be that keen if she had decided to make these changes and had carried them out in only a matter of days.

There was nothing at all mannish about her this evening as she placed her gloved hand on his arm and allowed him to lead her into the drawing room. Therese's parlor had been opened to the veranda in order to admit a cooling breeze. Amidst a cluster of potted palms and vases filled with passion flowers, the cream of Jamaican society had begun to collect. The air was ripe with the scent of tropical blossoms. Moisture from the sea filled James's lungs, adding to the overwhelming impression of heat. He had felt sweat beginning to gather on his

284

back since the moment Annie had appeared at the top of the stairs.

He would have taken her to introduce her to the guests he knew, but Therese came up to take that pleasure away. *"Non, mon cher* James! I will not allow you to keep Mademoiselle Bonny all to yourself. There are other gentlemen who must 'ave a chance with 'er."

James had to relinquish her, but he followed as Annie was taken first to meet four elderly couples. She had nothing to do but curtsy and say "How do you do?", while Therese supplied her history. By now, Annie had been told of the story he had made up for her, of a wealthy girl whose parents had died, leaving her a brig as dowry. James could see these people stare at her with interest. They eyed her unusual hair. The women seemed to approve of her gown. The men appreciated it even more, for they could hardly stop staring at the valley between her breasts.

A knot formed in his stomach. What a foul bunch of old geezers Therese had for friends!

A younger gentleman soon came forward to beg an introduction. Therese chastised him for being so bold, and Annie seemed to understand it was said in jest. Smiling graciously, she gave no sign of being bored or of taking offense. James wondered what sort of foolishness Therese had filled her ears with to prepare her to receive such a litany of social falderal without being bored to tears.

This younger gentleman, too, seemed to want to gape at her breasts. He did a better job of hiding his wishes than the older men, but James was not fooled for a moment. He could see the interest in the fellow's eyes and could certainly share his excitement.

Another young man came up, then another. Soon James was being elbowed out of the way, so eager were the young beaux of Kingston to meet his Annie. He felt like a fool standing his ground, but he had to make certain that nothing went wrong. He couldn't be sure that she wouldn't make a terrible mistake, and somebody had to stand by to cover it for her.

He grew very tired of the comments addressed to him, as if he were Miss Bonny's chaperon. These insufferable puppies seemed quite ready to resign him to the role of nursemaid.

One man, in particular, appeared to surprise a reaction from Annie. He was dressed as handsomely as the others, but his face had a hint of roughness that seemed to appeal to her. Therese called him Philip, and she whispered something to Annie that made her take greater notice of him.

"Miss Bonny." Philip bowed over her hand, moving so close to her, she must have felt the air from his breath on her face.

James stiffened as it seemed to him that Annie drew in a small gasp. She didn't seem offended by the young man's closeness at all.

"You seem to be a mystery, Miss Bonny," the Philip creature said.

"Me?" Annie looked flustered as the man leaned over her, letting his eyes wander from her face to the milky white tops of her breasts. His last exhalation had been so close to them it had ruffled her lace. James didn't care for the direction of his talk *or* his eyes. If the fellow weren't careful, he would find those eyes on the floor.

"Yes, you're a complete and utter mystery. I have yet to learn from anyone where you've been living."

To James, Annie's flustered look seemed very much like arousal. She had gazed at him remarkably like that the first time he had touched her between her legs. He could almost feel the pulse racing in her throat.

Her lips seemed to part of their own free will, and she glanced up to meet Philip's eyes. James could feel the challenge issued between them.

He had to put a stop to this. This behavior was most unseemly. If somebody didn't do something to stop this fellow's tongue, he might say something to provoke Annie to violence or worse.

As if he sensed the effect he was having, Philip moved his lips closer to her ear.

James strained to hear him over the laughing voices in the room.

"Miss Bonny?" He bent ever closer. "Won't you tell me where you've been all my life?"

James saw a flash of annoyance in Annie's eyes before she snapped, "I've been sailing on a pirate brig."

Philip recoiled, and James closed his eyes.

Patricia Wynn

His one anxiety had been switched for another. Why hadn't Therese taught her anything except how to show her breasts? For one dreadful moment, he thought she'd destroyed everything he'd worked for.

But when he opened his eyes, Philip merely looked bemused, then intrigued. He gave a laugh of pure delight. "So you've been raised as a buccaneer, have you? And what do you plunder? Gentlemen's hearts?"

With that flirting question, he stared at her so admiringly Annie had no reason to deny it.

Like a practiced courtesan, she rapped his wrist with her fan and said, "What do you think?" Then she brought the fan to her lips and dragged it across those plump little rosebuds until every man in the room must have wanted a taste.

James knew he did. He told himself he should be relieved that Annie's blunder had not cost them, that he should be proud she had managed to cover her own mistakes. But as Therese's young guests pressed around her until there was no place for him, he could only hover like an outcast dog, hoping to be thrown a bone.

The man called Philip stayed glued to her side. As word of her response rapidly spread about the room, every foolish young puppy in Kingston came to sniff. Unraveling her past became a parlor game, with each young cur weaving a myth.

To James's chagrin—and that of many of Kingston's young ladies—the myths were all

Capturing Annie

quite flattering. They declared that Annie must have been a captured mermaid or a nymph from the sea. Laughing, Annie seemed to enjoy their foolishness, even the attention of a bunch of gullible men. She alternately pouted and smiled at them like a seasoned flirt.

Damn Therese! She wasn't supposed to turn Annie into a simpering miss!

The idiocy of these men made James want to scoff. Couldn't they see she was leading them on? They didn't have an inkling of the truth, and they wouldn't know how to act if they did. Their parents should be ashamed to have raised a pack of sons no better than mongrels, circling and sniffing around a female in heat—and with her guardian standing right there watching! Not a one of them was worthy to wipe Annie's shoes. Not a one of them, thank God, had captured her real attention.

Except, maybe the one. The one who had stood by her all evening. Philip, who had had the infernal gall to take her in to supper, too, and to place his chair so close it was a wonder he managed to eat with his nose halfway down inside her gown. James couldn't blame him for being drawn to her. With her copper hair, those sea-green eyes, and her marble-white skin, Annie was as lovely as a flower and as alluring as a goddess. He could hardly take his eyes off her himself.

But he could blame the young bastard for declaring his lust so openly. He was a bit older than the others, too, which James did not like.

"Who's that fellow drooling over Annie?" he asked Therese later that evening.

She laughed. "They are *all* enchanted. I shall 'ave no trouble at all to find 'er a 'usband. Just look at them panting, James!"

He ignored her answer. "I can see them all very well. They're a pack of slobbering fools. But that older man—I don't like him. Who is he?"

Therese peered casually in Annie's direction. When she saw whom he meant, she let out a gasp. "*Mon cher* James! You do not know who that is?"

Satisfied by the shock in her tone, James thought it time to put an end to Annie's tête-à-tête. "No, but I thought he looked rotten. I'll tell him to keep away."

"*Mais, mon ami, non, non, non!*" Laughing delightedly, Therese pulled him back to her side. "That one is not at all dangerous! Except, perhaps, to young ladies' 'earts. That is Philip d'Armont, the richest young planter on the island. Do you see how our Annie has captivated 'im? I 'ave never seen 'im so entranced."

As James silently clenched his fists, Therese went on, "It would be good if Annie were to catch 'im, *non*? She seems to like 'im well enough. He is so rugged, *non*? And so 'andsome."

As James watched, Annie gave the young man a playful look that would have made any man go hard. He should know, because his own treacherous member was about to embarrass him in front of the company. She appeared to be enjoying herself. She even seemed to be attracted to the man he couldn't abide. James could almost swear she was encouraging Philip to move closer.

D'Armont was polished. He was dressed in the height of fashion, and his manners were impeccable. If Annie's laugh were anything to go by, he was also a wit. James felt like a coarse old sea dog, an ill-bred bull too gauche to stay in the room.

Well, if that was the kind of man Annie wanted, she could have him—and with her captain's blessing!

Abruptly, he quitted the room, leaving Therese standing alone. He had to get outside.

Chapter Fifteen

In the warm, heavy air, he strode through the garden and out onto the beach until the voices behind him were too far away to be heard.

He could barely breathe, but he would have to control his temper. He had brought Annie here to learn how to be a woman and to meet a future mate. She needed to find someone who would stay beside her. He had no right or cause to be angry if she did.

It had simply been a shock to see how easily she had drawn every man in the room, and how naturally flirting had come to her. And, on top of all, to see that she enjoyed other men, perhaps, even more than she had enjoyed him.

It had been a shock to see her in that revealing gown, dressed so beautifully for the soiree. Even though he had seen her much more revealed and had reveled in her body, he hadn't expected the mere sight of her to stop his heart.

No wonder all the young bucks had made fools of themselves, surrounding her like a swarm of bees. Any fool could tell what sort of honey he would find in her little hive.

James alone, of all the men she had sailed with, had tasted of that honey. He could almost taste her now, so strong was his need. But he couldn't go back on his word to himself. He had been selfish once. Now he must let Annie decide.

If only her fancy hadn't lit on the worst in the bunch, he could have borne it better. But she *would* have to choose the most virile man in the room, the kind that could eat twenty virgins for breakfast. Why couldn't it have been one of those damned little puppies?

Annie *had* been enjoying herself until she'd tired of James hovering around her like a shark too stubborn to feed. She hadn't understood why he'd stopped speaking, or why he'd slowly begun to act sullen. Therese had told her that he was sure to grow jealous when he saw her being admired by other men and that jealousy would make him change his mind.

She had done her best not to regard him. With so many admirers staring at her figure and her face with undisguised attraction, she had found it impossible to feel despondent. These silly boys acted as if she were a cherished prize in a race, with every one of them tripping over his feet to win. With Philip d'Armont standing close enough that his warmth spread through her body and the surreptitious glances from a host of males causing a tingling in her breasts, she'd felt a quickening almost like the feeling she'd had with James. She *had* enjoyed herself.

But as the evening had worn on, she'd begun to find them all a little bit silly. Not one of these men, not even Philip, would be able to hold his own against a crew. Not a man among them had the natural authority to be a captain. Not one of them was James.

She wondered why there could only be one man to make her happy. Why she should only want one man in her bed.

She had seen him pulling away, and only the knowledge that he'd kept his eyes on her all evening had reconciled her to Therese's advice. She could feel that he wanted her, even across the room. And she realized finally that the tingling in her breasts and the drumbeat of her heart were in response, not to these boys surrounding her, but to James.

She'd seen him standing with Therese, his brow growing darker and darker. The suddenness with which he'd left had made her falter in her speech. Dismayed, she started to excuse herself, until from across the floor, she spied a hint of Therese's delight. Grinning like a cat with a canary between its paws, Therese gave her a smug, gloating wink.

James left the next day. He made a polite farewell to Annie and Therese, but his goodbyes were strained. Annie tried not to show how much his leaving hurt her or how much she wanted him to take her in his arms. Instead, she followed Therese's tough advice. She smiled and professed her eagerness to taste the pleasures of Kingston society.

His eyes seemed to cloud as she spoke, but he told her he was certain she would enjoy her stay. Her voice seemed strangely disconnected from her lips, as she thanked him for bringing her. With Therese firmly grasping her arm, Annie recited her well-rehearsed lines; but all the while, visions of climbing James again raked at her nerves. She hungered for him. Her gaze lingered on his face and his body. If her eyes had been her fingers, she would have combed him from head to toe.

He left, and it was all Therese could do to keep her from calling after him. When she had got control of herself, she stared out the window at the drive where she had last seen him. Therese stayed with her, sympathetic but silent.

It took all Annie's courage to ask this one question. "What if he doesn't change his mind?"

"He will, *ma fille*. I am certain he will."

"But what if he doesn't?"

Therese gave a heavy sigh. "In that case, you will do what every lady must do when her heart has been broken. You will take your misery and you will keep it to yourself."

Time moved very slowly for James, despite the fact that his ships took part in many brisk engagements. As usual, luck seemed always to be on his side. With three more prizes delivered to His Majesty King George, James's coffers stayed full, and his men could rejoice.

But not James.

Not one of his victories brought him any pleasure. Taking enemy ships seemed to have lost its thrill. James worked through the motions of war without ever once losing sight of the interminable weeks that lay ahead.

He missed Annie. He wanted her. Not only in his bed, but in his every day. The fact that he missed her only confirmed what he had always feared—that he'd become attached. Too attached. He had done what he'd sworn he'd never do—he'd formed an entanglement. What he hadn't known was just how miserably sick her absence would make him feel. He had lost all the joy in his life, the pride in his ships and in his accomplishments. He had worried that a wife who cared for him might languish and pine. What he hadn't expected was being the one to suffer.

As the months wore on, he began to dread his return to Jamaica. The probability that he would return to find Annie betrothed to Philip d'Armont ate at his gut until it was raw. James knew that d'Armont was not good enough for her, but he could not imagine Annie choosing one of those weaker men. Unfortunately, he could picture Annie and d'Armont all too well. And the thought of them laughing together, stealing moments alone, was enough to make him snap.

His own wedding loomed like a prison sentence. He had lost all ambition to marry an earl's daughter. But he would marry Olivia and try to be a decent husband. The time had passed when a note from Therese might have spared him that fate.

His one transgression might have left Annie with child, and he had asked Therese to write to him if Annie increased. If she had become pregnant, a decision would have been so easy. She would have had to marry him, even if her love had fallen on someone else.

Selfishly, James had almost prayed for that letter. He'd asked for his mail in every port, but no word had come. And by the end of five months, he had been forced to conclude that their moment of passion had not forced her to become his.

He tried to tell himself it was all for the best. She would never be lonely as his mother had been. Until now, however, James had not fully realized how lonely his own life was. He had believed himself content. Now, he saw how much he lived apart from any human. A ship's captain had no friends.

Everyone under his command regarded him from a distance, with resentment mixed with awe. His decisions ruled their lives. If he ever forgot his authority and allowed himself to relax, he would lose his men's respect, with potentially disastrous results. That was why they

Patricia Wynn

kept up their guard around him and he kept his with them. No one should ever breach that wall, and no one ever had.

No one except Annie.

She had fearlessly battered it down in the short space of one day. Over time, perhaps, he could construct it again. But his life would never be the same. How could he forget the moments of joy he'd experienced? How could he forget what might have been his?

He would have to forget her. He would have to go on with his life as he'd planned, knowing that Annie had found true happiness in someone else's arms.

Ten months passed before James returned to Jamaica. He could no longer postpone the voyage. At the end of eight weeks he must be back in London for his own wedding. It was time to see Annie settled before then.

He docked his ship near the end of the day. After tending to his business, he dressed for an evening call and hired a vehicle to take him to Therese's. Not surprisingly, he discovered that the house was filled with guests. He hadn't written ahead, afraid of meeting Annie alone when he would have had a harder time concealing his emotions.

Therese's steward welcomed him into the house and directed him to the drawing room door behind which a loud murmur of voices announced a large company. In the doorway James paused to scan the figures. Amidst glittering silks and satins, his eyes went instantly to the only shock of red hair.

As his pulse fluttered into a roar, he noted the grace of Annie's figure, the measured lilt of her laughter, and the pleasure dancing in her eyes. He also saw the two men with whom she talked. One was d'Armont.

He stood possessively beside her. From time to time he touched her elbow as if he had the right. James's heart felt a stab that seemed to puncture his chest.

Then Annie saw him and, like a miracle, her eyes grew brighter, just for him. She gave a gasp—was it only from surprise? She started forward, then as if remembering her manners, she curtsied to her two companions. James could see the words of excuse forming on her lips before she calmly walked his way.

He feared he would lose the ability to speak. Her face was a vision. Her eyes, a pair of sparkling gems. Her hair was longer now, and it cascaded from the top of her head in a shining blaze of fire. And for a moment, her dazzling smile was only for him.

He took her bare hands to kiss. Stunned by their smoothness, he realized once and for all how much his Annie had changed. If he had not known better, he would have thought her an aristocrat. She had beauty, grace, and style. She walked like an enchantress, and she held herself like a queen. Where was his gamine?

James knew his face had fallen. He had made a terrible, disastrous mistake. After all his work and worry, he wanted her back the way she had been, even though her alluring airs were enough to make his loins tighten with desire. Before, with her little brown hands, she had been all his. Now, with her newfound grace, he could not doubt she'd been stolen by another.

"James . . ." She nearly breathed his name, and the softness of her voice came as another blow. What man would not want his name to come from those honeyed lips? They curved in the most delicious smile, their skin no longer chapped. Their smoothness made his very tongue go dry.

"Annie." Clearing his throat, he greeted her with all the courage he had. "I might not have known you, if not for your hair."

He thought a cloud passed over her face.

"Am I so easily forgotten?" She gave a playful pout that dispelled this illusion.

For the life of him, he could not respond as blithely as she could. "No." His throat felt raw. "I haven't forgotten you."

An upward glance from beneath her long, pale lashes told him she hadn't forgotten him, either. Their knowledge of each other seemed to suffuse the air between them. But how would Annie judge the touching they'd shared, knowing now how wrong it had been? Her lips parted as she stared into his eyes. James felt his groin inflame as visions of her naked in his hands came back to taunt him.

Just then, d'Armont appeared at her side. He took possession of her elbow. "Captain—"

Annie started. As James tore his gaze from her beloved face, d'Armont continued. "What a pleasure it is to see you, sir. You've been away much longer than Miss Bonny expected, and I, for one, have been eager to hear you were back."

James was not surprised when d'Armont asked to call upon him in the morning.

He was saved from a response by Therese's loud greeting. She appeared at his elbow, seeming just to have heard of his arrival.

"Mon cher James!" she exclaimed, before saucily presenting one cheek to be kissed.

James noted Annie's indulgent smile. He remembered the reaction she had made before to Therese's boldness. Now she didn't seem to care.

How much his Annie had changed.

Then, he had discouraged her resentment. Now, he would have welcomed any sign that she wanted him. But Annie seemed not to mind at all that he had kissed Therese.

James never knew how he survived the terrible evening. He was forced to speak of his voyages to all the guests. Their natural curiosity about the Spanish in the Caribbean kept him away from Annie's side, while d'Armont clung to her as if he couldn't wait for their wedding night. With James's emotions in turmoil, he couldn't sense Annie's feelings for the man. Her manners were too polished to give anything away. But he had to fear that d'Armont's constant hovering could only mean one thing.

Only once was James given a chance to speak to Annie, and that was when d'Armont called him over to settle a wager that apparently only Annie could solve. Yet, he said, she had refused to do it until her guardian's return. As a different man blurted out the question that had kept the young beaux of Kingston enthralled, James felt Annie's grave eyes upon his face.

"We have each asked her—in our different ways—where she came by that glorious copper hair. But all Miss Bonny is willing to say is that she must have been born with it. What do you say, sir? Was she touched by Neptune's golden trident, as I proposed?"

The question gave James a jolt. Clearly these fools expected him to invent one of the elaborate myths they had spun about her. But their thoughtless banter would be sure to make Annie question her parentage, now that she had been in society long enough to understand the importance of family.

James didn't know whether he ought to avoid her eyes. He had made a promise to Mr. Bonny to keep Sharkee's secret.

But Annie's voice cut across his hesitation. "It is all right, Captain. You may answer these gentlemen. I have kept the secret long enough."

Her voice teased him, but when he looked into her eyes expecting to find the ignorance there that her tone had implied, she fixed him with an unwavering stare, and he knew that she knew.

"If you do not tell them, I might as well. I

never knew my mother, but my father had a full red beard. Did he not?"

"Yes." James was waiting to see how Annie would receive the tidings, but nothing in her countenance gave her feelings away. "Your mother died in childbirth. Mr. Bonny told me himself. And, though I never saw her, I believe your red hair could only have come from your father."

He wasn't sure what he had expected to see, but surely not the rapid brimming of tears in her eyes or her tremulous smile. "My father was a very brave man, you know. He died trying to protect me. It was during a pirate attack."

"Yes." James cleared his throat. "I believe he did."

Annie broke their extended gaze to turn her smile on the other men, as if nothing momentous had occurred. "There you have it, gentlemen. The unvarnished story of my red hair."

James was so astounded, he barely heard the others' reactions to a tale which must have sounded flat to their ears. He had been stunned by the wisdom with which Annie had accepted the shocking fact of her parentage, for she had understood that he had been speaking of Sharkee. She had learned it. She must already have guessed it. And, like a woman wise beyond her years, she had accepted it as a beautiful thing. She had taken her father's measure and kept the good in him, while forgiving the bad. Even admiring her as he did, James had not expected such a maturity of heart.

He had known she could be loyal. What he hadn't known was that she had such a generous ability to love.

And how he envied the man who would have that love.

Before the evening was over, Philip approached him again about an interview on the morrow. James could do nothing but acquiesce. Then Therese insisted that he stay in her house to give them time to settle Annie's affairs.

Although he hardly knew what to say, James had hoped for a word with Annie before she retired. But their guests had no sooner left than Therese came to show him to his room. On the stairs, she chatted about Annie's conquests, her rapid progress and her clever ways, while Annie laughed them all off. With each sentence, Therese hammered the stake in James's heart until her yawns drove them all to bed.

They parted in the upstairs hall with Therese gazing on. James stumbled clumsily through a conventional goodnight. He expected Annie to give him nothing more than a similar response, but instead, she drew near and like an old and dear friend, holding on to his arms for support, she raised on tiptoes to be kissed. Her clear green eyes met his for only a moment, before her warm, tender lips brushed his cheek.

"Goodnight, dear James," she whispered. "I am so happy you are here."

James had barely recovered from the shock of her touch, the scent of her hair, before she was gone. He heard the click of her door. Its quiet closure boomed like a cannon in his head.

Alone in his room, he paced with a desperate longing. He had made a terrible mistake. How could he make Annie his again? Through his own stupidity he had lost her. He ought to have secured her to himself when he'd had the chance. If only he hadn't let his sense of duty sway him, she would have been his many months ago—not legally, but he was past caring how he got her now. Before she'd been tutored by society, Annie might have consented to be his mistress. Now she knew that she could get something better.

She deserved better, of course. With her grace and charm, she was worthy to be any man's wife. She deserved a notable position. And to all appearances, she had found one.

But he had to win her back. It no longer mattered to him that he was engaged. He only knew he couldn't live another day without Annie.

Late that night as he stood beside the window, brooding over his chances to win her again, he noticed a slim figure moving swiftly through the garden. Cloaked and furtive, the person might have been a burglar, but a flash of copper in the flickering light from the house revealed that the person who was escaping through the shrubbery could only be Annie. He would have called to her from his window, but she rapidly vanished down the beach.

He tore down the stairs and let himself out

through a casement window. The sugary aroma of flowers almost overwhelmed him before he left the garden wall. Then, on the beach, a damp tropical breeze brought the welcome scent of the sea.

Afraid that Annie might have left to meet d'Armont, James first moved with caution. But he soon discovered there was no need. The glow from the moon revealed a beach that was completely deserted for miles in either direction.

He searched it up and down, but all he saw was a shadow away to his right, no more than an irregular dark patch upon the sand. He set off at a jog. The warm air ruffled his hair. His boots thudded hard into the wet sand. Waves crashed to his left and roared into a mist.

He had not thought himself so far behind her. Starlight bathed the empty beach, mocking his search.

Arriving at the shadowy patch, he discovered a cloak and raised it. A suit of boy's clothes lay underneath.

"Annie!" he called out to sea, fear eating into his heart.

He pulled off his boots, and calling again, ran into the waves, leaping over low breakers and dragging his body through high ones. The sea lapped at his loins, and the night air chilled them.

"Annie, come back!" Water flew into his eyes, and the salt clogged his throat.

"James!"

At the sound of her voice, he turned and saw her, rising naked from the waves.

Relief flooded through him, even as the months of yearning burgeoned like a tidal wave at the sight of her.

Here was the woman he had missed, the mermaid who had come to be his joy. Water ran in rivulets from her hair, falling to her shoulders and streaming down her breasts. Waves lapped at the ruddy thatch between her legs, reshaping its strands into dark, mysterious ripples.

"Annie . . ." James whispered her name and felt her lure stealing over him like a warm summer tide. "I couldn't find you."

She walked toward him, the force of the undertow barely nudging her steps. His manhood hardened as she moved within reach.

She *was* his Aphrodite, then, risen from the sea.

His heart pounded in his throat. His knees trembled beneath the pounding of the waves. His fingers itched to brush the rosy peaks crowning her breasts. But above all, he wanted to touch her face.

"I was swimming," Annie said, pausing before him. Her voice came over the sound of the surf like a sigh from heaven. His awareness of her nipples teased his chest. Water lapped between his thighs.

James felt the pull of the tide pulling him closer to her as if Annie were the earth and he were the moon. "You frightened me. I thought you were gone."

"Would that frighten you, James?" Her face lay in his shadow.

"No. It would kill me."

As he reached for her, Annie whimpered and she leapt into his embrace. She flung her arms about his neck and encircled his waist with her legs. He caught her beneath the thighs to raise her as he sought to meet her lips.

Salt lips. Smoother than before, but still tasting of the sea they both adored. James thought his own tears might be coating them, mingled with hers.

"Annie, I love you," he breathed between kisses, unable to keep himself from saying it any longer. How he'd yearned to tell her those words, no matter how much they would cost them both.

Waves smashed into his back. The tide rolled in and pulled them out to sea. Warm, thick water swirled about them, coating Annie's smooth body with a wetness that made her slippery in his hands.

James felt for the spot between her legs. She grasped him harder, moaning into his ear. The sound sent a pulse to his groin. He pushed to meet her.

Annie began a rhythm, torturing him with her sweetness, her skin like silk beneath his hands.

Then she bit his neck. He responded to her wildness by grabbing her hair and pulling it back to nibble the skin of her throat. Her nipples glistened like crystals in the starlight. James took one of them between his teeth and felt her shivering against his thighs.

His clothes weighed him down like an anchor.

The surf made him stumble. He fell upon his back, taking Annie with him. Together, they worked to free him from his clothes. James struggled to loose his aching shaft from its flap. Waves washed them shoreward, and sand scraped his back.

"Annie, take me in you, love, before I burst."

But he hadn't needed to ask. Already her hand had found him to guide him where he belonged.

"James, I missed you so." Her voice rose with the current, words pulsing with the beat of the surf.

"Do you love me, Annie?" Her ecstatic moans filled his heart. He grasped her hair, and cried between gasps, "Tell me who you want."

"I want you, James. I love you." Annie felt his mighty thrust as he lodged himself inside her, gripping her thighs against his hips.

He was warm, and inside and around her. She coated him with her sweetness and stroked him with her grip.

"Annie, I've missed you so—"

A wave broke over their heads, tumbling them over on their sides. Like two otters, then, born in the surf, they rolled with every crest. Salt stung Annie's eyes, water clogged her nose, but she would not let go of James. She had won him, and he was hers.

When they both had reached completion, James staggered to his feet and carried her up onto the beach. Their gazes found each other in the moon's beams. Shadows darkened his eyes.

He laid himself beside her, throwing one arm

across her chest to hold her near. He kissed her eyes, and her cheeks then dragged his tongue across her lips. After one deep and final kiss, he pulled back a space so he could gaze at her hair as it spread in the tiny wavelets rippling in.

Still in a daze of desire, Annie saw the moon playing over his features. She traced them with her fingertips.

His beloved brow was so strong and dark, like the prow of a fighting ship. His lashes had clumped together as if with tears. His nose, lean and bronzed by the ever-beating sun. Lips curved with tenderness.

"I love you, Annie. I tried not to, but I can't fight it anymore. It drove me mad to think of you with d'Armont. Please tell me you don't love him."

"I don't. I tried to because I thought you wanted me to, but he isn't you."

"Thank God."

For the first of many times she'd heard him say those words, he seemed to mean them as a prayer.

"What about your fiancée?"

James closed his eyes in a drawn-out wince. He rolled over onto his back and stared up at the stars.

Annie turned so she could curl into his side.

James put one arm about her and pulled her up on his chest. "Annie, I have to go to England. I'm bound by a contract to provide for Lady Olivia and her father, Lord Figg. Until I can free myself from that agreement, I can't marry you."

He paused, and she felt the thump of his heart. "Marriages are often made between two people who have no love for each other. They are nothing but business. I want to find a way that you and I can be together. I *will* find a way. But I don't know, yet, what that will be. Will you trust me?"

Therese had said James must not make love to her again until he married her, but Annie had found it hard to accept that wisdom. She loved James. They had slept together once, and he made her happy. The only thing that mattered to her now was that James loved her, too. She had wanted him so much at the soiree this evening, she had hardly been able to conceal it. The moonlight swim had been meant to comfort her as it had every night they'd been apart.

Now, here he was, and he wanted to be with her, just as she did with him. Therese had spoken about the power of love.

She wouldn't have to pretend any more.

"I'll come with you, James," she whispered to him as his arms closed tightly about her again.

Chapter Sixteen

Armed with Annie's love, James dispensed with all her suitors, informing them with a forced show of regret that Miss Bonny had already formed an attachment. Philip d'Armont took the information hard.

James tried not to gloat. He knew it was his fault for encouraging Annie to find a suitor, and a nagging guilt made him eager to leave Jamaica as soon as his ship could sail.

This time, when Annie boarded the *Flying Swan*, she would be dressed in her skirts and accompanied by a maid. Therese had insisted that she must be chaperoned, and James had agreed. As much as he wanted Annie, he must spare her the insults of a shipload of men. He didn't know if he could win his release from

Lady Olivia, but he meant to try with every gun in his arsenal. And if he won his release, he wanted Annie to be free of any hint of scandal so society would accept her as his wife.

What he would do if Lord Figg refused to agree, James didn't know. He knew that time and money would both be needed. After his one meeting with Lord Figg, he knew enough to suspect that the earl would use the opportunity he offered to enrich himself. It would hurt to see his hard-won gains handed over to such a wastrel, but he would pay any price to have Annie. He only hoped Lord Figg could be persuaded to be reasonable.

In the meantime, James had decided not to discuss his plans with Annie, until he was certain he could make her his pledge. Nor would he consider any other option for their living together. The thought of Annie alone in a port waiting for him to return from his voyages still ate at his heart, but he could not give her up to anyone else. If that was the only way he could have her, that was how it would be. He prayed daily that she could become his wife, not banned from society as his mistress, that he could set her up in style and not in secrecy. Her future, and his, would depend on Lord Figg.

As James handed her aboard the *Flying Swan*, Annie's thoughts were occupied by her meeting with the crew.

She had said goodbye to Therese and Marie-Paul at the pier, screening tears with a flurry of embraces and promises to write. It was hard to believe how close she had come to them both, in many ways closer than to Mr. Bonny or even to James. She had learned that women had a strength of their own that had nothing to do with battles or knives. She had found a reason to be proud of her sex.

She carried a remembrance of these women in Marie-Paul's niece, Sophie, who was coming along as her maid.

Mr. Shirley helped Annie over the rail, before doffing his hat and bowing. Shyly, he stared at his feet. Annie suppressed a smile, wondering what he would say if he knew who she was.

The thought must have passed through James's mind, too, for his poise seemed to falter.

"Annie—er, Anne—this is my first mate, Mr. Shirley. He will see that you are comfortable during the voyage. Mr. Shirley, this is my ward who will be sailing with us to England, Miss— Miss Bonny."

When he had given her that name, Annie realized, James had not thought of the association his men would make.

But, to her surprise, Mr. Shirley did not appear to make it. At the name Bonny, a question seemed to wrinkle his sunburned features. He darted her a glance, but a shyness with females kept him from examining her long enough to see who she was.

"Pleased to have ye aboard, miss," he said, fiddling with his hat and looking as if he'd rather

314

be anywhere but here. "Whatever ye need, just let me know and I'll get it for ye."

Clearly anxious to have this unwelcome duty over, he asked the captain, "Shall I show her to her quarters, sir?"

Annie had the distinct feeling he couldn't wait to stow her away.

"That would be excellent, Mr. Shirley." James sounded relieved.

You're mighty anxious to be rid of me, the both of you, Annie thought. Piqued by their attitudes, she decided not to make things too pleasant for either one.

"I shall be happy to seek my cabin, Captain Avery. If Mr. Shirley will offer me his arm?"

The first mate's jaw fell open. As he swallowed, like a pirate forced to walk the plank, Annie reached for his elbow and leaned on him as if only his strong shoulder could hold her up on the rocking deck. He stiffened his back like a ramrod, for all the world as if it were a flogging he faced.

James frowned a warning over Mr. Shirley's head, begging her not to reveal herself. This made Annie smile more brightly.

"We won't be disturbing you, Captain," she purred. "I'm sure that Mr. Shirley can make me as comfortable as I've ever been on land. Now you run along now and do whatever it is that captains do."

James pinched his lips together, but a gleam of reluctant humor lit his eyes at the sight of his first mate's expression.

"Don't dawdle now, Mr. Shirley. We've got work to do."

"I won't," Shirley answered in a strangled voice. "No more 'an I have to, Cap'n."

Taking pity on him, Annie relieved him of part of her weight and allowed him to conduct her to the quarterdeck cabins. She plied him with questions—what piece of sail was this, what bit of tackle that—even though she knew every piece by heart. Mr. Shirley responded with a series of mumbles and grunts.

When they reached the cabins, Annie saw that hers was to be the one Mr. Bonny and Mr. Shirley had occupied. It had been enlarged, which meant that someone, perhaps even James himself, had been stinted.

As she noted this, memories of this room flooded through her, and she released Mr. Shirley's arm.

"Are ye all right, miss?"

"Yes"—she quickly recovered—"it is only that this cabin is much grander than I had expected."

"Aye, it is." He glanced about the cramped space as if it were a palace. "But the cap'n said as how he wanted ye to be comfortable. You and yer maid."

She fell silent, still overcome by the changes in her life. Mr. Bonny gone. She, a lady now—or what passed for a lady. James, her lover.

Mr. Shirley volunteered, "We had a chap on board once, a doctor, name o' Bonny. I don't suppose ye knew 'im?"

"Yes, I knew him very well."

Capturing Annie

Annie raised her face to trap his nervous gaze. Mr. Shirley stared back, frowning intently, as if to solve a problem that had begun to annoy him.

She sent him a wink.

He started, then colored and stammered, "That—would account for it, then." He fumbled backwards for the door.

"Account for what?" she demanded.

"For the feelin' that ye remind me of someone. That's all, miss, I swear it." A superstitious look had descended on his features. It was the fright of a man who's just been winked at by the captain's ward.

Stupid man! Annie felt the itch of her old restlessness. It rankled that no one seemed to recognize Jem. Could she be that changed? Excusing Mr. Shirley, she asked him to tell Sophie where she could be found and watched him back himself out.

Alone in the cabin, she realized how different this voyage would be. She wouldn't be allowed to work. In many ways, she would suffer the boredom she had lived with on shore. She'd be a burden to the crew. Annie chafed at the humiliation her new life had brought her. Why were women made to feel so worthless when she was proof they were capable of anything? Yet, even James wanted her to act the part of a helpless female.

He had not told her his plans. All he had done was insist she have a maid to keep them from being alone. For the first time, Annie began to question the wisdom of going with him to Eng-

317

land. He had not promised to break with his English fiancée. What if he didn't?

How, then, could she be with James? He had said she could not live on board, so where would that leave her? She would have given up her life at sea just to be an ornament for another woman's husband. And this barrier between them, the barrier of respectability, felt inexplicably wrong.

As James guided his ship through the treacherous waters of the Caribbean, making for the Atlantic, he found it hard to keep his mind on his job. The days were sun-filled and golden, the nights cool and breezy. Even his cabin, enclosed as it was, felt the freshness of the air.

Having Annie on board was like fitting a final piece into a puzzle. Just being with her brought him a special kind of peace. The sight of her red curls dancing in the wind alongside his sails, the sound of her laughter mixed with the murmurs of his crew, the rhythm of her walk across his deck—all these made him wish this voyage would never end.

He had to remind himself constantly of the danger in these waters, to maintain the state of alertness that kept his vessels safe. No captain should relax around these pirate-filled coves. But, though Annie did nothing to demand his attention, he found it hard to keep his mind on his work when all he wanted was to spend his every moment simply watching her.

Over dinner, he discovered the pleasure of discussing his life with her: his worry that a ship was overdue in Jamaica; questions about the merits of one route over another; concern about a sailor who'd managed to sneak a cache of rum aboard.

There was nothing he could not tell her. He had no need to fear that he might shock her, for Annie had seen more in her short life than he could ever throw her way. And, now that the partition between them had been breached, now that the very essence of each had been absorbed by the other, there was nothing left to keep their minds and their souls apart.

The only thing he had to conceal was his pressing need to make love to her again.

When she left the meal, escorted to her cabin by her childish maid, he longed to call her back. He wanted to announce to his crew that he and Annie would be married. They would sail together as mates across the seven seas, sharing adventure and laughter, and in the evening making ravenous love.

He would feel again the milky smoothness of her thighs wrapped about him, the pressure of her bosom against his. He would stagger under her weight as she rode him to exhaustion. Then they would sleep, hands and hearts entwined.

But this was fantasy. Even if Lord Figg released him from his contract and James was able to marry Annie, he would still have to leave her ashore or give up his life at sea. His business was war. Even if he resigned his letter of marque his ships would constantly be in danger from

French and Spanish privateers, their navies, and the pirates that roamed the coast. He could not raise a family on a ship. No matter how his affairs became resolved, he would have to live the greater part of his life away from Annie.

The *Flying Swan* passed between Hispaniola and Cuba and headed out into the Atlantic. The most hazardous part of the journey would soon be behind them. The only danger remaining besides the whims of wind and rain was the threat to James's equilibrium. He wondered how he would survive the repeated torture of bidding Annie goodnight when every time he would want to take her in his arms.

Unable to sleep, he strode the deck. The ship was sailing listlessly; the wind had diminished just a few hours ago. Hispaniola seemed only a speck behind them. James had made his nightly round of the deck, but he repeated it. The Spanish had recently stepped up their attacks on English ships, confident in the superiority of their own vessels.

The *Flying Swan* sailed with a load of sugar, a prize for any taker. More importantly, she carried Annie, and the need to protect her heightened all his concerns.

He called up to the lookout to ask if all was well.

"Aye, sir. No sails in sight."

A sharp wind would be welcome, but it was calm this time of year. The slow progress of his ship made it more vulnerable.

"I'm coming up." James climbed the ratlines to the masthead, then clambered over the edge, ignoring the lubber's hole like the experienced sailor he was. He borrowed the lookout's spyglass. With a faint breeze tickling the hair on his head, he scanned the horizon for any sign of a sail. A low bank of clouds obscured his vision. The sea appeared calm, and this corner of it, deserted, at least.

As he let the glass fall from his eye, he thought he saw a fleck of white, low at a distance. Raising the scope again, he trained it on the spot, but whatever he'd seen was gone.

"Who will be relieving you?" James asked the lookout, returning his glass.

"That would be Nichols, sir."

Nichols was the sailor who had smuggled the rum aboard. He had been given the prescribed number of lashes, but James suspected he had not exhausted his cache.

James frowned to himself, but said merely, "Keep your eyes south by southwest."

"Aye, aye, Cap'n."

James swung down and called his second mate to give the order for all lights to be extinguished until dawn. A dark ship would be hard to follow if that fleck of white had been a Spanish sail.

He thought of replacing Nichols, but was reluctant to disturb the watch. Nichols had been sober all day, and the men would resent him if James made someone else perform his work. There was nothing to do but to increase sail and hope the wind took them out of reach before morning.

James stayed on deck until sleep finally drove him to his berth.

Near dawn he was jerked awake by a sudden lurch.

"Captain Avery, sir!"

Bare feet hammered on the deck. A piercing cry chilled his gut. James sprang from his berth and heard Spanish curses cutting through the air.

Grabbing his sword and a pistol, James ran out to find the deck in chaos. Men stumbled up from their hammocks; the watch was nowhere in sight. Cuban sailors had swarmed over the decks, swinging their knives and cutlasses. The sloop they had sprung from hovered just off the starboard bow.

James spied his first mate racing for the quarterdeck. "Mr. Shirley! Secure the magazine!"

"Too late! Them bastards 'ave already took it!"

"Then take it back!" Without access to their weapons, the ship and all aboard her would be lost.

Anger burned in James. The lookout had failed to warn the crew. The sails were flapping, long abandoned. He took a shot at a Cuban who was trying to strike his flag.

Annie.

James had no sooner thought of her, than a boarder set upon him with a knife.

A woman's scream rent the air.

James whirled. *"Annie!"*

It was the last word he said before blackness filled his world.

Quick to grasp what was wrong, Annie had jumped out of bed at the first sound of danger. She woke Sophie and clapped her hand over the girl's opening mouth.

"Shhhh," Annie cautioned her, seeing Sophie's eyes go white. "Keep quiet as you can. We have to dress."

They threw on gowns, ignoring underclothes, and helped each other with the innumerable buttons. Annie muttered curses at her woman's garb.

Her nerves were calm, though a pulse beat loudly in her ears. She had no fear, but Sophie trembled and cringed. With no time for comfort, Annie quickly located her knife and buckled its sheath about her knee.

She had no sooner accomplished this than their door burst open. Sophie screamed. Annie would have drawn her dagger, but Sophie took one look at the man with blackened teeth charging for them and fainted dead away.

Annie caught her just as James's cry sounded from outside. She expected to see him racing through the door, but the Cuban kept coming, his eyes aglow at the sight of two defenseless women. Fear for James robbed Annie of her wits. He would have come if he hadn't been stopped.

For the first time in her life, she was helpless in a fight. Pinned by Sophie's weight, she couldn't draw her knife.

Other strange faces appeared at the door. Whistles sprang from the sailors' lips, with phrases she now understood. The Cubans clumped together in the passageway, jostling each other for a better view.

Annie squelched her fear. She had to live until she knew what had happened to James.

Remembering words she had heard aboard Sharkee's ship, she said in Spanish, "I surrender. Take me to your captain."

Ready to grab her, the first man halted. He scowled, thwarted in his intent. The others mumbled angrily behind him. She understood that they feared their captain's wrath if they did not turn her over to him.

"I claim your captain's protection," she said, recalling to them the law of the seas.

"*Sí, señorita.*" One shoved his way to the front and bowed. "*¡Ándale! ¡Váyanse!*" he yelled, shooing the others away from the door. Reluctantly, they obeyed.

Annie tried to revive her maid and was successful enough that the girl managed to walk. Annie was glad to be spared the horror Sophie would have felt if she had wakened in a sailor's arms.

James, please be all right, Annie prayed as they stepped out on the deck.

Wounded sailors littered their paths, splayed like beached starfish. Sophie buried her face in Annie's shoulder to stifle a sob. Though saddened by the loss to James's crew, Annie had seen too many similar sights to be stunned.

Anxiously, she searched every face for James.

His remaining men were being herded down into the hold. Annie whispered her thanks at seeing Mr. Shirley and others she knew among them.

Some of the Cuban sailors had climbed into the ratlines; their laughter and shouts rained down like flicks from a whip.

Containing her fear for James in a knot deep inside her, Annie followed her captors to his cabin. At the doorway, she braced herself.

The sight of her love—bloody, bound, but clearly alive—made her heart cry out for joy.

James was sitting with his chest laid bare, a pair of breeches still clinging to his hips. His face and shoulders were dabbed with blood, and a bruise had crowned his forehead. But even with both hands tied behind his back, Annie had never seen him look so handsome.

His eyes met hers and lit with a spark of thanksgiving. Then, anger clouded his gaze as he noted the man's grip on her arm.

Annie glanced toward the man seated next to James. A Cuban, impeccably dressed and unruffled by battle. His olive complexion was darkened by heavy brows and a neat, triangular beard. His black suit, trimmed at neck, cuffs, and knees with lace and gold braid, bore no sign of recent combat.

Seeing her, he rose ceremoniously to execute a bow. "Ah, *señorita*, you must forgive my men's abrupt intrusion. Captain Avery has just been inquiring for you. I am José María de Silva y Obregón, at your service."

Patricia Wynn

James's back straightened. Annie could see he was in pain, but he summoned his strength. "This is my ward, Captain de Silva, Miss Anne Bonny. I beg you will extend to her the protection due a lady."

Annie couldn't bear to hear the word "beg" on James's lips, not when he had suffered the loss of his ship. She knew that would hurt him far more than his wounds. Yet, because of her, he could not suffer those wounds with pride.

She took his cue, however, and curtsied. Advice from Therese passed rapidly through her head.

"Captain de Silva, I request the same protection for my maid. She has been frightened out of her wits."

Sophie still clung to her, her eyes wide with horror, but at least she had begun to breathe. Annie could feel the girl's trembling. The impatience she might have felt only months ago at such cowardice was stemmed by genuine concern. Sophie had not led the life she had led.

Captain de Silva obviously cared little for a servant's fear. "If you insist, *señorita*"—his smile was sneering—"although I hate to see such a waste of delicate feelings."

Annie swallowed her fury, though her eyelids burned with the need to retaliate. Instead she smiled coyly, as Therese had taught her, and curtsied low.

"You are merciful, Captain. If we had to be boarded, I am glad we have met with a true gentleman."

James sucked in a breath that she could hear across the room. She didn't know whether her answer had annoyed him, but she had her own game to play. She'd learned a thing or two aboard the *Merrye Laurie* and, now, with the subtlety she'd learned from Therese, she had a bigger bag of tricks than either man.

Captain de Silva eyed her figure with admiration. His gaze kept drifting to her breasts and uncorseted waist. Annie knew that her figure showed fuller without the stays. She only hoped he found her attractive enough to be easily distracted.

She smiled, then flicked her gaze to James. She hoped a look would be enough to reassure him. She shifted her stance, raising a wrist to her brow.

"Ooooh . . ." She drew the syllable out with a breathless croon. "I'm afraid the excitement has made me feel faint."

Captain de Silva took his cue and stepped quickly to her side. He supported her into a chair. As he stooped over her, his arm snaked about her waist and his breath felt hot against her neck.

"*Señorita*, you must compose yourself. My men will take good care of your maid."

At the threat to Sophie, Annie tensed. Still, she would be able to operate much better without the girl in her way.

"Captain," Annie begged. "I must be assured that nothing will happen to Sophie."

Irritation lit de Silva's eyes, but before he

could respond, she swayed against him, brushing her breast against his hand.

Out the corner of her eye, she saw James's sudden jerk. He started up, but the ropes held him down. Annie tried to check him with her eyes, but he glared.

"Please, Captain." She had learned how to make her voice low and seductive. "I would be more grateful than you can imagine."

Her smoldering look made him drop his jaw.

"Of course, *señorita*! How could I refuse such a charming request."

He barked to the man who had accompanied them. Annie strained to understand. She didn't know the Spanish for maid, but heard enough to be reassured. Sophie was to be locked inside their cabin.

"*Tráigame la llave.*" The captain turned back to Annie and stroked her hand, smiling confidently. "I have taken care of all, *querida*."

"Thank you so much." Annie heaved a sigh. He watched as her bosom stretched the thin silk fabric of her bodice.

James was glowering out of her reach, but she could still feel the heat of his anger reaching towards her. "Captain de Silva, I would request that my ward be confined with her maid for her own safety."

Cursing James for an idiot, Annie started to protest, but the Cuban's lips curled in a taunting grin. "I can assure you, Captain, that she will be most tenderly cared for."

"What do you plan to do?" James demanded.

De Silva looked down. Annie managed a pleading smile.

"As to you, *señor*, I very much fear that you will be executed as is custom. But your ward . . ."

Annie felt a grip of fear, but she knew she could beat any man if her timing was right. De Silva had already played into her hands. If James would only let her work her own way, she thought she could turn this ship around.

She let a feminine cry escape her lips and, falling to her knees, she held de Silva's hand against her cheek.

"Oh, Captain, please, you must have mercy on my guardian! I could not bear it if he were to be killed. He is like a *father* to me."

"For God's sake, Annie—!"

James exploded beside her, but she kept de Silva's stare trained on her face. She kissed his palm and let her voice grow husky. "I would do anything, *señor*."

De Silva's eyes began to burn with lust. "*Querida*," he murmured. "Such a charming plea would melt the Inquisitor, no? I shall have to consider your unusual request. But we have time. Nothing need be settled before tonight."

He surprised her, then, by saying, "I fear your guardian may be right. It would perhaps be better while we are securing the ship to confine you with your maid. This evening, we can discuss your request over dinner." He kissed her hand as his fingers stroked her palm.

Annie suppressed her frustration as he helped

Patricia Wynn

her to her feet. As he bowed, she revised her plans.

A whole day's wait. An interminable day to worry about James.

"Until this evening, *querida*?"

"And Captain Avery?" she asked in a throbbing voice. "Will you give me your word, *señor*, that no harm will come to him until we talk?" She raised her eyes to make promises she had no intention of keeping.

"I can give you my word that Captain Avery will be spared until we have been together." He cast a leering smile at James.

The bugger! He wasn't about to spare anyone longer than it took him to get inside her drawers.

But Annie smiled, hoping to trick him with a well-placed touch of naiveté. She couldn't do more, not with his crew swarming over the *Flying Swan*. She needed time for their number to be reduced, which it would be, once James's crew had been confined. Dinner with de Silva was beginning to sound like a better option. Spaniards ate late she knew, and it would be dark when he released her, the perfect time to free James.

"I would like to tend Captain Avery's wounds, if I might."

"No, *querida*. I shall keep him here. He must dress for his"—de Silva caught himself—"one of my men can tend to your guardian right here."

Perfect, Annie thought. *I don't want James locked away where he can't help me*. She only hoped that de Silva would keep him in one of

330

the cabins, according to the rules of the sea. In the event of capture, every captain hoped to be treated with consideration, so the conventions were usually observed.

"Then I shall see you at dinner, Captain de Silva."

The day passed very slowly for the two women locked away. De Silva had the courtesy to send Annie a tray at noon, though nothing for Sophie, so they shared. Annie did her best to comfort the girl, but judged it wiser not to reveal her plan. Sophie might be too terrorized to keep a secret.

As the bells signaled eight o'clock that evening, Annie dressed in a gown that made her bosom appear twice its natural size. Sophie styled her hair as if for a ball, and Annie placed two patches, one high on her cheek, the other near her lips to indicate her willingness to be kissed.

As her stomach began to growl in earnest, she heard a key turning in the lock. The same sailor who had returned her to her cabin motioned for her to come. Annie gave one last pat to Sophie's hand and made sure the door was securely locked behind her. Then, fearlessly, she went to meet her foe.

Chapter Seventeen

James had been sitting, trussed to the chair. He had struggled, but his strength had been sapped by the blow to his head. After what had seemed like hours, a Cuban crewman had come with two other sailors to wash away his blood. He resigned himself to their greater numbers and saved his strength for a better opportunity.

He knew that Annie had a plan up her sleeve. He had seen the mischief in her eyes, and he knew an act when he saw one. He only hoped she didn't think she could seduce de Silva to get him to change his mind. As the day wore on, his worry about this increased, so he was almost relieved when Captain de Silva appeared at his door.

"Ah, Captain Avery. *Buenas noches*. I trust you have been made more comfortable."

"I would feel better if you could dispense with these ropes."

The Cuban shook his head with mock regret. "My apologies, *señor*, but your freedom would not suit my plans."

James glared at him with hatred. "Harm my ward, and you will answer to me."

The Cuban bowed, and for one instant James was filled with hope. Then de Silva said, "She is safe with me. I treat all my women with kindness."

"She is not your woman!"

The Cuban smiled and said in a cunning voice, "Not yet, perhaps, but she can be persuaded. Her concern for you is very great, *Capitán*."

"You filthy—"

"But no, Captain Avery! The choice will be all hers."

James swallowed painfully. His head was pounding so hard he could barely think. He feared de Silva might be right. If Annie thought there was even a chance to win his release, she might give herself to procure it. And the Cuban would lie.

James bit his tongue, aware that nothing he said would sway de Silva. Keeping his head would be his strongest weapon.

They were interrupted shortly by Annie's arrival. James nearly froze at the sight of her, before a jealous anger dimmed his eyes.

Foolish girl! She had dressed within an inch of her life in the hopes of swaying the bastard. James's throat ached as she saw his distress and signaled comfort to him with her eyes.

The guard followed her inside. De Silva ordered him to stay.

"*Querida.*" De Silva's silky tone made James's skin crawl, but Annie smiled in a simpleminded way.

"You are beauty itself." The Cuban bowed over her hand, his gaze on her bodice. "It pleases me to see you recovered from this morning."

"Oh, yes, Captain," Annie cooed, gazing back with wide, eager eyes. "I have so looked forward to this evening."

If he had been at the theater, James would have laughed at her terrible performance, but fear made him sick. "Annie, don't believe a word de Silva tells you. He's going to kill me no matter what."

He was pleased to witness de Silva's annoyance. "Your guardian is raving, *querida*. He will tell you that I am not an honorable man, but I count on you to persuade me to do what is right."

"Annie, don't!"

Annie faced James. She looked so poised and beautiful that James's heart twisted into a knot.

"I never do anything I don't want to do, Captain Avery," she said in a sugary voice. "I only want to have a"—she turned back to the Cuban—"a pleasant evening with our host."

Capturing Annie

James tried not to curse at the expression that came over de Silva's face, wondering what smoldering look Annie had used to get him to reveal such lust. Another warning was forming on his lips when de Silva turned his blood to ice by saying, "Shall we excuse our friend, *señorita*? I fear he is not in the correct mood to join us."

"Excuse me from what?"

"From dinner, naturally. You will not mind if the *señorita* and I dine in your cabin? It is much more comfortable than mine. And there are so many men aboard my ship that I fear we might be disturbed."

"I do mind!" James exploded. "You'd better think twice."

"Now, James," Annie said, turning to fix him with a glittery eye, though her voice came as soft as velvet. "You don't have to worry. I have a small proposition to put to Captain de Silva, and it might be better if you did not hear it."

"Annie, please—" James was cut off by a furious movement of her lips. She was mouthing silent words at him—something about being an idiot—he could decipher that much. He couldn't distinguish all she said, but it was clear she wanted him to be quiet.

Torn between uncertainty and frustration, he was silent as de Silva signaled to his man.

"My servant will conduct you to the *señorita's* cabin where I hope you will be comfortable for the night."

"Annie—" James's words were cut off by a jerk

335

on his elbow. The sailor pulled him to the door as the others stepped aside to make room for his passage.

"Captain de Silva?" Annie had pressed against the Cuban in the need to move out of the way. "Might I bid my guardian goodnight?"

"Annie, you mustn't—" James halted at the sight of de Silva bending over her. His gaze was riveted on her bosom. Annie herself appeared to be swaying towards him. Her hand had inched up her skirt as if with uncontrollable passion. First her ankle, then her knee were exposed as she rubbed her leg against de Silva's.

James could hardly breathe past the pain in his chest.

The Cuban's voice had thickened, too. "*Querida*, if it will make you feel more generous toward me, I will grant your request."

"It would put me heavily in your debt." With that breathless promise, Annie dropped her hem to the floor and turned to James, who stood with his back to the door.

James fought the cobwebs in his head. When she came to kiss him, should he fight?

But when Annie reached him, she did not give him a kiss. She wrapped her arms about his body in a hug, and immediately he felt a tugging on his ropes.

His heart gave a leap as he searched her beloved face.

She gazed up at him with those devious green eyes. "Before you leave, I want you to remember what I was before you made me your ward. You mustn't worry."

James's hands silently broke apart under the sharpness of her knife. *Clever girl*, he signaled with his eyes.

She couldn't wink because the guard was staring at her face. Only human, he, too, had been distracted by that revealing décolletage. He stood next to James; but James's back was turned to the door, his own body concealing it. Pressed together in that small space like eggs in a nest, their very closeness acted as a screen.

"I love you for this," James said.

De Silva made an impatient sound behind her. Reacting, Annie slid the knife into the folds of her skirt, while raising her other hand. She brushed away a curl on James's head, and he sensed the other men's envy.

"Dear Captain, I can entertain Captain de Silva. But you must remember this guard, if you think to resist."

There, in a nutshell, was her plan. By now, the others were too mesmerized by her seductive voice to detect her hidden meaning. Annie moved to de Silva's side, swaying her hips with more effect than she could know.

De Silva licked his lips as she paused, then molded her body to his while taking his arm.

"Captain Avery—" De Silva's speech came huskily. He didn't bother to look up. "It is time that we bid you goodnight."

"That's right, James." Then a sharper note entered Annie's voice. "The time is now!"

As the last word left her lips, her arm swung forward and de Silva uttered a cry of pain. James didn't wait to see what Annie had done. He gave three quick blows to the guard's stomach. The man received them with grunts of surprise, falling forward with each. Then, James repeated his punches to the man's face, and he fell unconscious to the floor.

James turned quickly, ready to bound to Annie's aid, but he saw that de Silva had fallen backward into his chair. All color was draining from his face as he contemplated the blood dripping from his side. Annie stood over him, holding her knife to his throat, his hair in a ruthless grip.

James took the few steps between them and examined Annie's captive. A gash lay open between his ribs, blood sluggishly oozing from it.

"What a marvel you are, my dear." James straightened and gave Annie a quick kiss.

She flushed but held her grip. "Aw, it was nothing."

James took some handkerchiefs out of his seaman's chest to staunch de Silva's wound, then tore his sheets into strips to bind the bandage to his side.

"I'll tie him up," James said, using more strips for the purpose. "Better get the other one, too, before he comes around."

"Wait." Annie crossed to the guard and rolled him over. Quickly, she loosened the strings of his smock.

"What are you doing?"

"Undressing him."

"I can see that, Annie. But why?"

She glanced up impatiently, her fingers going to work on the flap of the sailor's breeches. "So I can take his clothes, of course."

"What for?" A chill of dread made its way down James's back.

"So I can nip on down to the hold and release our men."

"You will do no such thing! What if you're spotted?"

Annie grimaced good-naturedly at him. "Silly, that's what the clothes are for."

"A fat lot of good they'll do! You'll be recognized at once!"

"Do you think so?" Annie had stripped the poor sailor to his ankles, but now, she paused to shove her hair beneath his cap. "In the dark and in this codger's clothes, they'll take me for one of their own. He's about my size."

James couldn't believe his ears. Annie had planned their escape from top to bottom. Her competence floored him, but he couldn't let her take such a risk for his crew's sake.

"It's too dangerous. There'll be a man guarding the hatch, and I refuse to let you get into a fight."

With a look of exasperation, Annie rolled her eyes. "Why? Don't you think I can beat him?"

Amusement tickled his lips. "Whether you can beat him or not isn't the point. I don't want to lose you, Annie."

"Jaaames," Annie pleaded, raising her hands

Patricia Wynn

with impatience. "We've got to release the men, and fast, before the *Flying Swan* docks."

This was true. They had to retake the ship before it reached a Cuban harbor.

"I'll do it," James said, starting for the door.

Annie shook her head vehemently and blocked his way. "No, if you try it, they are bound to recognize you. You're too big, and they've all seen you, but they haven't seen Jem."

"I don't want you to fight!"

"Then I promise you I won't."

James fought the feeling that he was arguing with a superior. "So, you'll just stroll right up to the guard and say, 'Hullo there, chap. I've come to let me mateys out. You don't mind, do you?' "

Annie giggled. "No, I won't. You think I'm stupid. I'll say, *'A los órdenes del Capitán de Silva!'* " With a brisk salute, she clicked her heels together.

Astonishment took him aback. Annie had just given a respectable imitation of a Cuban guard. He had to admit, he was impressed.

"Where did you learn to speak Spanish?"

"Same place I learned French. Cap'n Sharkee had pirates from all over."

James recalled the extent of her French, and a new fear filled his mind. "You don't know enough to converse."

"Who wants to converse? All I need is enough to bluff my way through." She had pulled off the last of the sailor's clothes, and in the process, had discovered the key to her cabin.

The Cuban guard gave a moan.

James moved quickly to tie the man's hands. When he looked up, he found Annie awaiting his answer.

She must have seen the worry in his eyes, for coming near, she reached on tiptoes to kiss him on the lips. "Don't worry, James. Cap'n Sharkee got himself in messes all the time. He taught me more tricks than I'll ever have reason to use. When I was little, before a fight, he used to hide me in a barrel with a bunch of knives so I could pop out at night and free the crew if he needed. This is easy, believe me."

James couldn't deny that she seemed to have it all worked out. His heart burgeoned with pride. "All right. You're the boss. What should I do?"

Annie smiled back at him and reached over her shoulders to start working on her buttons. "You can sneak along to the magazine. I'll bet there's only one guard on duty now."

"Aye, aye, ma'am." James dragged the guard's body away from the door.

When he looked up, Annie's gown was loose in the back, but she had stopped to search about the cabin. Her eye lit on one of his brass instruments. She took it in her hand to judge its weight.

"Here," she said, tossing it to James. "Knock de Silva over the head with this."

Surprised, James turned to look at the Cuban, still conscious, but drooping miserably in his chair. At Annie's threat, his eyes grew narrow and he sneered.

James had to remind himself that she had

been raised without any principles. "Annie, I can't club a man who's bound and wounded."

"Him? When he would've killed you and poked me?"

"Yes, but—" James tried to explain to her the gentlemanly rules of war. "Yes, that was all very terrible, and he will be punished. But to hit a man when he's at our mercy . . ."

"All right"—she stuck out her chin—"then, suit yourself, but he'll get to watch me undress."

Without a second's hesitation, Annie started to pull the gown over her head.

De Silva's gaze had taken on a decided gleam. Whatever blood he still possessed was flooding into his cheeks.

James slugged him. The crunching sound made him want to wince.

"Changed your mind, did ye?" Annie was grinning at him, her dress draped across one elbow. He nodded, unable to keep from grinning back, as she kept removing her clothes, piece by lacy piece. Panier, corset, and chemise soon followed the gown.

When she had finished, and she stood there as naked as the day she'd been born, he could only whisper, "You're so beautiful, Annie, I could eat you."

She colored and bowed her head. Her eyes went to the unconscious sailor at her feet, and a look of deep regret came over her face.

"I would—that is, we maybe could—" she stammered and looked uncertainly at James. "But the ship—"

Capturing Annie

With a shake of his head, James tore his eyes from the heavenly vision, trying to stifle the heat in his loins. "Right. The ship." His heart was pounding as if he'd run for miles. "I guess we'd better hurry."

Annie scrambled into the sailor's clothes while James collected the cabin's weapons. Surprisingly, no one had removed his pair of dueling pistols. He loaded one for himself and the other for one of his men.

With de Silva's sword and pistol, his servant's cutlass and dagger—a small arsenal was soon ready to hand. James had forgotten Annie's knife, though she had not. As soon as she had dressed, she replaced it in its sheath and tucked it into her waist.

"Give me those others," she told him. Then, one by one, she stashed them inside the sailor's baggy trousers.

"Guess I'm ready," she said, practicing the stiff-legged walk required by de Silva's sword. "We'll have our ship back in no time."

"Annie—" James came to wrap his hands about her waist. "Promise to be careful."

"I already did!"

"Do it again."

Her lips quirked in a grin. "All right, sir, James. I promise. But, you know, I was beginning to think you led a pretty dull life aboard this ship."

"Dull for you, was it? Well, I'm glad we could arrange a little entertainment. Wouldn't want our guests to be bored."

As he finished his teasing, he felt the warmth

343

from her body stealing over him. His throat felt tight. "Annie, take this—" He bent and kissed her, so softly, just to taste her lips.

"What's that for?" He could feel her tremble beneath his hands.

"For good luck." He would have held her longer, but they mustn't forget the time. "Be careful," he said again.

"Jaaames! You're worse than Therese!" She peered out the door. "All clear now. You be careful, too."

Clutching the cutlass in one hand, the hilt of de Silva's sword in the other, Annie skirted the sleeping Cuban guards and made her way to the ship's waist.

"La llave, por favor. A los órdenes del capitán." She demanded the key to the lock on the hold.

The guard jerked out of a sitting posture and fumbled for the key. He must've been dozing, for he hadn't challenged her approach. She'd seen that his lantern cast a feeble glow and had taken pains not to put herself within its beam.

A heavy chain secured the door to the hold. The guard watched her as she turned the clanking key. He posed a question, something about Captain de Silva. Feigning an angry mood, Annie grumbled a curse she had heard Cubans use to signal a general disgust. She shrugged to discourage him from talking.

He took the hint, but kept watching while she raised the hatch. Annie swung around and snatched the lantern from his hand. It was a bold move. But he could hardly expect her to descend into a pit of enemies without light. She cast its illumination over the hold. James's crewmen were there, some sleeping, some moaning from their wounds. Mr. Shirley stood and shielded his eyes from the sudden beam.

"*Espérese,*" Annie told the guard. *Wait.*

He did as she commanded while she negotiated the steps of the ladder. At the first bend of her left leg, de Silva's sword cut through her trousers with a loud rip.

Sniggers came from the hold, and she fought down a giggle. A ribald statement floated down from the guard. She went on, holding her left leg stiff for the rest of the way and crimping with her right.

At the bottom, Mr. Shirley stood waiting, his eyes still unaccustomed to the lantern light. "Goin' to feed us, ye bleedin' bugger? We won't do ye no good if we starve."

"Hullo there, mate," Annie whispered, holding the lantern up to her face.

He started at her English voice, then bent to peer closer. Recognition came into his eyes. "Hullo there, Jem. Tooken' up with them Cubans, have ye?"

Annie smothered a chuckle. "Nope. Take another look. Where have you seen this face before?"

He stared, and stared again, but still he would not believe what he saw. "What ye doin' here, then?" He seemed determined not to make the connection.

"I'm here to free you," she whispered, wanting to shout. "The captain, my *guardian*, sent me."

"Did 'e now? There's a brick." Then, as her words finally made it through his thick skull, he stared round-eyed. "Yer a girl, ye mean? Same as that Miss Bonny?"

Annie nodded, then started pulling the weapons out of her clothes. He took a step backward in shock. Then, when he saw what she was doing, he grabbed the cutlass for himself.

"Been playin' a deep game, have ye, Jem? Well"—he tested the weapon in his hand—"I forgive ye for it."

"Thanks." Annie presented the hilt of de Silva's sword. "Wouldn't you rather have this? It's a fine blade."

"No, sir, not me. That's a gentl'man's arm. Look 'ere, lads! See what our ol' pal Jem 'as brought us."

The sailors had begun to rouse themselves. Now they clumped about her, exclaiming. As they started to grab for the knives, she shushed them and covered the lantern with a shirt lying close to hand.

"*Qué pasa?*" The guard on the deck sounded worried.

Annie called up to reassure him, then in a low voice, to her mates said, "I need some of you to pretend to be my prisoners. Mr. Shirley, you should be one. Who else?"

He chose five others, enough for one weapon each. Then, Annie, with a pistol pointed at their backs told them to precede her up the ladder.

She was the last to emerge from the hold. The guard had trained his own weapon on her mates, but without the lantern, it was hard for him to see. His back was turned toward her as he posed another question.

Annie clubbed him over the head.

"Sorry, mate, but I don't have the faintest idea what you said."

Within twenty minutes, it was over. As soon as Annie disposed of their guard, the imprisoned crew came scrambling out of the hold. On her instructions, they quietly made their way to the magazine, where they found James once again in charge. Properly armed, and with the element of surprise, the sailors of the *Flying Swan* overcame the small party of Cubans who had been set to guard their ship.

They might have attempted to outrun the Cuban sloop, but James saw no reason to forfeit a possible prize. Satisfied he had sufficient men, he gave his orders. Dressed in the Cubans' clothes, they made ready for battle on this moonless night.

"Mr. Shirley, make ready to sail quickly. No lights and no sound."

"Aye, aye, Cap'n."

"And lower the boat. I'll accompany the boarding party."

"I want to go with you," Annie said, putting her hand on his sleeve.

James grasped her by the shoulders. "No, I want you to stay here."

Patricia Wynn

"But you saw what I can do! You might need my Spanish."

"You and your Spanish are both wonderful, my darling, but we'll simply have to manage without you. I won't have you hurt in a fight."

Annie struggled in his arms, but he enveloped her, and squeezed her until her breath was nearly spent. "Annie, I love you. I couldn't bear to lose you. Please, do as I say."

"But what if you're hurt? Could I bear that?"

"Perhaps not. But I'm still the captain. I have to lead my men. And, besides, I have a score to settle with de Silva's crew, and I can't be content until it's done. They almost took you away from me. And that I'll never forgive."

Tears filled her eyes. Life would never be fair, but she could understand his fear of losing her. She would always be afraid of losing him, too. "May I kiss you for luck?"

"If you hadn't offered, I'd have to insist."

The night was so dark that no one could see them. The kiss took longer than either had intended, but neither wanted it to end. Annie sucked upon his lips, tasting the intoxicating flavor of his mouth. She relished the roughness of his cheeks as they scored hers.

She couldn't get enough of James, but a whisper soon told them that his men were ready. James emerged from their kiss with a shaky sigh. "I'm so proud of you, Annie," he whispered, cradling her head on his chest. "You can be on my crew any time."

With those words, he was gone over the side,

but Annie guarded them deep in her heart. He *did* understand her need to be useful and he wanted her by his side.

The fight was soon ended, and with the sloop added to his fleet, James was even richer when they sailed into London.

Chapter Eighteen

He installed Annie in a house of her own. He insisted she hire a companion, since society would consider it odd for a girl her age to be living alone. She reminded him that she had Sophie, but he told her only an elderly lady would do.

Then he went to call on Lady Olivia and Lord Figg.

In the past few weeks, James had experienced a profound change of heart. Now he knew without a doubt that Annie belonged at sea with him. Regardless of the danger and his previous opinions, she had proved she was the one woman who could flourish under the trials of life at sea. He could trust her more than he could trust his crew. There would be danger, of course, but

Annie would have the same chance of surviving it as he, and a better chance perhaps than in living on shore. She would be the greatest helpmate a sailor ever had, and he would never be alone. Leaving her ashore while he led a separate life would accomplish nothing for either of them. And the pain of separation would be too vast for either to bear.

All this he had realized by the time he rode up to Lord Figg's house. The scene that he met there caused his hopes to plummet. Several tradesmen with bills in hand were clamoring to speak to Lord Figg. Among them, James saw, was a wine merchant. This was a desperate sign, for a nobleman's winemerchant was the last tradesman he would cut off, since without a healthy cellar, one could hardly be received. As he forced his way through them to the door, ignoring their angry shouts, James knew how little Lord Figg would relish the proposition he had come to make today.

Presenting his card, James was admitted at once. Immediately, he noted the changes in his surroundings. The servant who'd admitted him no longer sported the Figg green and gold livery. Other hints of indigence confronted him on every side. The figurines and paintings he'd seen on his last visit had all vanished. The worn carpet had not been changed and had barely been swept.

After a few moments' wait, he was shown into the small parlor, where Lord Figg sat alone.

"Well, you've certainly taken your time about

returning," the earl grumbled. "It's a damned nuisance, I tell you. I had half a mind to marry my daughter to someone else."

His hope remounting, James overlooked the rude greeting. "I thought I had made my schedule plain, and that your daughter's period of mourning would prevent a quicker resolution to our affairs. But I will be happy to apologize if my absence has inconvenienced you, my lord."

"Enough of that!" A wave of Lord Figg's hand spoke nothing but impatience. "You are here now, and all can proceed. My man will call on you to make the final arrangements and the wedding can take place at once."

Even knowing how desperate the earl's circumstances were, James was stunned by the man's arrogance. It took a moment for him to marshal his forces.

As Lord Figg continued in his preemptory manner, James was forced to interrupt. "One moment, my lord, if you please. There is something I must tell you."

Fearing the outcome if he allowed the earl a chance to take control of the conversation, James pressed on. "I must tell you that something has occurred which will make a marriage between your daughter and me both unfeasible and unwise."

Lord Figg's brow contracted into a murderous frown. "Lost your fortune, have you?"

"Not at all." As much as James knew this would help his case, it would be useless to lie. His holdings were a matter of public record. "It is simply that my affections have been elsewhere engaged—quite unexpectedly, you should know. So, I cannot, in all honor, bind your daughter to me."

As he finished, Lord Figg's expression underwent a terrible transformation. James thought he had seen his prospective father-in-law at his worst, but nothing could have prepared him for the viciousness he saw unmasked.

"Your affections!" Lord Figg spat the words out. "What makes you think that I care, or my daughter should care, where your affections may lie? Do you think this marriage has anything to do with love? It's about money, boy. And do not flatter yourself that anything about you makes you acceptable to me other than your handsome fortune. Bourgeois sentiments will get you nowhere, so you had best leave them behind if you want to get ahead."

"I know my news is unwelcome. I could not fail to notice the tradesmen at your door. And I assure you I will settle all your debts. No one need ever know I have done it, if you will release me from our contract."

The earl's brows shot up. "So, you have found that pretty a piece? Well, make her your mistress, boy, for you will not be released."

"Sir"—James drew himself up, hardly able to restrain his temper—"I have offered to pay your debts. I do not doubt that some agreement can be reached between us."

"Then, think again, *Captain*"—Lord Figg's visage, when he spoke this last word, was both contorted and red—"and understand me. When I selected you to be my son-in-law, I did it with the belief that you would continue to increase your fortune, so that I might profit from your industry for as long as I live. You will not be released, and if you end the engagement yourself, I will ruin both you and this girl you wish to shackle yourself to.

"I tell you, make her your mistress. I will not begrudge her an allowance, so long as you conduct your affair discreetly. I do not imagine it will be your last."

"You are wrong, sir. It shall be my last."

Lord Figg gave a bark of laughter. "What a fool you are to be sure!"

"Only in that I ever indulged a wish to ally myself with one like you."

If James had wanted to stoke his lordship's temper so that he might indulge in physical violence, he was disappointed. The earl's face relaxed in a gloating smile.

"You may insult me any way you wish, but I will not meet you. Nor will I take a pet and ban you from my daughter's company. You are mine, sir, unless you wish your pretty lady's name to be dragged through the mud."

"I shall never supply you with her name."

"Another futile gesture. I can discover it with no trouble to myself. I happen to know that your *ward* has been lodged in a house not far from here. By all reports, she's a girl to tempt a man to foolishness."

James felt an impotent rage. Now that he

knew precisely the sort of cunning Lord Figg possessed, he knew no argument of his would succeed. He had come prepared to take the brunt of his fury, even the disgrace of reneging. But he was not prepared to sacrifice Annie's name to the vengeful cruelty of this man.

He had betrayed her by ever thinking that his conduct could go undiscovered.

He squeezed his hat under his arm, and since he had never been asked to sit, had nothing to do but take his leave. "We shall talk again, my lord," he said in a clipped voice. "May I inquire if the Lady Olivia is receiving?"

"It will do you no good to try that tactic, boy. My daughter will do as I say or she will find herself without a roof over her head."

"Is she receiving?" James persisted with his teeth clenched. "I suppose I might ask to see my future bride."

"Not today," Lord Figg said abruptly. "You may see her at a party to be given in her honor in two weeks. Now that you are returned, invitations will be sent to your lodgings both for you and your ward. Do not think to refuse. Your absence could only be ascribed to one thing, and the lady will suffer for it, I assure you."

James could make no answer to this threat without releasing all the pent-up anger inside him, so he made a stiff bow and walked out.

He wouldn't give up. He would delay the wedding as long as he could while searching for some new means to free himself. He would hire a solicitor. Surely, if he delayed long enough,

Lord Figg's creditors would become so loud that he'd have to find another pigeon to pluck. He could not *carry* James to the altar.

Meanwhile, Lord Figg's threats about Annie had been vicious enough to shake him. James did not doubt the earl would do what he could to harm her, if he thought she could ruin his plans. He had quickly discovered the one thing that could make James vulnerable.

Sick at heart, James decided he must stay away from Annie, to protect her reputation until he could find a way out of this mess.

Waiting in her London house, Annie grew impatient. She'd expected James to come directly from Lord Figg's house, anticipating the news that he'd been freed. Instead, he'd sent her a tersely worded note that he could not call on her for a few days. He would be spending them with his solicitor. She was not to worry, but she must prepare herself to appear at an affair to be given in Lady Olivia's honor, and she must try to trust him.

Annie couldn't fail to understand that something was terribly wrong. If James had won his release, he would have come immediately. That he had not threw her into a miserable confusion. She felt helpless in a situation in which she had no familiarity or control. And she hated feeling helpless.

She could do nothing, though, but prepare herself for the gathering planned. Once there, she'd be able to discover what was wrong.

* * *

Her days in London passed uneventfully. A mid-morning walk in the park, as James had insisted, a few trips to shops, and planning meals had to occupy her time. Annie chafed at so much inactivity. London was a cold place, as Therese had said. A muddy, bloody cold place without James.

His "few days" turned into two weeks and still he did not come. When the day of the party arrived, Annie received a note informing her that James would be obliged to escort Lady Olivia for the evening. It would be expected, and he mustn't insult his fiancée. This message filled her with alarm. She couldn't understand why James would continue this charade if he truly loved her. Her knowledge of society, still scant, was not enough to help her interpret every nuance, but she was certain that James's attendance on Lady Olivia would signal his intention to wed her.

Alarmed, Annie did what Therese had taught her. She dressed to attract every male eye. If James had to be reminded of the desire he'd shown for her and his pledge that they would be together, she would walk on hot coals to make him take note.

In spite of the cold that evening, Annie's hands had begun to perspire by the time she and her companion arrived at the imposing house where the dinner was to be served. An army of footmen in blue and silver livery stood poised to help them off with their cloaks. Hundreds of candles illumined the grand entryway and the drawing room, and clusters of delicate armchairs covered in gold-threaded damask flanked the walls.

If Annie had been taken aback by the elegance of Therese's friends, she now realized how simple they had been in comparison with London society. These aristocrats, in their diamonds and rubies, their sapphires and emeralds, their satins and their silks, could make any Jamaican gathering look like a Quaker meeting.

Her hostess, the Countess Fremont, received her in a wig more preposterous than any Therese had ever worn, a hideous confection with a tiny bird's cage nestled on a bed of curls. Annie peered at the canary inside it, but the bird had been stuffed—either that, or it had gone stiff with fright.

The countess in turn stared at Annie's flaming, unpowdered hair, and her extreme décolletage, and blinked. When informed that Annie was Captain Avery's ward, she reacted with a sharp arching of her brow. Her reception of Annie was quite chilly as she extended two fingers to press.

Annie could not be bothered by an offended look she did not understand, not when James and his fiancée stood just a few feet away. Both looked pale. Neither had the air of a person in love.

James finished greeting another guest just in time to witness Lady Freemont's frigid greeting. His gaze dropped to the front of Annie's dress, and his lips compressed into a thin, straight line.

His color changed to a ruddy glow as an older man at his side leaned to whisper something in his ear.

The shock of James's discomfort made Annie reel. He looked both angry and ashamed, and not at all glad to see her. Lady Freemont's hauteur, which she'd so casually dismissed, took on mammoth proportions now. She felt unwelcome and outclassed. She longed to be back aboard ship, or even in Jamaica, which seemed simple and familiar compared to the terrors that awaited her here.

Robbed of James's support, she nearly allowed dismay to overcome her, but she did not let it show. Hurt by his manner, she could only raise her chin and move forward through the line. If nothing else, she had learned that her charms were universally admired by men. She would use them to make James and every person who snubbed her feel as miserable as she felt.

With more poise than she knew she had, she said hello politely to James and turned to face the woman on his left. Lady Olivia was a pretty creature, if a bit older than Annie had expected. Annie had braced herself for this meeting. If anyone should resent her, it should be Olivia. Restricted in her choice of weapons, Annie knew she would have to employ the ones Therese had given her.

But to her surprise, Olivia did not treat her as an enemy. She only glanced at Annie's décolletage before flushing and averting her gaze, but nothing in her manner was unkind. She took

Patricia Wynn

Annie's hand and held on to it until Annie wished she would let it go. The woman clung to her as if for support.

She was surprisingly wan for a woman about to marry the man of Annie's dreams. Large dark shadows circled her eyes.

Perhaps she's ill, Annie thought, her mind taking off in all directions. Maybe James was afraid a disappointment would endanger her health. Nothing in his face betrayed the love he'd professed as he presented her as his ward, first to Olivia, then to her father on his opposite side.

"So, this is the chit we've been discussing?" Lord Figg surveyed her through his quizzing glass. With a lecherous gleam, he paused to stare at her breasts.

Annie suffered his rude scrutiny for James's sake. She could never be intimidated by such a pitiful specimen, though if society would permit, she would be happy to teach him a manner or two.

Then she heard him add, in a voice loud enough for her and James alone, "Now I see the *kind* of activity that has kept you distracted, boy."

This was uttered in a tone so insulting, Annie felt as if she'd been slapped. Through the sudden fury that clouded her eyes, she saw that James had gone rigid. Surely he hadn't told the earl that he loved her if the man could be so insolent? He seemed to know about their affair. But instead of punching Lord Figg in the face, James did nothing but stand in a mortified stillness.

The earl gave a barking laugh. "I'm tired of doing the pretty," he said, his eyes bright with mischief. "Miss Bonny, I expect you to entertain me while Captain Avery and my daughter greet their guests. I cannot resist a lovely face, especially when it's mounted on such a charming frame."

Again he let his gaze sweep her body. Annie had never felt so dirty. She would rather be coated in tar than support the leer of this man. He wanted to embarrass her. No matter how unschooled she was, she couldn't mistake the malice in his demeanor.

But, at least, his remark had startled James out of his complacency. He moved forward as if to step between them, only to be forestalled by Lord Figg.

"You will not object to a tête-à-tête between your ward and your future father-in-law." The earl's voice was sneering as he took Annie's hand and slowly drew it to rest in the crook of his arm. "We must become better acquainted, my dear. Once my daughter and Captain Avery are married, I shall hope to see more of you."

If Annie had expected James to display the same possessiveness he had shown in Jamaica, she was quickly disappointed. He did nothing but give her an angry, impotent look. It pleaded with her to go along even as it begged her to forgive his inactivity.

"There's a good boy." Lord Figg's tone hinted at a meaning Annie couldn't interpret. "I'll take care of Miss Bonny. You needn't fuss."

He led her away, aiming for an alcove in the large withdrawing room. Other guests stood about, conversing and waiting for dinner to be announced. Beside them, servants were laying the finishing touches on the tables covered with trays.

"Well, girly"—the rude label alerted her to his spirit—"I can see your pretty figure has bewitched our captain, but it won't do, you know. He is going to marry my daughter, as planned."

Enraged by his tone, Annie balled up her fists, feeling the bite of her fingernails on her palms, but she reminded herself that she could not resort to the kind of tactics she had learned aboard Captain Sharkee's ship. Lord Figg was acting in his daughter's best interest. James must have told him he wanted out, so Lord Figg saw her as a threat to his daughter's happiness.

"I am sorry if Lady Olivia will be disappointed, but you are mistaken. James is in love with me."

"Love!" he scoffed. "Lust is more like! But your *James* will soon tire of the charming delights you undoubtedly bestow upon him. I suggest you find yourself another protector before you end up in the street." He leered. "With your face and your more obvious assets, it shouldn't take you too long."

She would have been tempted to stab him if they had been in a less public place. The knife beneath her skirts called loudly to her, but Annie knew she couldn't cause a scene. If she gave in to her fury, James would be the one to pay.

For the first time in her life, she actually trembled with frustration. She had never borne an insult she couldn't avenge. If this was the kind of impotence ladies had to bear, she wanted no part of this life. Lord Figg knew she could do little to defend herself against mere words here. That was obviously why he'd accosted her now—the coward.

She refused to let the old bugger get the better of her. In a voice that was brittle and dry with sugar, she said, "I thank you for your solicitous advice, my lord, but surely Captain Avery will be the best judge of what he wants. If he decides to marry your daughter, he can inform me without your generous interference."

"That's where you're wrong, girly. The captain will do as I say. And so I've told him."

The image of Lord Figg trying to impose his will on James made Annie grin. "I have known Captain Avery far better than you, sir, and if he wants me, he will have me. It would take a much stronger man than you to keep him from getting his way."

That earned her a vicious look. "Stronger, Miss Bonny? Or smarter? You think I don't have a way to stop your captain, short of physical violence? I leave that sort of wrangling to the lower classes. Gentlemen like me have other weapons at our disposal.

"The captain knows full well the damage I can

do to him. He has already come to his senses, my sweet. If he does not go forward with this marriage, he knows that I will ruin him."

Annie felt a first real glimmer of anxiety. "Please explain yourself, Lord Figg."

With a sneer of triumph, he did. "Unless the captain lives up to our contract, I have only to make it known that he has refused to honor our agreement, and he will be a social outcast."

"James wouldn't care about that." Annie spoke quickly, but she felt a stab of fear nonetheless.

"No? Well, he seemed to care vastly about it when I confronted him. Perhaps he was affected by the realization that he'll be ruined financially as well. For who will enter into agreement with a man who's cheated an earl and reneged on promises to his daughter? And without a sterling reputation, I am afraid your privateer will lose his letter of marque, followed by one and then all of his ships. He might as well turn pirate for all the respect he'll be shown.

"No, dearie," his lordship continued gleefully. "The captain knows who has the upper hand. He's a plain nobody, up against the power of an earl. Why do you think he entered into this bargain in the first place? Your baseborn captain has aspirations to be a peer. He cannot afford to let a pretty strumpet get in his way, now can he?"

Annie stood, rooted to the floor by shock. Lord Figg raised his glass to one eye and stared at her until she felt her temperature burn.

"If you need another lover, my dove, you

might consider me. I'll be happy to keep you warm for a while."

His insulting words rang like cannon blasts in her ears. But they did nothing to add to her distress. His revelations about the hold he had on James had given her more than enough.

Annie was aware that society had more rules and complexities than she could ever have grasped through a ten-month lesson with Therese. These landlubbers had a system of laws. They all seemed to care for property. She had learned in Jamaica what it meant to have a title and a peerage. A captain might be king of his own ship, but she'd learned that the world was larger now. A captain was not as powerful on land.

To be important on land, one had to own some. To be the most powerful of all, one had to be a peer. If James had ambitions to be one—it didn't matter that he had never discussed them—she wouldn't be the agent to take his ambitions away.

She knew what it felt like to want something and have it denied. She had wanted to live at sea, but society had said she must live on shore. Society, as she had learned, could be very powerful. She wouldn't want to cause James to fall out with the powers that be, if they could take away his dreams.

Now she understood the expression she had seen on his face tonight. She had wondered what could account for his cold behavior and

his looks of shame. Lord Figg's jeering talk had
supplied her with the answers. If James dropped
Lady Olivia to marry her, he would lose the
sanction of the government. No one more than
she knew how James would feel if forced to turn
pirate.

Dinner was announced, recalling Annie to
where she was. With a smug expression, Lord
Figg proferred his arm.

She had tried to deflect his insinuations and
be civil in the face of his insults. She had learned
enough of the rules to know that she couldn't
make a scene.

But deep down in her gut, she knew that some
of Sharkee's lessons had been valid, too. And, if
there was one thing he had taught her, it was
never to let a bully get the upper hand.

With an air of graciousness and innocence,
she accepted his lordship's arm and prepared to
walk with him into dinner. Then, drawing inti-
mately closer, she whispered into his ear. "You
may have your own sort of weapons, Lord Figg.
But so do I, and I know how to use them.

"Just under this skirt, for instance, I carry a
blade that is ten inches long and three inches
wide. And, if once you refer again in any way to
what James has found between my legs, I will
find you, no matter where you sleep, and hack
off the pitiful thing that's dangling between
yours."

Lord Figg jumped away from her so fast, he
stumbled over a chair almost three feet away.
Two passing gentlemen stopped to help him to

his feet, but he kept his distance from her. His eyes were wide with shock. Annie gave him a sweet little smile before turning to put herself in the way of a solitary gentleman, whose escort she accepted into the meal.

At the table, she was dismayed to find that she'd been placed next to James. His cool demeanor could only mean that everything Lord Figg had told her was true. Hiding her feelings, she confined her attention to the plates the servants placed in front of her, though she never noticed the food. James threw her an occasional glance out the corner of his eye, but each so discreet, she had to assume he didn't wish for her to talk.

Halfway through the meal, between courses, his hand made its way into her lap, and he gently rubbed her thigh. The feeling of it shook her. She resisted the impulse to grasp for his warmth. After a moment, in which she showed no response, he slowly withdrew it.

Dinner seemed interminable to her. From where she sat, Annie couldn't see Olivia on his other side, but his meager efforts at conversation were directed that way. He held himself stiffly, as if conscious of his sins. Annie almost felt sorry for Olivia. If James couldn't be more loverlike, no wonder she was pale. Perhaps, as with Annie, something had occurred to break her heart.

As the ladies finally rose from dinner, the gentlemen stood, and James, taking advantage of the bustle to speak softly into her ear, said, "I want to walk you to your chair. Feign an excuse to leave the party."

He wanted a chance to tell her what he must do, but Annie had no intention of listening to him this time. She had had enough of this society that meant so much to him. It might hold what he wanted, but it had nothing for her if she couldn't live with him.

She ignored his whisper and curtsied as a matter of form, then joined the other ladies before finding her companion and making her excuses. Sedan chairs were called, and slowly Annie was carried home through the streets of London.

She had obeyed James—first, because he was her captain, and then, because he was her love. But now, she had to decide what sort of life she was willing to live and how much she was prepared to ask him to give up. If she stayed, perhaps he would install her in a house somewhere, if he was not afraid that Olivia would know.

She could share him, but she would have to live the way she'd lived these past few weeks. Alone and worthless. And that was no kind of life for a girl who had been raised by the likes of Captain Sharkee.

James was one of the first gentlemen to quit the table to join the ladies. He expected to find Annie there, ready to leave so they could be together if only for a moment, and he was astonished to find that she had gone.

He had wanted a chance to speak to her. He

could hardly do more, though he longed to hold her. Not with Lord Figg watching his every move. The past two weeks had been like torture as he'd struggled to find a way out of his predicament, living in his solicitor's office, but nothing would budge Lord Figg.

James had wanted to kill him—for his cruelty and his selfishness, and now for the way he had treated Annie this evening. But how could one kill a man of his lordship's age who hid behind his weakness?

Indecision had never been a problem in James's life—until he'd met Annie. Now it seemed that at every turn he had to weigh what would be best for her. He could walk out of his agreement and take his losses, but he couldn't bring himself to sacrifice Annie's reputation. He'd worked too hard to create a life for her. He had turned her from a scruffy pirate into a diamond of the first rank, and he wouldn't let Lord Figg or anyone rob her of that achievement.

She had looked like a goddess when he'd spied her this evening. Only the countess's frosty glance and Lord Figg's whispered insult had stopped him from greeting her with warmth. He'd felt the shame of being powerless to defend her when doing so could injure her more.

He was sick of society and its ills. He belonged only to his ships and the sea, and to Annie. Together they could brave storms and cutthroats. Why not this?

Worry that he might have lost her respect plagued him throughout the rest of the evening.

His hostess informed him that Miss Bonny had pleaded a headache and asked her duenna to take her home.

She was angry at him. Because of his churlish attitude? He ought to have spoken to her before tonight. He ought to have prepared her for the role he had to play. But he hadn't wanted her to know that she'd become the tool Lord Figg was using to hold him, afraid she wouldn't understand and would do something half-baked. And, too, he hadn't wanted her to know because he'd been afraid she'd find it all too easy to persuade him to forget the goal he had set for them both—a marriage with respectability.

Now, he feared that his reticence had hurt her. He ought to have had more sense than to keep her in the dark. Now, he would have to wait until morning to visit her, but then he would make her understand.

Chapter Nineteen

After a restless night, James got up, having made some momentous decisions. He would visit Annie and tell her what the problem was and that she must trust him to solve it. Then he would call on Olivia and persuade her to renounce their engagement. That would be the only way for him to break it off honorably. He would deal with Lord Figg the only way he knew how. He would threaten him with bodily harm if he so much as mentioned Annie's name again.

James went to call at her house. Surprised by the earliness of the hour, Miss Turner, her companion, greeted him with the bad news that Miss Bonny was still abed, sleeping off her headache of the night before.

James insisted on waiting—impatient, but still desiring to maintain an appearance of normality in front of a person who was not in his confidence. He was shown into the parlor, where he had to endure an hour of Miss Turner's conversation. Since he had been the man to employ her, Miss Turner obviously thought it her duty to entertain him. But, if this were her idea of talk, he could only be sorry he'd inflicted her on Annie.

Finally, unable to stand her useless chatter a moment longer, he interrupted her to say that he could wait no more. He asked her to wake Annie so that he could talk to her on a matter of urgent importance.

Plainly curious, Miss Turner left to do his bidding, demonstrating more than a slight disapproval. James was sure it was not at all the thing for a gentleman to waken a sleeping ingénue. If Annie's companion only knew the familiar terms on which they had stood, she would be shocked out of her mind.

She returned quickly, breathless from haste, to tell him that Annie was gone.

"Gone! Where?"

"I cannot imagine!" Frightened, Miss Turner wrung her hands.

"Have you searched the house?" He refused to be alarmed until he was sure, but at the mere idea, his stomach tied itself in knots.

"I've asked the servants, but no one knows where she's gone."

"Did anyone see her leave? Perhaps she merely went for a walk."

"Sir James"—Miss Turner drew herself up—"I hope you know I would never allow my charge to walk out alone!"

He thundered back, "Then how is she gone?"

Her indignation crumpled. "I cannot imagine how she contrived to leave with no one seeing her."

James curbed his anger, which was nothing more than a rising fear. He wanted to shout that if Annie had wished to escape, she would have found a way. But her absence confused him. It made no sense.

"I've done my best," Miss Turner was saying. "I cannot blame myself. Miss Bonny looked so wan when she returned from the dinner last night, I told her maid not to disturb her this morning. But, I assure you, she was here in bed last night."

Her maid. James had forgotten about Sophie. Surely Sophie would know where Annie had gone, and until he'd talked to her there was no cause for panic.

He made for the stairs. "Tell Sophie to meet me in Miss Bonny's room."

"You cannot mean to go upstairs!"

"I can and I do. And, Miss Turner, I am not accustomed to being disobeyed."

Sophie came tearfully. By the time she arrived, James had already examined the window. The outside wall was straight with little foothold, but undoubtedly she had gone this way. He knew how easily Annie could have managed it.

"Where's your mistress, Sophie?"

"I don't know, Captain! She just said she had to go away! But she told me not to be scared, because you would take care of me."

Until this moment, James still had not believed it. He'd been hoping that Annie had merely wanted to walk out alone. It must have been hard for her to be cooped up these past two weeks with this dismal woman and child.

"Did she leave me a note? Did she say why?"

Sophie shook her head.

"How was she dressed?"

"Oh, sir, she left all them fine clothes you bought her!"

"All? Think carefully now. Which gown did she wear?"

Sophie paused at the sharpness in his voice, but she seemed to know where he was heading, for she hung her head. "She didn't take a one of them, captain."

"Then what was she wearing?"

Sophie's gaze stayed glued to the carpet.

"Tell me, Sophie. What did she wear? Boy's clothes?"

In the background, Miss Turner gave a gasp, but Sophie admitted eagerly, "Yessir. Those from that Spanish man. She kept them."

"Why that—" James bit back the word, though his heart pounded with fear. So she had done it. She'd gone back to living like a boy.

And with no note. She had not even bothered to write him words of comfort.

He noticed the sheets had been pulled off the bed and asked for confirmation. "Were her sheets torn?"

Sophie nodded sadly. "Just there, along one end. The rest was fine."

James straightened his shoulders. "I'll find her. Rest assured that I'll find her."

Damn her! Fright ran through him, churning his anger. How could she do this? How could she scare him so?

A different voice spoke softly in his head. Had he thought that Annie would never run away, just because he couldn't bear it?

Had she gone back to sea? he worried as he strode from the house. The city had a thousand dangers for a boy. As he thought of what might have happened to her, he prayed she had her knife.

James's head was so filled with fears, it was a long moment before he could think. It still made no sense that Annie would leave him. She'd been hurt last night. That much had been obvious. But in spite of the irrationality of females, Annie had never behaved like other women. She was a creature without artifice, except for those few parlor games Therese had taught her.

Their night of passion on the beach had taught him that Annie was still herself. Still the honest, direct girl he loved. If Annie had merely been angry with him, she wouldn't simply have taken a pet. She would have stormed right up to him and demanded to know what nonsense he was up to.

She'd had a reason for leaving. Something had occurred to make her do it. For some notion, she no longer trusted him. He could only think of one person who could have managed that.

James struggled with a desire to find Lord Figg and break his neck. But that would have to wait. First, he would have to find his love.

Where? If she had gone back to sea, had she sailed with the morning tide? Fear almost paralyzed him when he realized that she could have headed out from London to any port in the world.

Without another second's pause, he flagged a hack and flew to the docks.

An hour's search told him he could not possibly do this alone. With tension mounting, he hired a group of idle seamen to comb the docks for a boy with shoulder-length red hair.

He kept up his own scrutiny, from ship to ship until the thought that she might have made for Portsmouth began to eat away at his gut. Twice, Annie had come into England through Portsmouth. James could do nothing but tell his hirelings to keep looking while he hastened to the other port. On the Portsmouth docks, he hired another army, engaging them to keep their eyes peeled for a redheaded boy.

At midnight, defeated at last, James returned

to the inn in London. Worry over losing Annie had roused him into a fury. He knew he would never sleep until he'd taken his fury out on the man who'd caused his unhappiness.

The morning found him at his lordship's club where Lord Figg often spent the night. Known to be the earl's prospective son-in-law, James was immediately admitted at the door. At this hour, Lord Figg could usually be discovered dozing in the morning room. James made his way there and saw him, sitting amid a group of other men.

Ignoring this audience, James stormed over to them, took his lordship by the neck and shook him until his teeth began to rattle. Startled and afraid, Lord Figg blustered in outrage.

"What do you mean by this? Take your hands off me, sir! Someone call the guard!" he issued in a strangled voice.

"Keep your seats," James commanded the others, gritting his teeth. He turned back to Lord Figg, aware that the other gentlemen looked on. "You've said something to frighten Miss Bonny. Tell me what it was."

The earl made an attempt to bluff in front of his peers. "What? The pretty ladybird has flown the coop, has she? Well, you ought to thank me. I've saved you the trouble of getting rid of her."

"What did you tell her?" James threatened. "I want it now!"

Even Lord Figg couldn't fail to note his menace. Alarm touched his eyes, and it was fairly clear that no help would be forthcoming from

377

members of the club. "If the chit has done something foolish, I can't be held to blame."

"Now—or it's your life!"

When he didn't answer, but sought instead to call the guard, James grasped him again by the lapels and yanked him over to a wall where he held him up, his feet dangling uselessly in the air. A muffled laugh behind him said that at least one gentleman was amused.

"You'll be ruined for this!" Lord Figg blustered.

"Fine. Ruin me. I don't give a damn. But first you will tell me what I want to know or I'll throw you across this room."

Since by now Lord Figg was entirely at his mercy, he had no choice but to comply. He spoke quickly. "All I did was suggest that her presence might cause some talk."

"Talk?" James scoffed. "You forget, I know you for the rotten scum you are. You told her it would ruin me, didn't you? Did you tell her, also, that you would be the one to do it?"

A hint of malice gleamed in the old earl's eyes before he hid it. James threw him down in a chair in disgust.

As he turned his back to stalk out, Lord Figg raised his voice behind him. "You'll be arrested for this! You cannot manhandle me! I'm a peer!"

James spun around and glared so threateningly that the earl shrank back in his seat. Still no man had lifted a finger to help him. "Indeed you are. A peer without peers, for which we English can only be grateful. But before you have me arrested, I might suggest that you consider what a magistrate will think of a man who put such fright into an innocent girl that she endangered herself by running away. If your reputation can withstand that scandal, go ahead and call a runner. But I don't believe it will." He looked around at the sympathetic faces in the club. "I cannot be the only man in London who knows you for what you are."

James turned again and reached the door before Lord Figg called after him. "Where are you going?"

"To call on your daughter, Lord Figg."

Out on the street, James realized he should have called on Olivia two weeks before. If he hadn't delayed the meeting, none of this would have happened. Instead, he'd allowed himself to be manipulated like a pawn. He'd fallen into a trap of cunning and deceit. He'd allowed himself to be forced into risking his happiness, all for the sake of Annie's reputation, which obviously meant more to him than it did to her.

What use had either of them for society's opinions? If he had thought them important, Annie had certainly set him straight. As soon as society had come between her and him, she had left it without a backward glance.

And so would he. They didn't need England any more. If he was to be ruined, so be it. They

379

could make it together in America where titles and peerages no longer mattered. Annie and he did not belong here.

As for Olivia, she had never wanted to marry him. If James broke their engagement, Lord Figg would surely find someone else. He would no longer sacrifice his own happiness simply to spare her grief. He would try to ease her condition to salve his conscience, and he would spend the rest of his natural life hunting Annie.

Olivia received him in her drawing room, where an earlier caller had already been seated. James was so annoyed by this circumstance, and so preoccupied, that at first he failed to notice a distinct difference in Olivia's behavior.

"Thank you for coming so quickly, Captain Avery," she said.

Startled by this greeting, when he had not announced his visit, James looked her in the face and was struck by her glow. He'd become so accustomed to Olivia's pallor and distasteful manner, he couldn't conceal his surprise.

Gesturing to a chair, Olivia noted his reaction with an embarrassed flush. "I cannot wonder at your astonishment. You have never received a summons from me."

"I received no summons," James said. "Other business has brought me here."

"Oh, dear." At this, Olivia glanced uneasily at

her other visitor, but still with an underlying confidence that had been lacking before.

Throughout all this, James had ignored the other woman sitting on the settee, but he turned at her snort of disgust. He found her glaring at him in open disapproval.

Noticing his question, perhaps, Olivia hurried to make the introduction. "Sir James, you must allow me to present Miss Thurston. I believe you have heard me speak in her praise."

Miss Thurston? James looked at the stern creature seated beside Olivia and tried to remember what had been said about her. Something about a governess, he recalled.

That was all well and good, but at the moment, her presence could only be a hindrance. What he had to say to Lady Olivia should be said when they were alone. He did not want to waste time that he could use to find Annie.

Impatient, he asked Olivia if he might have a word with her in private.

She flushed, as she always did whenever anything of an intimate nature was implied, but today even her flushes seemed different. They held nothing of her earlier fear. For a moment, James was afraid she might have overcome her aversion to their marriage.

But she surprised him by saying, "I have asked Miss Thurston to stay. I would rather she did, as I have something of a rather unpleasant nature to relay to you."

Patricia Wynn

James's exhaustion was making it hard for him to curb his temper. He started to insist that he must speak to her alone, and at once. He could not be wasting precious time.

Then, he remembered that Olivia had written to ask him to come and knew he must let her speak.

Miss Thurston took Olivia's hand and held it, as if to give her support.

Smiling shyly back at her, Olivia began. "Captain Avery, this will not be easy, but the situation would be worse if I were not completely honest with you.

"You may recall that I once mentioned an elderly aunt from whom I had expectations." As she ended on a querying note, Olivia's voice shook.

As James looked closer at her, he saw that her trembling stemmed from joy. Confusion clouded his brain, followed by hope as he recalled a portion of what she'd said.

"Yes . . ."

"Well, I am afraid—and I hope you will not be too disappointed—that my relative has indeed died, leaving me her fortune unconditionally. It is a small independence, but it should be enough to maintain me and my dear companion, Miss Thurston for as long as we are likely to live. There might even be enough to repay you part of the sum you advanced my father.

"You do recall that I said I never wished to marry?" Olivia asked, staring anxiously at James.

"Then, what you're saying is . . ." He held his breath.

When Olivia hesitated, Miss Thurston, who'd fidgeted, said loudly and firmly, "What Olivia is trying to tell you is that she releases you from your engagement."

"I am very mindful of the honor you have bestowed upon me," Olivia hastened to add. "But my wishes have never changed. I have never wanted a husband, and for once, I am free to do as I wish. I hope you will find it in your heart to release me from your contract with my father."

Relief poured through James until he realized that Annie was still gone. That thought alone helped him to hide his gladness. With the appearance of a failed suitor, he congratulated Olivia on her inheritance and wished her well.

She pledged to pay back whatever money he had advanced to her father, but he refused the offer.

"That agreement was between your father and me. And, since I doubt you were consulted in the first place, it would be unfair for you to have to settle the issue between us.

"Besides," he added with what tact he could. "Your father will undoubtedly make claims upon your fortune that you may find difficult to ignore."

Miss Thurston let out a "Hummppphh!" *Let him try*, her expression said, as she glared at James.

He saw no reason to linger. He made his excuses, convinced that in Miss Thurston, Lord Figg had finally met his match.

He took a hack to his agent's office where he had ordered his searchers to report if they found any trace of Annie, but no messages awaited him there.

He had offered a sizeable reward, so he'd had no doubt she would be found if she had climbed aboard any of the ships still in port. Tired and discouraged, he returned to Portsmouth and combed the docks again until late into the night. He couldn't believe she wouldn't try to ship to sea. He thought of the *Merrye Laurie*, sailing near Jamaica. She had been Annie's home. Surely Annie would try to hop a ship that would take her there.

It was nearly midnight on the next day when he stepped aboard one of his own ships. She was one he had mentioned to Annie, so she would have known to avoid it. In desperation, James asked the captain to search the ship, but he knew she would not be there. When she could stow aboard any vessel, why would she choose one of his?

He rested, leaning over the rail, watching the water lap against the side while the search took place. He was growing so discouraged, he'd begun to feel ill.

Where are you, Annie? he asked the lapping waves.

"There's no boy here, sir." The same phrase he

had heard a hundred times these past few days came from the captain behind him.

James's shoulders slumped before he whirled on him, anger and frustration sharpening his tone. "Are you sure?"

As he did, he thought he saw a flash of color vanishing above the masthead.

"Sure as can be, Sir James. We've checked the hold and every deck. Who is this boy, sir, if you don't mind my askin'?"

James didn't bother to respond. He was staring aloft, searching for that spot of copper. "Did you look on the masthead?"

"No, Sir James." The captain smiled, but he was clearly annoyed. "Why would anybody be up there when we're in port?"

"That's exactly what I'm wondering." With excitement filling his heart, James moved to a better spot and peered up.

The captain followed.

"Ahoy, there!" James called. "Masthead! Show yourself!"

Silence came from the place where he had seen someone duck. His pulse grew stronger. The captain plainly thought he was mad.

"I've already seen you," he called louder into the shrouds. "Surrender, or I'll have you dragged down!"

"Sir James, there's no one there!"

Ignoring his protests, James stripped off his jacket and cravat, his boots and his stockings, and started to climb, peering up from the ratlines to see if anyone emerged.

385

Someone did. Rather a spritely figure for a man. A figure that he knew so well.

Relief burst through him and out his every pore, admitting a radiance that brought tears into his eyes. Annie was safe, she was *safe*.

"All right, Jem," he called. His smile spread almost painfully as he rose. "You've had your fun. Now, come down here this moment."

She ignored him as she scurried up the lines, higher and higher. James reached the masthead and pulled himself through the hole. Irritation and anger came to replace his nights of worry. How long had she been hiding here, while he'd combed the docks in despair?

The little imp. First, he'd kill her. Then he'd make such passionate love to her, she'd never have the strength to leave him again.

Joy warred with his fury even as he saw her climbing ever higher. He was breathless with the chase. "Come down, Annie! You can't possibly escape!"

"Stop right there," she called down. "You shouldn't come any higher."

"Why?" He laughed. "Don't you think I know how? I was climbing these ropes and masts years before you were born."

"But you'll hurt yourself!"

"No, I won't. What do you take me for? A lubber? If you're so worried about me, you'd best come down."

"I won't go back to being a lady, just so you can marry someone else!"

"Oh, you won't? What if I catch you?"

"Go away! I don't want you on this ship!"

"Annie, please come down."

"You can't make me!"

"Oh, yes I can." James pulled himself higher, his body light with elation. He loved this woman. There was no one else like her in the world.

"James." Annie had climbed as far as she could go without risking real danger. "Don't make me fight you way up here. I'm sure you'll fall."

"Then, if you love me, you'll come here."

"That's not fair."

James could hear the painful edge in her voice. He almost regretted teasing her, until he thought of all the worry she'd caused him.

"Annie, I'm sorry. I'm a fool. But how can I marry you if you're way up there and I'm down here?"

"What?"

She'd heard him. Every sailor on every ship for miles around must have heard him, and not a few were gathering on deck below to watch.

James started to repeat himself at the top of his lungs, but she plunged down on a rope almost to within his reach.

He saw her stumpy red pigtail, her ragged fringe, and her bare feet, and his heart gave a thump.

"You'll have to take another bath before we're wed." The very thought of it made him go hard. He would watch her bathe this time and enjoy the sight without guilt. He might even join her. The image made him tremble.

"Did you say wed?" Annie slipped another foot closer.

"Yes, but I want to kiss you first. Could you come here now?"

She slid the rest of the way. He caught her with his right arm, and together they hung in the ropes.

"Why would you marry me?" She molded her body close to his as they swayed, foot against foot, both tangled in the lines.

"Feel the front of my breeches if you need to know."

She did, and the delicious pressure made his blood sing with desire. Still, she asked, "What happened to Olivia and Lord Figg? He told me he would ruin you."

Using his one arm to bring her closer, he whispered into her hair. "You don't have to worry about Olivia or Lord Figg. I know what he told you, Annie, but he lied. I've already broken it off. I was worried because he threatened to harm you, but we had a little talk and I've convinced him to see things my way."

Annie giggled. "I would have liked to see that little talk."

He couldn't help but laugh. "It was all very civilized, I assure you. In any case, I'm marrying you just as soon as I can find a priest, because I can't live without you. You know it's true."

She gave a nod.

"Why did you come here?" he asked.

Her voice was small against his neck. "I knew

I would see you sometimes, at least, if I could be on the crew of one of your ships."

"If I hadn't found you, you know I would have died."

"I know. I would have shown myself as soon as we got underway. I would have been your mistress."

He gave her a shake, then held her close. "Don't think I hadn't considered that in my stupidity, but I could never treat you so badly, Annie. I want us to have children. *Legitimate* children."

"Will we?"

"Aye, as many as you want. We can start right now, and we'll be married tomorrow." James glanced down and saw about fifty sailors peering up at them through the dark.

"But first we'll have to explain ourselves, or my men will think I've grown a mite perverted."

"Well . . . bugger 'em!"

He laughed out loud and squeezed her to his chest. "I'd rather make love to you."

As they kissed, her free hand explored him until he thought he just might fall after all.

"Don't you think," he suggested huskily, "that we might be a bit more comfortable in my berth."

"Ye mean, *my* berth."

"That's right, love. Though you might call it ours from now on."

Annie sighed contentedly and ran her mischievous fingers through his hair. Her gesture became more than provocative; it became the tender gesture of a wife. "And I can be your cabin girl forever now?"

"No." He spun them around until she whooped with pure delight. Then, with his mighty roar he shouted to his men gawking below, "I will never be happy until Miss Annie Bonny becomes my wife!"

Wink & A Kiss

THE BEWITCHED VIKING
SANDRA HILL

'Tis enough to drive a sane Viking mad, the things Tykir Thorksson is forced to do—capturing a red-headed virago, putting up with the flock of sheep that follow her everywhere, chasing off her bumbling brothers. But what can a man expect from the sorceress who put a kink in the King of Norway's most precious body part? If that isn't bad enough, he is beginning to realize he isn't at all immune to the enchantment of brash red hair and freckles. But he is not called Tykir the Great for nothing. Perhaps he can reverse the spell and hold her captive, not with his mighty sword, but with a Viking man's greatest magic: a wink and a smile.

___52311-6 $5.99 US/$6.99 CAN

Dorchester Publishing Co., Inc.
P.O. Box 6640
Wayne, PA 19087-8640

Please add $1.75 for shipping and handling for the first book and $.50 for each book thereafter. NY, NYC, and PA residents, please add appropriate sales tax. No cash, stamps, or C.O.D.s. All orders shipped within 6 weeks via postal service book rate. Canadian orders require $2.00 extra postage and must be paid in U.S. dollars through a U.S. banking facility.

Name_____
Address_____
City_____State_____Zip_____
I have enclosed $_____ in payment for the checked book(s).
Payment <u>must</u> accompany all orders. ❏ Please send a free catalog.
    CHECK OUT OUR WEBSITE! www.dorchesterpub.com

BUSHWHACKED BRIDE

EUGENIA RILEY

"JUMPING JEHOSHAPHAT! YOU'VE SHANGHAIED THE NEW SCHOOLMARM!"

Ma Reklaw bellows at her sons and wields her broom with a fierceness that has all five outlaw brothers running for cover; it doesn't take a Ph.D. to realize that in the Reklaw household, Ma is the law. Professor Jessica Garret watches dumbstruck as the members of the feared Reklaw Gang turn tail—one up a tree, another under the hay wagon, and one in a barrel. Having been unceremoniously kidnapped by the rowdy brothers, the green-eyed beauty takes great pleasure in their discomfort until Ma Reklaw finds a new way to sweep clean her sons' disreputable behavior—by offering Jessica's hand in marriage to the best behaved. Jessie has heard of shotgun weddings, but a broomstick betrothal is ridiculous! As the dashing but dangerous desperadoes start the wooing there is no telling what will happen with one bride for five brothers.

___52320-5 $5.99 US/$6.99 CAN

An Original Sin
Nina Bangs

Fortune MacDonald listens to women's fantasies on a daily basis as she takes their orders for customized men. In a time when the male species is extinct, she is a valued man-maker. So when she awakes to find herself sharing a bed with the most lifelike, virile man she has ever laid eyes or hands on, she lets her gaze inventory his assets. From his long dark hair, to his knife-edged cheekbones, to his broad shoulders, to his jutting—well, all in the name of research, right?—it doesn't take an expert any time at all to realize that he is the genuine article, a bona fide man. And when Leith Campbell takes her in his arms, she knows real passion for the first time . . . but has she found true love?

___52324-8 $5.99 US/$6.99 CAN

Dorchester Publishing Co., Inc.
P.O. Box 6640
Wayne, PA 19087-8640

Please add $1.75 for shipping and handling for the first book and $.50 for each book thereafter. NY, NYC, and PA residents, please add appropriate sales tax. No cash, stamps, or C.O.D.s. All orders shipped within 6 weeks via postal service book rate. Canadian orders require $2.00 extra postage and must be paid in U.S. dollars through a U.S. banking facility.

Name_____
Address_____
City_____State_____Zip_____
I have enclosed $_____ in payment for the checked book(s).
Payment <u>must</u> accompany all orders. ❑ Please send a free catalog.
CHECK OUT OUR WEBSITE! www.dorchesterpub.com

TEMPTED
MONICA ROBERTS

Well, tarnation! Apparently the man who mail-ordered Hope Savage didn't expect her, for he seems a bit taken aback by her language and her duds. But whooey, is he a looker! The parson's saintly face makes the Appalachian firebrand weak in her knees—and the preacher's perfect body makes her want to wail a hymn of thanksgiving. Still, every time she gets a hand on the rascally fellow, he manages to skedaddle, shrieking about the Good Book. Heck, she's seen a few good books and she hopes to learn if what she read is true. There she is, waiting to be set upon by her new husband, and all he wants to do is make a lady out of her. Well, maybe she'll let him. Then perhaps she can show him that it's sometimes nice to be naughty, and that something heavenly can come from being tempted.

___52353-1 $5.50 US/$6.50 CAN

A WANTED MAN.
AN INNOCENT WOMAN.
A WANTON LOVE!

Renegade Heart

Madeline Baker

When beautiful Rachel Halloran took Logan Tyree into her home, he was unconscious. A renegade Indian with a bullet wound in his side and a price on his head, he needed her help. But to Rachel he was nothing but trouble, a man whose dark sensuality made her long for forbidden pleasures; to her father he was the answer to a prayer, a gunslinger whose legendary skill could rid the ranch of a powerful enemy.

But Logan Tyree would answer to no man—and to no woman. If John Halloran wanted his services, he would have to pay dearly for them. And if Rachel wanted his loving, she would have to give up her innocence, her reputation, her very heart and soul.

_4085-9 $5.99 US/$6.99 CAN

MIDNIGHT FIRE

MADELINE BAKER

"Lovers of Indian Romance have a special place on
their bookshelves for Madeline Baker!"
—*Romantic Times*

He is a hard-riding, hard-drinking drifter, a half-breed who
has no use for a frightened white girl fleeing an unwanted
wedding. He tells himself he needs only the money she offers
to guide her across the plains, but halfway between Galveston
and Ogallala, where the burning prairie meets the endless
sky, he made her his woman. Now she is his to protect, his
to cherish, and he will allow no man—white or Indian—to
come between them. There in the vast wilderness where his
desire has ignited hers, he swore to change his life path, to
fulfill the challenge of his vision quest, if only he can keep
her love.

_4085-9 $5.99 US/$6.99 CAN

Dorchester Publishing Co., Inc.
P.O. Box 6640
Wayne, PA 19087-8640

Please add $1.75 for shipping and handling for the first book and
$.50 for each book thereafter. NY, NYC, and PA residents,
please add appropriate sales tax. No cash, stamps, or C.O.D.s. All
orders shipped within 6 weeks via postal service book rate.
Canadian orders require $2.00 extra postage and must be paid in
U.S. dollars through a U.S. banking facility.

Name_____
Address_____
City_____State_____Zip_____
I have enclosed $_____ in payment for the checked book(s).
Payment <u>must</u> accompany all orders. ☐ Please send a free catalog.

THE ANGEL & THE OUTLAW

MADELINE BAKER

Bestselling Author Of *Lakota Renegade*

An outlaw, a horse thief, a man killer, J.T. Cutter isn't surprised when he is strung up for his crimes. What amazes him is the heavenly being who grants him one year to change his wicked ways. Yet when he returns to his old life, he hopes to cram a whole lot of hell-raising into those twelve months no matter what the future holds.

But even as J.T. heads back down the trail to damnation, a sharp-tongued beauty is making other plans for him. With the body of a temptress and the heart of a saint, Brandy is the only woman who can save J.T. And no matter what it takes, she'll prove to him that the road to redemption can lead to rapturous bliss.

_3931-1 $5.99 US/$7.99 CAN

BRIDES OF DURANGO: ELISE
BOBBI SMITH

Elise Martin will do anything for a story—even stage a fake marriage to catch a thief. Dressed in a white lace gown, she looks every bit the bride, but when her "fiancé" fails to show, she offers ten dollars to the handsome gentleman who just stepped off the stage to pose as the groom. As a fake fiancé, he is all right, but when he turns out to be Gabriel West, the new owner of her paper, the *Durango Star*, Elise wants to turn tail and run. But she can't forget the passion his unexpected kiss at their "wedding" aroused, and she starts to wonder if there is more to Gabriel West than meets the eye. For the more time they spend together, the more Elise wonders if the next time she says, "I do" she just might mean it.

___4575-3 $5.99 US/$6.99 CAN

Dorchester Publishing Co., Inc.
P.O. Box 6640
Wayne, PA 19087-8640

Please add $1.75 for shipping and handling for the first book and $.50 for each book thereafter. NY, NYC, and PA residents, please add appropriate sales tax. No cash, stamps, or C.O.D.s. All orders shipped within 6 weeks via postal service book rate. Canadian orders require $2.00 extra postage and must be paid in U.S. dollars through a U.S. banking facility.

Name_____
Address_____
City_____State_____Zip_____
I have enclosed $_____ in payment for the checked book(s).
Payment <u>must</u> accompany all orders. ❑ Please send a free catalog.
CHECK OUT OUR WEBSITE! www.dorchesterpub.com